CURIOSITY
QUILLS PRESS

A Division of **Whampa, LLC**
P.O. Box 2160
Reston, VA 20195
Tel/Fax: 800-998-2509
http://curiosityquills.com

© 2014 **Richard Roberts**
http://frankensteinbeck.blogspot.com

ISBN: 978-1-62007-462-6 (ebook)
ISBN: 978-1-62007-463-3 (paperback)
ISBN: 978-1-62007-464-0 (hardcover)

TABLE OF CONTENTS

To Dana Simpson.
We always wanted to rewrite
our childhood together

CHAPTER ONE

O n the last day before I got my super power, I was sulking because I didn't have a super power.

"That's not going to work," Claire warned me.

"It will! I've been studying my Dad's notes," I snapped back.

She tilted her head down and looked at me over her glasses. "You can't give yourself super powers with a double-A battery, Penny."

"It's not the power," I explained. "It's the frequency. Get it just right and it resonates with your whole nervous system and gives it a jolt. I've seen Dad do it. If you have powers, they go off!"

I snapped that at her, too. I was frustrated! I clipped the wire another millimeter and looked at the wavelength reading on the meter. It went down a notch, like it was supposed to. I was dreading the next question. She was going to ask that question.

"So what's the frequency?" Claire asked right on time.

I collapsed on top of the workbench and confessed, "I have no idea."

Claire giggled, but at least she tried to restrain it.

"I was reaching. I knew I couldn't just guess. I don't know. I guess I hoped I'd get lucky," I grumped.

Claire put her hand on my shoulder. "We're supposed to be working on our science fair projects. Mr. Zwelf is being really nice about it."

I pushed myself back up and insisted, "This *is* my science fair project. It will work! I just have to steal my Dad's notes and do the math. And measure my body weight and stuff. There's a lot of math." A lot of math. A really stupifyingly tremendous amount of math. Pages upon pages of math. Even with a calculator, I'd be up all night handling the algebra.

"You know inventing and science are two different things, right?" Claire had the world's most teasing grin. Like, you looked at those teeth and you couldn't be mad at her for making fun of you, because it really was all in good fun. That's how it worked on me, anyway.

"So what are you doing for your science fair project?" I demanded. I actually hadn't wanted to know. Any excuse to be lab partners with your best friend, right?

"I'm already done! I blind tested photos of Mom when she's using her powers and when she's not using her powers on a bunch of boys. They couldn't tell the difference, which shows her power must be psychic, right?" she answered, so very casual.

"You want your super power as bad as I do!" Hard to sound accusing with a grin like the one stretching my face all of a sudden. This stuff was no secret, but, criminy, obvious much, Claire?

"It's still good scientific method," Ray pointed out, sliding down the workbench with his textbook. If Mr. Zwelf hadn't come down on me and Claire arguing, he wasn't going to pitch a fit if Ray made three.

I turned to him. "What are you doing for your project?"

He shrugged. "I don't know. I'm atrocious at science fair projects. I can never get an idea until the last minute. Right now, I'm looking through the book and hoping inspiration leaps out at me."

"You have trouble with science fair projects? You?" I asked, honestly blown away. Ray was the smartest kid I knew. My folks were celebrated super geniuses who had a framed letter on the wall from the UN thanking them for saving the world, and Ray was smarter than me. He could probably do the stupid math in Dad's notes. I wasn't looking forward to it.

"It's so meaningless and arbitrary. I might as well be measuring plastic cups to find out which ones are more dense," he griped, propping his elbow on the workbench and leaning his head on his fist. His blonde hair was so fluffy, it hung right down over his hand.

Ow! I still had the current on. I'd zapped myself on the antenna. Wasn't much of a charge, but still. I shook my finger and pried out the battery, but I didn't have time to dismantle the antenna. The bell rang.

"Lunch time!" Claire squealed with delight, stretching her arms above her head as Ray stared.

Love triangles suck.

"Why are you so dramatic today?" Ray asked as I sat down with my tray across from him. Just me and him at our table. I could listen to that inexplicable English accent the whole hour. He didn't know where it came from, and I didn't care.

"I'm not being dramatic today," I argued, trying not to be dramatic about it.

"Yes, you are."

I lifted my head in a show of innocence. "I'm not being dramatic. My parents are dramatic. Mom can reduce a mugger to tears with a speech about the statistical chance of ruining his life going up with every crime. You were there. He was bawling like a baby."

"Does she really prepare those speeches ahead of time?" he asked, grinning. Ray spends half his life grinning, and a third of his life sleeping, and the remaining sixth happens when I'm not around.

"She has a flow chart depending on circumstances. I got to draw the lines the last time she updated it. I was seven." I added that last part because, you know, it's beneath my dignity now.

"You're being dramatic for you," Ray pointed out, zeroing back in on the argument.

He was totally right, but I was saved from admitting it, because Claire had arrived. She brought her lunch, so she should get to the cafeteria early, but she'd never been big on hurrying. I bet her Mom trained her to be fashionably late.

She was heading straight here, so it looked like she'd be sitting with us today. Okay, I needed to watch that snippiness. Claire sits with me most days, it's just that Claire is welcome anywhere. Like most lunch rooms, the cafeteria of Northeast West Hollywood Middle is laid out in an intricate map of feudal kingdoms. The performing art kids have three tables, the computer science kids have a table, me and Claire and Ray have a table. Claudia has a table all to herself, poor girl. I'd invited her over to sit with us once, but she refused. Since Marcia had pulled the "sit with her, then make her the butt of all the jokes" trick on her once, it was hard to blame her. You can't help some people, much as you might want to.

Speaking of Marcia—thinking about Marcia, technically—maybe Claire wouldn't be sitting with us today after all. Marcia made her friends scoot over and pointed at the bench. "Space for you, Claire!"

No, Claire was sitting with us. She gave Marcia a smile and a shake of the head, trying to be polite, but walked right past. Marcia looked like someone'd stuck a rat up her nose. She should have let one of the other girls give the invite. Marcia is a Mean Girl, and she sits at the Popular Table, and, yeah, both exist and everybody knows it. I swear they were only popular with each other, but somehow they were the Popular Girls, even though it's Claire that everyone really likes.

I think our table is the "extroverted geeks" table. Or maybe it really is the "children of superheroes" table. Of course, both leave Ray out. He's quiet with other people. Eh, who am I kidding? The three of us were filed firmly under "other."

"Is Penny still desperate to get her powers?" Claire asked as she slid into place next to me.

"I had managed to distract her until now," Ray answered.

I threw my hands up in the air. "What's wrong with wanting to get my powers as soon as possible?"

"Didn't your parents' powers only surface in college?" Ray pointed out. I think I'd strangle myself if it took that long.

"Mom's power emerged at about my age." Claire was so breezy about it, but everybody knew she'd inherit The Minx's abilities. She'd be less like her Mom if she were a clone. Blonde, wavy hair, a curvy figure *already*, delicate, blonde doll face, all lips and eyes – pretty much the opposite of my shapeless stick topped with brown, braided pigtails. On her, glasses looked like fashion accessories.

"I can't even be positive I'll get powers. My Dad's thing with science is a brain mutation. He identified it. Mom's a regular human," I grumped.

Claire unbuckled her lunch box with a beatific smile. "My father probably had super powers. I should be a shoo-in."

Ray blushed visibly. Okay, maybe I blushed a bit, too. Claire really didn't know who her father was. Apparently there had been a lot of candidates, thanks to her mother's power of Clouding Men's Minds. If 'minds' was the right word.

And Claire was looking forward to inheriting those powers.

Thank goodness, Ray also wanted to move on. "There's no way your mother is human. Regular humans can't do that," he insisted.

"Chess grandmasters are regular humans. She says it's just focus and study, like Sherlock Holmes." Contrary to what I'd just said, I agreed with him. We'd been passed on the road by a police chase once, and she'd gotten on the radio and told them where to set up a road block, and they caught the criminals. She'd been able to explain it, but when she got to calculating how fast the criminals had intended to drive rather than how fast they were driving, I gave up. I knew she wasn't perfect, but, when villains heard The Audit was coming, they used to give up right there, and I couldn't blame them.

Claire passed me a cup of real gravy, which I poured on the school's bland Salisbury steak. Cutting a slice, I took a bite. The rich gravy made a world of difference. Claire's lunchbox is a collectible antique with Krazy Kat on the cover. Her Mom feeds her like a princess. My Mom makes me buy a cafeteria lunch. I would never have asked, but Claire shares the wealth automatically. She has those looks, and she's generous and kind. Is it any wonder her Mom got a full pardon when she retired? Of course, she'd saved the world a couple of times. What kind of crazy supervillain tries to destroy the world?

Half of them.

I stopped jonesing for super powers before I started and dug into my lunch. A little gravy made the mashed potatoes stop being pulped cardboard, too.

Claire gave Ray a chocolate cupcake, which must have made his sandwiches a thousand times more bearable. Ray eats like he's on the edge of starvation. As skinny as he is, his metabolism must burn like a blow torch. He got done in mere minutes and asked, "How did the big German test go?"

"Nicht so gross. Got a B," Claire admitted.

Ray looked at me.

I couldn't think of any way to brush it off.

I let out a sigh. "I got a C."

"Ow. Really?" asked the boy who never got less than an A on any test in his life.

Not that he was trying to be mean. He was trying to be sympathetic, which made it worse. "I'm pretty sure I'm going to get a C in the class," I admitted. I winced, my whole body tightening up, but it hadn't been… that bad to say. Just pretty bad.

Ray tried to comfort me. "Everybody has subjects they just don't get. Languages are yours, I guess."

Claire nodded.

"I'm not supposed to have bad subjects! My parents are the two smartest people in the world!" God, it dug at me. It dug right at my heart. How could I even explain this to them? "Can you imagine the look my Dad gave me when I brought home a B in Algebra II? He was trying to not let me know how disappointed he was. That's the look he had!"

"You weren't even supposed to *be* in Algebra II. You and Ray are the only kids going across to Upper High for Geometry, and you're getting an A in that," Claire pointed out. She was trying to cheer me up, not blow me off. She didn't get that it just didn't matter.

I couldn't help but feel bitter. Or cheated, maybe. Some kind of ugly emotion, anyhow. "I just want my super powers to activate now. I won't even have to worry about this stuff. I'm smart enough to get this frequency stimulator thing Dad designed working, at least," I grumped.

The bell rang. I wasn't done eating. Oh, well, I'd had the good stuff.

You want to know how good friends Claire and Ray are? When we got up, I noticed a plastic case in her bag. She'd gotten a new superhero collectable figure. She and Ray can geek out about them for hours. They'd kept their mouths shut about it not to rub it in. Then I'd spent the whole lunch period talking about super powers anyway.

We all had PE together. Half the class was spent changing into and out of our gym clothes, which I bet is why we only had the class on Wednesdays. Sometimes we could get together and talk, like when we were standing in line for the horse. Today was basketball, so no luck there.

The game went about like expected. Two random kids were picked as captains. The boy picked Ray second to last, and the girl picked me last. I wasn't the last person picked, though. The boy still had one more person to pick. Claudia, of course. Ray and I ran around the edge of the crowd until someone threw the ball over everyone's heads, and I jumped up and grabbed it.

Ha! I wasn't the greatest dribbler in the world, but I was in the clear because I hadn't been in the pack in the first place. I dribbled right past Claudia, who didn't even try to stop me, and found myself face to face with Ray. He wasn't a good runner, and he was already so winded I was able to duck right by him. Unfortunately for me, Claire had been lingering on the edges too. She snatched the ball in the middle of one of my clumsy dribbles and passed it to Li, who was a way better shot than either of us.

Still, face to face to face on the basketball court had been cool. I was considering chalking up this gym class as a rare success when the boy captaining his team started to yell. Not "yell," exactly, but he had a nasty tone as he told Claudia, "What is wrong with you? You just stood there! You really are slow in the head, aren't you? At least try to play the game!"

I wondered if I should get Miss Theotan's attention, but it wouldn't do any good. If she'd witnessed it personally, she'd come down on bullying like this like a ton of bricks, but she was on the other side of the court, and if a teacher doesn't see it, it didn't happen. Instead, Claudia turned away from the boy without a word. The crowd of kids taking the ball away from each other again and again turned and lurched in our direction with Claudia in the middle of it. She grabbed the ball as it went past, tossed it over everyone's heads, ran through the crowd, and caught it herself, then launched it from the three point line and sank the basket.

You'd think that would get everyone gabbing and circling around Claudia and she'd finally be popular, right? No, that's not how it works. All of a sudden a girl was complaining to Miss Theotan that it wasn't fair that one team had one more player than the other team, and, as Ray and Claire and I stood around feeling helpless and guilty about it, Claudia ended up sitting on a bench for the rest of the game.

That put my mood right back in the dumps. I dodged Claire and Ray both when class ended, and with it the school day. I didn't step out the school doors until it was exactly time to meet my Mom, driving up to take me home. She didn't ask me about my obvious bad mood, so I didn't have to tell her about the test.

Nothing eases the sting of social injustice like knowing you'll soon have super powers to help you combat it. Nothing eases the sting of lousy test scores like knowing you'll soon have the ability to absorb and then apply abstract data far beyond mere human limits. If they ever really integrate psychological theory, my Dad will be impossible to live with. Until then, us normal humans have a shot at outwitting him.

Not a good shot. He's still a genius. Still, I had the advantage of experience. I wandered into his office. To my delight, I found him at his computer with an e-reader laid on either side of his keyboard, scrolling slowly down a web page with lots of text and a few teeny, tiny diagrams. The curiosity bug had caught him. He was researching. He'd have no attention left for anything else until it all came together in his head.

Or not. As I picked my way through the stacked up books and lifted the first pile of printed paper to peek at the title "Subliminal Paralyzation Cascades" he spun around in his seat and greeted me. "Hey, Pumpkin! How was school?"

I pointed at the "Pumpkin" jar. He put a dollar in it blithely. It hadn't made him stop, but the penalty really supplemented my pathetic allowance. "Princess" is five bucks, but I'm saving that jar for emergencies.

I needed a plan.

"Where's that paper on the antenna thing that resonates with the human nervous system?" I asked. My plan? Pretend it was something totally normal to ask for.

Dad took off his work glasses, which folded up as he scratched his head. "If you want me to build you one, the answer is 'no.' The shock is too dangerous to be used casually, and not dangerous enough to be a weapon. It didn't even bring Marvelous' powers back. Really a failed project."

That was not good news. Not for my plans, and not for one of the nicer superheroines. "Is she okay?"

"Beebee took a look at the release records and worldwide superhuman crime reports. She says the odds of any criminal being near enough to LA and crazy enough to try a hit on a depowered hero are insignificant," he answered. Beatrice Benevolent Akk, would be my Mom. Officially retired, as was my Dad, but still neck deep in the community.

"Not what I meant, Dad. Will she get her powers back?" I pressed.

"She says her powers will return when the curse is broken."

Oh, the weight on those words. We had this argument again. "Dad, I can't believe you still don't believe in magic."

He argued back as if this were the first time. "Pumpkin, I've done the analyses. She's inherited a tone of voice and sensitivity to electrical currents that allow her to initiate some very complex energy chain reactions with precisely formulated sound wave patterns."

I pointed at the jar. Money in the bank.

"So she can cast spells," I translated back to him.

"They just happen to sound like incantations," he insisted.

We glared at each other. Then I realized he'd taken off his glasses, so I took mine off to make it fair. We glared at each other a few seconds more, then both broke down laughing at the fuzzy-edged blob arguing against us.

"So, where is that paper on the nervous resonating antenna thing?" I asked.

He looked around the room, then his eyes drifted down the rows of piled up books, drives, notebooks, clipboards, and sheaves of paper. Got him! He'd started analyzing his own pattern of clutter. He knew it well enough to figure out the system when he needed to. "Under the Audubon Field Guide. I'm still not going to build you one."

I scooped it out. No title, but the first paragraph talked about matching neural electromagnetic resonance. He loved printing out his work. Good for me!

"I need to do it myself anyway," I evaded. "It's for the science fair."

"How is school? Report cards will be coming in soon. Were you ready for that German test you were worried about?"

EEK.

Okay, shake it off. Not literally. He didn't notice me freeze up. I flipped through the pages laying out the engineering of the antenna. "I don't think I have time to talk, Dad. I have to do a lot of math. Really a lot of math. Really, really a lot of math." A different sort of horror crept over me at the thought. Urgh.

"Yeah, I bet. Good luck, Pumpkin," he urged me. I pointed at the jar silently. I would have liked to gloat that I was cleaning up today, but I was trying to keep from fainting.

I could do this. I got the trig and calculus textbooks off of the kitchen shelf, praying I wouldn't need to use them. I got my custom smart phone (like Dad would let me use a brand name when he could spend three weeks making one that works across all platforms) to use the calculator functions.

So many equations. Okay, I had to know the percentage by mass of each element in the antenna. I ran into Dad's electronics workshop and copied down the label on his cheap spares. It didn't matter what they were as long as I had the numbers, right? That gave me three variables he had down with Greek letters, and I plugged them into the next equation, which... took differentials of sines and cosines. He had to be kidding me. I dug out both books I'd been hoping not to use. I'd seen this stuff before. I just had to find the cheap rules and apply them... Okay, no. No, this was too complicated. I had to understand what I was doing. How did you get the first differential of a sine function?

I didn't know. It just... it just didn't make any sense. There was something there. I had to know because the waves from the antenna when they traveled through my skin had to become waves that would merge with waves in my axons, causing a chain of...

I could almost see it, but those words didn't make sense. What was I doing? It was like trying to call The Mona Lisa a painting. Just work out the math the cheap way. I'd need my body mass index; that was in the next equation. Of course, I needed my real, exact body mass index, not just some rough approximation by comparing weight and height, or whatever the rule-of-thumb trick was.

I didn't even know the rule-of-thumb trick. I'd need a machine just to get my body mass index.

Whining in frustration, I threw Dad's papers across the room, then threw my notebook with my fumbling math after it. I'd probably gotten the math wrong anyway. And I was good at math!

I lay down in bed and put the cover over my head. It wasn't nearly bedtime. I would spend the rest of the day sulking and trying to avoid the issue and maybe tomorrow I could come up with a new idea. I had to hurry. I could hide a C on a test from my Dad, but not my report card.

And what was I going to do about the science fair anyway?

The alarm on my phone woke me up the next morning. I didn't want to get out of bed. I stared at the ceiling for a while, but I'd already outsmarted myself. The phone was out of reach of the bed, and I had to get up to turn off the alarm, and after that I might as well go take a shower.

The sky was black outside, and I was all alone in the house. Technically, I wasn't alone. Mom and Dad were there, they were just fast asleep. I tied my pigtails into braids myself. Dad made me a machine for when I don't feel like putting forth the effort, but he'd tinkered with it yesterday. The little hands had extra fingers, and the access plate looked new. No matter how lazy I felt, I wasn't going to risk it. I could tell just by looking that he'd messed something up. Dad's inventions always do what they're supposed to do, but sometimes don't do what you think they're supposed to do. Something about the extra grabbers looked wrong to me, and, if I couldn't put a finger on it, I wouldn't let them put a finger on my hair.

The scrambled egg maker, on the other hand, was a godsend, since it's a miracle if Mom ever makes breakfast. She's right; I'd hate it if she pulled her Audit routine at home, and she needed a break. Not that she could stop herself completely. Halfway through my cereal bowl I heard her door alarm squeak, and, as I reached for my backpack, she stuck her keys in the side door and opened it for me.

As she pulled the car out of the driveway, Mom asked me, "Still brooding, Penny?"

I'd just sat through breakfast grumbling about my parents' super powers. "Yeah, I guess. I don't know what to do for the science fair."

Just saying that gripped me. That's all I needed, an F for not presenting anything at all. I had no ideas for what to do to replace the antenna. None. I still wanted to make the antenna.

"Want any advice?" she asked.

"No." If I talked over the science fair thing with my parents, sooner or later my grades in German would come up. Most likely sooner. I was hemmed in on all sides.

At least my Mom has a light touch. She let it go, although she gave me a concerned glance. I wouldn't be at all surprised if she'd timed it precisely to give the maximum amount of sympathy without making the recipient feel pressured.

The brooding didn't stop when I got to school. What was I going to do for the science fair? I wanted to invent something, really bad. I wanted to make that antenna. It wasn't even about zapping myself with it for super powers now. It clawed at me that I'd stared at a few pages full of math and they'd beaten me utterly. I'd had reference books, but they didn't help, because none of it had made sense. The device and the calculations were two different worlds that I couldn't connect.

Making that connection was Dad's super power. I didn't have it. I didn't even have a hint of it, like I was going to grow into it.

The bell rang. I was sitting in my chair in History class, and I hadn't heard a word. I'd read the whole chapter ahead of time because World War I was such a bizarre war, but that wasn't the point. I'd been wrapped up, brooding the whole time. This was tearing me apart.

I slipped out into the hall and laid my back against the cement block wall of the hallway. I had to do something. I had Geometry next, across the street in Upper High. I'd always kind of known it would be easy to skip out on that class, because nobody was tracking that I'd been to the other school that day. It hadn't been important until now.

I walked around the school to the science lab. I'd left the parts in there. It would work. I couldn't do the math, but it ought to just work. It was the most obvious thing in the world. If the antenna was the right length and you touched it, it would zap you.

I stopped in front of the classroom. I could see kids at their benches through the door's window. Of course, a class was taking place now. There'd be a science class every period.

"You are entirely unable to leave this invention thing alone, aren't you?" Ray asked from behind me.

I flinched. Of course, there was one person who would track whether I'd been to Geometry, because he took the course with me. He'd even guessed where I would come.

I turned around to see Claire standing right next to Ray. They were both missing class to talk me out of being an idiot.

"It's driving me crazy, okay? I just need to try. I need to fiddle with it until I've proven to myself I can't do it and I don't have any choice but to let go." I hunched my head down between my shoulders. Guilt clawed at me, but I'd be in more trouble going to class late than skipping it anyway. I wasn't walking away from this.

"Were you able to get hold of your Dad's notes?" Claire held her hands clasped behind her, the picture of innocent concern. Even her dark blonde hair just made her look more sincere and charming than if she'd been a pale blonde. Claire was so much better looking than me; her power would come out any minute.

That was crazy thinking, getting mad at Claire for being such a good friend. I was just so frustrated. "It was like Dante's Calculus Inferno. There was no way," I whined.

"You're not Brian Akk, and you don't have to be. You're Penelope Akk," Claire reminded me. I wanted to pop her for that gentle, talking-me-off-the-roof voice—so imagine if she hadn't used it.

"It doesn't matter. I can't get to the parts now. I just can't let it go!" I growled.

"If you get an hour to show yourself that it doesn't work, will that help you?" Ray asked.

He knew something. "Yeah, it will."

He started grinning again. I must be seriously flipping out if he'd been frowning this long. He did know something. "Come on," he told us, and we followed him down to the other end of the hall, past the computer science lab to the... other computer science lab.

I'd never actually been in this one. He pulled the door open, revealing a lab empty of kids or teachers. Half the computers were in bits. This wasn't a schoolroom.

"Miss Petard lets me help her with hardware repairs when I'm ahead of the class," Ray explained grandly. That "when" would be "all the time," but he didn't say it.

"I can't steal the school's computer parts!" I squeaked in horror.

"You don't have to," he promised, as smug as if he'd been waiting for that objection. He stepped over to a set of shelves, scooped up a pile of cards and drives and cords, carried them over to the nearest table, and dumped them on it. "All broken. She never throws anything away. You just need the parts, don't you?"

Claire, bless her as the best friend a girl could have, heaved a toolbox onto the table.

I grabbed a screwdriver and opened up the casings. A length of copper wire, any battery, it wasn't a complicated device. It had to... what was the word? Modulate? It wouldn't be exactly the same signal constantly. It had to work in a pattern. I needed... I didn't know the name of the part I needed. I tried to pry some electronics off of a circuit board with a screwdriver, and it snapped in half.

"FRACK!" I didn't quite swear.

"What are you looking for? Maybe we can find it," Claire asked.

I shook my head. "I've got what I need here. I just need to rearrange things."

"You can't rearrange a circuit board. They're made that way in a factory. You'd have to recycle the whole board and start from scratch. We don't carry blanks." Ray was trying to be gentle, but it was useless because he was wrong. Or he was right, kind of.

Recycle. I'd have to recycle the whole board.

"I need... metal cutting tools," I begged. Was I begging? My voice sounded so quiet. Yes, I needed those tools. I couldn't let this go.

"I don't think there are any in a computer lab, Penny," Claire warned.

Ray's eyelids lowered, and his grin widened. He'd thought of something. "There aren't, but nobody's using the shop classroom in the morning."

"There's a shop class?" Claire and I asked simultaneously.

"It's downstairs," Ray told me, grabbing our hands and pulling us out the door.

"There's a downstairs?" Claire and I asked simultaneously.

He dragged us down to the corner stairway. There were the stairs going up, like I'd expected, and there were stairs going down. I'd been to Northeast West Hollywood Middle for three years, and I'd never had any idea these were here.

It was like a sign. The tools I needed were down there. I skipped down the stairs ahead of Ray and ran down the short, blankly white hallway. One of the doors said "Shop," and I flung it open. I walked inside and was surrounded by ugly, crude versions of all the mad machines in Dad's workshop that I'd have to find the names of.

I knew what I needed. Gears, lots of gears. I found them. Magnets, electricity. I flipped on a saw and sliced pipe into thin slices, then squeezed them in a vice. It was obvious, wasn't it? You could recycle anything. Even energy, sort of.

Stop trying to find words. I didn't know what I meant, but I could see it.

I twisted the top segment into place. It looked like a centipede. I sighed, put the soldering iron into its brace and turned around to lean against the table until my muscles stopped shaking.

Ray and Claire stared at me like I'd made a second head instead of—

"What is this thing?" I asked, looking at the contraption in my hands. Large portions of it had no cover plates. There was just no way I'd made gears that tiny, much less fit them together.

"Shouldn't you know?" Claire asked me. She and Ray really looked scared. No wonder. Was that a psychotic break? I felt so tired now, but relaxed. Well, if I'd stressed out so badly I'd made this ridiculously intricate piece of modern art, my parents would be sympathetic. Therapy wouldn't be so bad.

"I think it's just—" I started, absently twisted it in my hands. It resisted, but turned, like a crank. And just like a crank, it kept turning. Then it flipped, grabbed my hand with its many legs, and crawled up my arm.

Claire squealed, but I wasn't afraid. I'd made it. I knew it wasn't going to hurt me. That was about all I knew.

Ray got there before either of us. "Penny, you made that. You have super powers!" he announced.

My eyes stung. He was right. He was so right! I lunged forward and grabbed both of them and squeezed them in a hug. I felt a little electric feeling as Ray's not-as-skinny-as-I'd-have-thought chest pressed against me, and he must have felt the same about Claire, but... forget that!

"I have super powers!" I crowed, my voice squeaking like a mouse. "Just like Dad's ... ! Almost like Dad's." I saw Dad work all the time. He had to do research, lots and lots of research, and he knew exactly what he was building ahead of time and what it did when he finished.

"I made this," I said, pulling back and holding up my hand as the little automaton crawled up that arm and fastened itself around my wrist like a bracelet. "I have no idea what it does."

"It's an inscrutable little machine, isn't it?" Ray admitted, leaning down to peer at the snowflake gears.

Who cared about the details? I was a superhero!

CHAPTER TWO

I had my weird little machine, and I had my super power. Now I had to do the right thing. Before, that would have been humiliating and terrifying. Not now.

Claire tried to argue with me. It was her decision, blah blah blah. She shut up when I pulled the door to the biology classroom open.

"Claire Lutra, Penelope Akk, Ray Viles, what are you doing, and, Miss Lutra, why are you so late?" Mrs. Golgi demanded, pausing in her lecture to give us a frosty glare. I imagined Claire and Ray fainting behind me, but I was in front on purpose. I couldn't feel her anger at all, just the wonderful high-tech metal bracelet around my wrist that I'd made myself.

The right thing would also be the smart thing, if I was brave enough to do it, but that wasn't the point. It was the right thing.

"Mrs. Golgi, I'm here to apologize," I told her solemnly. "I'm the reason Claire missed class. I've been having a hard time, and I broke down, and, if Claire and Ray hadn't found me and gotten me through it, I don't know what I would have done. I really lost it. I know I'm going to be in trouble, but please don't blame Claire for being a good friend."

It was all completely true. Talking about super powers would have confused the issue. What I'd said had been the important part.

Mrs. Golgi could tell. She looked stumped, like anyone caught between anger and sympathy. I'd had her last year, and she was a good teacher and a good person. All my teachers were.

Her face and tone never gave away exactly how she'd decided to feel, but she ordered, "Claire, take your seat. You'll have just enough time to copy down the homework. You two, get to your next class. If you don't show up on time, you can expect to be in even more trouble than you are now, Penelope."

"Yes, Mrs. Golgi," I agreed. I felt like doing the Japanese thing and bowing, but she'd think I was insulting her when I meant it. I did the next best thing and obeyed immediately, backing out into the hall.

"You have German. I've got to get back to computer science," Ray told me sheepishly. Our classrooms were in opposite directions.

"You're not abandoning me." Lifting up my right hand, I showed off the segmented bracelet wrapped around my wrist. "See you in science," I promised. I smiled, and it felt like contentment shot straight from the bracelet into my heart, then spread out everywhere. I had a super power. All that worry and tension were over.

So he went one way, and I went the other. I got to German class right as the bell rang to let out the last class. I learned immediately that my super power hadn't opened up some awesome wealth of new brains. I spent the hour struggling to figure out which nouns had which gender.

I was fine with that. My German grade was a sideshow now. If I could pull it up, that would be great.

What was important was my invention, which I had no time to investigate while trying to give German the focus it desperately needed.

That had to wait until the next period, in science. Not the same as biology, or computer science. "Science" wrapped up chemistry and physics in one bag. It was often a fun class, and today we compared elastic and inelastic reactions, throwing cue balls and toy cars and rubber balls at each other and doing lots of calculations to figure out how much force was lost when they hit.

It was a perfect excuse for me, Claire, and Ray to huddle together. Plus, we had the measurements and calculations of each experiment finished in half the time anybody else did and didn't even have to concentrate. It gave us time to talk.

And we had a much more interesting scientific conundrum on our hands. On my wrist.

"You still don't remember what it does?" Claire asked as she scribbled down the calculated force of our slingshot.

"No! It's not a blank. I remember putting it together, but I can't make sense of it. I didn't know any words for what I was doing," I whispered.

"You may not remember long. Memories you don't have words for disappear quickly," Ray suggested as he smacked a toy car against a wall.

I measured the distance it traveled back. "There has to be some superhuman dexterity thrown in. These levers and gears are beyond tiny." I peered into one of the open panels at the bracelet's intricate guts, my heart burning with pride.

"I hope you can take it off," Claire pointed out. We were all feeling pretty whimsical.

I was sure I could, but I wasn't going to experiment while performing a lab experiment. It would have to wait until I had real freedom, during lunch!

I only had the patience to go through the cafeteria line because I knew I'd regret not eating big time by the time I got home. We get a lot of Bel Air kids whose parents don't go for the private school thing, but the food is still bland. So bland that I picked up a couple of pieces of cafeteria pizza without enthusiasm. It's all just different colors of cardboard.

Claire had to be developing superhuman lateness superpowers. Ray watched me and my machine approach the table like a hawk ready to pounce, but Claire was nowhere to be seen—

until the instant I sat down she walked in the door and made an impatient beeline to settle beside me.

"It can't just be a bracelet. Look at all that machinery. And we saw it move!" Claire cooed over the machine. It was rapidly becoming The Machine in my head, the mystery device my life now orbited around.

Ray leaned over the table, adjusting his glasses like magnifying lenses as he squinted into one of the open panels. "The internals are purely mechanical. I noticed that while you were building. It doesn't run on electricity. Your first doomsday machine is a malevolent, inscrutable wristwatch." I left my right arm stretched out over the table for them to study while I ate limp brown cardboard with gooey yellow cardboard on top of it. I wasn't going to ask for my hand back from Ray, nope. Not even after the "doomsday machine" crack.

"Does it run at all, now? It moved before. How do you trigger it?" Claire asked.

I washed the "pizza" down with milk. At least milk is milk. I minded more that having to eat something had kept me from my own investigations. Wiping my hand on a napkin to get less grease on The Machine, I made my first attempt to slide it off my wrist. That didn't work. I was pretty sure the segments clenched tighter together when I pulled.

"It's not stuck there, is it? Like, forever?" Claire asked, suddenly anxious.

I breezed that question aside. "Worst comes to worst, my Dad can get it off. I knew what I was making when I made it, even if I didn't have words. I'm positive it wasn't meant to hurt me."

"We can mark off 'malevolent,' but we're still left with 'inscrutable.'" Ray chuckled.

"Maybe your powers don't have to do with inventing in general, but with this—" Claire started to suggest, but she suddenly stopped. Half the conversations in the cafeteria stopped when some adults opened the doors.

Not just any adults. My Mom and Dad. Brian "Brainy" Akk and The Audit didn't have much of a secret identity, so a lot of the kids knew on sight that these were my parents.

I ought to have been mortified and terrified, but instead I had trouble keeping my expression solemn and apologetic like it ought to be. I stood up, grabbed my book bag, and walked around to the door to meet them. Nobody in the crowd said anything mean. Maybe they knew, in some secret mob psychology way, that this was my moment of triumph rather than shame.

Ray and Claire fell in behind me. I wanted to tell them not to. As much as I no longer cared, there might be serious trouble on the way. I'd like to have kept Ray and Claire out of that, but that would be taking away their chance to share my triumph.

No teachers waited with my folks out in the hallway. Superheroes had to be trustworthy, right? Mom and Dad were trying to look noncommittal. They didn't know what was going on, yet. Mom's poker face is amazing, but Dad looked worried. "Penny, we got a call from the Principal's Office. You told them you missed math class because of some kind of nervous collapse." My heart thumped in my chest. He had the most serious expression in the world, and the sharply planed face for it. I had the best parents.

I couldn't leave them in suspense. As solemnly and respectfully I could, I explained, "It's true. I've been going crazy with stress, but I think that was a side effect. I had to get a little crazy to make this." I held up my wrist and grinned. I couldn't hold it in anymore. They'd understand, now.

They knew what it meant, but they didn't want to just leap to the obvious conclusion. "You built this yourself? What does it do?" asked my Dad, taking my hand and holding my wrist up high so he could peek in at the machinery.

He ought to have turned around and told me what it did. That he didn't got my Mom's notice. "Even if it's just jewelry, Brian, that's not middle-school level craftsmanship. That's not even prodigy-level craftsmanship." Her eyes turned on me with her professional look. Yikes, now I knew why criminals sometimes surrendered without a fight. I felt like I'd been disassembled and weighed and every part tagged. "What tools did you use, and how long did it take?"

"I had power tools from the shop, and about half an hour?" I glanced at Ray and Claire for confirmation, and they nodded.

"Less than forty-five minutes, Mrs. Akk. We got Claire back to class before the bell," Ray agreed.

"Even if it's junk…" Mom began. She didn't get to finish.

"Stop fighting the obvious, Beebee. Your daughter's powers have arrived! Congratulations, darling!" Claire's Mom squealed. I was suddenly engulfed in platinum blonde hair and strong, slender arms. Only Mom had seen her coming. Well, only Mom didn't look surprised.

"We don't know anything for sure yet, Misty," Mom argued. Even she was starting to crack a smile. This argument was lost before it started.

"Can you think of any explanation that does not involve Penny having super powers?" The Minx shot back. She set me down, but gave me another quick hug. "This is the proudest moment of your life so far, Penny. Throw caution to the wind and enjoy it."

"As for you two…" Claire's Mom went on, rounding on Claire and Ray. She gave both of them a playful hair ruffle, and praised, "You two are such good friends. You're not in any trouble at all, Claire. Skipping class to help a friend you're worried about? Getting to see that shining moment when her power comes out for the first time? I'm proud of you. Both of you."

That last came with a wink at Ray, who looked stunned. I could tell Dad was staring, just less obviously. Rather than having to work to use it, Claire's Mom had to work *not* to use her powers. Her control must be slipping today. I hope I look that good when I'm nearing forty, but she had to be using superpowers to keep a boy as young as Ray mesmerized.

I was one of those people with super powers now!

My Dad had more self-control than Ray. He pulled his attention back to The Machine on my wrist. "What does it do?" he asked. The million-dollar question, right there.

"I don't actually know," I admitted.

"We'll take you home and analyze it, Princess. We ought to do that anyway," Dad assured me, placing his hand on my backpack to start me moving.

"Mom?" I asked. She understood what I meant and nodded. There'd be five more bucks in the Princess jar when we got home.

"You two are finishing the school day. Sorry, kids!" Claire's Mom told Claire and Ray as I walked away from them.

Being sent home from school early never felt so much like a victory parade.

Keeping my hands off of The Machine during the ride home was a labor of Hercules. Keeping from bouncing off the ceiling of the car was a labor of Hercules.

"Go over the process of building it for me, Pumpkin," Dad urged from the front seat.

"Mom?"

"One Princess, one Pumpkin," she acknowledged.

"The question stands," my father insisted.

"There's not much to go over. I've been getting more and more stressed out, and I felt like building that power-revealing device would fix it. This morning, it got so bad I cut class to try to build it. It was the only thing I could think about. Then I got some tools, and, when I figured out they weren't enough, I got an idea of how to fix that. Then I ran out of words. That's why I don't know what it does. I knew what I was making, but I don't know what that knowledge meant. I was really wrapped up in it. Totally obsessed, lost track of the world." That was pretty much all I knew.

"That's not my power," Dad mused.

"It might be an early stage. She has the comprehension skill you do, but she doesn't know enough science yet to communicate that comprehension with her language centers," Mom countered. I ought to have felt incensed that I'd been brushed off with "doesn't know enough science," but compared to Dad? No, I didn't know enough science.

We pulled into the driveway. Dad set a speed record getting out of the car.

"To my workroom, young lady. We're going to find out what you built, and what you can do," he ordered.

Maybe a "young lady" jar next to the other two?

I beat Dad to the lab. Workroom, laboratory, whatever you want to call it. Me, I'm getting a lab. Since Dad's specialty is applying other people's theories rather than research, it was actually a fancier version of the school's shop class. Much, much fancier.

I had to wait, hands clasped and grinning like a mad scientist, while he unlocked the door. I felt like I'd float right up to the ceiling. The master was going to take a look at my handiwork and tell me what it did! Eagerness scampered up and down my spine. Come on, door!

Dad was in a hurry too, but not enough. It must have taken him thirty seconds to unlock the door, turn on the lights, and ask me, "Okay, Pumpkin. Can you take off your creation safely so I can have a look at it?"

Good question. "I don't know. I think so? Let me try."

So I tried. The bracelet was too tight to slide over the wider bones of my wrist. In fact, the segments squeezed together, getting tighter, when I tried. Not a great sign, that. Pulling it back the other way didn't help. I twisted it, and the segments turned against each other with a grinding resistance.

Oh, right, that's how I got it moving the first time! I grabbed the band and rolled my fist around. The Machine began to writhe on my wrist. The head unbuckled, the tiny legs came out, and it crawled sluggishly around my arm. Sluggishly? It picked up steam, spiraling up my arm like the crazy metal bug it vaguely resembled.

"Hey, stop that!" It stopped. "Sit on my hand, not my face!" I yelled. The Machine scuttled forward again, now twining down my arm with purpose and crawling up on my hand.

"Voice commands?" asked my mother from the doorway.

"She's thirteen," my father threw back skeptically.

"Sit up!" I ordered The Machine. HA! It reared up on my palm like a snake!

"Voice commands," my mother repeated. She sounded amused, and her folded arms and lazy posture as she leaned against the doorjamb shouted her sarcastic amusement at my Dad's cautious attitude.

"Unless you think she found a voice recognition unit in her middle-school shop class, she built one in less than half an hour. We're well into superhuman territory here already," she added.

HA! I resisted my urge to stamp my feet and laugh. HA!

"It is an advanced-placement middle school," Dad tried. Neither Mom nor I dignified that with a response. He hadn't been serious anyway.

"May I examine it?" Dad asked when we'd been silent at him long enough.

"Sit still, and don't do anything," I ordered The Machine. It didn't respond, which was good, right? I picked it off my hand with two fingers—kind of heavy to carry that way—and put it in Dad's hands. It stayed in its reared up posture like a statue.

Good enough!

He unlocked his computer, laid The Machine on his scanner, closed the lid, and started tapping buttons. "An interior layout will tell us the most. We'll try scans all across the wavelengths, but we'll begin with a simple x-ray."

The giant virtual screen he built just to prove that it could be done lit up. There was The Machine, a white cylinder with little legs sticking off of it. Solid white. Dad magnified one of its segments. The straight edges weren't straight, they were blobby in this representation. The interior was solid, unvarying white. Plain white.

"It's made of metal, so I guess x-rays were never going to penetrate too well," I said.

"At the intensity I bombarded it, I should get at least a blurry interior picture," Dad countered. I watched him adjust the wavelengths. I watched nothing whatsoever change on the picture. Okay.

He switched to magnetic imaging. Same thing. "Well, it eats a very broad range of energy types. I might be able to overload that effect, but if I succeeded I'd only damage the device," he observed.

28

"Please don't." This was my first invention as a superhero. Even if it did nothing we hadn't seen already, or stopped working in ten minutes, I wanted to keep it to show my grandchildren one day!

"We'll try passive mapping systems," Dad assured me. He clicked a few menus. There, that was the passive magnetic scan.

Well, I guess it worked. "All I can tell is that it's full of junk," I said. It looked like a regular medical x-ray, all cloudy bits inside solid shell.

"You really packed in the gears, Pumpkin," he told me. Complimented me, I guess. I held up a finger, and Mom nodded. I was cleaning up on the Pumpkin jar this week!

"What's the bright rectangle?" I pointed at the one shape that stood out in the body.

"I think it's a 9-volt battery. It's mostly drained. I'm not seeing signs of electrical current," Dad answered. Then he sighed, clicked off the scanning program, unsealed the scanner and heaved up the lid. "Eyeball examination will have to do."

He picked up The Machine, and, on an impulse, I ordered, "Straighten out." It did, extending into a straight line maybe a foot long. Less, really. So it was still active!

Watching Dad put it in a vise and pick up his screwdriver made my heart seize up, but I just had to be cool. He wouldn't risk breaking it. Not something this valuable. His glasses rearranged to magnify as he peered into the many gaps in The Machine's plates.

Right now, his own super power was working, trying to connect what he knew about science with the thing in front of him, analyze the pattern, and distill it into a practical result. "Your guess is as good as mine as to what it does. I'd swear it's purely mechanical. I can't find a power source at all," came the answer.

Wow, I'd outfoxed Dad's super power. Go, Penny!

"Superhumans with creative powers traditionally create artificial life or perpetual motion the first time their powers emerge. Looks like our Penny pulled off both at the same time," Mom told Dad. She sounded proud, but…

"There's no such thing as perpetual motion, even for us," I argued. "Us." HA! I get to say "us" from now on!

"Photosynthesis looks like perpetual motion if you don't know anything about chemistry. How could shining sunlight on chemicals keep reactions

29

going forever? There's always a price, always entropy being made and fuel being consumed. We still call something like this a perpetual motion machine because it looks like it's ignoring those rules. Like your Mom said, they're the first thing most mad scientists make." Dad leaned back in his chair and put his elbows on the desk as he explained all this to me. His glasses whizzed and clicked, rearranging to their normal configuration.

"Mad scientists are villains, Dad. I'm not a mad scientist," I scolded him.

"I'm not sure you're anything, yet," he countered. Wait, what? I looked back at Mom. She wasn't correcting him.

When I went back to staring at him, he explained, "It's normal for superhuman powers to go off without—"

I cut him off, throwing up both hands. "I know, I know! You don't have to give me the super- powered Birds And The Bees speech!" Criminy, he was probably right. I'd worked completely on instinct. Maybe my powers hadn't emerged yet, after all.

"Can I have my Machine back?" I asked immediately. I knew I sounded like a begging baby, but when Dad pulled it out of his vice and set it in my hands, when I tried to bend it around my wrist and it got the hint and locked up like a bracelet again, I felt so much safer. This was my proof. I'd done something no regular human could possibly do.

"It's fine, Penny—" my Mom started, her voice gentle.

I interrupted her. "I really don't want the super-powered Birds and Bees speech, Mom!" Being patronized would make this worse.

"I was saying, it's easy to check," she corrected me. "Brian, you don't mind if she uses your work room for this, right?"

"Go right ahead, Pumpkin. Make another. Make anything," Dad urged me, sliding out of his chair and stepping over by Mom.

Eek. Okay, pressure time. Big, big pressure time, Penny. I looked around. Dad's machines made even less sense than the ones in the shop. Well, no, that wasn't true. Everything here was nicely labeled, and, even if I didn't know how to work it, that machine over there stamped microchips, and there was his micro water knife, and... well, I sort of understood everything I saw.

Okay, build another Machine. I looked at it, wrapped snugly around my wrist. I'd felt so inspired. I'd needed to recycle circuit boards, right? What was it like to think that way?

It wasn't coming. Maybe something simpler? I had all the parts here. I knew how Dad's nervous system antenna worked. Funny now that building it would do its job for it.

I still didn't know the math. I didn't know what I was doing.

I must have signaled my defeat somehow. I became aware of Dad standing over me, and he reached down and wrapped his arms around my middle and picked me up. I didn't think he was still strong enough to do that.

"Okay, I'm going to be serious, Princess. The bad news is, you'll have a flash like this every few months, not as impressive, but you shouldn't expect your power to emerge for at least a year, maybe three or four." His voice was low and smooth as he laid it out. Not comforting, exactly. Professionally respectful, one superhuman to another.

Then he turned me in his trembling arms, as much as he wanted to pretend I was still eight and he could do this easily, and he leaned his head down until his glasses tapped mine. "The good news is, your powers are on their way and they're amazing. Maybe you're not a superhero now, but you will be one day. You proved that today. The only question is where we go out to eat to celebrate."

"Pizza Place!" I answered instantly. The prospect of the best pizza in the world soothed my disappointment considerably. I wrapped my arms around Dad and hugged him, and our glasses clinked again. His were way more complicated and high tech, but you know what? Now it was only a matter of time.

"The Audit! Run for it! Everybody run for it!" the owner yelled. Cooks and deliverymen scrambled around like scared ants.

"This must be the twentieth time you've made that joke," Mom told him as everybody smirked.

"Twenty? Really?" he asked her. Everyone settled down and got back to cooking.

"Contrary to rumor, I don't count everything, Mr. Grigoryan," Mom informed him. Her hands at her side flashed me seven fingers.

It was easy to enjoy the humor as I climbed into my seat. The tables and chairs in Pizza Place are really high. I've never asked why. It's Los Feliz, so

I'm not sure there has to be a reason. The smell of cooking cheese hung thick in the air, and I just couldn't wait.

A meal at Pizza Place really eases the disappointment. Of all the tiny little restaurants that litter Los Feliz and serve amazing food, this is my favorite. It's small—two tables inside and one outside small—but the pizza is so good. So good.

Forget cafeteria pizza. They brought ours to the table, with the fluffy, dark brown crust and the pepperoni slices curling up on top of the cheese, and I grabbed the first slice and stuffed it in my face. It was greasy, but not grease. Hot cheese, greasy, full of flavor, with a sharply spicy sauce.

"I'm really proud of you, Pumpkin," Dad told me after a couple of measly bites. I reached for my second slice.

I glanced up at Mom.

"Three Pumpkins, two Princesses," she recited.

And that was just since I got out of school. Once I made a deposit in my bank account, I'd be buying the Candy Chainsaw expansion pack to Teddy Bears and Machine Guns this weekend. That was a pretty good bonus reward.

"I'm serious, Penny," Dad went on, all stubborn. "Every parent in the community wonders whether they do or don't want their children inheriting their powers. It's a dangerous, crazy life, sometimes." I shot a glance up at Mom. Yeah, she had that wistful look too. "I've asked myself that question more than once in the last year, but, when I looked at the mechanisms in your little creation there, I felt so proud I thought I would explode. I know it's going to hurt waiting four years for your power to really emerge, but when it does it's going to be something else."

"Until then, you'll have to be patient. Like the other Birds And Bees speech, you can't rush this. It will happen in its own time," Mom added. They'd switched roles, and now she was the designated Bad Cop.

I bit into another slice of pizza. So good! So good! Was it any wonder this little hole-in-the-wall restaurant was where superheroes went for their pizza?

Speaking of which, I gaped as a suit of shiny brown armor hit the sidewalk. I wasn't alone. Yeah, the superheroes ate here, but in costume?

And Mech himself?

Mr. Grigoryan had to slap his workers around to get them moving again. I could have used a slap myself as Mech entered the store, walked right up to our table, took off his helmet, and told me, "I hear there's a new mad scientist in LA. Welcome to the brotherhood, sister." And he winked at me.

I was going to fall out of my chair. I couldn't feel my butt. And he took off his helmet! Yes, the goggles and the flight suit underneath with all the metal to fit into the suit were nearly as good as a mask, but it was still a risk.

I should have protested that mad scientists are villains, but if Mech and my Dad both used the term…

Dad just couldn't let me enjoy it. "Tell the rumor mill they're jumping the gun, Mech. Penny's powers showed themselves rather spectacularly today, but it's only a flash. She won't be one of us for a few years."

Bah.

"Those few years will disappear, Brian. Be ready for it. So, what did you make?" Mech looked at me again!

I held up my wrist. Then I felt like an idiot, so I told The Machine, "Uncurl." It didn't. I'd have to restart it.

"Artificial life and a perpetual motion machine in one go," Mom filled in. Now she looked pleased. Both of my parents did. Proud.

"I can't figure out how it works. It appears to eat ambient energy to keep moving and stores it in a nine-volt battery, of all things. It isn't even electrical. The actual method of operation is a mystery," Dad explained.

Mom flashed a whimsical smile. "And it crank starts."

Yes, I'd had to grab it and twist it around, feeling it grind reluctantly until it picked up speed and came to life. Uncurling, The Machine climbed up onto my upraised hand and reared up facing Mech.

"May I?" Mech asked me, personally.

"Absolutely."

I knew I blushed. I sounded like an idiot fan girl. It's just that Mech was talking to me, and he'd taken off his helmet, and, even with the gold mask of the flight suit, he had a jaw that rounded down in a way that was almost pretty, and his dark skin (Indian, maybe? I didn't know him out of the suit) and his black eyes ….

Get a grip, Penny. Get it fast. Mech is just the top of the game. Smart, powerful, dedicated. When those aliens with the drone army attacked, Mech was one of the heroes who went out to destroy their warp gate.

Actually, as a superhero's daughter, I was one of the very few non-heroes who even knew that had happened, and I was in the process of "superhero."

He had a thousand idiot fan girls, but treated me with respect regardless. While my brain raced, he picked up The Machine.

I heard a nasty scraping noise, like metal fingernails on a blackboard. It came from The Machine. What the frog? Was it chewing on the thumb of Mech's suit?

"Stop that!" I scolded. It went still.

"Voice commands, no identifiable power source, and it's packed with gearwork. I'm impressed. The first thing we invent is often our greatest creation. Your father has warned you about that?" Mech asked, peeking up from squinting into The Machine's open panels. They were convenient for showing off, but it looked half-built with a casing only on some of its segments.

"Yeah," I answered. Was absolutely everyone going to try and give me the speech?

No, he was going another direction. He gave me a warm smile, and he looked impressed. He really looked impressed. "If the rest of your inventions are only half as brilliant as this, I look forward to adding some of them to my armor."

I laid my hands carefully on the table and tried not to geek out. Sitting on them would have been safer, but more obvious.

Dad smirked. "Throwing me over for the younger model, Mech?"

"I wouldn't even be in the same league I am without your additions, Brian. All I invented was the armor," Mech assured my Dad, giving him that warm smile now.

"Which I still can't replicate. As efficient and adjustable as it is, you could go to anyone for weapon systems," Dad answered in the same tone.

"Mech, how is Marvelous?" Mom inquired, slipping into the mutual congratulations.

"I got her a sample of dragon blood this morning. The real stuff, not a mutated super science lizard. She believes with that she can break the curse."

"Dragon blood might help. Dragon genetics makes guppies look simple. Their blood is full of so many unusual enzymes, I've seen it spontaneously induce super-powered mutations," Dad mused. Me, Mech, and Mom all had the same expression. Dad would fight to his last breath to describe magic as anything but magic.

"Where did you get real dragon blood?" Mom asked.

"From Malachi. Are you aware of another dragon who isn't deep in hiding?" Mech replied. There was definitely a sardonic element in his tone.

"How did he take it?" Mom asked back, with the same tone.

"I need Brian to replace the shield supercharger, that's how he took it," Mech answered her.

They were drifting into superhero shop talk, which could be pretty cool, except I didn't know anything about Malachi and I didn't get the joke. It would only get worse from here. Anyway, I wanted to play with The Machine, now that I'd woken it up, but Mech was still holding it in his hands.

I reached down into Mom's briefcase and pulled out a paperclip. I couldn't play with The Machine, but paperclips had potential. They stored energy in tension well, like they were waiting to be springs. There was a lot you could do with that. I just had to twist, and twist, and use the edge of the table to make a sharp kink there, and I set the paperclip down on the table and watched it walk half a dozen steps before it fell over.

What...?

I picked up the paperclip, or at least the thing I'd made out of a paperclip. I'd made a thing out of a paperclip. My parents hadn't noticed, but I could show them right now. I set it down to walk again, and it fell over. Oh, right, the tension had wound down, and I... had no idea how to reset it.

So much for showing anyone.

Wait! Dad told me it would be months before I had another flash like this. It had only been a few hours. My parents were expecting it to be years before my powers emerged properly.

My parents were in for a big surprise, very soon.

CHAPTER THREE

The next morning, or technically noon, I sat down at lunch with Ray; Claire was hardly a heartbeat behind us. I'd had just enough time to give them headshakes until now.

Claire laid her lunch box on the table with a clink. "So what's the word?"

"'Inscrutable?'" Ray suggested.

"Did your Mom tell anyone I got my powers?" I asked Claire. The tone of accusation went right out of me when she unpacked her lunch and passed me her turkey pot pie. Where did a woman like The Minx, who never had to be domestic, learn to cook like this?

"Anyone? Everyone! And then I got home and they're calling her back saying you don't have your powers after all," Claire filled in, cutting her lump of fried potato hash in half and slipping it to Ray.

"I'm fairly certain I remember standing there for half an hour while you giggled and your hands moved like lightning. That seemed a touch superpower-y to me." Ray tried to look serious, but his voice cracked and couldn't hold the deadpan.

"It's a little of both. I've got super powers, but they're not here yet. They're just hinting at what they'll be," I replied, then took a bite of the pot pie before I had to speak again. It wasn't pizza, but the crust was nice and fluffy and bready and blended perfectly with the chewy turkey. Even cold, it was good stuff.

"Ah, a super-powered adolescence. I've heard that happens." Ray was much better at keeping the disappointment off his face, but now the noncommittal solemnity betrayed him.

"Mom's happened all at once. She said it was scary, but it got her out of all the trouble it got her into. What timeline did your folks give you?" Claire asked.

"They said a year to four years. They meant four years minimum. I could tell," I answered.

Claire and Ray looked at me. Apparently my poker face sucks, too. I had to go on. I hunkered closer and lowered my voice. "They're wrong. I had a second episode while we were eating dinner. Just a little tiny one, but if it's really going to be years that wouldn't happen." I might keep this secret from my folks, but there was no way I wasn't sharing it with my best friends.

"So what are we looking at?" Claire pressed.

"Dunno. If they keep happening, maybe days? A week? I'm betting no longer than by summer," I non-answered. I wished I had a real answer.

Claire frowned. "Six months would be a long time to wait."

"I don't know. I'm looking forward to six months of random super-science inventions," Ray countered.

"That sounds fun for us, but the guessing is going to kill Penny," Claire told him.

"I've got a distraction right here," I assured them both. I held up my wrist, letting my shirt cuff fall away from The Machine.

"I know this thing does more than just move around. We need to find out what." My co-conspirators grinned.

I was smart enough to text my Mom before my last class that I'd be sticking around after school to hang out with Claire and Ray. She wouldn't object. How the two biggest nerds in all of superherodom could worry that their daughter spent too much time playing computer games and not enough outside in the healthy fresh air baffled me.

It's pretty safe around the school, which helps. The poor heroes all live south of here, and do a lot of patrolling in South Central, and the rich heroes live just north. Me and Claire were the only kids of openly admitted superheroes in school, but muggers and drug dealers and what all knew this was the most dangerous neighborhood in the city for them. Here, and Chinatown. I couldn't tell you why Chinatown, I'd just heard my folks say it. Superhero gossip.

We're on our own against bullies, unfortunately. I wish it was a surprise to step out the side door onto the recess grounds and see Marcia bee-lining toward Ray with three of her friends watching.

He was reading while he waited for me, so, of course, she grabbed the book right out of his hands and snarked, "Class is over. Do you ever spend five minutes without your nose in a book?"

"Please give my book back," Ray said, quiet and serious. That's Ray with other people.

Marcia smirked at him. She was blonder than he was, the perfect LA princess like everybody sees on TV, and taller than him, and cheerleaders are pretty strong. He looked so skinny and helpless, and she looked like what she was, just plain mean.

Then she glanced at the book itself, and it got worse. With that nasty drawn-out twang her voice has, she laughed. "Oh, please. Look at this, Rachel. It's not even a book. It's a catalog for superhero toys! Guess who wants to get his hands on a page full of superheroine figurines?"

Ray gets really expressionless at times like this, but that just tells you how mad he is. I didn't want to look at it, but I also wanted to do something. "Stop acting like a harpy and give him his book back!" I snapped at her as I stomped up.

Like that did any good. "Oh, please, now he needs a girl to rescue him. And it's the Akk girl, whose superpower is the biggest pair of glasses in the world." I tried not to wince. My glasses look great! I could have had contacts if I wanted.

"Here. You can have your pictures of women in spandex back." Marcia turned around and tossed the book over her shoulder. Ray had to grab twice to catch it.

He didn't want to look at me. I had to get control of my breathing and stop trembling. Why would anybody enjoy being mean like that? At least I'd scared her away.

No, I hadn't scared her away. That made no sense; I was another target. Claire had rounded the corner and was walking toward us. Picking on Claire doesn't make you look good. "I'd like to say a few things about

38

her, but my mother says that swearing isn't classy for villains or heroines," she muttered as she joined us.

"Forget her. We're supposed to be celebrating." Ray still sounded sour, but he was right. We wouldn't stop being sour by stewing.

Claire knew the right thing to say. "Is that the new Dynamic catalog?" she squealed, crowding up closer to peek into it. While Ray blushed and looked stunned, she crowed, "They came out with the classic Minx figurine. I've got to get one for Mom. And that's Marvelous in her old costume! I'd forgotten how blatant it was. That's less than Mom's costume. Do you two want to go down to Rocket To Earth and see if the new stuff has come in yet?"

"Normally, sure, but I wanted to try and find out what The Machine does," Ray demurred.

"We might as well go. I can wind it up and make it move around, but, other than that, I don't even have a clue where to start," I assured them.

Ray's grin came back. "I have an idea or two. Come on," he promised me.

He led us right back inside. I wondered where we were going, but it turned out we were going right here, back to the computer labs. We'd just caught Miss Petard closing the door behind her.

"Miss Petard?" Ray greeted her, with a hopeful tone and a big smile.

"It's Friday, Ray. Shouldn't you be going home?" she replied, with a smile almost as big.

"Actually, Claire and Penny and I were interested in forming an official club, maybe lure out any other children of super-powered parents. You know who Penny's Dad is, and I thought she might have some insights on our broken supplies." I was a little surprised he'd lie to her, but… was it a lie? A club for kids of superheroes. I'd have my powers soon, and so would Claire.

Letting us fool around in her repair lab was a ridiculous request, so she must have really liked Ray. "All right, I suppose. Lock the door when you leave, Ray?"

"Of course, Miss Petard," he promised. He stood and watched her, smiling and grateful, as she started walking away. She didn't look too certain about this, but she'd agreed. When she stopped looking back, we let ourselves into the repair lab.

"Why are we even in here?" I asked Ray when the door shut behind us.

"I don't know how much you remember, but you got your inspiration when you were trying to build that antenna and didn't have the parts. I figure The Machine has something to do with electronic parts. If you try to build the antenna again, maybe you'll figure out what you needed The Machine for," he suggested.

It wasn't a bad idea. I grabbed an old hard drive and a sound and video card and dumped them on a table. Then I stared at them. What was supposed to be happening?

"Okay, I… was building the antenna," I needed a wire. Anything would do, really. Claire handed me the toolbox. It had a wire stripper, so I cut a wire out of a spare internal power cord. It didn't matter, right? And I'd have to send an electrical current through it.

This was going nowhere. Without that obsession, I knew I had no clue what I was doing. I didn't even have the tools or the supplies. I hadn't when I built The Machine, either. I'd been so annoyed by it…

"…I built a machine to recycle parts," I finished out loud.

Ray and Claire stared. They were trying not to jinx it. I grabbed The Machine and twisted until it began to roll around on my wrist by itself. It uncurled, but this time I didn't let it crawl up my arm. Instead, I dropped it on the table and pointed at the video card.

"Eat that," I ordered.

By all the stars and little fishes, The Machine did. It pounced on the card like a cat on a mouse, and a grin split my face so wide my cheeks hurt.

Behind me, Ray laughed. "He's getting fat. That's so funny!" He was right. Flakes of metal laid themselves over the gaps in The Machine's armor, and through the holes that were left I could see green plastic circuit board lining the interior. The little robot centipede looked plump.

Well, that was half the job. The Machine took voice commands, and I knew what I'd really wanted from it the first time. "Give me a blank circuit board."

It did. The Machine twisted, lurched, and ejected the original video card, blank and green and smooth with none of the attachments or holes punched in it.

"That was so cool!" I gushed, scratching its little metal head. It sat there, reared up off the workbench, perfectly still. Aww.

"Mom thought it might be alive, but I think it's just a really fancy machine," I added, looking back over my shoulder at Claire and Ray.

Ray nodded. "A very useful machine for an inventor."

It certainly was. What couldn't I do with this? "Transistor," I ordered The Machine. Off the top of my head I didn't know what a transistor was exactly, but it spat a little chunk of metal attached to wires onto the tabletop.

Now, if only my power would come in! Then I'd know what to do with this. Maybe it would even let me do something about my German grade. I had a page of vocabulary to learn for Monday, and it all looked Greek to me, pun only partly intended. It'd be nice if my power made me smarter, but maybe I could at least build something to help me study.

"Eat that. I need wires, a six-inch diameter shell, and three circular magnets," I ordered The Machine, pointing to the hard drive.

Trying to program a computer to speak a language I didn't know wouldn't work. I had to go past that, to something universal. I... stop the words, Penny. You know what you're doing!

The Machine was wonderful. It ate and it spat out parts for me, over and over, until I screwed the upper dome of the shell into place and sighed. "That's it!"

"Das ist alles!" the little metal ball immediately echoed, in a raspy metallic voice.

"It translates English—" was as far as Claire got before the ball copied, "Es English übersetzt—"

That little lever... that was the volume control. Yes! I remembered. I switched it down to zero, then I asked, "Wait, did I just invent something again?"

"You should have seen your hands move. And, apparently, The Machine makes a good wrench and screwdriver," Claire answered in a hush. She and Ray realized how close they were standing and took a sudden step apart.

I had to ignore that. "Another episode already, and that one was almost under control. I can still feel it! I need... to make something. Flying boots would be cool! I've always wanted flying boots! Now, how would those work?"

I had no idea. Well, I had some ideas. Flying boots were all over the place, although they mostly relied on exotic power systems or other components nobody but the creator could reproduce. Some of them manipulated gravity to repel the Earth as the largest body around, and you could do weird things with magnetism, and there was simple propulsive force… and the feeling I'd had when I was inventing was totally gone.

I thumped my head against the desk in despair. OW! Not doing that again.

"Not working?" Ray asked. I appreciated the wry, sympathetic tone. Perspective. That's what I needed.

"It's gone. I think we can be sure it's not gone for long." I scooped up the round metal… I guess it was a German grenade, huh? I held it in one hand and laid my wrist over top of The Machine, which curled around it obediently.

The glee hit me again. "And I know what The Machine does!"

"Part of what it does," Ray corrected me. Interesting idea, that.

"Now we can go shopping in triumph!" I told them both.

I stood back, examining a fan-made chart of Mech's tools and weapon systems. The secondary boost systems in the wrists were accompanied by a photo of him lifting a cruise ship out of the water. It was too ludicrous a weight for him to actually lift, and now I recognized those glowing, spinning wrist cuffs. That was Dad's ferrous gravitic rejection device, wasn't it? It had to be. My dad's craziest toy was installed in Mech's armor, and he was using it to move weights he shouldn't be able to budge. I'd seen the theoretical papers behind the device. Nobody else could understand them, or how Dad had turned a painfully abstract mathematical model into a functioning, if weird, invention. I sure couldn't. So how could I do the same thing? Saying it made iron's easily magnetized properties exactly cancel out gravity sounded great, but how did it work? Without lots and lots of math? Could I just… line up the…

"Hey, Penny?" Ray interrupted. Not that there was anything to interrupt. It didn't make sense, it just felt like it should. Ray, on the other hand, was really leading up to something.

Might as well be direct. "What is this leading up to?"

From me, a sarcastic tone was no discouragement. "When I told Miss Petard we were making a club, I thought it might be a good idea. You want to surprise your folks when you've got control of your powers, and, I will not lie, Claire and I want a pile of mad science devices to play with."

Claire hunched her shoulders, avoiding looking back at us for a moment. That only lasted a few seconds. Embarrassment is foreign to the Lutra genetics. Chattering enthusiasm resumed. "I should get my powers soon. A club for super-powered kids could be useful. If we're official, Upper High will transfer the club with us next year. We'll have regular time to practice our powers without our parents asking questions, because we're being all healthy and extracurricular."

"I will manfully endure being the token regular human in the club," Ray announced airily. I snickered.

I took off my glasses and scrunched up my nose, considering. Claire and Ray did exactly the same thing, just to be goofballs. "I like the idea, but it won't be much use unless I can get a laboratory set up. The school might let us use a room for club meetings, but a dozen other clubs will be using the room. We won't be able to build or install anything."

"Your Dad could set you up," Claire pointed out immediately. She slid glasses back up her nose with one finger. Elegantly, of course. Maybe her Mom taught her how.

"I'd lose out on surprising my folks, and now I really want to. They don't want to believe it's happening, so I'm going to wait until I can blow their socks off and they can't deny it." For now, though… "I don't know. Maybe having a clubhouse with a real laboratory would be worth spoiling the surprise."

Ray's smile turned sly. I'd almost missed it, since he was now one of two blonde blobs in front of me. I put my glasses back on with just enough time to catch that wicked grin before he suggested, "If you want a working laboratory, you don't need a clubhouse. You need a lair."

"Thanks for bringing me home, Mom!" I piped as I shoved the car door closed behind me. "Could I get into the basement?"

"Why?" She'd just been sitting there in the car and hadn't bothered to open the door, luxuriating in not having a schedule. Right up until I asked my question and got the pointed look.

The key was to tell most of the truth. A direct lie would not get past The Audit. Not while Mom was alert. "Me'n Claire'n Ray were thinking of starting a club. You know, kids of superheroes. It means a lot more now that my own powers are on the way, and maybe we could figure out if any other kids in the school had superhero parents. Anyway, Claire and Ray love superhero memorabilia, and it's all in the basement."

There. Lots of plausible, rambling truths that weren't the actual reason at all. Come on, fall for it!

"Trying to uncover the secret identities of your classmates is a disastrously bad idea, Penny. They could take it personally," she warned me. Gently, though. That was the voice that trusted me to do the right thing.

"You're right. It didn't occur to me, but that's how bad they'd freak out. It doesn't make a big difference. If there's a club, some of them might join us on their own, and if they don't we'll still have fun. I still want to poke through your mementos." I put on an extra-relieved smile and didn't have to fake it. It hadn't occurred to me, and her advice might have prevented a lot of trouble.

"If you want. You know what not to do," Mom finally conceded. I waited, swinging my arms behind me while she got out of the car, then followed her inside. She unlocked the door to the basement stairs and wandered over to Dad's office.

Ha! Rule one of living with super genius parents, play it light. If they suspect at all, it's over. I felt smug as I tromped down the basement stairs and flipped on the light.

For the one millionth time, I wished my parents had kept some kind of superhero headquarters beyond my dad's laboratory. This was a storage basement. It looked like a storage basement. Gray cement walls, green cement floor. Those boxes over there? Camping gear and thirteen years of my old clothing. Those file cabinets held every receipt and financial and legal form that had ever crossed my mother's hands. She never even opened them. Pure packrat instinct.

The file cabinets on the other side were different. I scampered over to them.

Mom kept papers. All kinds of papers. I pulled a drawer open. Mostly newspaper clippings. "Who is The Audit?" "Brainy Akk Captures Spectral Burglar." Maybe I should pull a couple of these. We could put them on the walls of my new lair. Claire and Ray would flip. Here were a bunch about The Minx. My Mom and Claire's Mom must have known each other forever.

I tried the next drawer. "Akk and Audit Announce Espousal.""Audit Reveals Identity To Marry Super Sweetheart." Did these fill the whole drawer? How big a story was my parents' marriage, anyway? No, they only filled half the drawer. The other half was announcements of my birth. The excitement over that disappeared fast.

Ah, this next drawer was it. I hadn't poked through these in forever, but I knew she had a bunch of files on supervillains. This stuff was all ancient, pre-internet printouts. A KGB dossier on The Last Soviet? Freaky. The inner pages were all in Cyrillic. So much for the cool factor. A scrapbook of photos of some villain in ugly spandex in action. The cover read "Unknown Villain 1993" and over that had been glued a label "Coincidence (deceased)."

Okay, who was a local mad-scientist-type villain Mom and Dad had taken down? The Thief Of Parts had stolen a lot of Dad's old crime fighting inventions when I was tiny. Dad had told me that a few times. He hadn't committed a crime in years, so info about him must be low security and might be in here. After Coincidence was Lubricia, then a thick stack of foot and fingerprints all labeled "The Hope Chest." Not alphabetical order, then. By date? No, The Last Soviet held on until nearly 2000.

This wasn't in any order. Or, if it was, it was some system only my Mom understood. I slammed the drawer shut in irritation. I should have known. They wouldn't keep any information anyone could use in our basement!

I looked at the boxes on the shelves by the filing cabinets. Most of that stuff was just as useless. The very few items that weren't were dangerous enough that I wasn't going to go opening random boxes.

That left two possibilities. My mother's laptop, sitting on its shabby little desk right here next to the filing cabinets, or Dad's computer upstairs. The location of every secret villain lair ever discovered in the world was probably on that laptop, along with the rest of Mom's important files when Dad scanned them into electronic format. It wasn't hooked up to the internet for good reason. Who knows what security systems Dad had put on it?

Time to find out. With the laptop pointing away from me, I lifted up the lid and pressed the power button. A grinding noise. Was that an alarm?! I tried to restrain the feeling that my skin was trying to jump off my body. It was just a computer noise. This was an old laptop. I knew Mom kept her Audit research on it, but...

Blue screen of death. There it was on the laptop screen: "Fatal Exception." This old broken piece of garbage didn't hold anything. My Mom had suckered me with a fake.

I grabbed my bracelet, then forced myself to let go. No, I was not going to let The Machine eat this piece of junk. I didn't know what was actually going on. Maybe this was a trap for any supervillain who just couldn't believe that Brainy Akk and The Audit had really retired. Maybe I was overthinking this, and it was an old, dead laptop, and Mom had moved her files elsewhere.

I could forget aboutgetting into Dad's computer. I needed a new plan.

"Penny, Claire's here!" Mom yelled down from upstairs.

"What, already?" I asked.

I didn't wait for an answer. What did I have down here? I ran upstairs. Claire still stood on the stoop, so I ran out to meet her, leaving my Mom to shut the door behind us.

"I struck out. Nothing," I leaned up against the car and puffed a little. Stairs, okay?

"I didn't," Claire returned.

"How did you find one this fast?" I asked in shock. I wanted to disbelieve, but she had her hands clasped behind her back, and her smile radiated smug pride.

"I asked my Mom! She thought a clubhouse in an old supervillain lair was a great idea. You're going to love her recommendation, but I have to show it to you." She was going to explode from smug. There had to be some kind of joke here, but it was a joke that got me a laboratory!

Although it wasn't a laboratory without equipment.

Something about Claire's pride was infectious. I had the craziest idea.

Opening the door again, I leaned way in and yelled, "Dad, can I have your junk bin?"

"For what?" he yelled back. He didn't sound suspicious, he sounded baffled.

"To put in our clubhouse! I'll need equipment when my powers arrive, right?" I yelled.

"You can't hurry nature, Penny. You'll get your powers when they're ready!" he called back, his voice softer with parental understanding. Parental misunderstanding. He was so sure of his own timeline for my powers, he'd gotten entirely the wrong idea about what I wanted. I had him!

"Can I have it or not?" I demanded, just as impatient as if he were right and I refused to believe him.

A moment of silence. Mom making her opinion known, I was sure. Then, "I suppose. Do you need a ride to move it?"

"Nope, Claire's Mom wanted to help with that. Thanks, Dad!" I pulled the door closed.

This was delicious. "You're sure we've got a lair?" I asked Claire.

"We could have a dozen, but one of them is perfect," she promised me.

"Then I have what we need to set it up. Watch this." I skipped around the back of the house. Yes, it was twee. I was so eager to try this.

Dad's junk bin is a huge thing. He's not great at repairs, only building things the first time, and he racks up piles of equipment that can't be regularly thrown away. Until he makes arrangements, he dumps them in a big concrete bin in the back yard. I pulled the bar out and hauled the double doors open. There was one of those saws, and his old special welding and soldering rod with the broken handle, and that was the old scanner before he built the new one. He hadn't emptied the bin in awhile. None of it worked, but there were treasures in here, if only they could be recycled.

I grabbed The Machine and twisted until it let go of my wrist and flopped around in my grip on its own. Then I tossed it into the bin. "Eat that whole pile. I'll want them back later, but with anything broken fixed back together."

With a grinding noise, The Machine began to eat. With its little jaws, this might take an hour, but it would be an entertaining hour.

Or it might take a lot less. Plates formed over the empty patches. Then they pressed out, and more plates made out of the metal it was eating slid up to fill in the gaps. New legs emerged near the front, shoveling mechanisms into larger jaws that hinged like a bear trap. Every bite made it bigger, and, as it got bigger, it ate faster.

I watched the bloated, turtle-like metal monster filling the bin suck up the last bits of wire, loose screws, and a tiny screwdriver lying on the bottom.

"Come here, boy!" I ordered, my voice hoarse from excitement.

The Machine stepped out of the bin on four bladed, multi-jointed legs. It was the size of a car.

I giggled. I wanted to laugh out loud, but if my parents hadn't seen what was going on yet, I wanted to keep them in the dark. This was the last real hurdle that might get them suspicious.

I tucked my foot into a wedge sticking out of a metal leg, grabbed the edge of an armor plate, and hauled myself up. Then I extended an arm down to Claire, who just possibly might have been radiating as much glee as I was.

"Where are we going?" I asked her.

"Head down toward Santa Monica Boulevard."

I slapped The Machine. "You heard the girl. Get moving!" It lurched, rocking underneath us as it stepped over our fence, walked up the driveway, then turned and followed the sidewalk down the street. Walked? It moved way faster than I could run.

Wait. "We're heading toward Santa Monica? It's not. It can't be—" I gaped at Claire.

She giggled back. It must be.

It was. The ride was surprisingly smooth. The Machine was obviously a superhero's kid's toy, so a few people pointed and laughed with delight, but nobody minded clearing the sidewalk as we trundled down toward West Hollywood. Right until Claire pointed and told me, "Over there."

She was pointing across the recess yard of Northeast West Hollywood Middle School. The old villain's lair was on school property.

"Go on!" I told The Machine. It picked its way across the concrete yard, and I was glad it was late Friday afternoon and every kid I knew was as far away from here as they could get.

"Those doors on the corner," Claire said as we got closer. The school is huge and capital-J-shaped. It had lots of plain locked doors on the outside I'd never worried about. On the opposite corner, there had been stairs going down to the shop class. I knew there weren't any stairs going down on this side.

A supervillain's lair was taking up that space. It had to be.

When we reached the doors, I slid off The Machine and tugged at the doorknobs. Locked, of course. I could have The Machine eat the lock.

I didn't have to. Claire's feet hit the concrete next to me, and she pulled a key out of her pocket. "Mom broke into this place right before Baron Overlord got himself banished to another dimension."

"Baron Overlord? Quite a title for a villain I've never heard of," I said as she unlocked the doors.

"Nobody's heard of him. He lasted about five minutes. Major overconfidence problem. So now his lair is ours!" Claire crowed, pulling the doors open.

Inside was a metal platform. An elevator. An elevator with lights. It still worked.

"In!" I instructed The Machine. It stepped around Claire and drew in its legs to fit in through the doors and onto the elevator. I'd programmed it to be gentle, apparently.

We squeezed in around the Machine, and I pushed a button that lit up bright green. My stomach fluttered as the floor dropped quickly, then smoothed to a halt. Wire gates opened in front of us. The lights on the elevator's posts were just enough for us to see that we faced a big, dark room.

I peeked around the corner and slapped the button on the wall. Sure enough, lights came on in rings on the ceiling of a huge, domed room. Open electrical panels gaped along the walls. I saw five more doors, two open into dark tunnels, but not much else. This place had been stripped.

I pointed at the middle of the floor. "Start upchucking, Machine. Remember, I want everything back like it was, but fix any broken parts." Would that work?

The Machine shambled past me, metal spikes clanking on the floor, and, with a loud clatter, spat my Dad's welding rod onto the floor. The rod fit perfectly into the handle.

"Penny? Claire? Are you down there?" Ray's voice called from above.

The Machine started horking up a much larger machine. "Hit the elevator button!" I yelled up. "You have got to come see this. We have a secret lair!"

CHAPTER FOUR

Monday I told Mr. Zwelf I'd be submitting The Machine for my science fair entry. He gave me the bad news immediately.

"It's an impressive invention, but it's not going to get you a good grade, Penelope," he told me as The Machine wiggled around in his hands.

"Are you kidding? I built a robot that takes voice commands and has no identifiable power source. Forget a middle-school science fair, my Dad can't reproduce it or even figure out how it works. It's as Science as it gets!" I shouldn't have sounded peeved, because Mr. Zwelf's was a good guy and I knew this was coming, but what was wrong with the world if I didn't get an A for something like this?

He explained to me what's wrong with the world. "Building something new, no matter how brilliant, isn't the same as science. Did you have a hypothesis when you made it? What were you testing?"

"I just made it. I was trying to find a way to recycle equipment better," I answered, trying not to glare.

"What process does it use?" he asked. I was fighting a losing battle, and it gnawed like acid in my stomach, but at least he really was impressed. He couldn't take his eyes off The Machine and kept trying to spread its joints to see how they connected.

If only he hadn't asked that exact question. "I don't know. I knew when I made it, but then I forgot," was the best answer I could give him.

Now he looked pained, and his voice got slow. Here came the bad news. "Penelope, I can't guarantee the other judges will believe you made this yourself."

I didn't say anything. My expression must have said volumes.

"As amazing as this invention is, I recommend you turn in a traditional project. You deserve better, but you'll be lucky to get a D if you present this," he concluded.

I took a deep breath. I'd known I might hear most of this. It still stung, but I'd made up my mind. "Thank you, Mr. Zwelf, but I'm going to go ahead. I know I'm getting an A in the rest of the class, and I can swallow an F on the science fair project if that happens. I'm proud of my Machine, and it's more important to me to show what I can do than to get a good grade for it."

"I understand," he acknowledged, dropping The Machine back into my hands.

I knew how to soothe my considerable rancor. As soon as the school bell rang, I ran down the stairs and past the shop room to the second entrance to my new laboratory (there were four!). On Saturday, I'd picked up a book from a hardware store about electrical wiring. I had all these pieces of high-tech shop equipment The Machine had salvaged for me, if only I could plug them in!

I'd opened up the book in terror, expecting to have to splice wires, grade them by voltage, hook them up in careful order to hard-to-identify terminals, and make decisions based on amperage. My jaw almost dropped at how simple it was. One of the devices The Machine had spat back up was a volt reader, so I didn't even need to buy one. I dumped the contents of my Pumpkin jar on a few grounded outlets and rubber gloves for safety, and that might be all I needed.

So, now, as I heard the door open and close, I was on my knees, using one of The Machine's jaws as a screwdriver to twist a screw drown and lock the power wires into place.

"Don't touch any switches!" I yelled back.

"Why are you working with just a flashlight?" Ray's voice asked.

"Circuit breakers," I answered. I gave the outlet a tug. Felt secure. I twisted the screws that fastened it into the wall. "Okay, flip them back on!"

Ray ran down to the circuit breaker box open and exposed at the far end of the lab. Whoever'd taken out Baron Overlord had ripped out his machinery and the power outlets they were attached to, but left the wiring in the walls intact. I was sitting pretty. I should be sitting pretty. We were about to find out.

He flipped the switches, the ceiling lights turned on, and my outlet failed to burst into flame. I stuck the volt meter sensors into the holes. 121 volts. Success!

I jumped to my feet, slapped The Machine back onto my wrist, and dragged over the metal press. I'd never used one while I was completely conscious, but the idea seemed simple enough. I plugged it into the socket, grabbed a copper rod from the pile of raw materials, stuck it into the gap, and pulled the lever. Thunk. Clank! Half a copper rod hit the floor.

I slapped my palm against Ray's. "YES! It works just like it says in the book. It's even easier than it looks!"

He grabbed a traditional screwdriver, then walked back over to the circuit breaker box. "We need more light. I'll turn off one breaker, and you can find which outlets that makes safe."

The elevator whirred, and a few seconds later the gates opened and Claire stepped in. "You look like you're in a good mood," she told me immediately.

I gave a little shrug. "Mr. Zwelf told me to expect an F if I use The Machine as my science fair project. I can't dress it up to look like an experiment. I'm gonna do it anyway."

Ray winced.

"Ow," Claire echoed.

"Don't worry. I'm fine, because I did this during Art. Watch!" I unzipped my backpack and pulled out my box of pencils, paperclips, and random stationary crud. I only used them once in a blue moon, but I hated not having a thumbtack when I needed one. You could do a lot with a thumbtack.

Don't think about it. I reached in, picked up two thumbtacks, and used the jaws of The Machine to crimp them together. Then I put them down on the floor, sticking off from each other at an angle, and spun them.

They kept spinning, whirling around in a blur without falling down or sliding away.

"What did you just do?" Claire asked, crouching down to squint at it.

"I built a simple gyroscope. I think. I don't know!" I threw up my hands and started to giggle.

Ray knew why I was laughing. "But you meant to do it!" He looked around. "We have to get this place fixed up fast. You're going to need tools before the week is over."

"I controlled my power for less than ten seconds, Ray. We've still got a few weeks," I corrected him. A few weeks. Oh, man! Let it be that soon!

Claire, smarter than either Ray or me sometimes, announced, "These wires over here have no power."

I knelt down between the two of them and walked them through the process of securing the hot, neutral, and ground wires, and wonder of wonders both outlets had screw holes to fasten into place. We all flinched as Ray flipped the breaker back on, but my laboratory again failed to erupt in flames. It must be a mad scientist record.

Not that I was a mad scientist. I just felt very giggly as we plugged in my dad's water knife table and flipped the switch. I could barely hear the hissing as the stream of water shot from overhead pump into the hole in the workbench.

"What is that?" Claire asked, doubt creeping into her voice.

"You've never seen a water knife?" I asked. I just had to keep the grin off my face as I picked up a shiny iron pipe from the pile of parts The Machine left me with, and waved it through the stream of water. I didn't even feel the resistance as the knife sliced it in two, but Claire let out a squeak of shock when the other half fell onto the work table with a clonk, rolled off the end, and fell to the floor with a louder clonk.

"That was amazing. You'll be able to build anything with this kind of equipment," Claire wheezed, leaning against the wall as she calmed down.

I flipped off the water knife. As cool as it was, it also scared the dickens out of me.

"We should make plans. Don't you want to be the girl with her own sentient supercomputer in the middle of your base?" Ray suggested.

They were both so excited! I hated to break it to them. I nudged a heating coil from what had been a microchip press with my foot. "I'm a long way from building a traditional supercomputer. The Machine is awesome, but it's not good at anything but raw materials and repairing clean breaks. Most of the stuff we brought back it spat up in bits. I've got the tools for simple metal shaping and macro electronics work, but my superpower's going to be working crippled until it builds me better machine tools. If I can get it to build me better machine tools. All the cool big machines will require custom shaped metal parts. I really need a miniature smelter with adjustable molds for casting. I've almost got the parts for one." Like that heating coil I'd just kicked over. I'd still need—

Stop thinking, Penny!

Ray caught me before I hit the floor. That was so sweet. My own prince charming, my hero. Sure, he wasn't strong enough to hold me, but, when he landed on his butt, neither of us took much of an impact. Lying in his lap with his arms around me was what counted.

What was that thing in front of me? Had I fed The Machine? So many tubes and domes.

That was my metal caster. I put metal into the bin at the top and worked those levers to adjust the prefabricated forms for the molds. With its help, I could make better molds. The whole thing was modular.

"I have to try it out. I don't want to forget how the controls work!" I gasped. I was still panting for breath, and sticky with sweat. Ugh. My legs wobbled. They wanted to rest a minute before I stood up again.

"I don't think we have time, Penny. Our folks are going to get worried if we don't get home before it's fully dark," Claire corrected me. She still sounded nervous. Or maybe excited.

Fully dark? "How long did I spend building that?" I asked.

Ray flipped open my smart phone and pressed the button. A glance at the welcome screen later, he answered, "About four hours."

I looked back up at the metal caster. It was huge. It would be so useful. Something I felt told me that and itched to try it out.

Looking up at Ray, I asked him, "End of the week?"

"I'd say, yeah," he chirped back smugly.

Tuesday.

"Were your parents suspicious?" Ray asked me as I sat down for lunch.

"Nope. A little grumbling about how hard it is to put Dad's junk back together, and they think it's a phase I'll get over. I'm going to blow their socks off when I get this under control. What do you think I should build first?" I gushed. It was a little much, but we'd had no chance to talk all morning!

"It'th not my plathe to thay, Marther," Ray played Igor back at me.

"Ho ho ho, mad scientist humor." I didn't get to tell him I was serious. He suddenly looked too puzzled.

"You don't remember?" Ray asked. Claire slid into the seat next to me, all attentive curiosity and ostentatious lunchbox opening.

"Not a thing. I go into a world without words when my power turns on. I can't hold onto it afterward," I explained to Ray. To both of them, really.

"Oh, you had words," Claire corrected me. She and Ray had the same pinched, failing to-control-a-smile expression.

"They weren't very good words, so she might be onto something." Ray tried to juggle being almost serious with dancing around an explanation.

"Spill it, minions. You're creeping the mad scientist out," I ordered.

"That's how you acted, like we were minions. Every few minutes you'd surface to shout at us to help you rearrange your tools," Claire supplied, finally.

Not that I liked the answer. "Wow. I'm sorry."

Ray raised an eyebrow. "You weren't nasty, just impatient. Maybe desperate. You might be right about the words, because it was all 'Move that here!' and 'Plug that in!' This isn't ringing any bells?"

"Total blackout. It's a little bit disturbing to find out I turn into someone else and can't remember it when my power turns on." Understatement. Maybe I needed help?

Claire passed me a plastic dish with a slice of chicken on a bed of rice, then poured a thick, transparent sauce on it from another little container AND laid a slice of her Mom's fudgy brownies on my tray. "Here. This will make you feel better."

I cut off a slice and took a bite. It was sweet, peanut-ty, and, after three seconds, I grabbed my milk carton and drank the whole thing. My tongue was burning! It was so good, but…

I twisted The Machine desperately on my wrist, and, when it let go, I ordered, "Water! Bring me cold water!"

Then, of course, I had another bite. My tongue screamed at me. This stuff was great!

I opened my mouth to thank Claire and realized there was no way I could talk like this. My glasses were fogging up, and my body wanted to bolt to the nearest water fountain. That duplicitous little minx!

Ray leaned in to reassure me. "Don't let it worry you, Penny. Your powers are supposed to get a bit crazy when they first emerge. In Evolution's biography, I read he turned into a tree for a week when his powers came out."

"I heard about that. It was in that article in National Geographic about whether he was the cause of the super power boom, with all the pollen he released and all. They can find traces of his DNA in every human on Earth," Claire chatted back to Ray.

Ray waved a forkful of pasta at her. "Think if it's true. Ten years later he fights Bull and Chimera, getting even more powers from villains whose powers he created in the first place."

This was what they talked about when I didn't set the topic. Claire had outmaneuvered me, and there was nothing I could do about it. Oh, thank Tesla, The Machine was waddling back, distended like a gallon jug. I heaved it off the floor and drank. Ice cold water from the fountain!

Claire still had me. Any time not spent finishing the chicken or slugging down water was time with my mouth on fire.

I had the best friends.

They conspired against me after school, too. They were both waiting in the lab, arms folded identically, and, as I opened the hatch, Ray announced, "No working yourself until you collapse this afternoon, Penny. We've taken a vote and decided you need a break."

"More specifically, we've decided we haven't had a game of Teddy Bears And Machine Guns all weekend. I put too much work into my zombie rag doll army for you to sneak out of being on the receiving end of it," Claire filled in.

That sounded pretty good. I'd made a pile of money off the Pumpkin jar, and those zombie rag dolls were in for an ugly candy chainsaw surprise. Except for one thing.

I held up my hands. "I provisionally surrender. I have only one condition. I need to try and build something, and remember doing it."

Claire looked suspicious. Ray figured it out. "You've been freaking out all day about this, haven't you?"

I let out a huge sigh. "Yes! I know it's fine, it's just been needling me. I don't remember anything from yesterday. I don't even know how that works." I flapped a hand at the metal caster, and went on. "And you say I ordered you around while building it? I'm going to be creeped out until I try to explore this, and there's no way I could do it in class."

"Okay, but keep it small," Claire warned me.

Like I had that kind of control. That was part of the problem. Could I even turn this on? A three-second invention made out of a pencil wouldn't count. It wouldn't tell me anything.

If I didn't get this figured out, I'd be on edge all night. I picked up a screwdriver and one of our spare outlets, and went over to another wiring gap. Dropping down onto my knees, I looked at it.

Wiring gap was the problem. There had to be something I could do with it.

My brain remained blank. The wrong kind of blank.

At least we had electricity. I didn't know if it was part of the school's circuit or what. I could plug in most things, and, if I needed higher voltage or amperage equipment, maybe I could…

I'd started something. Wires. I twisted The Machine to rev it up, and, as I scrambled to pick up a pile of copper wires, I ordered, "Plastic sheets, quarter-inch thick. No, better idea." I hadn't turned off the circuit breakers yet. Who needed to? I smacked The Machine into the open gap. "Divert and store the electrical flow."

What was I—don't think about it. Just do it, but pay attention. I grabbed pliers and twisted around a length of wire. The loops had to be exactly this width apart, because the electricity would flow…

I lost it. I'd tried to put words on it and strangled the understanding in my head. Bah.

I grabbed The Machine, and told it, "Let go." It did.

"You still in there, Penny?" Claire asked.

"Clap once for Penny, and bark twice for Mad Scientist Penny," Ray suggested.

That did it. I snickered. Pushing myself back up to my feet, I snapped The Machine back onto my wrist. "I messed it up, but I messed it up in a way that makes me think I can get it with practice," I confessed.

"So you feel fine now?" Claire asked, all sweet and careful.

"Yeah, as long as I know it's not totally out of control," I assured her.

"Good." She nodded at Ray, and they stepped forward together, grabbed my shoulders, and pulled me toward the elevator. "You can't spend all week down here," she lectured me. "Your powers don't need a push, they're already racing. We're going upstairs, you're going to call your Mom and get us all a ride home, and then you will be crushed under the unstoppable might of my zombie rag dolls."

"Uh-huh." I pretended to concede. I'd let her find out about the candy chain saw the hard way.

An hour later, she found out about the candy chain saw the hard way. I found out that zombie rag dolls had a nasty reassembly mechanic, and, as fast as I could kill them, she could spawn two more. Then we both got ourselves stomped by some horrible hybrid thing Ray had been building without telling us. He called it "The Thresher," and we might as well have been standing in front of a combine harvester when he launched it at us.

Who was the mad scientist here, anyway?!

Wednesday.

Mom was awake when I got up. It was Pancake Day. Nobody told me it would be Pancake Day, but a wise superheroine never questions good fortune. Needless to say, I questioned my good fortune. While shoveling buttermilk pancakes soaked in more butter and maple syrup into my mouth, of course. What was going on?

"Are you going to need a ride home this afternoon?" Mom asked as she passed the dishes through Dad's latest model of dishwasher.

So that was it. Mom didn't make me these pancakes. The Audit did. Another tell—you could have set a metronome to the rhythm of my mother's hands through the dishwasher. Dishes were stacked, then slid into place on the shelves with perfect efficiency.

No point in lying to her. "Probably the opposite. I've got a lot more work to do on the clubhouse. I want my lab assembled as soon as possible."

The Audit smiled, and walked over to the table, and it was Mom who bent down and kissed the top of my head. "You're in such a rush. Your powers will arrive when they're ready."

Yep. I was guessing Friday. Or maybe tomorrow. One week after first emergence? That'd be perfect.

But that wasn't what Mom meant. She was so sure about the four years thing she'd gone in totally the wrong direction. HA! I was out of the woods!

Honesty was now an even better policy. "I still want a lab. It'll make me feel better."

My Mom gave the head shake of adults dealing with children. My secret was safe for another day.

One morning of classes later, I slid my lunch tray down onto the table across from Ray, eyed the ravioli suspiciously, and wondered if I could get The Machine to recycle it into raw starch and tomato sauce and cheese proteins. If I just ate the ingredients raw, they'd taste better than this mushy paste.

"That's quite a smile. It's as if you won last night, instead of being churned into sugary goo." Ray gloated as he unpacked his sandwiches.

"Sugary goo would be better than pasta frappe." I poked whimsically at the ravioli with my fork.

"I never pick candy. It's all reflexes and offense. You can't build something that's greater than the sum of its parts, like the junk heap can," he explained.

I chuckled. "You'd think that would be how I play." Greater than the sum of its parts was inventing in a nutshell. Even chemistry was like that. The starch in this so-called-ravioli was a long, boring chain, but if you attached something more reactive to the end…

I'd killed the idea, but I'd meant to. I did not want to flip out and go into inventing mode in the middle of the cafeteria. Much safer to think about Teddy Bears and Machine Guns. If we hadn't been busy with each other, I bet Claire's zombie rag dolls could have taken that Thresher. Going

Von Neumann on cloth and making dolls that infected other dolls with mobility was an idea with such potential. Maybe some kind of internal framework…

I had to gush. "I am so inspired this morning, Ray. I can't tell you how it feels, like my power will pop any minute. I swear you were right and I'm going to get control of it before the week is over."

"Does this good mood mean you also got a good grade on the German quiz?" Claire asked as she dropped heavily onto the bench next to me.

I shrugged. "High B. I spent a lot of time on the homework after our game last night. I think if I keep doing that, I can pull out a B, and that would be fine."

"I hope my powers activating will make me that happy. I'm sorry about…" Claire trailed off, waving a hand at the popular girls' table.

"About what?" I asked, looking around. The cafeteria looked normal.

"You didn't hear? You're better off," Claire said.

"Her brains are full of Science," Ray explained.

"I'd still like to know what I missed," I insisted. Claire opened up her lunchbox, which bulged with food today, and passed me and Ray sandwiches. These weren't like Ray's flabby peanut butter and jelly offerings. She had fat submarines on crisp Italian bread. I kept looking at her. I wasn't that easy to divert!

"Marcia just implied they won't let me join the cheerleaders if I keep spending time with you two." Claire successfully kept her tone light and avoided the actual insults I was sure had been flung.

"I still can't believe you want to join them," I told her, then bit into my sandwich. Real mayonnaise and tuna and so many spices, mmm! I still had the ticklish idea that mayonnaise must be made of all kinds of useful chemicals.

"It's in the blood. I love showing off and wearing short skirts," Claire answered me before biting into hers.

Ray turned beet red, but we weren't going to embarrass him by mentioning it.

Wednesday meant another PE class, walking into the gym to see every piece of athletic equipment we had lined up and Miss Theotan shouting,

"You thought PE didn't have pop quizzes? You were wrong! It's time for your national physical fitness tests!" Miss Theotan was a woman who struggled day after day with the inappropriateness of cracking whips and yelling, "Hyah, mule!" while we exercised. She settled for, "Be aware, your performance will be permanently recorded next to millions of others on a national database with no names attached that no one will ever look at!"

If we weren't a gifted school, what followed would have been a walk of shame. Claire could manage eleven pull-ups. My arms turned to jelly after seven. Ray started wheezing after six. I couldn't pull myself so much as an inch off the floor at the rope climb. Our salvation was that nobody was any better off than we were.

Technically not nobody. A dozen or so kids could bob up and down on the pull-ups, keep doing sit-ups like they'd never get tired, that kind of thing. Marcia could even climb the stupid rope. She was the head cheerleader, after all. The other cheerleaders and the kids on the sports teams—we had an okay soccer team, apparently—did fine. The rest of us were troglodytes by nature and didn't get that kind of regular exercise.

Marcia at least got some whistles when she climbed to the top of the rope. Nobody else could do it. Claudia of all people got a quarter of the way up, then hung on like she'd had an attack of acrophobia until Miss Theotan pulled her off. Two of the boys did very well on the weight lifting, but nothing else. About a third of the kids could do cartwheels. Claire could almost pull one off, but she overbalanced at the end and landed too hard.

"Is it just me, or is this like a free ticket to the circus?" I whispered to Ray as we stood in a line, waiting to fail to climb a wall. Nobody knew how it was done. Even Marcia couldn't do it. One girl managed by jumping so high she grabbed the top edge, and we were watching a boy as skinny as Ray who'd gotten two feet off the floor by clinging to cracks in the boards, and couldn't go any higher.

"I'm guessing it all seems entertainingly trivial to a newly fledged superheroine," he whispered back.

I thought about that for nearly half a second. "Yeah. It does. It's my powers I want to be testing right now."

Time passed, and gym class ended. My arms and stomach ached, but I wouldn't let them stop me. I grabbed my backpack and trotted innocently down the stairs to the shop class and thumbed the hidden latch of what looked like a service door and let myself into the long, gloomy cement corridor that let me into the back of my laboratory.

Ray had gotten there first and was screwing together another outlet. As I threw open the hatch, the elevator hummed. A few seconds later, the gate opened, and Claire lugged in an apparently heavy ice chest.

Ray and I looked at it. Claire opened up the lid and explained, "Mom thought we needed some food if we intended to spend all afternoon messing with wiring."

On top were what looked like individually wrapped cuts of fried chicken, a cheese wheel, a tub of the crazy, spicy stuff Miss Lutra pretends is potato salad, and several bottles of root beer packed in ice. The kind that came in brown glass bottles that looked like real beer, of course. Claire's Mom loves that.

"I'm starving after all that exercise," I realized.

Ray gave a screw one last twist and left the new outlet in the socket. "You sure you can put off a power outbreak long enough to eat?" Hopping to his feet, he flipped the breaker back on and trotted over to join us.

It might have been a serious question. "I hope so. My arms are killing me," I answered as I dug under the chicken. I pulled out a tub and opened it up to reveal either macaroni and cheese with a lot of extras, or casserole with a lot of gooey cheese.

"So is mine," Ray echoed, flexing the hand he'd held the screwdriver with. "Can I request your next invention be an automated outlet installer?"

I fed myself a forkful of the macaroni-and-everything-else-and-cheese and considered that as I chewed. That seemed simple enough. It could be purely mechanical. All it had to do was hold wires into place and tighten five screws at once.

That was as far as the idea went. "No good. I still don't have control."

"That invention might not be exotic enough. Your power seems to like the grandiose," Claire suggested.

"Too much practicality, not enough super science," Ray conceded.

I snorted.

They might be onto something there. I couldn't guess how the German grenade worked. Even Dad couldn't guess how The Machine worked. The metal caster wasn't super science, just diabolically involved mechanics. The itch to create usually came when I was thinking about science I only distantly understood, like when I was at lunch wondering about the chemicals that made up food.

I closed up the tub of casserole-ish, and peered into the ice chest for something else. Was that strawberry ice cream, or bubblegum-flavored? I wasn't placing any bets.

"Why do they make bubblegum flavored ice cream, anyway? Isn't regular bubblegum good enough? I guess the taste…" I rambled, then stopped.

I could feel it. I could see it. More bubblegum. Don't think too hard about it. I just wanted to observe and not black out.

"Materials. Chemicals. We hardly have any chemicals!" I complained. Ray and Claire stopped and stared at me, mid-chew.

"You have some salts and a lot of metals. What do you need?" Ray's eyes were so wide. So were Claire's. What did I sound like? What did I look like? They couldn't see the picture in my head!

"I need…" No! Don't try to name it. You'll lose it! "Organic chemicals! Lots of them!"

"Can we break her out of this? We don't have any raw materials like that!" Claire leaned over and asked Ray in a hush. I could hear her, but I didn't have time for that. Didn't we have—we had plenty of raw materials. They just weren't raw enough!

I activated The Machine and dropped it in the ice chest. "Eat!" I ordered.

"There were cupcakes at the—it's eating the ice chest, too!" Claire squealed.

"Of course. Polyesters!" I barked at her. Didn't she see what I could?

The inspiration faltered. Just ride it, Penny. I could see what I needed. I didn't need to describe it.

I rushed over and pawed through my equipment until I found a bunch of heating coils, then lined them up in a row. Containers! I had so many metal and plastic tubes and cups and bowls. No problem!

Metal feet clicked as The Machine waddled sluggishly back over to me and began vomiting powders, grains, and blocks into bowls. I grabbed the one I needed, ran back, and scooped up a handful of ice, tossed the ones I didn't need to The Machine, and dumped them into the bowl. I split the last ice cube before putting just the amount I needed in. Now to heat it and let it—

Walking the edge between slipping into that wordless world and slamming the brakes was hard.

I couldn't pay too much attention to what I was doing. My hands scraped and mixed and poured, and I set things to heat. It took a delicate touch to put in exactly the right amount sometimes.

"I'm still in here, guys. I think," I told Ray and Claire as I added this stuff to that stuff drop by drop so that they would combine the way I saw in my head.

"Do you need us to talk to you?" Ray asked.

"No!" I barked back, then took a deep breath. "No. I'll lose the idea. I'd rather lose me."

I ran a tube between one container and another, so the gas could bubble through. As it did and purple stuff formed blobs around the edges, Claire asked, "What is that smell?"

It was bad. This stuff smelled terrible. Of course, it would. It was downright dangerous.

Fumes! I had a few seconds. I bent down and grabbed The Machine, and slapped it on top of the desk. "Filter the air!" I snapped at it. It spread its mouth wide and inhaled, and kept inhaling. Not perfect, but that would do. The chemical residue pellets might be useful later.

I wouldn't need them in this invention. I could see all the steps along the way.

I did need… need… don't lose it, just one word.

"Glycerol!" I yelped.

"What about it?" Claire asked from behind me.

I shook, trying to hold myself back long enough to explain this. "I need it. I need it bad. I can't make it fast enough. Go get it!"

"There's bottles full in the science lab, but I don't know how to get it," Ray said.

"Find a way. Get it! Please!" I begged.

I was losing it. I couldn't lose it. Just look at the picture. I understood the whole process in my head. A hatch clanged behind me. I had good friends. I hoped they could find what I asked for, but all I could do was walk through the steps and hope the glycerol was there when I needed it.

It was. That step was coming right up on me when Claire pressed a glass beaker into my hand. That sweet smell. This was what I needed!

"Now, wood. That's all I need now, is wood," I told them as I stirred the glycerol in to be chewed up and reassembled into my elegant organic mix. Almost alive.

"Will paper do?" Claire offered.

"There's a broken chair left in there," Ray noted. I didn't care where they got it. I cared that, just as my gooey mass sat warm and ready to be fed in its bowl, Ray laid a wooden pole in my hand, and I slid it in to be absorbed, inch by inch.

"What is that?" Claire asked over my shoulder. As the lump ate the wood, it turned pink. Just like I wanted.

"Bubblegum!" The glow of success lit me up. The process was so close to complete, it didn't matter if I lost the image. Even now, I wasn't sure how I got here. How did it work?

It made bubblegum, that's how it worked. What else mattered?

"Is it safe?" Claire asked again.

"Yes. Yes, I remember. It's safe. It's bubblegum. The purple thing in the middle will burn your hand, but the pink is regular bubblegum." More pink frosted over the top, enough I could twist off a knot and toss it into my mouth. I'd been able to see what it did to humans while I made it. It was perfectly harmless.

It tasted like bubblegum. Pretty good, actually. Sharp flavor, very sweet, and the flavor lingered as I chewed. As Claire stared at me, Ray snapped off a bit and started chewing himself. Pursing his lips, he blew a bubble. Aww, man. I didn't know how. His bubble was big. It stretched out farther and farther, growing to the size of his head before he sucked it back in.

Pulling the chewed up chunk out of his mouth, he tossed it into The Machine's. The Machine stopped ventilating and gobbled it down happily.

Ray approved. "I don't know if it's the best bubblegum in the world, but it has to be in the running."

"How much is it going to make?" Claire asked, bending over the bowl to peer at the big, squishy pink lump.

I grabbed at memories as they tried to pour away. "It's like a catalyst. As long as it's fed, it will keep making bubblegum, and it's not picky about food." It liked wood. I remembered that. Wood was the best, but I'd also known that the core would eat the dead skin off my hands.

Claire rephrased her question. "I mean, how big is it going to get?"

How big? I hadn't fed it much, but I didn't need to. "I think… maybe… room-sized?" I guessed. That couldn't be right, but that was the picture I'd left in my head. A ball of bubblegum the size of this room. After that, it would run so short on conversion material it would slow down to a crawl.

Until then…

"Penny, it's growing faster." Claire's voice went up a notch.

"Yeah, it will do that." Now I felt sheepish. That's what she meant. The ball of bubblegum was the size of a soccer ball already.

"Are we in danger?" Ray asked calmly. That was the important question.

"No. There'll be a big mess," I answered.

I really needed to contain that.

I took a deep breath. "Guys, give me quiet for a few seconds." They did.

We could throw the stuff out, or fill a back room with it, but any way around it'd be a giant problem. Containment was what I needed. Not just a container, a container that slowed down the reaction, let me control it. Reactions only happened until they met too much resistance, right? Equilibrium.

That was the spark. I'd fitted together the first pieces of the puzzle, and the rest of it laid itself out in the back of my head.

I didn't have time. I had to be fast. I pressed the bowl into Ray's hands. "Hold this!" I ordered him. Then I turned and grabbed some insulating circuit board. I had to…

I couldn't balance it all. I chose to stop thinking.

There were only two more soccer-ball-sized lumps of bubblegum ripped off and sitting in buckets as I locked the plastic shell into place. That hadn't taken too long. I opened the hatch on one side, let enough bubblegum bulge through to rip off a chunk, then sealed it again.

"We're safe?" Ray asked, his voice quiet.

"We were never in danger, but yeah. It's controlled. The hatch on the other end even lets you feed it more wood. As long as the shell is shut, it can't grow." I wheezed. I was tired again. My arms had been sore, now they trembled. Whew!

All of a sudden, I had to laugh. "Super bubblegum. That has to be the most ridiculous invention, ever."

"No." Claire and Ray said it together. They were right. I'd seen the elephant attracting umbrella in the Museum Of Unsolved Science myself. I was a mad scientist piker.

"If you don't want it, do you think I could have it?" Ray asked me, his voice cautious and trying not to press.

Way too much concern for a question like that. "Sure, but why do you want it?"

"Part of it is the last invention Penelope Akk made before she gained control of her powers, and the other half is the first invention Penelope Akk made when she gained control of her powers," he explained.

Still way too much effort to sound calm-

He was right. I'd made the containment unit absolutely deliberately.

HA! And it was only Wednesday.

Thursday.

Oh, yeah. There had to be a next day after I'd mastered my powers. This time Dad was up early. He wasn't making breakfast, and it didn't have anything to do with me. As I walked past his office to take my shower and then walked back to dress, he sat in his office looking at three different computer screens, and on one of those screens he was designing a schematic.

I wandered in to have a chat. You know, super brain to super brain. "What are you making?" I asked over his shoulder.

"Aren't you up a little late, Pumpkin?" he asked back.

I pointed to the jar. When he didn't look, I turned his head. "I'm about to go to school. You've been up all night again."

He had to stand up to get a dollar out of his wallet and drop it in the jar. That produced a groan. "Thanks, Pumpkin. I got wrapped up in a new idea. There's no reason I can't finish after a few hours sleep."

I tapped the jar. He put another bill in it.

"What are you making?" I asked again.

He pushed up his glasses and rubbed his eyes. "Quantum machines. I think I've finally got a teleporter design that conventional science can build."

I looked at the screen. I saw math. I didn't recognize half the symbols. The schematics did look molecular. "How does it feel when you use your power?" I asked.

"I don't know what it feels like to not use it. The science makes sense, like it makes sense that it takes two one pound weights to balance a two pound weight. If I study enough, someone's figured out the answers already. I just have to make an object out of their math." Now he sounded tired. His voice was getting soft.

I looked at the screen. The math was math. I couldn't attach it to anything. I looked at the second screen. Some paper entitled "Distances, Cohesion, and Quantum Tunneling." I looked at the schematic on the final screen. It was wrong. It wasn't what I saw in my head!

I shook my head, hard. Which hurt. Could you get super power hangovers? "You get to bed, Dad. I'm running out of time to eat breakfast."

"Patience, honey. You'll know what it feels like in a few years," he mumbled as I walked out.

I'd been hoping for a third Pumpkin.

"What are you working on?" Claire asked me while our sugars decomposed in science class.

"I'm trying to come up with a good presentation for The Machine for the science fair," I explained.

"You deserve an A. You deserve a college degree, or something," Claire whispered.

"I'm not going to get it. I've decided to go Ray's route. I can still get an A in the class if I get a zero on the science fair, so I'm not going to let it get to me. It would just be nice to make it fit the scientific method rules so it can win. I don't think I can do it, but I'm trying." I shrugged, and it felt surprisingly casual.

Ray inched a little closer along the table and hissed, "It's wrong that you can't get a good grade on this. If it doesn't fit the rules, then the rules are wrong. A student got her super powers right here in school. The principal should have declared a holiday just to celebrate!"

I shrugged again. "I don't need the grades, but they keep me in school and I need the classes. I can make stuff way beyond anything I understand, but knowing theory seems to be the spark. That happened yesterday. I thought about reaction equilibriums, and my brain took off to make that shell." That popped another thought into my head, and I segued. "Where did you get the glycerol? Mr. Zwelf doesn't seem upset, like he's got ingredients missing."

"We only took a few ounces from a gallon bottle. He doesn't know it's gone," Claire mumbled. Yeah, we should keep our voices low about this.

Still, I had to glance over at the chemicals closet. "You really stole it? Did he leave the door open?"

Claire unsubtly leaned up to peek inside our crucible. She wasn't going to answer, so Ray did. "Guess whose mother taught her to pick locks?" he whispered with considerable glee.

I gaped. "No way!" Then I felt a little dumb, because I shouldn't have been surprised.

Claire still didn't say anything. Quietly again, I asked, "Claire, is something wrong?" Had we upset her? She was usually proud of being The Minx's daughter.

"Nothing big. I'll tell you later," she murmured back. Ray scooted down to the other end of the table, and Claire took our crucible down with the tongs and set it on the scale. I took the hint. Mr. Zwelf was watching us.

Later came. Specifically, Ray and I were waiting to pounce when Claire sat down with us at lunch.

"Spill the beans, girl. What's wrong?" I ordered.

She did not spill the beans. She took them out of her lunchbox in a big covered bowl, and scooped us both out a portion. How can cafeteria chili be meat goo, but this stuff is red and packed with whole beans and has a smell as sharp as a knife?

I refused to be distracted with good food. I kept giving Claire the eye until she confessed, "It's not a big deal. It's just annoying. I can't be a cheerleader because I'm out of shape."

Ray must have physically bit his tongue not to say anything. I wanted to hug Claire and curse the world for her, but, "I have to admit, that almost sounds reasonable."

"Almost, except the only reason Sue and Helga are in shape is because they attend cheerleader practice." Now she was letting it out, at least enough to scowl angrily at her chicken salad.

"And it has nothing to do with Marcia wanting to be tyrant princess of her own little clique," Ray observed, his tone sharp with sarcasm and disgust.

"Maybe. Maybe not. Just let it drop. It's like you and the science fair. Cheerleading seemed like fun, but it's not important. My best friend got her super power. That's important. My second best friend's winning streak with his junk yard abomination is going to end tonight. That's important. This is a nuisance."

"It's still not fair," Ray said for both of us.

"Topic over," Claire told us firmly. "New topic: What should Penny build to surprise her parents?"

That did make for a more pleasant lunch between bites of chili even more tangy than it was hot.

Not that we got to discuss it much. We had to eat, and then there were afternoon classes. Afterward, Claire, Ray, and I ended up outside the door at the corner of the building at the same time, and then stepped in and descended the elevator together. Ray and I, of course, stared fixedly at the big brown bag Claire carried until the gate opened at the bottom.

"Yes, it's food," Claire admitted as we stepped into my lab. "Mom said that if you're going to destroy her ice chests, you'll have to be happy with sandwiches and a fruit basket."

"Sandwich" hardly described the corned-beef-on-toast monster half the size of my head that I pulled out of the bag. I did my best to look sorry.

"Before I build anything else, I need more equipment," I told Ray and Claire as I unwrapped it. "I'll need to shape glass and plastics, better chemistry containers and tubing, pressure chambers, a microcircuit presser, lifts and braces… and that's just basic stuff so I can make sophisticated tools. I may have to dig out my savings and buy some of it. The super noggin doesn't seem to like building anything simple."

"How does that work, Penny? Inside, I mean?" Ray asked as he rooted through the fruit basket. He didn't like any fruit that I knew of, but I couldn't identify half of these. One was covered in big thorny spikes, for pity's sake.

"I haven't done it enough to be sure, but so far I focus on some scientific concept and I get an image... it's not a picture exactly, just an understanding of how to do something with it."

"So, if you started thinking about how to make Claire athletic enough to join the cheerleaders, the answer would pop into your head?" Ray inquired, in the absolute worst attempt to sound casual I'd ever heard.

Claire was as shocked as I was and squeaked, "Ray!"

My own voice spiked. "That would be cheating, Ray!"

"Cheating who? How? She'll attend practice. She's not doing this to win a competition. Does it matter how she gets in shape, if she really is in shape by tomorrow morning?" He didn't sound the slightest bit guilty, and he stared at me really hard, like I was the one who had to be convinced to do the right thing!

"Yes, it does. It's like taking steroids!"

That ought to have ended it, but he was ready for that argument. "No, steroids are banned because they're unhealthy. If vitamins were that effective, no one would care. I know you wouldn't give her something that would poison her like that."

No, I wouldn't. Anyway, it wouldn't be steroids. They were so inefficient. Everything came down to the quality of her muscle fibers and the nerve...

"I can see it. It would be so easy. Why hasn't anyone done this already?" The wonder in my own voice recovered my focus. I gave my head a shake.

Claire's hand settled on my shoulder. "I agree with Ray. It's not wrong; it just sounds wrong."

"What?" I asked, looking up at her. I could barely see her. Chemicals drifted in my head.

Had I ever seen Claire look shy, before? "Can you really do it? Just get me into shape so they won't have an excuse to turn me down? Nothing more?"

"Easy, Claire. Easy! There's only one big chemical, and it wants to be made. Everything I need is in… is in that fruit basket!" I clenched my fists to stop myself from grabbing The Machine.

She leaned in, resting her forehead against mine, our glasses clinking together. Very softly, she said, "Then let me worry if it's right or wrong. Do this for me. Please?"

I stirred the metal bowl very gently. I shouldn't have used metal, but the contaminants wouldn't make a difference.

Oops. I'd blacked out again.

"How much time did I lose?" I asked cautiously. I didn't feel exhausted, so that was a good sign.

"Not much. Less than an hour. It only took that long because you said the chemicals had to mix slowly," Claire answered. I looked back in time to see the hungry expression on her face. "Is that it?"

"Yeah. It's stronger than you wanted, but that's the only way it works. It's funny, because, you know, supervillains try to make this stuff all the time, but they keep trying to make soldiers. They design it to make people more aggressive, better fighters, and that always goes wrong. If they just tried to give you better muscle tone and stuff, it works. So I'm calling it the Super Cheerleader Serum. Do I sound drunk?" I had to tack on the last, because I sounded drunk to me. Drunk on pride, maybe. Like creating life, this was another milestone every super-powered scientist went through, but mine would work because I hadn't overreached.

Claire reached out and took the bowl gingerly in both hands. "So I just drink this?"

The image in my brain objected. "No! This is way too much. Here." That plastic bottle cap would do. I poured just enough in, and set the bowl down on the table. "That much. About a milliliter." I knew because…

The picture in my head was gone. I let out my breath heavily and leaned against the bench. "It's up to you if you want to drink it."

Claire grabbed me suddenly, yanking me up onto my feet and giving me a tight hug. "You are the best friend I could have, do you know that?" she whispered into my ear.

"Say that after you've tried it," I warned her. Now I was tired. Not in a muscle ache way, just drained.

She let go of me, picked up the bottle cap, and drank it. That fast, with no ceremony.

I stared at her. So did Ray.

"I can feel it. It tingles! No, it stopped. Um," Claire reported, staring at nothing. She stepped away from the table, took another long step, stretched out her arms, and did a lazy cartwheel. She let out a loud giggle, turned, and took two much faster steps, then jumped up and did a front flip in mid-air, landing heavily on her sneakers. She wobbled, but didn't fall.

"It—" I started to say.

I didn't get the chance. Claire sprinted across the room and yanked me up off the floor, arms squeezing me tight as she spun me around. Ow. She was stronger, all right!

"You are the best friend I could ever have, Penny! I wonder what more of the serum would have done?" she crowed, while I got dizzy from the spinning.

Ray picked up the cue. "Only one way to find out."

Claire put me down, hopefully to tell him that she wasn't going to take more. Instead, we watched Ray lift the bowl and drink the whole thing in three swallows.

Holy carp.

"Ray, that's dangerous!" I squeaked.

"I'm sure it's fine," he snorted, setting the bowl down. Then he grabbed his shoulders, and his voice turned hoarse. "Did you say it tingled? Because my muscles are burning!"

"Ray!" I bolted a step toward him, only to be met with raised hands.

"I'm kidding! I'm kidding! It only works on Claire. You talk to yourself while you work," he assured me with a huge, sly grin.

I punched him in the shoulder. Hard. Of course, I personally have the muscle tone of a plate of spaghetti noodles, and I winced more than he did. "You idiot. It wasn't funny this time!"

His grin didn't falter. "Claire, who's your best friend?" he asked over my shoulder.

"Penny is!" Claire let out a squeal, and I got yanked off the ground and hugged from behind again. Then she let me go and started cartwheeling around the room in circles.

The Super Cheerleader Serum was a success. Could I make some for myself?

Apparently not. Nothing popped into my head. Maybe the super brain didn't like repeating itself.

Friday.

It had been quite a week. I ate breakfast in silence and lurked in the seat of Mom's car. I was looking forward to a quiet day, and then the weekend. Maybe I'd talk to Ray and Claire about skipping out on rebuilding the lair this afternoon. We could go shopping instead, or get in a few games of Teddy Bears And Machine Guns, or both. There had to be one day this week without a major life event.

That quiet feeling lasted right up until German class, when the bell rang to start and Claire wasn't in her seat. Sure, she liked to be fashionably late, but not tardy. Not that I had any reason to suspect that something was wrong, except that when last I saw her I'd fed her an unidentified mutagen produced in a fugue state by a child with still-developing super powers. And she hadn't been online last night.

My growing panic must have been obvious. Frau Donsky looked straight at me and said, "Fraulein Lutra will be joining us late, if at all. It seems the cheerleaders are holding a last minute tryout, and the principal feels this is more important than mere academics."

I melted into my chair. Not only was Claire okay, the Super Cheerleader Serum must have worked spectacularly. I still wasn't sure it had been the right thing to do, but I wasn't sure it was the wrong thing to do, and either way it was done. If it was done, I was glad I'd done it well.

She showed up for Science class, scooting in right before the bell like usual and setting up beside me as we listened to Mr. Zwelf tell us about solvents and disassociation and polarity, with a lengthy discourse on how water was just plain weird. I knew he was right because my super power kept distracting me with inspirations more like hints than images.

Neither distraction kept me from noticing Claire's expression. She wasn't smiling like I'd have expected, but she didn't look depressed. She half focused on Mr. Zwelf, sitting up and leaning just a little forward in her seat with a distracted and thoughtful air. Even the crossed ankles added to the effect. If she'd propped her elbow on the work table, someone could have carved The Girly Thinker.

Mr. Zwelf set us to measuring how much salt and sugar dissolved in water. I measured a beaker and then the salt added to the beaker, and wrote it all down, and asked Claire under my breath, "Marcia found a way to turn you down, didn't she?"

"Not exactly," Claire hedged.

"Come on, spill," Ray whispered, sliding down the bench.

I grabbed the beaker he'd been spinning on the tip of a finger and scolded him, "You're the one who's going to spill everything. If you break that, Mr. Zwelf will split us up!"

He immediately looked sheepish. "Sorry. Claire was saying?"

Right. I looked back at Claire. I gave her my sharpest look. She gave me back a pout, lips slightly pursed, blue eyes staring at me from behind glasses that magnified them hugely. If she wanted to get out of talking about it this badly, maybe I shouldn't have pressed.

"I thought everything was going fine. The girls were all over me, and I could do anything. I had to tone it down because I was worried they'd get suspicious. Marcia was fine; she wasn't catty or anything. I thought I was a shoo-in, but then I asked if I was on the team, and they said I should be the mascot. Mascot, mascot, mascot, over and over, it was all they would talk about!" Lifting her glasses, she put her hand over her eyes.

I wanted to give her my sympathy. I did. I really did. It's just that I could see it. Claire, skin painted blue, with that bouncy fake tail and the big fuzzy ears and the fake paws, prancing around the sides of a basketball court with all of her strutting and attitude.

I put my fists in front of my mouth, but I couldn't hide it. I started to giggle. "That would be perfect!"

"Penny!" she squeaked, looking so cross with her eyebrows jammed together.

"It would! You'd be so good at it, Claire! Wouldn't she look great in the mascot costume, Ray?"

He grinned hugely. He could see it, too. "She would. They'd stop the game so she could give everyone the look she's got right now. I mean it, Claire. We're not kidding you. You'd be adorable."

She so would. Even Ray thought so, and his reaction to Claire in a costume that showed off that much skin should have included a lot more drooling.

Wait.

I looked back at Claire. She folded her arms over her chest and gave me the most perfectly put-upon glare. I couldn't stop giggling, but I managed to squeak, "Claire, can you turn it down?"

"It?" she echoed. She almost got what I meant, because she looked all confused and thoughtful again.

"Your power. Can you turn it off?" I locked my jaws together to avoid telling her how much I was enjoying seeing her like this, because I totally was, but she'd rather I think clearly, wouldn't she?

Claire's eyes flickered. She took a very deep breath, and, if I'd needed any further proof, Ray giggling instead of fainting gave it to me. Then she exhaled slowly and deliberately, and, as she relaxed, so did I.

All the other kids in class turned back to their experiments. Thank goodness we weren't doing anything with open flames.

"Is it turned off now, or is it just my imagination?" she asked, slow and cautious.

I checked. She'd look good in the mascot costume, sure, but she'd have been happier as a cheerleader. That sounded like a rational opinion, didn't it? "It is."

Awkwardly, Claire leaned closer and whispered, "Penny, I'm pretty sure you don't feel 'that way' about me, so if I'm not clouding men's minds with lust...?"

"I'd say you cloud everyone's mind with cuteness."

Claire's mouth opened, but she didn't say anything. Ray filled in the silence by leaning forward and asking, "So Claire, whose Super Cheerleader Serum activated your super powers?"

It hit her. I could see it hit her as her eyes widened. And then she hit me with her whole body, yanking me off my feet and hugging me again. "Eeee! Penny! My best friend Penny! I have super powers!" she squealed at the top of her lungs.

"Claire Lutra, I'm glad you're having a good day, but—" Mr. Zwelf started to object.

She didn't let him finish. She spun around, clasped her hands behind her back, and gave a little bow. I had to echo her sunny smile, despite my sore ribs. She even cocked her head to one side, a single ash-blonde curl hanging over her eyes as she apologized, "Sorry, Mr. Zwelf!"

He smiled back. "It's all right. Just get back to your work and talk *after* the experiment. Okay?"

Claire gave a little bob of her knees. "Thank you, Mr. Zwelf!" Triumphantly, she turned back to the workbench.

Claire and I both had our super powers. It had been quite a week.

CHAPTER FIVE

I summed up the next week with a checklist:

1 expanded smelter, glassworks, and plastic shaper
1 utility jumpsuit
67 assorted crystal batteries
2 static cling gloves
1 projectile air conditioner
1 lie
1 psychotic episode, courtesy of Ray Viles

"Ow!" I flexed my hands. Those burns hurt!

I was getting better at staying conscious while I worked. This thing in front of me would be an expansion of my metal caster. I needed to mix and smelt metals and shape glass and plastics, and this baby would do it. In fact, all I had to do was twist this around to define the dimensions, then pull this lever—

POOF. Ow! Glass had burst out of the machine and hardened in a globe as designed, then rolled into a little catch tray. Pulling the lever also clued me into a burn way up on my arm. On my arm? I held out my arms and looked myself over. Criminy, I had black ashy smudges and little burned holes all over my blouse and pants. Nowhere seriously embarrassing, but what a mess! I'd been floating so high on inspiration I hadn't noticed.

I'd be working a lot with high temperature materials. I was lucky these burns were only first degree, maybe just scalds. I needed safety equipment, and my super power wasn't going to provide anything that blandly conventional. To get it interested, I'd need some kind of heat distribution network under the fabric.

Something moved in the back of my head. I tried to lure it out. I might need serious protection. A full body suit with layered materials. Could I composite a metal protective mesh with plastic threads? Embed a modular electrical system to plug myself into future inventions? Goggles were a must, but they'd need to adjust to my nearsightedness no matter which direction I looked.

There. I could see it. So many tiny details. I'd just built machines that could help. I fed chunks of plastic and metals into the parts synthesizer. Fibers. I needed conventional fibers. I could feed The Machine my hair—no. I needed fibers. I needed them! I kicked off my shoes, stripped off my thick socks and dropped The Machine on top of them to devour. Then I scooped up a pile of electrical components and grabbed the soldering rod.

I let myself drift. I had to watch out just enough to not grab the metal threads until they cooled and not bump the heated pressure core with my arm. Needles. Thread. I didn't know how to sew. I knew where the threads had to be. *Stop thinking and just do it.*

I didn't seem to have any new burns when I pulled my blouse and pants off. I lifted a leg to slide it into the jumpsuit I'd made when the elevator whirred.

EEK! Bad timing! "Ray, if that's you, eyes shut right now!"

"It's me. Your modesty is safe," Claire promised as the elevator slid to the bottom and the gate opened.

"I haven't been able to get a hold of Ray since Friday," she added, giving me a worried look straight in the eyes. She had to look me in the eyes because… right. I pulled the jumpsuit the rest of the way on and zipped it up. Then I wedged my feet into the boots. This was unexpectedly comfortable!

"I didn't see him online. We could try calling him," I suggested.

Claire was ready for that. "I tried that on the way here. No answer."

Hmm. "He's only got a land line."

"I wouldn't be concerned, but last week was weird." Claire was right.

I wasn't too worried. A voice wrenched my attention away. "Requesting permission to see the scientist's laboratory?" Adult woman's voice—it took me a second. Claire's Mom!

Well... she was here. There was no way to keep it a secret. "Sure, come on down, Miss Lutra!"

The elevator whirred up, then down again, and Claire'sMMom stepped out. I pulled my jumpsuit's gloves on, wincing at the hot, sharp pains from touching my burns. I needed to test the flexibility. Nice. Very nice, considering the gloves were layered with tubes and circuitry whose purpose I couldn't quite remember. The circuitry was so I could plug things in, right? I had little outlets along my arms and shoulders and waist.

"This is the laboratory of a starting mad scientist," Claire's Mom told us in a hushed voice. Then her finger pointed right at me. "You made that outfit yourself. I know Brian's style, and that isn't it. And this thing." She walked up in front of my metal, glass, and plasticworks. Seeing her next to it made me realize just how big the machine was. "Amazing. Look at all those levers. It's not a joke that the only thing a stranger can operate on most mad-science inventions is the self-destruct."

"That's over—" I clapped my hands over my mouth. Ohmygod. I'd built a self-destruct lever into my smelter.

To cover, I slipped off my glasses and tried on my helmet. The visor was supposed to... forget "supposed to." All I had to do was focus on Miss Lutra's eyes to get a close-up of a striated blue iris.

"Could I convince you not to tell my parents?" I asked. "They're rock certain that it'll be years before my powers fully emerge. I want to build up and bury them in proof that they're wrong."

The smile she gave me wasn't just warm. She had a devilish glee in her stare. "Of course! That's why I'm here to invite you to celebrate only the first hints of Claire's power."

I felt my eyebrows shoot up. "You're covering up Claire's powers, too?"

"Half-truths make the best lies, girls," The Minx lectured in a brisk, easy tone. "We all expect two girls who don't quite have their powers yet to spend a lot of time together and keep secrets. Claire needs the time to learn control before I throw her at the super-powered world. Everyone wins!"

Scrunching up her nose, Claire commented, "It's not hard to turn off my power, but it's like keeping my fist clenched every waking moment."

"Not just when you're awake. Lucyfar dropped by to congratulate you after you went to bed last night and spent ten minutes watching you sleep before I took pity and dragged her away," Claire's Mom added with slyly deadpan amusement.

Claire gave me a stare of melodramatic resignation. "Mom's immune."

"One day, you'll be grateful. I couldn't handle the temptations my power put in front of me at your age, and your power is much more dangerous. It doesn't seem like that without the boys drooling all over your shoes, but trust me." Miss Lutra wasn't saying this for Claire's benefit. Instead, she looked right down at me again and told me, "You're her chaperone from now on. Like I said, everyone wins!"

What? The Minx didn't want her daughter having the same fun she'd had? I bit down on that before I said it. All this inventing had left my brain raw.

Claire felt no such restraint and shot back, "You don't regret anything."

You only had to glance at her Mom's playful smile to know Claire was right. Miss Lutra didn't look any more guilty as she bent down and put an arm around Claire and kissed the top of her head. "No, I don't. If you followed the same path I did, I would still be proud of you, but, if I'd known then what I know now, I'd have made different choices. I'm hoping I can pass on my harder lessons and you can have all the fun without the mistakes."

Failing utterly in her attempt to sound resentful, Claire snarked, "I'm not going to have half the fun you did. Boys want to pinch the wrong cheeks when I turn on my powers."

Miss Lutra stood up straight. "Which reminds me." A second later, I got yanked off the floor and squeezed in a savage hug as Claire's Mom squealed, "You gave my daughter her super powers! Thank you so much, Penny! Come on, let me treat you to ice cream." Serious deja vu struck, along with minor asphyxiation and the certainty that Claire had inherited her Mom's personality down to the tiniest detail.

When my feet were allowed to touch the floor again, I wheezed, "Let me put my clothes back on." I glanced down at the ragged, lightly charred pile of fabric. "And maybe take me home to pick out new ones."

A hand rubbed the top of my helmet, expertly making a mess out of my hair even though she couldn't reach it. Back to "brisk with a touch of playful," Miss Lutra told me, "I'll buy you some clothes while we're out instead. Your secret's covered, and your parents know I'm feeling generous right now. Everybody wins! I just wish we could find Ray."

Ray turned up on Monday. Claire, Ray, and I all have homeroom together, for all the good that does us. There's no time to talk in homeroom. It did reassure me when he turned up almost like normal. Exactly like normal, except for his clothes. All Ray wore was black today. Black tee shirt with no logo, black pants, black shoes, black belt. Here he was, and I wouldn't have thought the clothes were weird if I hadn't been wondering about him already.

There was no time to talk during math class either, but perhaps there would be while we walked across the street to Upper High. I kept an eye out as I stepped out of the building, and his black clothing made Ray easy to spot.

I drifted over and fell in next to him. As he gave me a welcoming grin I asked, "What's with the black?"

"I think it might be my new look," he half-answered. Sly blue eyes dared me to ask more. The smile had always been there anyway. Okay, Ray was just fine, and certainly himself.

Except for the black. "Why black?" I asked as we hurried across the street between momentarily stopped cars.

"I thought I'd look good in it." I couldn't tell if he was serious, except he had to be serious, because he looked good in it.

Sure enough, he asked, "Do I look good in it?"

He had to ask that question? What did he expect me to say? To come out and admit that wearing black gave him shoulders I'd never noticed before, and he looked sleek instead of gawky? That I'd thought he was cute already, but this made me want to invent a—

NO, brain, no love potions! What is that chemical? The one like a crystal around a—there, the inspiration broke.

I settled for, "Yeah, it never occurred to me, but black is your color."

He pulled open the front door of Upper High, and as I stepped through he echoed, "Me neither, but it is. Black is definitely my color."

"So where were you this weekend?" I asked as I sat down at lunch. "No answered emails, you weren't online to message, and you never logged into Teddy Bears And Machine Guns. A change of clothes can't take the whole weekend."

"You'd think, but it can. I know I must have missed some inventing, and I'm sorry. Any progress on what you're going to show your parents?" He did sound sorry.

I gave him a head shake. "Not really. I just built utility items for the lab, then Claire's Mom took us out for ice cream to celebrate her 'almost' having her powers."

Ray snickered. "I should have known that rumor came from Claire's Mom herself."

That stopped me in my baked-beans tracks. Laying my spoon down, I asked, "What, you heard about Claire's power? I mean, other than being there?"

"The online superhero fandom is all over these things," Ray explained with a bemused and tolerant look. "There are still websites devoted entirely to The Minx, and a rumor's going around that her daughter's inherited the power but can't quite charge it all the way up to sex appeal yet. It's not big news, but it's going around. Speaking of which…"

Ray slid out of his seat, and I followed his gaze behind me. Claire had just stepped into the cafeteria. Ray slid around the table and did an impressive job of not looking at all hurried as he intercepted her and held out his elbow. "May I escort the newly fledged superheroine to her seat?"

I stared. I might have gaped. A lot of other people stared. Neither Ray nor Claire showed any sign of noticing. She gave him a pleased smile, he walked her over to the table, and she sat down next to me as he returned to his seat across from me. Then they acted as if nothing had happened, although the first thing Claire did when she opened her lunchbox was pass Ray a cupcake.

"So what do you want to make?" Ray asked, reminding me of what we hadn't had a chance to discuss.

Had something happened between Claire and Ray? No, Claire's attention was entirely on me as she suggested, "You should hold out for something actually superhero-ey. A jet pack or freeze ray or something."

I'd been thinking about this. "The problem with a lot of that is power. You may have noticed that everything I've made either plugs into the wall or was just chemistry."

"Except The Machine," Claire corrected me.

"And that thing that talks in German," Ray added.

That got to the crux of the matter. "I don't know what's with the German grenade. I think it's purely mechanical, just weird. The Machine has the awesome power source. It sucks up energy. Bright light, heat, radiation, electricity, even some physical force. Anything beyond regular room temperature it absorbs, stores, and uses to power itself. I wish I could duplicate it." I couldn't. The idea was intriguing. Just divert and convert the energy that's always around whenever it reached any sort of imbalance. I really, really wanted that thought to inspire my super power. It didn't.

"You can't plug a freeze ray into a wall socket. That defeats the purpose," Ray agreed.

"I might be able to build something crazy like miniature fusion reactors, but the whole idea scares the daylights out of me. Dad knows exactly what his inventions do. I have to hope they're kind of what I asked for. That's not a good place to be with nuclear power." I really had been thinking about this. And more than that. If my power didn't like duplicating itself, coming up with different power sources could get complicated, fast.

Ray put on Whimsically Thoughtful Smile A. "I like the miniature fusion reactor idea. I bet, instead of blowing up, it would give the whole school super powers."

I sighed, with a touch of growl. "That would be great. I'd live just long enough for my parents to kill me."

Claire passed me some Chinese stir fry. "Eat. We'll try to figure out power sources this afternoon. I'm sure if we can't think of anything, your power will answer the question for us."

How could I argue with that? I ate.

I didn't see Ray on the way down to the lab after school, and he wasn't in the lab. Had he disappeared again? Just for this moment, I was grateful. I ducked into one of the empty back rooms and changed into my jumpsuit as fast as possible. Just in time because, as I slipped my glasses into their pouch and lowered the helmet visor, the elevator hummed.

It was Claire who stepped out as I reentered the lab. "Is Ray not here yet?" she asked, echoing my thoughts.

"Not yet," I answered, hoping "yet" really was the operative word.

Claire wasn't just echoing my thoughts; she'd gone past me. "If he shows up, I was thinking of asking him to help me practice my powers."

It had been a question, really. I responded with one of my own. "Why Ray? If you're practicing turning it on and off, you can use me as a target. Just warn me."

"No, it needs a boy. I want to find out if small amounts of my cute power make me more attractive, and how much it takes to flip that to a purely platonic interest." She snickered, and I giggled nervously. Maybe Claire did need a chaperone.

My objection had nothing to do with Claire's virtue. "I think that would be cruel. The only question is if it would be a little cruel, or really cruel."

Claire scowled, crossing her arms and pursing her lips in the classic protruding lower lip pout. Even prepared for it, I wasn't sure if her powers had slipped a fraction, or if she was just being theatrical. Cute wasn't hard for her to pull off to begin with.

It had to be her power. I normally didn't notice or think about it like this. And she'd just shut it off again. "I wish you were wrong, but you're right. He seemed like he'd loosened up so much at lunch today, I thought it would just be, you know, fun."

"He's different today, isn't he? Not 'pod person' different, but different."

That perked Claire up again, bringing out a cheerful smile. "I was worried that his best friends both getting super powers would make him feel left out. Instead, it's given him confidence."

And that was all the gossip we got to do, because the elevator hummed and rose back up to ground level. A few seconds later, it descended with Ray lugging a big and heavily loaded plastic bag. We both squealed, "Ray!" He handed me the bag, and I nearly dropped it. "Heavily loaded" was an understatement. What was in this thing?

I opened it up to find out. "Batteries? A lot of batteries? AA, watch batteries, 9 volts, Ds... is that one of those big block batteries for flashlights? Did you clean out a whole store? How did you afford them all?" Oops. I immediately felt stupid for asking. Ray never has money, and I didn't want to rub his face in it.

Fortunately, he didn't bat an eye. "The question is, what are you going to do with them?" he returned.

"Not much. They don't solve my power problems. Like they are now, there's no way..." I trailed off. I didn't want to scare away the ghost of an image in my head. Like they were now, they couldn't store enough electricity or provide it in the amounts I needed, but what if they were better batteries? Not filled with acids and metals, but something more exotic. I couldn't duplicate The Machine's power source, but maybe I could store what it—

That did it.

I was breathing heavily but not really exhausted when I came to, bent over a pile of batteries scattered across a work table. They all had new, shiny black plastic casings.

I'd blacked out again. Come on, couldn't I get a handle on that?

No, not completely blacked out. Just badly lost track of time. I couldn't remember how I made them, but I remembered using my metal press to clamp the battery casings back into place around a series of purple crystals. Crystals that could be charged with power. Power that I would get from The Machine, which clung to one of the still-empty wall sockets, jaws clamped around a power cable. I'd stuffed him in there before I started working, and he must be holding a lot of power by now.

Lifting my visor, I wiped my forehead and announced, "I'm back. Let's see if this works."

Claire shook her head. "Super batteries. I don't know if I should applaud you or Ray. How did you know what she'd do?"

"I trusted her to be the best at what she does." He threw it off as if it were no big deal, but my already weak knees threatened to fall out from under me. Would lowering my visor again just call attention to how hot my cheeks had turned?

"Time to test your faith," I told him as I kneeled by the outlet and pulled out The Machine. I inserted the battery I'd been holding into his jaws and ordered, "Charge this."

Purple light flicked on. Yes, that's how I'd know how charged a battery was. I'd left a clear plastic strip, and it turned purple, then glowed purple. The Machine hadn't frozen up when the battery stopped getting brighter, so he must have more juice. I plugged him back in and stood up.

Then a disappointing thought hit me. "Too bad I don't have anything for it to power yet."

Ray shrugged. "Chicken and the egg. You have the egg, so a chicken's on the way."

I set the battery down on the workbench to pick up another. The bench was already covered in tools. How many screwdrivers did I have, anyway? "I need to find somewhere to store these. Somewhere to store *everything*."

"Shelves can't be hard to build," Claire replied, walking up next to me and picking up the glowing battery. Ray scooped up one of the big converted D cells, and walked over to The Machine to fill it.

"They'll be ugly. My mad scientist super power thinks it's too good to build anything as trivial as a shelf," I grumped.

"Maybe some kind of automatic storage system?" Claire suggested.

I shook my head. "Rotating storage bins? An unfolding system? It's not biting. Maybe it's waiting for an idea that uses electricity." I gave a snorting little chuckle. "Like using static cling to stick the batteries to the wall with their own power. Not that that would work. You'd need to—"

It hit again. I hadn't been expecting two inspirations in a row. "I've got another. Back up."

Claire obeyed, fast. The batteries wouldn't stick on their own power. I needed just the right electrical field. That pattern I saw in my head. *Don't think about it too much.* This one was easy. Electrical circuits. I stripped off my gloves, grabbed an exacto knife, and slit them open. Snip the circuits. Rearrange them. Build up charge in this ring, shape it in—my inspiration flickered, but that's fine. I let myself keep rearranging the circuits. Wrench a few levels around to make the smelter extrude a plastic cover, slip the fabric back over the circuitry, heat seal it to the edge of the plastic cover. Take two batteries from Ray and plug them into place. Pull the gloves back on.

"…that didn't take long, did it?" I asked. I remembered almost everything. I didn't understand what I'd done, except at that deep level where it all seemed obvious but I couldn't put it into words.

"Five minutes?" Claire guessed..

Ray nodded. "Fifteen, tops. What do they do?"

Yes, that was the question. A question I had an answer for. I picked up the largest battery in my left hand and clenched my right fist. Position was important. Instead of just a fist, I had to form a tight ring.

I nearly let go when blue lightning arced around my fist. Then purple. They were hardly more than sparks, but the arcs got brighter, lasting long enough to crawl. My brain nudged me. I'd overdone it. If I charged any more, I'd have trouble taking the battery off the wall again!

I released my grip, pointing my right hand at the battery. A dozen beams of twisting blue and purple lightning shot out and into the battery. Okay, now I just had to place the battery against the wall and let go…

The battery stuck.

Claire did clap this time. Ray's words came slowly, distant and stunned. "That is the coolest device I've seen in person. It has to be one of the inventions you show your parents. It looks superheroic."

I pulled out the battery and checked it. If it wasn't still full, I couldn't tell. "Doesn't eat much power, either. That or these are super super-batteries." Half a dozen of the batteries on the table had glowing purple stripes now. Ray had been busy while I worked.

Ray was right. This, finally, was a superhero toy. I wanted to play with my new gloves, but while my batteries were still charged, I personally felt drained.

I leaned against my work table, hard. "Tell you what, guys, I've had enough inventing for today. I'd like to go home and get in a game, if a certain someone will log in when he gets home instead of disappearing."

So we did. I walked home to clear my head. Home was just close enough that it would be faster walking than trying to call my Mom. Now was not the time to get her thinking about the lab anyway. A few more days and I'd be ready to spring my surprise.

Tuesday Ray was still wearing black, but I had more important issues on my mind, like an upgrade tree to candy chainsaws that would counter the regeneration and duplication of zombie rag dolls. That, and one other thing.

"How is the science fair display going? You have to put it up tomorrow, correct?" Ray asked over lunch.

I put my arms over my head. I'd have dropped my head on the cafeteria table if pudding weren't in the way.

"That bad?" he guessed, wincing in sympathy.

I grunted. "Yes. Not really. I've been hoping a blinding ray from heaven would illuminate me as to how to make the judges swallow an invention. I get it. Technically it's a really fancy baking soda volcano. I just wanted a way around that, and it's not coming."

"It bugs me. The only reason The Machine won't change energy and manufacturing forever is that there's only one of it. That should be more important than the rules." The scowl on Ray's face didn't look right, and I was glad when it disappeared. I glanced over my shoulder. His welcoming smile was directed at Claire, who didn't seem at all ruffled by the flirty tilt to it. Had something happened between them? Was that why Ray was so laid back and distracted this week? I had to be imagining it, because they both turned their attention right back to me. Maybe Claire's power hit Ray harder than it hit me.

That was a slightly less welcome topic than the science fair, and the venting had eased my nerves already. I kept up with it. "You've just described half of the inventions mad scientists make." I needed a better term than that for people like me, but if it was good enough for Mech, maybe I was too sensitive. "Dad is It, he's the top, the best, because he can duplicate and record his processes, and he can only copy maybe half the stuff captured from supervillains. Then when he hands his notes and samples over to regular engineers they tell him it might as well be moon language."

"That just makes my point. You've built something beyond the scientific process, not beneath it," Ray insisted.

"Never found a good way to present The Machine?" Claire asked, giving me a pained grimace like Ray's.

"Nothing good. I'll have to try to describe what it does as a test and pray for a C." I shrugged, hoping to convey that I was okay with that. And I was, honestly.

Anyway, that raised a thought. "What about you, Ray? What are you turning in?"

He stared at me. Then he let out a sudden, sharp laugh. "Hah! Absolutely nothing! We've been so busy with super-powered stuff, I completely forgot."

Yikes. "I'm sorry, Ray."

He shrugged, and unlike me, he pulled it off. "Why? It's a tiny part of the grade. I'll still get an A. I dragged my heels so badly last year I never turned anything in. This time it's for a good cause."

Claire set a stack of cold pizza slices in front of me. I dug in, because I wasn't sure what I wanted to ask.

End of the day and I still wasn't sure what I meant to ask, but I meant to pin Ray until I worked it out. I headed for the side door he uses to leave school as soon as the closing bell rang.

Instead of the ambusher, I became the ambushee. As I came down the stairs and caught a glimpse of him standing by the door, he turned and charged up to me, grabbing my hands. He grinned at me. He had so many teeth. Okay, a stupid thought, but seeing all that shiny white, that's how it hit me.

"Come here. Watch this!" he whispered to me. He pulled me down the stairs, and then left me to stand at the door while he wandered outside. Pulling out a pocket watch, he glanced at it, then took a book out of his backpack, and leaned against the wall to read.

Marcia and two of her friends walked past. He'd set up a mirror image of the confrontation two weeks ago. He couldn't think she'd try the same thing.

He'd pegged her better than I had. She didn't seem to notice him. She was looking at one of her friends instead, and I caught the words "Wait until you see it!" Her hand still darted out to grab the book.

The book moved, dropping a couple of inches just as she struck. She missed. Her head turned, and her face set in anger as she grabbed again. She moved so fast, she should have gotten it. The book only dipped, but she missed.

Ray had a moment's advantage as she glared at him, stunned. He closed the book, folded his arms, and told Marcia, "I don't get it. You're obsessed with being better than everyone else, all the time. Why? You've got enough going for you. You'd be really cute if you weren't so mean."

That got her laughing, sharp and sarcastic. "Oh, please! Are you hitting on me?"

The contempt in her voice made me wince. It rolled right off Ray. "Not likely. Dating a shrew like you would be a nightmare. I just kept thinking there had to be a better person underneath. I guess not!"

That wiped the sarcasm from Marcia's face and replaced it with a stiff mask of hate. I didn't see her move, but her friends each grabbed her by the arm. Her feet dragged, but she let them walk her away. Ray didn't rub it in, except by watching with the same solemn concern.

"What did I just see?" Claire whispered from behind me. I'd been too distracted to notice her approach. All I could do now was shake my head and push the door the rest of the way open and walk out to meet Ray.

"Ray, what was that?" I asked him, hearing my voice peak in surprise.

That didn't faze him either. On the contrary, he tucked his book away and stepped up to Claire and me, turned, and scooped an arm around each of our waists. "Exactly what it looked like. I meant every word. I decided I couldn't be the better person if I didn't try, just once, to find the other side of her."

I had trouble listening. He'd slipped his arm around my back so casually. His hand stayed high on my hip, not intruding, but his arm was around my waist. I would never have expected him to do this to Claire, much less me. He had his arm around Claire, too, but that was it. Even if he didn't make a single move further, he'd just made it clear that he knew exactly whether I was a girl or a boy.

I could feel my heart thumping in my chest as he pulled away from both of us, leaving us at the front door to the lab. "I'm sorry, ladies, but I'm going to play truant again this afternoon. I still have a lot to think about. Life seems different since my two best friends became superheroes."

He walked off. I tried to slow down my heart. Not that I had any idea how to do that, but slow breaths helped. Realizing I'd just turned into a frightened rabbit and made a giant fool of myself did not.

"I guess if he wants to be alone, we have to let him. Do you want to get any building done today?" Claire asked me, her voice completely noncommittal.

I shook my head. "My Mom will be picking me up out front in a minute. I don't have time to build today. I have to go home and try to put some kind of science fair project together for tomorrow."

The day came. Wednesday, the first day of the science fair. I woke up in the morning expecting to be terrified, but I felt okay. I had other things on my mind.

I didn't get to pursue those things immediately. There was no time to talk in homeroom, and I didn't catch Ray on the way to Math, and Science was all lecture—most of it about the science fair and how we would set up, which left me drumming my fingers and staring at Claire and Ray, impatient for lunch.

It took its own sweet time, but lunch did arrive. I made myself get a tray of food, but, when I slapped it down on the cafeteria table, I had no interest in it. My eyes were on Ray's hat. The hat had taunted me since homeroom. It sat low and wide-brimmed and velvety black on his head, matching the black clothes he was still wearing. Another question for the pile, but they all tied together.

I didn't have to wait for Claire to bring this out. "Fashionably late" today meant thirty seconds. She slid down next to me, folded her hands over the top of her lunchbox, and stared at Ray's hat, too. Her expression was more affectionately amused than my interrogating stare. Ray's face remained blankly indifferent, as if we weren't even there while he chewed away at baby carrots from a little plastic bag.

Might as well go for the kill. "You got super powers from drinking the Serum, didn't you?" I demanded.

Ray let out a sigh—a relieved sigh. He sagged in his seat like he'd started to deflate through his blissfully wide smile. "Thank goodness. I was praying you'd figure it out. I didn't know how to tell you."

I picked a nominal tater tot off of my tray and flung it at his forehead. He caught it before it hit, plucking it out of the air like I'd gently lobbed a softball. "You twit. You lied to me and drank the Serum on purpose, then you tried to hide it from us!"

"He didn't try very hard," Claire pointed out. She still had her blandly amused version of a poker face on.

Ray finally looked guilty. Not much, more exasperated than guilty, but he put his hand to his forehead and lowered his face and told us, "I was an idiot for hiding it. At first I wasn't sure it worked. Then I thought I'd surprise you like we're going to surprise your parents, then I couldn't figure out how. I didn't really want to keep it a secret from you, I was just stupid, stupid, stupid, and I'm sorry."

I spotted the hole he was talking around. "But you're not sorry for stealing the Serum."

He looked up at me, right in the eyes. "Not in the slightest. It worked. I have super powers. My two best friends have super powers, and now I do, too. Would you regret it?"

I clenched my teeth. I scowled. The answer was as obvious as The Machine clamped around my wrist. No, I wouldn't have regretted it.

"So you really have super powers? How super are we talking?" Claire asked. Now that I'd had to swallow Ray's apology her detachment had disappeared, and she leaned over the table eagerly to hear.

"I drank twenty times as much Serum as you did, and I got maybe five times the effect. You can't put numbers on it, but look," he whispered. Grinning like I would grin, probably did grin, he pressed his thumb against the metal tabletop. Pressed hard. Cafeteria tabletops aren't the sturdiest metal in the world, but should it have dimpled that much?

He pulled his hand away. He'd left a dent. A deep, obvious dent.

"That is superhuman," Claire whispered back. She was smiling, too. Oh, criminy. So was I. Ray had me. This was awesome.

Ray glowed with pride. "I'm not sure about superhuman. Maybe extreme end of human. I can't lift a car, but I can lift the front end."

I gave up the last bit of resistance and joined in. "I saw how you moved with Marcia. I could hardly believe how fast she could grab, but she couldn't touch you."

"I think they'd disqualify me if I tried out for the Olympics. I wouldn't know where to start telling you all the crazy things I did this weekend. This is, with absolutely no contest, the greatest thing that's ever happened to me," he whispered.

"That's how I felt, too!" Claire and I answered at the same time.

We all stopped. People were staring. They couldn't hear us, but they knew something was up. Claire flipped open her lunchbox and gave me a carton of real tater tots. "Eat. We have to eat. You know what's after lunch."

After lunch we all filed into the gymnasium. Not for PE this week, or the rest of the semester—as pitifully short a period as that would be. The bleachers and equipment had all been tucked away, and tables lined up in rows for kids to set up their science fair displays.

At least I had something. Claire's looked nice and smooth and professional, with charts and photos of her mother—sure to please. I'd managed to pretend the experiment was using The Machine to determine raw materials of household items, and set out a small tray of scissors, batteries, crayons, and so forth for people to try themselves, with lists of ingredients that would be produced. We had two hours to set up, and, for most people, it took five minutes, which left everyone wandering around looking at each other's projects. Intentional, I was sure.

Ray fed a battery to The Machine to watch it separate water, crystalized base, organics, and metals into little bins. I set up the "DO NOT TOUCH" sign over the potassium hydroxide bin as he wandered off to look around. Hopefully, no one would be stupid. The lye was already absorbing water from the air, but I hated to think what it would do to a finger.

I nudged The Machine over; it drank the goo out of the bin and spat out a pellet of dry potassium hydroxide that stayed dry for about a second. Then Ray stepped out of the crowd and grabbed my sleeve. "You have to come see this." His face and voice were way too flat. What could have crushed his mood already?

He led me around a couple of aisles, and it quickly became clear where we were going, because one display had students and teachers gathered around to gawk at it. When we got around to where I could see, I had to admit that the small metal footlocker and the colored charts glued to a sheet of laminate made a nice display. They didn't explain the crowd, of course. The glowing super science device sitting on the laminate sheet did.

Blue lines traced over a gray surface that might be ceramic. The device twisted like a bowl, with a purple crystal ball floating just above and another imbedded in the base. Light crawled through the blue lines, making it look alive. The volt meter sitting next to it looked positively pedestrian, except that it registered a circuit attached to a sneaker that glowed faintly blue like the machine.

I looked at the title. "Conduction Of Energy Not Found On Earth" by Marcia Bradley. I felt a distinct urge to swear. She'd somehow borrowed a piece of actual alien technology from the museum, and her project compared how it could be used to charge ordinary elements and random devices. She admitted smugly in her presentation that electrical production could only guess at the real charge, since this energy was not understood and human technology could not directly measure it.

Ray pulled me up next to Claire, who was already glaring at the display.

"There's no way she just borrowed that. Museums don't lend out irreplaceable exhibits like that. One of her parents is a superhero," Ray hissed to us.

"An important superhero. That's tech from the invasion, the one that officially didn't happen," Claire whispered back.

"It doesn't have to be a parent. A family member, even just a friend of the family. A lot of successful heroes are extravagantly generous," I argued.

Ray made a little growl in his throat. "They're still practically outing themselves."

Claire shook her head. "No villain will follow it up. That would be getting personal."

I shrugged and tried to look like I meant it. "I don't care who she knows. I have my own super powers."

I walked away from the table, circling back around to my own display. Nobody would try to steal The Machine, but I was having trouble getting used to the feeling of leaving it there for the next couple of weeks. It was so useful in my work, and, unless I was inventing, I kept it wound around my wrist night and day.

There was Mr. Zwelf standing by my display, looking grim. Ah, well, might as well get the bad news.

I walked up and told him immediately, "It's fine, Mr. Zwelf. I know the experiment involved is pretty flimsy. I wasn't doing this for a good grade." He really, really looked grim. "What did I get, a fifty out of a hundred?" I asked.

On his lean, angular face, that frown looked tragically bleak. He seriously felt bad about this. His voice dragged reluctantly as he answered, "Most of the grades aren't decided yet, but yours has. You've been disqualified. Not all of the judges believe you made The Machine yourself.

Don't ask me to tell you who. Because we don't all agree, you won't get in trouble for cheating, but you get a zero. I'm sorry."

He was. Obviously, whoever thought I was trying to pass off one of my Dad's inventions as mine, it wasn't him. I could find out who the other judges were, maybe guess which of the five did this to me, but it wasn't worth the stress. I took a deep breath, then let it out slowly. No, it just wasn't worth the stress. "Don't worry about it. I knew what could happen, and I don't regret it. My grades are good enough I should still get an A."

"A B+ at worst," he promised me.

"I'm fine with that. Go on. You've got a lot of grading to do," I told him.

"I'm sorry, Penelope," he repeated and walked off. He'd really wanted that to be over. Fair enough; so did I.

My heart sat heavy in my chest, but that would clear. I was fine. A cracking sound told me Ray wasn't. He'd squeezed the edge of the table so hard, the wood broke.

I had absolutely never seen this expression on him. Pink lined the whites of his eyes, like he was about to cry, and his eyes glared stonily through the lenses of his glasses.

I put my hand on his shoulder. "It's fine, Ray."

The wood started to crack under his other hand. His head sank another inch. "No, it's not," he whispered back. "It's not fair. I had enough trouble swallowing that you wouldn't get a good grade. This is disgusting."

"It's not the right kind of science, Ray. I knew I wouldn't get a good grade just for showing off an invention." His shoulder shook under my fingers. This really had infuriated him.

He lurched up straight, and his voice rasped as he demanded, "But do you know who's getting a good grade? Look around, Penny. Who's getting a hundred and winning the science fair? Can you tell at a glance?"

"Why do you care what grade Marcia gets, Ray?" Claire asked. I was glad she asked it. She could make her voice sound gentle, not accusing.

"Because the only reason she'll win is that alien device. She'll be treated as if she made it, but she only got lucky enough to borrow it. Penny made hers, actually made it herself, and she's getting a zero," he rasped.

He was so mad. My own eyes stung with sympathy as I tried to reassure him. "I'm fine with it, Ray, honestly. We're both getting zeroes. Mine doesn't bother me any more than yours." It did, but not much. Not like this.

"I didn't try," he snapped back. "I earned my zero. You earned a celebration in your honor, but you're getting a zero and the real cheat is being treated like a genius. I can't stand it." His fists balled up at his sides, quivering with effort. It was a wonder he didn't hurt himself, with that strength.

I wanted to tell him it just happens, but he didn't give me a chance. Pointing straight across at Marcia's display, he growled at me, "And the worst part is, some superhero is an accessory to this. They gave her that thing so she could crush kids better than her in a competition."

I got a peek of tears running down his cheeks, and more than a peek of clenched teeth, but he twisted aside and stomped away from me, heading straight for the gymnasium door and barging his way outside.

I shared a look with Claire. Should we follow him? A teacher was already headed for the door. He'd just cut school early, after all. But they couldn't possibly catch him, and neither could we.

When the bell rang and school let out, I still couldn't see any sign of Ray. Now that he had super powers, he could be anywhere. Claire and I trooped solemnly over to the elevator and took it down into my lab.

"Ray?" I called out as the gate swung open. My voice echoed. No luck. No one else was here.

A guilty suspicion nagged at me. "Do you think the Serum did this? It wouldn't be the first time something that gave someone super powers made them crazy."

"No, I think this really means a lot to him," Claire answered in a quiet but confident voice. Maybe she knew him better than I did after all.

"If I'd known—" I started, but Claire put her fingers over my mouth. It was a sweet gesture, the touch against my lips calming, and her smile made her face glow with gentle kindness. She was using her powers on me, but I didn't care. It helped soothe my own heart.

"You're not going to worry about that now. You're going to invent something and remind yourself that you have super powers, and so does Ray, and so do I, and those are going to change our lives so much we won't even remember what grades we got in the science fair." My shoulders sagged. She gave me a small, quirky grin and an immaculately raised eyebrow. I shuffled into the other room and pulled off my shirt and skirt and pulled on my jumpsuit.

"I don't know what I'm going to create," I grumped as I emerged. My heart felt a lot heavier after being out of the room and away from her power. "I'm not feeling very inspired."

Unruffled, even wryly playful, Claire put her hand on her hip. "I know what you're going to invent. You're going to invent an air conditioner. Have you noticed how warm it is down here? It's winter. Imagine when June Gloom hits, and it's ninety degrees and overcast and wet outside every day. This metal cave will become an oven."

I could imagine that. The soft plastic of my jumpsuit kept me nicely temperate and dry of perspiration, but I could still feel the warmth on my face. I wouldn't want to set foot down here in summer.

"An air conditioner isn't exciting enough for my super power," I argued lamely.

"I have faith in you," Claire answered, completely unmoved.

"I don't know how I'd even make a good one. I'm scared to open the air vents yet, and without better circulation you'd need to chill the air without displacing heat, which—" My complaint solved itself. My super power seized on the challenge, and I watched a design take shape in the back of my head. That was some crazy circuitry, but not too small to build by hand. The way it worked was almost like The Machine. Almost. Not as good.

My hands started working while I admired the schematic in my head. That was fine. I just wanted to feel my hands work, laying out circuits in concentric circles, firing ceramic tubes out of the smelter, burying one of the larger batteries in the middle. The system was wonderfully efficient. It just needed a jolt to get it started.

Finally, I set the box on the floor, closed the telescoping projector until it looked like a regular fan, and turned it on. Just a little power on the fan, about two thirds of the way up the refrigeration slide. It could heat, too, but that drew more power.

Wonderfully icy air poured out over me, filling the room with a gentle wind.

"Feel better?" Claire asked

"I do," I admitted, taking off my helmet and lifting up the fan to steam cold air through my hair. I extended the tube to make it more directional, and my hair flew around behind me in the strong gusts.

Claire stepped up next to me, tilting her head to look at the telescoping tube from one side and the other. "It looks like a gun," she commented whimsically.

Tesla's Electrified Elephant. "It *is* a gun!" Understanding washed over me. I could still remember just enough of my inspiration about how it worked. "I guess it was because I had Ray being mad at superheroes on the brain. You get so many supervillains who have a minor power and turn an already advanced refrigeration system into a freeze ray, something like that. That's all the super power they really had. My brain clicked and made an air conditioner cannon without asking." I telescoped what I now knew was the barrel all the way out. I couldn't freeze or burn well, but if I turned the force all the way up the blast of air would hit like a real cannon. It even had fasteners for the arm and back of my jumpsuit. My super power had wanted a cannon, all right.

"It'll be a good toy to show your parents. Very superhero," Claire pointed out.

I smirked. "More like supervillain. The guys who make these things are all crazed on revenge."

Understanding hit me again. I saw the same revelation in Claire's expression of growing horror. Desperately, I told her, "Claire, we have to do something. Ray's a superhero now. He's so mad, he'll destroy the science fair and think it's a good deed."

"Not until after dark. Too many staff hanging around until then. We'll come back after dark. We can talk sense into him. If not... well, we have powers, too," Claire answered.

CHAPTER SIX

I got home. Mom noticed me staring out the window, of course. "Something happen at school?" she asked as we drove up. The school is so close I can walk if I'm patient, but the short drive took forever. Ray was out there planning something nuts.

Not actually lying had worked so far. I made sure to grumble, which didn't require any faking. "I put The Machine up for the science fair, and now I'm reaping what I sowed."

Mom is too good at reading people for her own good. Since I didn't want to talk about it, she let it drop.

Now I had cover to trudge into the house and straight into my room and lock the door behind me. Those audible but unintelligible voices would be Mom telling Dad I had to work it out for myself. Right? That was what Mom would do?

Seconds crawled past. Dad failed to come knocking at my door as I turned on my computer. Mom came through. I had cover for tonight.

Ray wasn't online. Hadn't been online all day. I was going to need that cover.

Claire was online, but I didn't feel like talking to her, and she didn't seem any more eager.

Time crawled. Around sundown I went to stage two. I found a multi-hour video of the championship tournament of Teddy Bears And Machine Guns and put that on. That would be my alibi.

It got dark. I couldn't wait anymore. I pried open my window, crawled out, snuck my bike out onto the street, and pedaled off toward school. This could go wrong in so many ways.

As I pulled up to the school, out of breath, one of those ways nagged me, tensing my stomach. What if Ray couldn't be talked down? He had super powers now!

I unlocked the lab's front doors and rode the elevator down. I could stash my bike safely here so it wouldn't get stolen. Even in this neighborhood, someone might try that.

The gate slid open. Ray wasn't here. My heart sank a little further. It would have been so much easier to talk this out here. At least I could use the back door to get into the locked school.

I looked around at the clutter. I'd hardly stuck any batteries to the wall yet. Pieces of circuitry formed a pile on a work table against the wall, and bars of plastic and metal sat in piles on the floor. My jumpsuit hung over one of the levers of the brooding anemone mass of my smelter. The air conditioner cannon lay right in the middle of the room, still gently pouring out chilly air.

Ray had super powers. So did I. I had a cannon. Okay, a souped-up air conditioner, but it might convince him not to just push me out of the way.

I wished I'd had more time, more inspirations, more weapons. Armor and a disguise in case I was seen. Not good for either, but I slipped into my jumpsuit. And the helmet. And the sticky gloves. And I grabbed the German grenade and stuffed it into a pouch at my waist. I was armed for Bar Mitzvah. It would have to do.

I walked down the long tunnel to the door behind the shop classroom. For the first time I noticed how bleak and shadowy it was. At the other end, I snuck into the (hopefully abandoned) school. The blank white hallway was empty. I crept upstairs. The institutional, dirty beige hallway was empty. The gym was on the very far end of the school, at the tip of the J, and I walked as softly as I could. Any minute a janitor, security guard, or late teacher could spot me, and then what would I do?

They didn't. I reached the mud brown, oversized twin doors that opened into the ground floor of the gym. I pulled on a handle. The door came open, and I stepped in just in time to see Ray kick over a display table.

At least, it had to be Ray. Skinny, my height, wearing black. Not a black T-shirt and pants. A black suit. Dress shirt, jacket, crisply creased slacks, shiny black leather shoes, that same black hat, and a pitch black mask. Not one of those skimpy generic hero masks, but a masquerade ball mask with a sharp beak that hid the whole upper half of his face.

He kicked another table over. I didn't recognize whose glassware broke, whose papers scattered all over the floor and turned purple with chemicals. I did recognize his next target. He walked over to Marcia's exhibit, broke the lock as he yanked it open, and lifted out the alien machine.

I had to say something. What could I say?

Someone else knew. "Put the energizer down, and your hands up," a girl's voice ordered.

The gymnasium was three stories tall. I had never looked at the metal struts that crisscrossed the ceiling like rafters in an attic. Now a girl in pink plunged down from them, sliding down a cord and then letting go to land with expert delicacy on her feet.

She held a long pole in her other hand, an extended cheerleader's baton. With the full body pink leotard, the little dress, the sparkles everywhere, she had to be a superheroine. A superheroine our age? A sidekick. It hardly mattered. This was now officially a disaster.

"I knew it," she lectured Ray smugly. "I knew there were supervillains' kids mixed in at this school. All I had to do was make the bait too good to resist." The baton twirled, and she leveled it at Ray. "Energizer down, hands up."

Ray lifted the glowing alien machine up in one hand, and threw it. He didn't throw it at the girl, but still threw it so hard it sailed all the way across the gym and bounced loudly off the wall. Then he cracked the knuckles of both black-gloved hands theatrically. Ray couldn't possibly be this stupid.

They lunged for each other, so fast I had trouble keeping up. The girl pushed aside his fist with her baton and they slammed together, except she'd tangled her foot with his and Ray went down hard on the flat of his back. The baton didn't wait for a moment. She prodded it right into his throat, pinning him with the threat of it as she laid a foot on his stomach. She was good. Who was she? A memory turned over. Miss A, the Original's sidekick. I'd never met either. Like Mom, the Original had no powers, which meant he had to be one of the toughest, fastest, smartest men around. Ray was in trouble.

My heart squeezed into a knot in my chest. I flicked the power on the air conditioner all the way up, the focus to the tightest blast it could deliver, raised my arm, and fired at her back. The barrel fastened to my forearm jerked, and the gymnasium echoed to a violent crash as a hole punched through the wall behind Miss A, level with her head.

Thank goodness for terrible aim. If that had hit, it would have taken her head off. I thumbed the force down to a more moderate level as I stepped out onto the gym floor. I hoped my voice would be steady! "Killing you the first time we met would be bad form. The Original might think this was personal. Still, I thought you should know how badly you're outgunned here. Hands up, or run away, or whatever it is sidekicks do when they lose. We'll finish our business here and go."

Sarcasm dripped like venom as Miss A drawled, "Oh, please! Who do you think you're fooling?"

Marcia's favorite vocal tick was unmistakable. Yes, that was Marcia's voice, and her size and shape and blonde hair where the mask let it loose. Marcia was Miss A.

Ray's peculiar English accent was also unmistakable. A word out of his mouth and she'd know. I pulled out the German grenade, turned its volume to max, and tossed it out into the room. It hit a table and rolled off, nowhere near Marcia.

"You have the worst-" was as far as her sarcastic reply got. The grenade screamed out over top of her, "SIE HABEN DAS NULL!"

Marcia flinched. In that flicker of focus, Ray rolled out from under the tip of her baton.

"That is-" Marcia started to say, and the grenade screamed, "DAS IST!"

Ray was back on his feet. Marcia swung her baton to face him, and he lifted his hands, fingers spread instead of bunched up into fists this time. I clenched a fist, walking over toward the German grenade, lifted my hand, and released my grip. Blue and purple lightning arced out to ground into Marcia. Even if she couldn't feel it, the flash of light made Marcia spin around to face me. Her foot planted again, stuck, and she lost her balance before ripping it free of the floor. It would take a lot of charge to keep a determined human stuck to anything.

Thank goodness her squeal didn't set off the grenade again. My throwing arm really was terrible. I bent down and picked it up off the floor. Dramatically, I clicked the volume down to zero again.

Marcia's roll took her under a row of display tables. As she hopped up on the other side, Ray kicked a table out of his way and advanced on her, each step slow and cautious. Her mouth curled into a sneer. "Do you amateur clowns think you can toy with me?" She sounded confident and she looked poised, not tense, as she waited for Ray.

"Uh-huh. That's exactly what we think," another girl answered for us. She shuffled into the gymnasium. She had to shuffle. The full body brown teddy bear pajamas with the loose teddy bear hood had loose teddy bear feet. Her voice squeaked. She looked and sounded six. The hood shadowed everything but a broad, white-toothed grin.

Marcia laughed. "This gets more sad by the minute. You can barely walk in that outfit. How could you hurt anyone?"

Marcia wasn't exaggerating about Claire's costume. Claire. That had to be Claire. Claire's floppy bear feet dragged as she waddled up to Marcia. I clenched both fists. Marcia smirked at her. Then Claire punched her in the gut.

Not the gut. The solar plexus. I'd heard it didn't matter how fit you were, a punch right there below the ribs hurt. Now I saw it in action as Marcia stumbled backwards, bent over and wheezing loudly, fighting for breath.

Ray stepped forward, but I shook my head at him. Marcia forced herself upright, and I pointed both fists at her and unleashed the charge I'd been building while Claire's power distracted her. Then I swung my air cannon around, twisted the focus to a wall of force big enough I couldn't miss, and fired. I still had the force set too high. Tables tumbled, and Marcia didn't just fall over, she flew off her feet and landed on the floor against the wall.

She hit hard enough to stun, but no more. As I walked toward her, she lurched up – and couldn't move. I'd poured a lot of power into her, and it worked. Everywhere her body touched the wall and floor was stuck. In that awkward rag-doll position she couldn't even get leverage.

I lifted my air cannon and slid the focus back up. I kept walking as Marcia clenched her teeth and glared hate at me, but no matter how she tensed up she couldn't move. I lowered the barrel of my cannon and pointed it at her face.

"You've figured it out, right? We sprang your silly little trap for fun. I only wish you'd been smart enough to bring help. Three against one, this wasn't even a fight." My own voice sounded giddy and glib in my ears. The visor on my helmet zoomed in on her face as I focused. Yes, that was Marcia, and, in a close up, I could see her trembling. Whether with anger of fear, it didn't matter. No one deserved this more.

I shrugged, turning away from her. "I suppose it doesn't matter how easy it was. We've made our statement. Congratulations, Miss A. Maybe one day you'll tell your grandchildren that you were the first to fall to The Inscrutable Machine! HA! HA HA HA!" I couldn't help it. Fake laughter became real laughter, bubbling up inside me. "AH HA HA HA HA HA HA HA!"

I braced a boot against a display table and shoved it over. Photos and carefully light stained papers flew. I kicked another table out of the way. "But I don't want you to feel you lost for nothing," I called back. "We'll fulfill our half of the bargain and trash the place. In fact…"

I bent forward, pretending to read my own display. The Machine curled up eagerly as I reached out for it. Still active. I laughed. "Oh yes, I love the irony. Let's see how well this thing works." I closed my fist around The Machine, but only long enough to toss it lightly across the row at another table. "Eat. Recycle the entire room."

The Machine dug in, crunching up metal plates and rulers, and then wood and the metal lining of the table. By the time the table broke and fell over, The Machine was the size of a dog, and snapped up the remains in big gulps.

"HA HA HA! So much for the daughters of superheroes!" I crowed

"We're done here," I called out to Claire and Ray. Claire giggled, and Ray tipped his hat at Marcia with a sneer. I walked out through a side door—a side door without a handle to keep it closed. Only I had taken the easy route tonight.

When the door swung shut behind us, I whispered to Ray and Claire, "Split up. We have to get out of here."

Ray leaned in close, showing me his toothy smile under the mask, and whispered. "You're a wonderful friend, and an even better supervillain." He didn't give me time to react. He turned and ran. Ran fast. He was around the corner of the school and racing up the street in seconds.

Then Claire threw her arms around my neck and squeezed the breath out of me. "That was so amazing! We can't talk now!" Then she ran away, too. Not as fast, but she could run just fine in those ridiculous pajamas. Without running out of breath, either. I wanted some Super Cheerleader Serum!

I'd collapse if I tried to run, but I jogged over to the elevator of the lab. I started stripping off my jumpsuit before the elevator hit bottom, struggled into my clothes, dragged my bike back out, and pushed open the doors again.

No one around. No sound of sirens, no visible signs of trouble. I locked the elevator doors, got on my bike, and pedaled as fast and as hard as I could.

No one chased me. By the time I got home my lungs hurt and my legs wobbled, but I crawled back in the window to find my door still locked and the game video still playing. It had hardly been any time. I turned off my computer, flicked off the lights, and fell into bed.

I didn't get to sleep through the night. Quiet scratching and rattling woke me. I sat up. The Machine was shuffling around outside the window. It had vomited up its cargo somewhere and returned to normal size.

Automatically, I pried the window up and fastened The Machine into place around my wrist where it belonged. A little more weight lifted off my heart. I'd hated leaving him behind.

Then I about jumped out of my skin as someone knocked on my bedroom door.

"Pumpkin? I'm sure you'll think this is good news, but there's no school tomorrow. Talk is that they may go straight to Christmas break," Dad's muffled voice informed me.

My body went cold and my heart seized up again. This was it. Someone had found out. Hope and playing innocent were the only cards I had now. I swung tiredly out of bed, shambled over to the door, and opened it enough to peek out. "Something happened, didn't it? Something happened to the school. I know it did, because The Machine came back," I told him, holding up my wrist. I couldn't keep my voice from fluttering.

Dad looked down at me with his most gentle and concerned frown. "No one was hurt, and the structural damage will be fixed by New Year, but, yes, something happened. Supervillains attacked your science fair. Supervillains your age."

I stared up at him helplessly. He pushed the door open and bent down to put his arms around me, hugging me to him tenderly. "Your invention came back because they used it to eat the whole science fair. Don't worry, Princess. That's all they did to it. I've seen the security tape. They weren't after it, or you. It had nothing to do with you. You're safe. You're completely safe. Okay?"

"Okay," I whispered back as my body went limp. We'd gotten away with it. No one knew I was a supervillain.

CHAPTER SEVEN

D o all superheroes—okay, supervillains—sleep like the dead after a battle? I did. It helped that I got to sleep in, with there being no school and all. I was awake and had my hair washed by the time the nerves hit me again. I was a supervillain. I was in so much trouble if someone found out. Had I done anything to give myself away like Marcia had?

Forget that. What was this going to do to my superhero career? I could get this all straightened out somehow, but I'd have to work with Miss A eventually. She was unlikely to forgive being blasted with an air cannon. A gigantic ego like hers would hold onto the memory of tumbling helplessly through the air, smacking against the wall, and then being fastened to it like glue by super-science weapons with particularly ridiculous themes.

I had the best equipment. And now I couldn't use them for real superheroing because they'd be too distinctive! Not the jumpsuit, either. I couldn't even let anyone see that in the lab. What a mess.

My mood bounced up and down while I got dressed, and as I drifted into the kitchen my Dad completely misinterpreted it. Right out of nowhere, I got lifted off my feet and the life hugged out of me. "It's okay, Pumpkin. This isn't your business. The community will deal with it. You'll have no shortage of villains to deal with when you're a fully fledged superhero yourself."

So, nobody had figured it out overnight. That was one weight off my shoulders. "I guess," I non-answered as I plopped myself down into a kitchen chair. I felt enough relief to sniff the air, and I liked that sweet, buttery smell. Just as I identified it, Dad poured some pancake mix into a skillet and started frying it up.

Buttermilk pancakes. I blow holes in the school gym, humiliate a prominent sidekick, destroy the entire science fair, and force the school semester to end early. My punishment? Fresh buttermilk pancakes. That certainly took another level of sting out of my worries about last night.

The first stack landed on a plate in front of me. As I carefully applied butter and thick maple syrup to every layer, Dad suggested, "If your powers fully emerge before you finish high school, your Mom and I could find you a hero to teach you the ropes. Starting as a sidekick may seem like a joke, but no one is ready for their first super-powered battle."

No kidding.

"We'll have plenty of time to decide, honey, but I'd rather not," Mom broke in, wandering into the kitchen. Her hair looked like an electrocuted badger. Since she didn't have to take me to school, she must have decided to sleep in. As she grabbed a plate of pancakes for herself she explained, "Can you think of a single parent in the community who made their child become a sidekick that you'd want to be like? The Original is an—a jerk, and Miss A has obvious emotional problems. She should not have been there last night." I smirked around my mouthful of gooey pancake as she restrained herself from swearing in front of me.

Dad was unruffled. "We'll have to let Penelope decide. When the time comes. If there are more supervillains this young, it may be healthier to let them fight kids their own age." Silence reigned for about three seconds before he failed to hold back a snorting laugh and added, "I can't believe I just said that."

"I can't believe life gave you the chance," Mom sighed more seriously.

At that point, my phone roared. "Hey, Penny, if you're up, do you want to come over to my place?" Claire asked on the other end.

"Mom, Dad, can I go over to Claire's?" I dutifully repeated.

"Yes," they both answered together.

Dad seized the chance to follow up before Mom. "You have the day off school. We want you to go out and enjoy it." You know, and not mope. Dad wasn't subtle today.

"I'll be there as soon as I finish breakfast," I assured Claire.

First things first. I stuffed myself to bursting with pancakes.

I took my bike over to Claire's. Mom wanted to drive me, but I'd have felt like a heel. Claire's house was closer than school after all. Even on the edge of Bel Air, I wasn't going to leave my bicycle outside and not locked up, so I walked it up to the front door and pressed the doorbell. Then I tried not to yelp as Ray jumped off the roof, landed next to me like it was nothing, and opened the door for me without waiting for it to be answered.

As I tried to force my heart back down my throat into my chest again I turned on him. "You are really getting a kick out of this super agility thing, aren't you?"

"Yes," he said, voice sharp with glee.

After last night I wanted a little less glee and a little more apology, but Claire met us at the door, grabbed both our hands and dragged us inside.

"You know I could hear your footsteps on the roof, right?" she asked Ray.

"I'll know from now on," he assured her.

"Mom could give you some great cat burglar advice," Claire suggested as she pulled us through the living room. I knew Miss Lutra must tidy up occasionally, because the clutter on the pretty red furniture in the pretty white room was entirely different from the clutter the last time I'd come over.

I felt like no one else was taking this seriously. "Aren't we in enough trouble as it is?"

"Not as long as you don't get caught," Claire's Mom commented as she stacked my bike against the clutter. Oh, of course, she knew.

"Just let me show you something, Penny. Okay?" Claire begged. She gave me the puppy dog eyes and everything. I reluctantly kept my mouth shut long enough for her to drag me into her room and up to her computer.

Flipping on the screen, she grabbed her mouse and clicked on a bookmark on her web browser. In half a second, a website called Villain Hunting popped up, the latest entry trumpeting the headline "THE INSCRUTABLE MACHINE."

Holy…

I couldn't complete the thought. I had to start over. The blurb was tiny. The supervillain team that destroyed the Northeast West Hollywood Middle gymnasium but left behind the alien device were rumored to be named The Inscrutable Machine. That was all they knew, but they could make a lot of guesses because a single still frame from the battle had leaked out to the public.

In front of me the screen displayed a huge black and white image from the security cameras, blurry and out of focus but clearly showing me blasting Miss A off her feet, with Claire and Ray watching.

There could not possibly be over a thousand comments on this picture. I had to be imagining that. Then Claire clicked another tab on her browser, and another, and another. Two more web sites with almost identical articles. The last was a forum instead, with thread after thread entitled "The Inscrutable Machine."

Ray gasped. "We. Are. *Famous.*"

Claire's take was more smugly practical. "There's all kinds of speculation about what our supervillain names are. We'll have to come up with something fast, or there's no telling what the fans will name us."

"We're not supervillains!" I yelled at them suddenly.

Ray looked theatrically over at the computer screen, then back at me. "I'd say we are."

"I was hoping we could cover this up! How are we going to be superheroes now?" I wailed.

"From personal experience, it's never too late to switch sides," Claire's Mom called from the other side of the house. I'd been a bit loud, but shock and anger still boiled hot through my blood.

"Of course, we're going to be heroes after all, Penny." Claire sounded so calm about this, although if she smiled any wider her head would fall in half. "Brand new villains find their conscience all the time, and everybody's fascinated by the superhumans who you never know if they'll rampage through a neighborhood or foil a bank robbery next. Lucyfar's got to have three times the fan pages Mech does."

"That might have something to do with the outfit." Ray leaned back against the wall, folded his arms and tucked his hat down enough to show off only his grin.

That he pulled it off just infuriated me more. "Ray, you ought to be a little more sorry. You got us into this!"

He lifted his head again and smirked. "Sorry? Sorry I made a fool out of an arrogant bully? Sorry I trashed a science fair rigged by that arrogant bully? I'm only sorry about one thing." He took the hat off, holding it in both hands, and suddenly he did look sorry. In fact, his face pulled away from mine, and he obviously had to force himself to look in my eyes as he explained. "I sold your bubble gum invention to buy my suit. Leased it, technically. I'll get it back eventually. I know it was ungrateful, but there's a fortune in mad scientist collectibles and I got a little bit crazy. And about that, I'm sorry. Really, really sorry."

I wanted to be even more mad, but his confession took too big a weight off my shoulders. "Yes, you got crazy. I was worried you'd stolen the money to buy that stuff. I thought you wanted to be a supervillain."

"It was a lot of fun, and we can switch to being heroes whenever we want," Ray half-answered. That speculative tone indicated he didn't mind how things had gone at all.

I did. "We're switching to being heroes right now."

Claire waved her arms in mock grandeur. "The scientific mastermind is always the leader. We, her minions, can only obey."

I nearly snapped at her, but I caught that glance between her and Ray. Oh. They were teasing me. I really needed to lighten up. I'd just been so nervous!

"We have to do something. Immediately," I insisted. I sounded sullen, but that was better than mad, right?

"Then it's a good thing we've got all weekend free, and I had a long talk with my Mom already about this, right?" Claire nudged. She beamed at me. Tension I didn't know I'd had eased out of my shoulders.

"You've worked out a plan already?" I really wanted to believe they did.

"I kinda got lucky. When I show you, you won't believe how stupid some people are. First, you two have to see some of these comments threads. In one of them a guy actually guesses I'm The Minx's daughter and then gets laughed off the forum because the pajamas are so unsexy." A little more tension went out of me, and Claire slipped up and gave me a quick, tight hug. "See? We're not in any trouble. We can start fixing our reputation tomorrow. Right now, come see how famous you are!"

CHAPTER EIGHT

My sense of urgency might not have been universally shared. I had great friends. Everything turned on its head on Thursday, and, thanks to Claire, by Saturday I was poised to set it all right. It's just that while I folded my arms and tapped my foot and tried to not draw attention from the street, Claire…

"These are so much fun!" she squealed as she slid down the concrete drive on one foot. She held the other foot raised, perfectly balanced despite the clunky bear pajamas, then pirouetted and zoomed back in the other direction.

"Somebody's going to see us!" I hissed. In the sense that someone had already seen us. Quite a few people. The street our school is on isn't busy by any stretch, but pedestrians still passed by. The last couple took photos of Claire skating around in her frictionless bear feet. With me standing next to her.

I wouldn't mind, but there was the whole "wanted supervillain" thing.

"It's fine!" Claire assured me. The Super Cheerleader Serum had done wonders for her. She looped around the driveway in quick circles, usually on one foot, leaning wildly but always balanced. As I watched her skate she explained. "I think I've found just the right level of juice to give my powers. They see a couple of kids in costumes, sure, but they're not thinking about us. We're too cute to be supervillains."

She had me. When I saw a middle school girl in hoodie bear pajamas skating around like she had butter on her feet, evil supervillain was not the first thought in my head.

Claire swooped and swooped in tighter and tighter circles. I watched her feet. I'd made the inserts hidden between her feet and the soles of her pajamas, and I still couldn't tell her feet didn't really touch the cracked pavement. She glided like an ice dancer, right up until she grabbed my shoulders with both hands.

"Did you try them? They're so fast, and so much fun at the same time, and I love them! Have you been keeping them as a surprise? When did you find time to make them?" She made no attempt to hide her bubbling glee.

"Yesterday, after I left your place. I was too nervous to go home, and I thought building us some equipment for today would take my mind off of things." I was fudging. I'd wanted to putter around in my lab until I exhausted myself, yes, but I didn't have a plan. My power came up with this latest round of toys in a blackout. That thought felt creepy, but I'd have to get used to it. My parents got one thing right. My powers were here, but controlling them wasn't even on the horizon.

Fidget fidget fidget, fret fret fret. I couldn't even enjoy watching Claire sliding around on her... what? Reverse friction pads? They pushed away instead of clinging?

Claire let go of my shoulders and pushed off again, spinning in tight circles, hopping from one foot to the other. Her voice lilted, spiking with giddy enthusiasm. "No wonder the mad scientist is always the team leader. These were exactly what we needed! What do Ray's do?"

I fiddled with the pouches on my jumpsuit, and the half dozen fat bracelets they held. "Teleport, I think. I don't actually know."

My heart only lost one beat as Ray landed on the ground in front of me. "It doesn't matter. I don't need them!" Ray assured us.

"Is this jumping off roofs thing going to be a habit?" I asked sarcastically. Okay, I was kind of grinning a little.

"Did you find our target?" Claire asked. Maybe I wasn't the one with her mind on business.

Not too far away, a girl shrieked. That brief yelp sounded strangled.

Ray become mostly business. "That would be a 'yes.' Follow me. I'll take the slowpoke."

I was the slowpoke. That became really clear as he swept me off my feet and into his arms, and it felt like I'd leaped fifteen feet into the air all at once. Then I heard his shoes hit the roof and he crouched over me to take the impact. Oh. We *had* jumped fifteen feet into the air.

His feet pounded over the flat rooftop as he held me to his chest. Wait, he'd jumped from ground level onto the roof carrying my weight? How strong had I made him, anyway? That heart-taking-off sensation signaled another jump, and I got enough sense to peek down and see a fence pass by under us before we landed on the roof of... next on this street was a string of shops, right?

I could feel his chest heaving next to me. Okay, running like this while carrying me must have been a strain, but he seemed completely steady about it. Even carrying my weight he tore up the distance. The scream hadn't been far away. After the shops was...what? That boarded up auto depot? Ray jumped again, landed, jumped again, and seemingly light as a feather we landed in the parking lot behind the car sales place. The shop might be abandoned, but the parking lot sure wasn't. Cars in disorderly lines, and, in the corner of the building, a bulging mass of gray muscle held a high school girl against the wall by her throat.

Well, Claire had been right. One of our schoolmates wasn't just a budding supervillain. He wasn't just planning to go on a rampage to prove himself just like we had; he'd also been dumb enough to post that plan on the internet.

The thing heard Ray land, and looked back at us over his shoulder. His eyes widened, which merely left them tiny, piggy, and black. "You brought her. You really are The Inscrutable Machine!" His transformation had given him a wheezy, squeaky voice I couldn't hope to match up to one of my classmates. I might even be imagining how excited he sounded; it was that garbled.

And boy, the transformation. I had to feel bad for him, inheriting a power like this. He had all of the ugly. All of it. He hadn't left any ugly for anybody else. No hair, his head fusing into his shoulders in a mass of blubbery gray muscle, skin like armadillo or rhino hide, and the grossly distended face that brought attention to his sharp teeth—that was just the first glance. He couldn't look more like a supervillain if he tried.

Speaking of...

I lifted my air conditioner cannon and pointed it at his hideous face. "That's us. I'll sign your head just as soon as you put down the girl. This is your first time, so I'll give you a hint—hostage dramas give us more time to surround you."

That set off a wheezing gusher. "You would sign my head? Really? What about my shirt? You can't write on this monster skin, I've tried. Meeting you means so much to me. My uncle and his friends are always telling me that I'm not ready, and a superhero would clean the clock of any kid my age, but I'm stronger than any of them. Everybody knows Miss A couldn't touch you, and she—" He leaned toward us as he babbled, and the girl behind him got enough free room to let out another yelp and start squirming. Pressing her back against the wall and choking off her scream, he finished lamely, "Sorry."

"Listen, Lumpy—" I started.

He cut me off. "Sharky."

My silence must have said it all. "I can come up with something better," he mumbled.

"There's, like, six guys bigger than you already using it," I pointed out. With any luck, my voice dripped contempt.

That thick skin didn't show expression well, but the way he lowered his head looked pretty embarrassed. "I know, I know. I just didn't expect to need a good name 'til I was eighteen, and then you happened!"

"Yeah. About that," I echoed, scrambling to get my thoughts back on track. Drama. I needed to scare him. My cannon didn't need to be cocked like a shotgun, but I grabbed the levers for the settings and yanked them from one side to the other so they clacked loudly. "You've been dangerously misinformed. We're not on your side. Put the girl down and surrender, and we'll give you a chance to convince us not to give you to the police."

Was he shaking? I was a little girl in a tight, gray spacesuit with a china pipe on my arm! I couldn't be that scary! Those were definitely big breaths he was taking. He couldn't possibly be psyching himself up to fight me. Except that's exactly what he was doing, and, by the time I forced myself to believe it, he rasped, "It's okay. I get it. I knew it would happen when I came out here. I just got a little star struck, right? It's your territory, and that means I've got to take it from you."

It was going to take a lengthy explanation of the difference between a superhero and a supervillain to make those shark brains understand which side I was on. Before I could even find the words to start, his body bulged. Muscles swelled like inflating balloons. He grew another six inches. That stony hide couldn't cover him anymore, and big gaps ripped in it, then flapped slowly like gills. He'd actually found a way to get uglier. The wet, pink crud showing through those flaps was hard to look at. So much yuck.

At least he dropped the high school girl. Sharky's foot thudded as he took a clumsy step toward me. Compared to that, Ray slid in front of him as smoothly as a snake. Sharky swung a wide punch, and it couldn't have been that slow. It just looked that slow when Ray ducked under it.

I cleared my throat loudly, looked straight at the cowering teenager, and gave my head a jerk. Even through the visor she figured out that was for her and ran hunched over down the length of the wall toward the street.

I'd also gotten Ray and Sharky's attention, and I pointed my air conditioner cannon upward and announced, "I think I'm the one he wants to fight."

Sharky nodded clumsily. "Yeah. Yeah!" He lurched toward me. Ray stepped out of the way, and I shot Sharky dead on.

He was tough. I liked the setting that blew Marcia off her feet, but it only pushed him back a half step. It might as well have been a stiff breeze.

He couldn't dodge. I turned the force way up, left the focus wide, and, as he took a step to charge me again, blew his legs out from under him. He hit the asphalt with a wet, loud smack as gross as the holes in his skin. I slid the focus lever tighter, let the visor's magnifier help compensate for my lousy aim, and, as he tried to lift his head, I shot him in the face with a cannonball of pleasantly chilled compressed air. That rolled him over onto his back. Had I hit him too hard? No. As long as he lived, no such thing.

With that in mind I shot him again, rolling him back over onto his belly. He didn't seem eager to get up this time, but I still stayed out of arm's reach when I walked up toward him. "You're so not ready for this, Sharky. Not now, not ever. Go home and think about it. Think about how you'd be going to enhanced-abilities jail right now for mugging if I was on a regular superhero patrol."

"I'm a superhero on patrol, and that sounds like a great idea. In fact, why don't I send all three of you together?" Marcia's snide voice announced.

Not this! I looked back to see her drop lightly off the roof down by the street entrance, all dressed up in her Miss A costume. People jumping off roofs still looked weird to me. I'd have to get used to it.

I tried really hard to keep hold of my temper. "I'm pretty sure I just stopped the mugging and beat up the mugger."

"And I'm pretty sure there's a charge for gang war. That's the DA's job to figure out. Mine is to leave you gift-wrapped for his convenience." She sounded so snippy..

As an alternative to shooting her in the face, I played the shrew right back at her. "A job you're doing so well. Outnumbered against opponents who've beaten you once already, you just gave up the element of surprise so you could get in some quality sarcasm time."

That only made her smirk more annoying, and she upped the gratingly snide tone another notch. "I'm sure your mirror is all quiet and appreciative when you give your villainous monologues. I'm so sorry to spoil your moment. Would now be a bad time to point out I'm also not outnumbered?"

Orange, flickering light presaged flames, hot and roaring, sheathing a high school boy in a red and black superhero costume as he walked calmly around the corner. Oh boy. Fire-based powers. This had gotten dangerous, fast.

"I don't know if you keep up with the other team, but this young man's called Ifrit. I think he's Marvelous's younger brother," Miss A explained with a sadistic grin.

"She's wrong about that," Ifrit sighed. Apparently Marcia got on everyone's nerves. "But she was right that we'd catch you here this weekend." Fire powers, and the look he gave me was way more serious than Miss A's.

"We're barely a block from the school, and the ego that put on a show there just had to return to the scene of the crime. Oh, and have you met Gabriel?" Marcia got more venomous every second. Wait, didn't I know that name, Gabriel?

White wings fluttered, six of them, as Gabriel landed. His white suit made him look like an inverse of Ray, except Ray didn't have those six huge wings that could do way more than fly. This wasn't fair. This wasn't even close to fair. Gabriel was new to the superhero scene, but he certainly wasn't a sidekick. Those wings were scary. I knew because—

"Gabriel! I read your blog! What are you doing here?!" Claire squealed. She was a high-speed, brown blur skating around from the opposite entrance to the parking lot. Of course, she'd been watching, and now she zoomed up to the white-winged young hero, grabbed both his hands, and they spun like dancers as he dragged her to a skidding stop.

He chuckled. I might have, too, despite the seriousness of the moment. "I'm doing my job. Fighting supervillains. Supervillains like you, young lady," he answered her.

Claire gave him a knowing look, her head tilted to one side. "Kind of my point, isn't it? How did Little Miss Sore Loser rope you into an obvious grudge match like this?"

Claire was obviously laying it on thick. I mean, she was wearing bear hoodie pajamas! Still, she had a point, and Marcia didn't like that.

"Grudge match?" Marcia screeched. Ha! Claire had hit a nerve.

At that, Ray stepped forward and bowed floridly to Marcia, arm curving underneath his body and then lifting up and back. She spun around her baton, bared her teeth, and marched on him. He lunged for her, fist raised, and, exactly like Thursday night she twisted, but, this time, they both fell, then back-flipped to their feet like twins.

It was on. Gabriel's wings extended, but Claire gave his hands a tug. "Seriously, Gabriel, look at that. Will you be proud of yourself when you post online that you took part in this? Right after the video of you talking down Lucyfar?"

"You really read my blog?" Gabriel asked her, the dumbfounded tone telling me she'd scored a point. I turned my head. I couldn't tell who was scoring points between Ray and Miss A. As I watched, she jabbed the end of her baton at his throat. He grabbed it, and she swung the baton and her whole body, tossing him past her into the wall. Except he climbed back to his feet easily and she crouched, wheezing. He'd hit her, and I'd missed it.

"Does the name E-Claire ring a bell?" Claire asked Gabriel as Ray grabbed for Miss A, got his arm twisted into a painfully awkward looking angle, then yanked her off her feet and threw her over the next car. Had he been trapping her with his strength, or had he barely escaped a trap himself?

"Yes. Yes, it does. So that's your online and your supervillain handle?" Gabriel asked her as fire roared up all around me.

Oops. I heard Ifrit's voice outside the not quite opaque flames. "I don't know what's going on, but we can figure it out after you three are under control." He held both hands out toward me, controlling the cage of snapping flame I'd been trapped in. Let myself be trapped in.

I'd just made a bigger fool of myself than anyone else here. Ifrit had been right. Business first. The walls might not be physical, but walking through them would put me in the hospital. I could feel the flames, muted by my jumpsuit. I clenched my fists.

"E-Claire is right, Ifrit. Miss A's lost a screw. We shouldn't get involved in this. We don't know what's really going on," Gabriel chided him.

"Seeing supervillains in costume is usually good enough," Ifrit answered.

I heard Claire's voice next. "Come on. I know you can't trust me, but look at Miss A and tell me this is on the level." Everyone was a vague shape through flickering orange and yellow to me, but the fast moving shadows would be Ray and Marcia, and I could hear Marcia's grunts and snarls of anger with no difficulty.

"If we don't win, it won't matter who we decide is right," Ifrit shot back.

Okay, I'd let him argue enough. I took two quick steps forward, eyes and mouth shut, and tried not to yell at the feeling like I'd stepped into an oven, then out of an oven. I felt like I'd gotten a sunburn on my face and wrists, but my burn resistant jumpsuit had done its job. I lifted my hands and opened them so that the charge I'd built up arced out and grounded itself in Ifrit *before* I announced, "I agree."

The lightning wouldn't hurt, but surprise made him jump a step back, and when his first foot touched the asphalt I had him. I raised my air cannon and fired a couple of merely stunning shots. The cage next to me disappeared, and instead he swung his hands up and spun arcs of fire that exploded every time one of my blasts hit.

I deliberately and visibly thumbed the levers of my cannon higher. "Nice shields. I guess I can turn up the juice without worrying I'll kill you."

His eyes narrowed. He looked and sounded very serious. "Nice fireproof suit. Looks like I can do the same."

I saw the flicker around his hands and threw myself down. I fired a shot somewhere in there, but it didn't have a prayer of hitting. My jumpsuit was really not sufficiently padded, and I got a jolt of pain when my shoulder hit the asphalt. The flame that swept past me hurt even though it didn't touch me. I needed to get behind a car, but I wouldn't have the time. I swung up my cannon instead.

Miss A and Ray spun past Ifrit in their latest grapple, and Ray's elbow shot out and hit the back of Ifrit's head.

The little devil. "Reviled!" I yelled, hoping Ray would know who I meant. He did. He dropped and pushed Miss A up and into the open, and instead of blasting Ifrit I blew Miss A off her feet.

She hit hard, but she got her feet under her and tried to flip up. Ray hooked his foot behind hers, and she smacked onto her back again. Ifrit was more of a threat. Flames gusted up around him, but the blow to the head left him too muddled. I had a half-second to point my cannon at his face.

I didn't have time to fire, because a huge, white wing extended and wrapped itself around Ifrit like a blanket. Another scooped up Miss A.

"Just give up." Gabriel scolded both of them. "You lost, and the whole fight was stupid from the start. I can't believe the adult here is the supervillainess in pajamas."

"So that's it? The fight's over, and you're not getting involved?" I asked, more sharply than I wanted. I couldn't take anything for granted, and if Claire couldn't hold him I'd need the first shot.

"I don't like grudge matches, and I won't let myself be dragged into one. The only person I saw committing a real crime is the chump on the ground. He's had his beating." One of his free wings gestured behind me. Oh, yeah. Sharky.

"Leave him. I'm hoping he'll figure out he's not cut out for this." That sounded more like a demand than a request. I lowered my cannon arm, so at least it didn't sound like a threat.

He didn't like it. He watched me. He had the greenest eyes. It seemed odd to notice right now, but with his white hair and white clothes and white wings, they stood out. He chewed over his words, then finally told me, "It's a cliché, but... when next we meet, we meet as enemies. I'm hoping that won't happen."

From inside Gabriel's wing, Marcia growled. "It'll happen. I've met supervillains like her. She'll turn up like a bad penny."

If I'd spent the rest of the day telling her I wasn't a supervillain, she wouldn't have listened. I might as well get in a dig back. "Aren't sour grapes delicious? E-Claire. Reviled. Let's get out of here."

I slapped the control on my chest, and a bike made of blue light spat out in front of me. I climbed on, grabbed the handlebars, and pushed with one foot. The bike and I leapt forward, curling smoothly around the edge of the building and down the street. Claire caught up with me before I hit the next intersection, feet pumping like a speed skater. Ray just ran, keeping up like we were both dawdling.

"That was so cool! I met Gabriel, and I got to cloud his mind, and Ray, by the end there you were mopping the floor with Miss A!" Claire yelled.

"Once I learned her tricks, she had nothing. It was great!" Ray crowed back.

I corrected them as sternly as I could manage. "Okay, it was cool, but it was not great. I was as clumsy as a penguin out there. I need better defensive gear, and they still think we're supervillains."

"At least I've got a great supervillain name. 'Reviled'. I love it. Thanks!" Ray laughed.

Marcia's last words came back to me. "I'm glad you're happy, but I think I just got stuck with the dumbest supervillain name ever. Worse than Sharky."

CHAPTER NINE

I jingled the bracelets in my pockets as I walked up the street toward my house. I'd stowed everything else away. A bike of light made it pretty easy to visit the lair and drop off my supervillain gear. I really had to get that redefined as "superhero" gear!

I'd kept the bracelets. They didn't look like anything much, and, even if Ray didn't want to figure out how they worked, I did.

Anyway, I needed more toys. Way more toys. I'd been a useless lump back there—although I had to admit, Ray and me taking out each other's opponents had been pretty cool!

I wandered up the driveway and stepped up to the side door and heard my parents' voices in the kitchen.

"We have two video samples now. I can work out their height and approximate weight. There's an eighty-five percent chance at least one of them is the child of a known superhuman. Someone on the team has technology powers, most likely the girl who keeps her face hidden. I'll get my figures. At least seventy percent of tech supervillains use their own equipment. I have the exact number. Brian, I can identify these children!" That was my Mom. Her voice came fast and clipped, but kept derailing into little spikes of emotion. She was wobbling between being my mother and The Audit, and it made chills creep down my spine.

"Let it go, Beebee," I heard Dad insist. His voice was calm, at least, but so serious. I was in so much trouble.

"It's not the eighties anymore. It's not even the nineties. This won't take me a week. All the information I need is online, or our friends still working have it. I could have The Inscrutable Machine's secret identities in an hour," Mom begged him. That's what she sounded like. She was begging him to let her catch us. She could. If she said an hour, I'd set my watch.

I had an hour to figure out how to get out of this mess.

"Absolutely not. This is not going to get personal." My knees wobbled, I relaxed so much. Dad sounded firm, and my Mom was a wreck. He was going to win this argument. I really hoped he was going to win this argument.

"They're just kids, Brian. We're not stalking real supervillains back to their homes," she argued with the desperate tone of someone losing a fight.

Dad's voice stayed level. "No, we'd be stripping a supervillain's children of their secret identity and stalking them back to their homes. Most likely three supervillains. This will get way beyond personal; the whole supervillain community will explode. How would you react if a villain tracked down Penny's identity?"

"Everyone already knows Penny's identity." Mom voice sounded hoarse. Was she crying? "The Machine just attacked and defeated three superheroes' children—"

"Two superheroes' children. Gabriel didn't attack them, so they didn't attack him," Dad corrected her.

"And Gabriel's behavior makes sense to you? The difference from normal was too subtle for mind control, but it was there. Probably a chemical agent the girl in the bear suit delivered," my mother babbled, slipping back into The Audit's rapid speech.

A little louder, Dad warned, "Beebee—"

"It just happened!" Mom shouted suddenly. "Penny is out there right now in the same part of town they're hunting, and she's got a giant target painted on her because we didn't want to keep who we were a secret!"

Everything got real quiet for a few seconds. I could hear my heart and my breathing, and the traffic a block away, but nothing from inside. Finally my Dad said in a really low voice, "Penny is in no danger unless we put her in danger by making this personal. These kids aren't Spider or Winnow. They're joyriders with super powers. What percentage of the community, the adult community, is just in it for the brawl? On both sides?"

Mom didn't answer. When that became clear, Dad kept talking. "I don't like that middle-schoolers are getting into the business either, but this will sort itself out. They'll be defeated, or they'll get scared or bored and give up, or, most likely, they'll see what supervillains are really like and switch sides."

That was exactly what I wanted to do. It was just easier said than done! I didn't hear a response from Mom. Well, I heard a sigh, but that was it.

I was out of the woods again. News had gotten out about the fight already, but my folks just didn't want to put two and two together.

Still, not a great time to go home. I wanted to experiment with these bracelets, and, especially with my Mom keyed up, ""at home was not a great place to do that. Being spotted by random strangers would be way safer. I didn't know which was more common in LA, goofy performance artist stunts or superheroes showing off with their powers. Being out in public suddenly sounded way, way safer than being at home. Maybe I could walk down to Griffith Park.

Walk down there? Yeah, right. Bike, maybe. Or maybe these bracelets. I'd made them for transportation.

No time like the present. I pulled all six out of my pockets and slipped three up onto each forearm.

They did nothing. They might not even work for me. That super-powered thing in the back of my head had Ray's powers in mind when it built this.

No, they had to do something. I walked down the block, trying to figure out how to activate the bands. No obvious controls. Pads on the inner surfaces. Maybe it was in how I moved my arms? I just wanted to teleport to the end of the block.

My next step took me to the end of the block. My knees about gave out underneath me, and I looked back over my shoulder. Had I traveled a hundred yards in one step? How had I activated the bracelets? I'd taken a step, and here I was, as tired as if I'd run the whole distance. My heart pounded, not from fear but effort. I took a few deep breaths as an alternative to sitting down.

Was every teleport going to knock the wind out of me like this? How did I activate the rings, anyway? Maybe I'd try something easier. I'd walk down to the next mailbox and pay very careful attention to what I was doing until it activated and see if—

The first step. The very first step, and I ended up leaning against the mailbox I'd aimed at. I'd held my arms out a little, yeah, but not in the same position as when I'd teleported the first time. Man, I felt tired, but that was still mostly from the first jump. I'd felt this one, but not too bad. So distance made a difference. And were these things thought activated? Let's say I thought about moving into that square of sidewalk two cracks down.

Nada. But if I took a step, everything jumped and my foot came down in that spot. I'd made high-tech seven-league boots. No wonder I'd made them for Ray, if the wearer's body had to power them. With his slimly muscled, superhuman physique, he wouldn't even notice the exertion. Kind of weird to think of Ray as being muscular, but I guess super powers have fringe benefits.

It really felt like I'd run these three or four paces. Maybe I had, and what the bracelets did was mess with time? Easiest way to test this was to try and teleport somewhere I couldn't walk or run. Let's see. Inside that SUV in the driveway next to me.

I took a step, and that's all that happened. I took a step. Maybe the problem was I still didn't understand the controls? Trial Number Two. The top of that house. I took a step… and lost my balance and sat down on my butt hard on the rough shingles. I wasn't in shape for this. While I caught my breath, I looked out over the rooftop at the street. There was the SUV I hadn't been able to get into, and the mailbox I'd been standing next to a moment ago. A tree blocked the street lights. Probably somebody saw me up here, but nobody seemed to care.

I might love these bracelets more than anything I'd made since The Machine. Plus, they blended in with the segmented hunk of metal on my wrist. It'd be nice if he was a little less recognizable.

My phone beeped. I wasn't going anywhere for a second, so I pulled it out and flipped it open.

I'd gotten a text message from Claire. "You won't believe the invitation we just got. Meet me at the Red Line down by the library ASAP."

I sent back "That's downtown! Now is not a good time to ask my folks for a ride!"

A few seconds later, my phone beeped again. "Don't tell me the mad genius girl can't find a way to get to a Red Line station."

She had a point. There was a station, like, a mile away tops. I had a bicycle. And teleport bands.

I wanted to ask Claire a million questions, but one question was way more important. Would the bands and the bike work together?

I typed in "You win this round, E-Claire."

If my parents were freaking out about this Inscrutable Machine thing, would they start setting times I had to be home? This situation was awkward enough as it was. That was the kind of nervous thought that plagued me as I wheeled my bike out from beside the house.

The moment my butt settled on the seat I had a different question. Was this going to work, or was it going to get me killed? I pedaled a couple of times, and I couldn't wait. There, on the other side of the intersection. I shoved down hard on the pedal... and the houses skipped around me. I wobbled, mostly because I felt like I'd been riding uphill to get here, but my tight muscles eased up in seconds. So, it worked with a bicycle. Would it work with my light bike? A car?

A crawling nervousness itched between my shoulder blade at those thoughts. How far could I take these experiments before failure got me killed? Was this a warning straight from my super power, or just nerves?

Pedestrians up ahead. My body tightened as I teleported past them, then relaxed. Then I looked back over my shoulder at their bemused faces. HA!

Just keep an eye out on clear spaces ahead. Coming up on the next intersection, I waited until I got close, aimed past the dressed up couple standing at the corner, pushed down, and appeared perfectly in place, still zooming along, AH HA HA!

I headed down to Hollywood Ave. Biking past the hospitals would normally be impossible. On Hollywood, the buildings went from tree lined residential to densely packed urban real fast. I turned the corner. There were the hospitals ahead of me, alright. Packs of pedestrians everywhere.

I was so going to kill someone, starting with me.

I couldn't help myself.

Across the intersection. Jump past the nurses at the hot dog wagon. Pedal a few times through an open stretch. Before the doctors ahead of me could try to dive out of the way, I teleported past them, and—yikes, wheelchair! Down the block, across the intersection, I shoved down on the pedal and jumped!

That had been too far. The world skipped, and I was on the other side
of the big intersection, but my arms and legs felt like lead. But I'd made it. I
took it easy down the peaceful stretch as Hollywood turned into Sunset
before it turned into Cesar Chavez. Well, peaceful-er. Skipping little
intersections and bouncing past an occasional shopper wasn't hard at low
speed. Being able to coast on a bicycle really took the sting out of the
teleports.

I should have gotten on the Red Line, but I just had to take this
downtown. Without having to stop at intersections, I zoomed. The street
got more and more urban, and I saw the big buildings of downtown off to
the right and turned down Hill street, which was really easy since I could
just hop right across to the other side of the street to do it.

I started to feel like a bit of an idiot. Without my parents to take me or
hopping a Red Line train, I didn't know where the library was or where
Pershing Square was. That was the subway exit I was looking for. Sure, it
was down here somewhere, but I could be wandering around for a while,
and this hill I coasted down now was going to be a major pain getting back
up even with teleportation powers.

Or I could get lucky, and, as I pulled up to an intersection between two
huge ratty buildings, that could be Pershing Square right across from me,
layers of concrete like an ornate but barren park. Ray could be standing
there by the subway exit, leaning against a pay phone and scanning the
crowd under the brim of his big black hat.

I gave the pedal a gentle push, teleported right up in front of him, and
shoved on the brake. Then I slid off the seat and tried not to breathe hard
from that last jump. I couldn't look less cool than my minion, right?

He wasn't going to make it easy on me. He tipped his hat, dropped it
back in place, and grinned like a maniac. "Come here often, beautiful?"

I might be the first girl in history with giant brown braided pigtails to be
on the receiving end of that line. I didn't have a comeback, so I changed the
subject. "Is Claire not here yet?"

His eyebrows tilted up. Apparently I'd just said something hilarious.
Okay, so I guess I'd made pretty good time. To cut off whatever joke was
fermenting in his brain, I asked, "Does that girl look familiar?"

Ray followed my gaze to the young woman with the long, straight, black
hair. In jeans and a hipster tee-shirt with a summoning circle on it, she sure

didn't stand out from the downtown crowd, so why was she standing out from the downtown crowd? Besides the way she looked right at us.

"I think that's Lucyfar," Ray answered in a hush, just before the blackness started crawling up the woman's legs.

Black shapes crystallized in the air. I got a glimpse of one of them plunging toward my face, then the world tumbled around me. The tightness was Ray's arms, and we hit the ground with me on top of him, rolled, and he swung right back up into a crouch.

Three of Lucyfar's signature black knives hovered in the air like snakes. Really? Twice in one day, and the second ambush by Lucyfar? I was going to murder Claire, if I lived to have the chance.

One of those knives eased forward. Ray's arms tightened, but I shoved both hands against him, shouting, "I can take care of myself!" He let me go. All three knives swerved to focus on me, and I didn't give them time to strike. I lurched forward. Even in this position the teleport rings activated, and I staggered to my feet behind a palm tree. I looked around to spot Lucyfar, and we caught each other's eyes as she looked around to spot me. Black knives moved in a blur, and I leaped forward, aiming for the far side of the street.

That was too much. I collapsed against a parked car and gulped air as black edged around my vision. I had to be stronger than this, or at least smarter.

Across the street I saw the notch missing from the palm tree I'd hidden behind. Lucyfar had returned her attention to Ray. He ducked behind the railing of a subway escalator as a knife went over his head, then catapulted back over top in its wake. The other two knives slammed down at him, and he backflipped, ducked behind a trash can and then out the other side as a knife blow made the metal frame ring.

It didn't matter. She still had a knife between herself and him. This was not a fair fight. Black hair floated around Lucyfar's head, and liquid black magic covered her like a gown. Her knives were more like spear heads, phantom fleur-de-lis blades made of the same black magic.

No one was screaming. Sure, the crowd had parted, but cars rubbernecked instead of fleeing. I saw a college student in a backpack just circling around and going on her way up the street. My parents joked about how jaded LA had become with superhero battles, but criminy!

I didn't have time for that. As long as Lucyfar kept her attention on Ray, he couldn't close. Sooner rather than later, she'd hit him. But she'd stopped looking for me.

We were downtown. I scanned the sidewalk until I saw an old glass bottle. With one step I teleported over to it, grabbed it up off the ground, and, with another, I teleported back across the street and threw it at Lucyfar's head. It wouldn't hit her. With my aim? Forget it. But her head turned at the motion, and one of her knives swung around to smack the bottle out of the way. Ray saw a chance and charged forward. He could really move, but he wouldn't beat the knives swinging in to intercept him. I took a step, and, after the world stopped whirling, I saw the black thing I'd jumped next to was Ray. I latched hold of him, and, as he dragged me forward, I threw out a foot and aimed right behind Lucyfar.

We appeared right there. She loomed right in front of me, a skinny figure clouded in floating black like the reaper himself. Ray pivoted, jumped up, and kicked her in the middle of her back below the shoulder blades.

That knocked her off her feet, bent at an awkward angle. If she'd been a regular human, that would have meant "goodbye, spine," but she so wasn't a regular human. Before she hit, four more blades appeared in the air between her and us. Pointed at us, of course.

I needed to teleport us again. There was the little problem that my arms and legs felt like concrete and I was only upright because I clung desperately to Ray.

Lucyfar landed on the pavement. The knives didn't so much as flicker. Her laugh, crazy and bouncing up and down, rang out over the plaza as she pushed herself up on her arms.

"I can't believe you guys are twelve! What a ride!" she cackled.

"What in heaven's name do you think you're doing?!" Claire squealed behind us. She skated right past us, past the knives that rolled out of her way, and propped her fists on her hips to glare down at Lucyfar from the hood of her bear pajamas.

"I don't do anything in heaven's name. You ought to know that by—" Lucyfar started to joke. Then she made the mistake of looking up, and immediately threw her arms over her face. "Okay, okay! Turn off the juice, please!"

Looking at the stumpy little bear body in those loose pajamas, it was way too easy to imagine Claire's baby blue eyes glowering behind her oversized glasses and her mouth squeezed into an angry pout—

I put my arms over my eyes. Maybe it would help a little. At least I knew what was happening to me.

Visions of how adorable Claire must look no longer plagued me. Maybe she had turned it down after all.

I risked a peek to find Claire sliding back up to Ray and me, holding out her hands. Ray took one. I couldn't take the other. My whole body hurt, and the only thing holding me up was being draped over Ray. I probably should have been enjoying that, but my lungs and muscles were too busy screaming.

"I was just testing them. Gabriel's video sucked. I can tell you're new, but you kids have a lot of talent. I never expected you to get a hit in," Lucyfar explained. She was all casual now, although, as she walked over to us, she winced and gave her back a twist to stretch the spot where Ray kicked her.

"Lucyfar comes to visit sometimes. She didn't say she was inviting us down here for an ambush," Claire told me and Ray in a gruff aside.

Lucyfar took Claire's irritation in stride. "If I hadn't seen your costume hanging in your closet, I'd never have guessed. That thing you do with your face works."

I was too tired to ask, which gave Ray a chance to break in. "Speaking of which, one of us is in her civilian identity." His face jerked at me. Sometime during the fight he'd managed to put on that black bird mask of his.

Lucyfar nodded. "It'll be fine, but we'll get you out of here just in case. Put this on." A black baseball cap writhed into existence in front of me, and I tucked my braids up underneath it and pulled it as low as I could over my head.

What was Lucyfar up to? I let go of Ray, settling wobbily onto my own feet, but I still couldn't hide my suspicious expression. With a not-at-all-guilty grin, she apologized. "I'm sorry about that. I invited you here for a social occasion, but I just couldn't resist."

"It was an honor. We learned a great deal," Ray assured her. I guess if he didn't mind, I didn't have much place to. The knives had mostly been pointed at him.

"I bet you did. That's the scary part." Lucyfar pointed down at the next intersection. "Come on. I want you to meet my friends. We've got a place right down there."

Walk right off a main thoroughfare downtown and the looming skyscrapers become dingy mixtures of boarded-up windows and tiny hole-in-the-wall stores. I swear we passed five pawn shops in a row. These bracelets were going to be the death of me, but I was recovering quickly. By the time we crossed the street again, Lucyfar strutting ahead of us with her hands in her pockets, I didn't need to lean on anybody and only felt kinda stiff.

"It'll be Pandemonium. I'd place money on it," Ray told me with a whisper and a nudge. He meant the dusty bronze sign over the door three shops ahead.

Clashing beeps and pops drifted down the street from that door. A secret lair in an arcade? Still, "No way I'm taking that bet."

"We need a ridiculous pun to name our lair," Claire whispered into the huddle.

"Can we not refer to it as a lair? How about a base? Or the morality-neutral 'secret laboratory'?" I asked helplessly. That helplessness nagged at me. I was having enough trouble turning around my reputation without palling around with Lucyfar, who was famously on whatever side she felt like that morning.

Actually, Lucyfar might be the perfect person to get tips from.

Another shoulder nudge from Ray interrupted my descent into brooding. Lucyfar swerved left into the arcade's front door. I gave Ray a look of exasperated concession to reward his triumphant grin. He'd figured it out first, after all.

We followed Lucyfar into the arcade, and it occurred to me I'd never set foot in one before. Seen them on TV, heard about them from my parents, sure, but never actually been in one. It immediately became obvious why. The rows of machines were all complicated driving games and shooters with fake guns as controls. Not my thing.

I began to wonder if we'd get a fancy secret door or elevator as we threaded our way toward the back. There weren't a lot of customers to see us use it, but nope. Lucyfar opened up an Employees Only door in the back wall, and we stepped in after her into a relentlessly brown room. Beat-up, brown leather sofa, wood walls, not well lit, that sort of thing.

The room was occupied, and not by regular folks. "You did it. I can't believe it. How can you already know The Inscrutable Machine?" the floating gray girl in the shadowy back corner gasped.

"The devil's own luck," Lucyfar answered. She'd gone quiet and casual during the walk, but now she grinned, sauntered around a brown table, and threw herself into a ragged, brown easy chair.

"Assuming those aren't fake costumes. These could be any three kids," objected the brown skinned guy with the spiky, gelled hair and all the muscles. His old denim jacket and loose jeans made him look like a rougher thug than pants around his knees ever could. My heart skipped faster as he stepped up to us, scowling in disbelief. His eyes looked straight into mine. Brown, then green, then gray, they changed with his breath as he reached for my chin.

He didn't get there. Ray's hand shot up and grabbed his wrist. The guy even tried to pull back and dodge, and it didn't work. Muscles tightened on both their arms, but the wrist stayed exactly where it was.

"The young ladies are not to be touched," Ray informed the thug, his English accent thicker than ever. Please don't let me be blushing, and please don't let Ray get us killed. Two fights in one day were enough. I was unarmed and didn't have the stamina for a third!

The guy's muscles relaxed, and so did Ray's. He grinned. Criminy, he had sharp teeth, an irregular hacksaw set that made Sharky look tame. He straightened up, and Ray let go so he could pull his hand back. "Well, you're sure the real Reviled. Okay, you win. They're The Inscrutable Machine." Digging a hand into his pocket, he pulled out a rolled-up stack of bills and tossed them across the room, where Lucyfar caught them effortlessly.

"Kids, meet Chimera," Lucyfar introduced as she counted off the bills.

"Chimera's dead," I blurted out like an idiot. Well, he was! And this guy was too young to be the original, even if somehow he'd survived.

"Not even Chimera Junior, Chimera Two, anything? Someone's going to get real, real mad you took that name," Claire echoed, just as disbelieving.

"Evolution missed a piece. You still had the hydra's powers," Ray said in a much quieter voice.

Chimera didn't answer immediately. Ray had nailed it. Barely remembered antiquated TV footage wasn't much to go by, but this guy had the right look. It had been years. Lots and lots of years. But then, Evolution hadn't left much to regenerate.

Chimera finally laughed. "You kids are way too sharp. I'm glad to meet you already. Sit down, make yourselves at home. We're not formal here. This is just the place we hang out."

Ray looked around at all the brown. "I would have expected a bar. I suppose that just shows off how new I am to this."

Lucyfar giggled, a little too hysterically for my tastes. Chimera gave his head an amused shake. "Yep, you are, but not for the reason you think. The only drinks here are for Cy." As he explained, the half-sized brown refrigerator the brown lamp sat on opened up and a brown beer bottle floated out, sitting atop a black knife. The knife flipped, tossing the bottle over to Chimera, who caught it in one hand—a hand that red and black scales flickered across as his arm swung.

He held the bottle out to Ray. "Have a drink if you want, but it won't do you any good. If you've got a physical power, forget getting drunk or high. Super metabolism."

Ray took the bottle and flicked the metal cap off with his thumb curiously while Lucyfar added, "And I'm pretty sure E-Claire's out of luck as well." Ray passed the bottle over to Claire automatically. She gave it a sniff, and wordlessly handed it back to me. I sniffed too. Yuck, smelled way too much like coffee.

I held the bottle back out to Chimera. "I don't think we'll be putting underage drinking laws on our crime spree."

"If you don't want it, I'll take it," the guy on the couch offered immediately. That left me to step away from my friends and hand it to him. I could tell he was a mad scientist automatically. I'd never seen a coat with so many pockets, in rows down the front and all of them bulging. Plus, he had leather goggles pushed up on his head. They were clearly a badge of office.

I had to make me a pair. Could I get away with wearing them when not in costume? I totally could; my dad was Brian Akk. People would think it was a father/daughter thing.

Without them, I got this skeptical stare from the couch guy. As he tilted back the bottle to take a pull from it, Lucyfar said, "Bad Penny, this is Cybermancer. Cybermancer, Bad Penny. You may feel free to commiserate about your supervillain names."

I did wince. I knew it was coming, but… "It's been like two hours. Am I Bad Penny already?"

"I don't know. Are you? How does that lightning attack work? It didn't hurt Ifrit, but it sure threw him off balance," Cybermancer questioned me.

Lucyfar broke in again. "Why would I bring Reviled and E-Claire, but a ringer for Bad Penny?"

"Princess of Lies, remember?" Cybermancer shot back. Lucyfar pressed her hand to her chest and gave him a wounded look. It was all fun and games between them, but, when his eyes turned back to me, they weren't convinced. He was waiting for an answer.

An answer I didn't have. "It glues you to the next thing you touch. I stuck his foot to the floor," I hedged.

I'd been totally obvious. He took another swallow of the beer, and pressed. "But how does it work? If you're Bad Penny, you built it, right?"

I didn't know how it worked. My heart tightened with embarrassment. It got worse because he wasn't even being a jerk about it. He wanted proof, yeah, but he gave me a minute to think while he peered into his beer bottle, pulled a vial of glowing green liquid out of a pocket, and cracked it open.

I had to say something, but only the thing in the back of my head knew the answer. The same thing that took the sickly sweet smell of that green liquid and painted pictures I didn't understand in the back of my head. Cybermancer had almost forgotten me as he lifted the vial up to the mouth of the beer bottle.

Those pictures in my head clicked, and I lunged forward, grabbing the bottle in both hands. "Don't do that!"

He recoiled back into the couch. "Why not?" Now his voice had gotten sharper, and he really was angry.

Why not? Because I didn't want to be… be… "Does anyone have a pencil?"

A black knife pulled open the drawer of a little brown table and flicked out a black magic marker. Relief flooded me as I caught it in both hands. I rushed over to the wall. I didn't have words, but maybe pictures? I drew a bunch of interlocking lines. Grids of them. Make those two really thick, okay. Were these arrangements of atoms? They looked kind of like diagrams... okay, okay, the thing in my head didn't like that. Just draw. It would let me go far enough to draw that this bit connected here, and to here, and to here. But those were physical shapes. I drew sweeping ovals to show how different parts were linked, then filled in the arrows for how the energy moved. There were a lot of them. A lot, a lot of them. I hoped Cybermancer got the message.

Okay, that was close enough. The best I could do without making my power lock up. I sighed heavily and slapped the marker down on top of the fridge.

"I surrender. She's Bad Penny," Cybermancer announced beside me. He twisted around farther to the opposite end of the couch so he could look over what I'd drawn. To my considerable relief, he also closed the lid on his vial of sludge.

"Cy, what does that diagram say?" Lucyfar asked, her thin black eyebrows going up and her tone sharp.

"That you don't mix beer with magic science goo." His worried, guarded tone and the hard stare he gave the wall filled me with even more relief. Yes, he'd understood.

Lucy picked a small brown pillow off her recliner and threw it right past my face to bounce off Cybermancer's head. "You ninnyhammer. The rest of us aren't wearing protective shields!"

"Yeah, I... sorry," Cybermancer clumsily apologized, still staring at the wall.

"Lucy?" Chimera broke in.

Shooting him a suspicious glance, she asked, "Yeah?"

"He ain't wearing it, either." A grin forced its way across Chimera face.

Lucy let out a loud, incoherent growl and threw herself backwards, leaning her chair way back and sprawling her arms and legs over the edge. She lay there in melodramatic defeat, and that seemed to be the end of the fight.

"You've captured the whole reaction," Cybermancer murmured to me, not looking the slightest bit guilty anymore. "I'm impressed, yeah, but why couldn't you just tell me?"

No point in lying, I guess. "My power doesn't work that way."

"Oh, one of those." Eh? He'd accepted it immediately.

"What, do a lot of mad scientists not understand what they're building?" I blurted out.

"You must have regular human parents. Or they've got a physical power, right?" he asked me. I didn't answer that, and he went on as if he hadn't expected me to. "A regular brain can't hold a superhuman intellect. Everybody's different, but it takes someone real scary like the Expert or Brian Akk to know what they're doing in detail. Not a problem for me. I'm a puny little normal human, not a super brain."

He winked at me, and I dropped onto the couch at the far end from him. "Normal humans don't carry around that..." I knew what it was. The information was there in my mind, but in the itchy way of a word I couldn't quite remember.

"I call it magic science goo. I've got three magical teammates, so it's easy to make." He lifted the bottle of beer to his lips, paused, and dropped it in a brown waste can. Laying an arm over the back of the couch so he could turn and look at me properly, he explained, "I don't have a power, just a talent. I figured out how magic interacts with basic chemistry. It's a separate layer of energy storage. Caused a big stir, then I got slapped down when I sent my theory to Brian Akk and he proved it was wrong."

"I've met him. He's got a serious chip on his shoulder about magic," I offered, hoping I wasn't revealing too much.

Cy shrugged. He didn't look mad at all. "My theory may be wrong, but my model works. All I'm good at using it for is making explosives, but the community loves them. Even heroes buy from me sometimes. Speaking of..." He plunged his hands into two of his pockets. Not finding what he wanted, he sat up and tried again, and a third time. That one paid off. Out came a folded up pile of bills that he tossed into my lap.

I stared at the cash. How much was that? The bill on top was a hundred, for pity's sake! What was he doing? He'd just given me a stack of money, and yet he leaned forward and looked at me with wide eyes, like he was begging for a favor. "Can I buy that recipe on the wall off of you? A thousand is all I've got on me. I can't steal someone else's idea, but if I understand your markings it doesn't just explode, it curses everyone caught in the blast."

Another cushion came sailing over to bounce off of Cy's head. As he yelped and threw his arms up, Lucy snapped, "You are the biggest goober I've ever met! If I could find your pea brain, I'd feed it to a goldfish! It's not enough blowing up the rest of us, you could have blown up Apparition!" That stopped her. Half-raised out of a still horizontal easy chair, she waved a hand at the shadowy corner next to her, and the gray girl floating in it. Looking suddenly guilty, she added, "Uh... kids, meet The Apparition. Apparition, The Inscrutable Machine."

I had just enough time to mumble, "Yeah, sure... you can have it," before Claire came charging across the room.

"You really are The Apparition! I know, I'm sorry, I'm gushing, but I've only seen drawings of you. Your image doesn't capture on film! But, I mean, you know that." Claire squealed all of that in a rush, then giggled nervously and twisted her hands together. Her paws together, since she bear suit pajamas covered everything.

I should give the money back. I couldn't sell a supervillain an explosive recipe. It would be better just to give it to him. It would.

As I gave up and stuffed the thousand dollars into my own pocket, I tried to cover by giving The Apparition a good look. Her feet didn't touch the ground, and I could see the brown wood paneling through her gray. "Is she a ghost?" I guessed.

Everybody looked at me. "I don't follow supervillains, or even superheroes much," I explained, feeling pretty lame.

"And that's what I like!" Lucyfar rolled forward out of her chair, snapping it upright as she stood up and raised her arms toward the brown ceiling. She almost clipped the brown ceiling fan. "So many of our comrades in arms are poseurs. They want the fame, or the money, or they're imitating a big name villain. They're not having fun! Let someone else judge if I'm a hero or villain. I'm free to enjoy my powers however I want!"

"I thought we didn't ask these kids over to talk business," Apparition cut in. Cold, calm, and a little sour, or was that a very deadpan playfulness?

"I love watching Lucy rant." Chimera certainly didn't hide his whimsical tone. Cy wasn't even paying attention. He was scribbling down my formula. I wished him luck making sense of my super power's wordless imagery. I wished him a thousand dollars of luck.

"You've had your turns. Now it's mine. Forget business. What do you guys do for fun? What are you into?" Apparition asked us.

Chimera grunted. "They're middle school kids, App. It'll be stuff like computer games."

That dragged up Cybermancer's attention long enough to give us a curious glance. "Do you all game? What do you play?"

Shame is something that happens to people not named Lutra, so Claire answered for us. "Supervillainy is eating up our free time lately, but we're Teddy Bears and Machine Guns players."

A high pitched shriek sent me jumping an inch into the air. What the… ?

I didn't get time to finish the thought. "You play Teddy Bears and Machine Guns?!" Apparition demanded. She flew out of her corner, grabbing Claire's shoulders first, then Ray's, then mine. I felt her fingers gripping me, but at the same time they felt more cold than a physical touch. I guess she really was a ghost. Her pale face floated right in front of mine, and even her giddy enthusiasm couldn't completely erase lines of heavy tiredness from her face. "What side do you play?"

"Toybox. I like my adorable armies," Claire answered.

Ray's turn. "Junkyard. There's always a new combination."

"Candy?" I hazarded. It was a little harder to be glib while seeing the room through Apparition's transparent head.

"I'm a Candy player, too!" Apparition squealed. She let go of my shoulders and sank back into her dark corner with a heavy sigh. "Not as often as I like. I've only gotten to play a few times. I can't touch a computer without possessing someone first."

Claire did the curious head tilt. "I would think you'd like Toybox for the tricks."

That got a giggle. Okay, a wistful giggle, but Apparition clearly liked talking about this. I couldn't blame her. Who doesn't love discussing their Teddy Bears and Machine Guns strategy? "That's the beauty of it. I win with Toybox and Junkyard. Candy builds up so fast I can push an early raid, but instead of trying to do damage I steal parts with Want Some Candy, and then use my raiding force to fight off the other side while I build. It's risky, but if it works I crush them with their own powers!"

Claire hmmed. "I've tried to do that with Wind Up Keys, but if I devote that much time to building them, someone rolls over me." Motion caught my eye. Cy beckoned me with a finger. He held up the notepad he'd been copying my formula onto.

Chimera stepped away from the wall, and addressed Ray. "Hey, Reviled. How long have you had your powers? You gotten into Parkour yet?"

"Wait! Wait wait wait wait wait," Apparition interrupted us all, floating out into the middle of the room and holding out her hands. She looked over her shoulder at Lucyfar, who'd fallen back into her recliner again. "Is today Saturday?"

That yanked Lucyfar up. "We should take them to Chinatown," she announced.

"Yes," Chimera and Cybermancer agreed together.

"I don't think we have the time," Claire half-answered.

She was right. Besides, they were so gleeful, it freaked me out. I tried to sound apologetic. "If we don't get home before dark, our secret identities are busted."

"We'll go tomorrow!" Lucyfar offered, leaning forward out of her chair with a look of, well, demonic eagerness.

The Apparition slapped it off of her. Literally, although I didn't know what that spectral hand across the cheek actually felt like. Lucy's head did recoil maybe an inch, but the blow didn't make any sound. "We're making them feel pressured, Lucy. They're cool, but they're kids, and the community is brand new to them. They're not even used to being supervillains yet." She looked straight at me and added, "I'm sorry, but it's pretty obvious."

Lucyfar raised her hands. "Okay, okay. We'll let them bow out gracefully just this once. Maybe later." She gave Claire a wink, and added, "I know I'll be seeing you. The Inscrutable Machine is welcome here any time. Especially weekends."

I looked at Claire and Ray. They nodded, although I wasn't quite sure what question I'd asked or what they'd answered. Ray opened the door, standing on the other side and bowing deeply. "Ladies," he offered with an outstretched arm.

Claire and I hurried out into the arcade. Just on the other side of the door, I glanced back. The Apparition was closest to us. She'd floated nearer the door.

I lowered my voice as far as I could without being drowned out by the arcade's noise. "I'm sorry I asked about your origin. It can't be a fun topic. It was thoughtless of me."

"You're not sure which side you're on yet. It's written all over your face. Trust me, Bad Penny, you just proved you're meant to be a supervillain," came the breathy reply.

I nodded to that, turned around, and scurried a few quick steps to catch up to my friends. What could I have said? I thought I'd just proven the opposite!

Ray pulled off his bird mask, then suddenly slapped his other hand over his face. "I was talking to Lucyfar, and I didn't get her autograph."

Claire grinned wickedly, and leaned in to give him a nudge with her whole body. "Pretty soon, they'll be asking to trade."

CHAPTER TEN

I ended up taking the Red Line most of the way back. There was no way I could manage biking all the way from downtown, even with the teleport rings. My serum-enhanced best friends, on the other hand, were fresh and eager to return to their homes the hard way. Claire giddily assured me before gliding away that a girl skating down the street in teddy bear pajamas got photographed by everyone.

I wasn't mad, but I really wished I'd saved a couple of drops of serum for myself by the time I pedaled up to my parents' driveway. I pushed my bike into the empty garage and hoped my knees weren't visibly wobbly. With the car gone, my parents might be out and it might be moot. I slid the teleport bracelets into my pockets anyway.

I'd just stepped into the kitchen when Dad leaned out of his workshop and looked down the hall at me. "Hey, Pumpkin! You look tired."

Yes, I bet I looked tired. From his casually cheerful tone, he didn't have an inkling why. "Yeah. We ended up going down to the library," I acknowledged. Telling ninety percent of the truth had worked for me so far.

He tapped away at his phone instead of answering me, so when he did look up it was to explain, "Just sending your mother a message that you're home and she had nothing to worry about."

This was Dad and not Mom, and I was all the way down the hall. I could get away with, "Why would she be worried? Nobody attacks three kids on the subway in the middle of the day."

"The Inscrutable Machine defeated a couple of sidekicks again this morning," Dad answered me.

I'd known he knew. I just still didn't know what to say about it. "Already?"

Apparently, I sounded nervous.

"They move fast. Gabriel was there, and he videotaped it for his internet project. Come back here, and I'll show you the footage. That might take all your fears away," he called down.

I couldn't refuse. I padded down the hall and into his laboratory. He'd rearranged his equipment with an ease that made envy nibble at my gut. What was this plastic machine with all the readouts arranged around a big cylindrical tank? What was the not-quite-clear green liquid inside? I smelled chlorine, but my power didn't react.

Dad lifted up and put back down his keyboard and mouse, then cleared the screen of the programs linked to the new machine. Instead he brought up a video file, "TIM2c," appropriately enough.

"Trust me, Pumpkin. This will make you feel better." I couldn't see how watching a recording of my own supervillainy with my father could make me less nervous, but I didn't have any good excuses. I grabbed a pen and wrote "P Jar – II" on a sheet of paper by his keyboard as the video sprang up.

The video was terrible. What was that white mess I was looking at? Over a lot of rustling a girl said something about gang wars. What a snotty voice. Then another girl answered her, and, as hard as it was to make out the words, the two seemed to be in a competition for who could be most sarcastic. In fact, I caught the words "quality sarcasm time"—

Wait, was that me? Was that what I sounded like? In answer, the white mess of a wing cleared away. Gabriel was watching from the roof, back out of my range of vision like an actually serious superhero. I got to watch Marcia answer, and I could clearly make out the words "quiet and appreciative when you give your villainous monologues." What a lousy video. It didn't sound like her at all.

Marcia made her comment about not being outnumbered, and the parking lot disappeared in favor of roof asphalt as Gabriel crept around some more. People talked low. I couldn't make out the words, until I caught "Gabriel" and I heard Gabriel sigh into the microphone. The view jolted as he stood up, then jumped lightly down, drifting to the thumping of his six wings until he settled on the pavement of the parking lot. Oh, geez. That was me and Ray. My jumpsuit looked like stormtrooper armor from this side.

And then, "Gabriel! I read your blog! What are you doing here?!" squealed deafeningly out of the video, and rather than a superhero/supervillain battle, I found myself watching the Girl in a Bear Suit Show.

I stared. I was being treated to what should have been a close-up of Claire as she and Gabriel chatted, but it wasn't. Who was this girl? Claire didn't have a dimple. I'd been seeing Claire's smile most of our lives, and she didn't.

Or did she, with her power turned up high? What exactly did she look like then? All I could remember were eyes and a mouth, those oh-so-serious expressions she was giving Gabriel now.

You little vixen, Claire. You knew all along your secret identity was completely safe. Your Mom must have known as well. You little shape-changing vixen.

My mouth was hanging open. I closed it, and unwound The Machine from my wrist to cover my embarrassment. Dad read that his own way. "This is why I wanted you to see this. Your mother and a lot of the adult community are having fits, but for no reason. Gabriel saw it immediately. These kids aren't evil. They'll pick fights with other supers until they lose. Until then, maybe they can teach our children this isn't a game. Watch what happens next."

Dad had been chatting away over top of Claire and Gabriel, but Claire hadn't been able to hold Gabriel's attention entirely. I saw Ray and Miss A (even though I knew who she was, she didn't much look like Marcia on video) going at it like a Kung Fu movie. Just like a Kung Fu movie, where Miss A started out throwing all the attacks at first with Ray in retreat, until slowly it turned exactly the other way. Every time she'd swing or kick he'd lunge past it, and all she could do was fall back.

Then Ifrit twisted his hands around and a cylinder of flame roared up around the girl in the armor. Me. Ifrit and Gabriel argued about the situation casually.

"Ifrit's not trying very hard, is he? I think Miss A's trying to kill the boy she's fighting," I suggested. I'd been there, so I had some idea of how Ifrit was fouling up. Watching it had me twisting The Machine around in my hands until it crawled around them with hyperactive energy.

"That's it exactly. He assumes he's caught her. Miss A's lost her temper and Ifrit is overconfident and not giving this his all. Watch what happens to both of them." Man, Dad sounded calm and professional.

I watched myself step out of the flames and nail Ifrit's foot to the floor with my static gloves. I'd felt like a cow in the exchange that followed, but from here it was obviously Ifrit who couldn't dodge, couldn't do anything but get smacked in the back of the head as Reviled waltzed past. Miss A was way too mad to avoid getting blasted.

All that was left was a lot of banter. Dad talked over it. "A lot of our tools and powers in superheroing are tricks, Penny. Those gloves glued Ifrit's foot to the ground. Ifrit's fire cage is hard to get out of. Half of martial arts is supplying someone small like Miss A with trick moves that put her opponent at a disadvantage. If you figure a way around those tricks, they become liabilities. When it's you out there one day, pay more attention to your defenses than your weapons, so you'll have a chance to escape anything. Then when you have the advantage, press it. Don't assume you're going to win until your opponent is immobilized, and even then watch him."

My Dad was giving me supervillain advice and didn't know it. Great. The Machine squirmed as I gripped it guiltily, staring at him. The video ended, and Dad peered behind the monitor, then into the cord-strewn chaos behind his desk.

"Did you drop something?" I asked automatically.

"An iridium electrode. Not easy to replace, even for me," Dad answered.

It gave me something to talk about other than my career as a supervillain, so I began to circle Dad's lab, peeking around the edges of his fabricating machines, eying the bits of wire, forceps, and screws cluttering any flat surface. Man, I wanted his 3D printer, but I forced myself to peek through the clipboards and magazines stacked on top of it, letting The Machine scurry up my arm with its little metal claws.

"Sounds exotic. What do you do with it?" I asked. After all, my power wasn't telling me anything.

He spun his chair around and thumped the new glass tank. "You heard me talk about knowing the other guy's tricks? I've been asked to analyze an

144

exotic chemical sample from a supervillain attack. It's highly caustic and behaves so strangely when it should be inert that it looks alive."

Even under the circumstances I had to flash a grin. "Sounds like magic."

Pavlov's dogs could not have been more faithful. "Because people call it magic is exactly why I need to identify this formula and chart out its properties. Dump an easy label on it and you fool yourself into thinking it's all powerful."

Well, the topic was on magic, and this was my Dad, not my Mom. Today had left me with a lot of questions. Maybe I could get away with one or two. "Dad, what do you know about Lucyfar?"

"Why would you ask that?" he shot back immediately. I grabbed The Machine in both hands again, but he looked puzzled, not suspicious.

I had to remind myself that I could risk a sufficiently white lie here. "I met her at Claire's Mom's place today. Then we went downtown, and I saw her at the library subway station fighting that Reviled kid. I'm not sure they were really fighting. She's kinda weird."

Dad sat up straight in his chair, hand resting on his desk, and sighed loudly. A smile spread across his face. "Thank you, Pumpkin. That's the last little doubt removed. You were right next to them, and The Inscrutable Machine didn't care. They're just goofing around. You're not on their radar, and never will be."

"And Lucyfar?" I pressed.

"She says she really is Lucifer, the demon princess, and she might be crazy enough to believe it. I think she's just playing around, drunk on her own unfortunately considerable power. She's playing a game with the rest of the community, stopping a robbery one day so she can rob the same place the next. We put up with it because she doesn't kill civilians and we'd like her to feel like if she gives up villainy for good, we'll accept her. In practice, that means we only fight her when we have reason to think she's actually committing a crime," he related.

"She seemed really friendly, but she couldn't hold to the same topic for thirty seconds," I hedged.

"Not someone I'd have wanted to introduce you to at your age, but it's better you learn now how weird the community can be." Dad sounded entirely noncommittal, but he'd also been sucked into another fruitless search of the wires behind his desk.

I peeked into the cracks between the tank and the machinery surrounding it. *Come on, power. What is this stuff? You pounced on magic science goo like a wolf on a rabbit. Why can't I turn you on and off when I want?* I'd almost gotten some sense I could take back to the regular world from that meeting with Cy.

My power ignored me. I used The Machine's teeth to pry a crack wider to peer into it. I knew that was useless, but, barring an iridium detector, we'd have to keep checking places we swore we'd already looked.

"Hey, Dad, do you have a really pure crystal lying around?" I asked as curiosity hit me.

He slid over to a cabinet of little drawers, and opened one up. "How about an industrial diamond?" I snatched it out of his hand immediately. Awesome. Well, a start. I needed… what did I need? I didn't need to understand, just know what to ask for.

"Sheet aluminum?" I spat out before I knew what the word would be.

"How big?" he asked back, lifting a strip out of another drawer.

"That will do." I knew it would do. He dropped it into my hand, and I made The Machine crimp the aluminum into a band around the diamond.

"Uninsulated copper wire? Silver? Gold?" I asked. Each time he deposited them into my hand. This was easy. I wouldn't need any of his fancy machines. I had my own Machine, fancier than any of them. This was just a little addition, and, once I bent the wires right, I pried open The Machine's mouth and stuffed the diamond down its throat. The wires clicked into place.

That would do it. I dropped The Machine onto the floor, and, after the metallic bang when it hit, I instructed, "Find the iridium."

How well would this work? The Machine scuttled on its hundred little bug legs toward Dad's desk, then veered off in an arc and crawled underneath the frame holding up the tank. Three seconds later, it crawled out holding a gleaming blob in its mandibles. I lowered an arm, and as The Machine crawled back up into its proper place on my wrist I extracted the electrode and held it up for Dad. For a little tiny thing, the electrode had a weight I could feel.

I looked up into Dad's face for the first time as he took the electrode from me. He looked like he'd just swallowed the sun, like he could cry from joy and pride.

"Penny, do you know what you just did?" he asked, his voice soft and hoarse.

I was pretty sure, yes. I'd just shown off my supervillain powers to the person who was most likely to recognize them.

Except he hadn't. "Your super power just sparked again. It hasn't even been two weeks, and you had another episode. May I see?" He held out his hands for The Machine. It had just curled up around my wrist again, but it let go with a single twist. It still had some juice left from when I'd woken it up a few minutes ago.

I plumped it in Dad's hands, and he lifted The Machine up and peered into its mouth at the sensor apparatus. "Your power is coming faster than I ever dreamed, and it's powerful. I can guess at how your chemical detector works, but the design is so simple that's all I can do. You might be able to turn your power on at will by summer and have a fully emerged super power by the time you enter high school."

"Really?" I asked, feeling weirdly helpless.

"Since your second invention is an upgrade for your first, there's a good chance all of your inventions will center around this device. If that turns out to be true, don't fight it. You'll learn so much and this bracelet will become so powerful, you'll have all you need to be a fantastic superhero. Mech's power isn't half this impressive, but he kept improving his armor until he became a powerhouse and improved his skills as he did." Dad was gushing. My Dad had the same wide-eyed stare Claire gave Gabriel.

"You should start thinking about a superhero name with the idea that your powers will center around this invention. It's a pity The Inscrutable Machine is taken," he went on, dumping a bucket of ice water down my spine. This was a bad, bad direction for the conversation to go. What could I say?

And then he gave me a sober stare, and, as the cold gnawed toward my heart, he told me, "The public is even starting to call the tech based girl on their team Bad Penny. I'm sorry, Pumpkin. There's no way to change their mind once these things get started. Even if she rejects the name, it's likely to stick. I know that the confusion is going to be annoying and embarrassing for you." He reached out, laying The Machine back in my hands and pulling me over for a tight hug as he went on in a wry, sympathetic tone. "Ask your mother about Dr. Brain and The Brain Auk sometime. If I try to tell that story, I'll beat my head against the wall." He ended with a little chuckle. I echoed it, feeling suddenly weak and giddy.

I held back the urge to laugh hysterically. HA! The epiphany rolled over me, easing every tension, making me feel looser, stronger than I had in weeks. I wasn't going to get caught. Not just now... period. The evidence was already all in front of them. Unless I did something flat-out stupid, my parents were never, ever going to catch on. I had all the time in the world to deal with my supervillain reputation however I wanted. I really wanted to laugh. I also wanted to fall over.

"The Brain Auk does sound like a mixup waiting to happen," I conceded, letting my grin at least peek out.

Dad's mouth twisted in momentary disgust, and he changed the subject. "Why don't I call your Mom and we can go out to dinner to celebrate your power flashing again? She's only getting groceries."

"I'd pass out in my pizza plate. I've been out all day, and I just want to heat some of the leftover fish and take a nap." I refused as gently as I could. I love going out to eat, but this had been the longest day I could remember and it was only early evening.

Dad gave my hair an affectionate rub, making a mess out of everything not pulled back into my braids. "Your power just activated for the second time. Even a purely mental power can take a lot out of you. Sleep well, Princess. Your Mom and I may be out when you wake up, assuming you don't sleep through the night. When she hears you were ten feet from The Inscrutable Machine and they didn't give you a second glance, she'll feel like celebrating just for that."

I did sleep through the night, so if they went out I wouldn't know.

Technically, my phone going off woke me the next morning. I went through the process of groping for it and turning it on in a drowsing blur, so the first thing I actually remembered was Claire squeaking into my ear. "We're going to get together today, right?"

I fell back onto my pillow and stared at the sunlight through my window. I glanced at the phone's screen. Eleven a.m. I guess I should be grateful she let me sleep that long. Dad might have had a point about my power exhausting me. I'd slept more than twelve hours!

"Sure," I mumbled groggily, "but no supervillainy, or superheroing either."

"Aww," Claire protested, but her power didn't work over the phone, and I didn't let her go ahead with it.

"One of us has a puny human body, remember?" Hopefully my croaking voice would make the point.

Well, it got a giggle. "Yeah, I have the proportionate strength of a girl my age who exercises," she quipped back. I started to grin too, as her good humor pushed back the fog of sleep.

"I need to take the day off. We're all strictly secret identity today, okay?"

Claire's light and philosophical tone immediately told me I'd won. "I'll have to tell Ray to stop hanging from a tree branch in my back yard, but we outvote him together. When do you want to get together?"

"Give me time to get cleaned up, dressed, and eat," I suggested, my voice growling again as I registered that I was lying in bed and achy. Yesterday had been full of crazy things.

One of those crazy things was a supervillain paying me a thousand dollars. I groped off the edge of my bed for the pants I wore yesterday. A fat bundle of bills remained in the pocket.

Now I really grinned hard. "Actually, take your time, but come on over. I won't need to eat. I'm going to buy us all lunch on Melrose instead!"

I beat them to my front door because I let my dad's automatic braiding machine take care of my hair. I wondered if my super power would tell me if this version had any bugs, but I wouldn't get that question answered today. The machine worked just fine, and my five hundred pounds of hair got tied in ribbons and out of my way for the day.

A shout of "Mom, can you take us down to Melrose?" before I hopped into the shower spurred her to get ready. When the doorbell rang, I yanked the kitchen door open. We all piled into the car in a chorus of, "Thank you, Mrs. Akk!"

Melrose isn't far, although you have to drive down a bit to get to the fun shopping section. It wasn't long before Mom asked, "Are you going to need some money, Penny?"

Not hardly. I had a thousand dollars in my pocket. I answered a bit more tactfully, "I just emptied the Pumpkin jar last week. I've still got plenty."

That answer did not seem to thrill. Not that she was obvious, but the lack of an instant answer told me I'd messed up.

Ray caught it, too. "Mrs Akk, did Penny tell you we got to see Lucyfar dueling the kid from The Incredible Machine downtown, yesterday? Well, I did. It ended just when Penny and Claire showed up." Criminy, Ray, that had to be the stupidest attempt to change the subject... or, well, maybe it wasn't.

"I caught it all. It didn't take very long," I insisted.

"It's the first time I've seen a supervillain battle in person. It was amazing! Lucyfar threw knives everywhere, and Reviled bounced around like a spastic squirrel. Then they walked off together like it didn't happen. Are villains often that casual about trying to kill each other?" Ray asked. He didn't have to fake enthusiasm for the subject.

"Frequently."

One word. She was still troubled. I reached over and put a hand on her shoulder and promised, "Mom, we'll be fine. How many supervillains attack Melrose on a busy Sunday?"

"Red Dawn, Chimera, and Logo three times. That's if you don't count Bullet Bob, Weasel Fingers, or Jim," Mom listed without a pause.

"Wasn't Bullet Bob the guy with all the guns but terrible aim?" Ray asked, drawling with glee over the thought.

It got a smile from Mom, too. "That's why he doesn't count."

"We're here! Let us out right here!" Claire squealed, and Mom pulled the car up into a no parking spot long enough for us to pile out.

"Have fun, kids. Give me a call when you want to be picked up," Mom offered as she pulled the door shut. Her moodiness had vanished. Score one for Ray.

We filed into the burger place with the little stone wall around their courtyard, the one I don't know the name of because it doesn't have a sign. Leaning closer to Ray and Claire, I offered, "I brought the money Cybermancer gave me, so order whatever you want. I'm paying."

They did, and we sat down at a stone table with trays heaped with food and bowls of ice cream. Then we said nothing at all, because we were too busy stuffing our faces.

There did come a moment when I wasn't sure I could eat anymore. I pushed my tray away, rubbed my mouth with a napkin, and complained in a discreet hush, "All this cash is burning a hole in my pocket." It wasn't entirely a metaphor. I could feel the lump of money, an intrusive presence hard to ignore in my pocket, constantly reminding me that it was there and should be spent on something.

Ray swallowed a last bite of fried chicken strip and agreed, "I spent the bubblegum money immediately. Partly because I had enough money to buy whatever I wanted, and partly because I just wanted to look good for once in my life."

Scarecrow thin, but immaculate in black long sleeved shirt and slacks, with his big black hat and that grin just a little too wide to be sane... he did. He looked good. "Immaculate" might have been the wrong word. The fabric had a few rumples, but that didn't matter. He still looked sleek.

"You succeeded," Claire promised him while I was still thinking it. I should have said it first. That gnawed at me, and I wanted to believe the smiles they were giving each other were just friendly, but it wasn't easy.

"It looks like we're all done. Where do you two want to go first?" I asked, piling my cup and plasticware onto my tray.

The answer came as inevitably as the tides: "Lost World!"

Two blocks down sat the comic book store, or at least the only comic book store I knew of on Melrose. My friends dragged me through the door physically by my wrists as I complained, "I'm not into this stuff!" Theatric, and only mostly true. They ignored it. Having dragged me over the threshold, they left me waiting on the rubber mat and scattered.

Sometimes I wonder if stores have to go through some kind of gladiatorial contest to get a place on Melrose. Lost World was a great example. Technically, it was a comic book store, and sure there were the racks of popular comics in that corner, but they were dwarfed by the carefully sorted archives of obscure collector's editions on the long wall, the racks of costumes, the shelves of actual books, and oddities like a globe of the heavens, nested crystal spheres outlining what Apotheosis claimed the universe was really like.

To be polite, I wandered over to the comic racks. Dramatizations of superhero battles had never drawn me, but there were the science fiction comics and the weirdly artsy graphic novels. My eye caught on Volume Twelve of Sentient Life. The series finale. I plucked it out of the rack and flipped through cautiously. I didn't want to spoil the ending, and I'd always wanted to read this comic. That had to be Delph, the evolved dolphin boy. What had happened to his body in the volumes I hadn't seen? In one frame, he pressed his hand against a screen as restraints fastened him down. In the next, the outline of a hand formed, an illusion of another, more delicate hand pressing against his from the screen's other side. So Vera had survived to the end. Well, almost to the end. This page was near the beginning of a long graphic novel. That was why I'd never properly read Sentient Life. Twelve fat books, and I'd never been willing to spend the money to read all of them at once. Even with collections, it would be well over a hundred dollars. Who had that kind of money?

Me, that's who. And all for thirty seconds of scribbling a formula on a wall in a code I couldn't be sure Cy would even understand. The wages of sin were amazing.

Not, however, the wages I wanted. Ray stood a shelf down from me, poring through a book of maps of LA, of all things. Claire wasn't much farther, failing to control her giggles at a corset modeled after her mother's old costume. I stepped between them and offered quietly, "You guys know I'm buying, right? I have a thousand dollars of supervillain money I want to get rid of as soon as possible."

Ray's face bent in his most maniacal grin. Claire's eyes merely twinkled. She'd lost control of her super power for a second. They had to have known this was coming, but they hadn't wanted to assume.

Maybe they'd even discussed it. They swept right past me, beelining to the long display of statues that took up so much of the store. Statues? Statuettes? Figurines? Whatever. Claire scooped up two boxes, and set one in front of herself and the other in front of Ray. Then she delicately pried open hers and lifted out and set on the rack…

…a foot-tall statue of Lucyfar. Criminy.

"Come on, you two, this is a civilian day! I just want to be normal!" I hissed, rolling my eyes. Rolling my eyes didn't feel like enough, so I rolled my head, too.

"This is what we talk about buying on normal days. We just can't afford to!" Claire was right. I couldn't deny it.

I examined the statue instead. I immediately had to giggle. "No one would wear that." Lucy's costume amounted to... well, not much. A black leather bikini, a few skull ornaments, some random straps, and very impractical looking boots.

"Lucyfar did." New, shameless, super-powered Ray didn't bother hiding the subtle growl of appreciation at the thought.

"Is it really so hard to believe, now that you've met her?" Claire asked, then gave me an impish grin. I had to return it, because the image of Lucyfar flopping onto her stuffed recliner in that getup started forcing hysterical giggles out of both of us. I tried to calm myself down by focusing on other details. This statue had Lucy's black knives on the end of bony, black wings coming out of her back. Was that made up for the statue, part of the old costume, or an aspect of her powers she hadn't shown us?

Wistfully, Claire noted, "I wouldn't mind wearing something like that in a few years when I've filled out, except my power will completely cancel the effect."

My cheeks warmed up. Thanks, Claire. "Don't let that stop you," Ray purred in delight. Thanks, Ray.

Then, to my considerable surprise, he changed the subject. "As much as I do like the costume, *this* is the Lucyfar statue I want." With a little hop, he reached up to slip a big box off the top of the shelf behind the display counter. It dropped into his hands with perfect delicacy. Tesla's Alternating Current Motor! Would it be too much to ask to repeat the Super Cheerleader Serum recipe, super power? I wanted some of that. My power ignored me.

He lifted the statue out as if it weren't two eighteen-inch tall ceramic figures that must weigh half a ton. The broad base looked like pavement, with tiny fake dollar bills strewn over it. The statue needed the support, because the statue of Lucyfar stood on the ground with the statue of Gabriel held up only by two wings wrapped around her, the other four spread to keep him hovering. At least Lucyfar was better dressed in that black gown she'd materialized fighting us.

"Oh, wow," Claire concluded succinctly.

"This was the first time anybody'd seen Gabriel in action. He hadn't started his blog yet," Ray whispered to me. To me, specifically. Claire would know this stuff.

Wait- "This really happened? They made a statue of an actual event?"

Ray looked surprised at the question. "Sure."

Claire bolted away from us over to the comic racks, then scurried back and spread out a magazine. "Compendium: Lucyfar" it read. She flipped through it to a page with a photo of, well, exactly what the statue in front of us depicted—Gabriel hovering and wrapping her in his wings from behind.

'Lucyfar and Gabriel, The Archangels', the section was titled. The page was mostly photos because there wasn't too much to say. Lucy claimed to be the actual fallen angel and that Gabriel was her divine brother. Gabriel said she was making it up, but for all that he freely talked online about what it was like to be a superhero, he never explained who he was, how he got his wings, or how he knew Lucyfar. They did seem to have a connection, and their frequent meetings were half super-powered battle, half bickering about morality. Gabriel had notably caused Lucyfar to go from working with Arson to fighting and defeating Arson, mid-crime. The conversation was unrecorded, but witnesses claimed the winning argument was that Arson's bombs would level the library next door, and it still had children inside.

Wow. Lucy had a whole magazine packed with this stuff. I flipped a few pages and saw in one header the question that had nagged me earlier. "Where Did Her Wings Go?"

A different question struck me now. "Is there one of these books for The Apparition?"

Ray nodded. Apparently I'd asked a solemn question. Claire returned the Lucyfar magazine to the racks and brought back another one, much more sedately. Chilly nervousness tiptoed up my spine. The Apparition was dead, after all. This might be gruesome.

Unlike Lucyfar's packed volume, "Compendium: The Apparition" was slim, only half a dozen pages. The only photo showed Lucyfar standing over a prostrate, terrified man in a suit. Next to it was a copy of the same photo, with an artist's sketch of The Apparition crouching over the man, holding his face in her hands. There were other pictures, and the one on the cover looked exactly like her, but they weren't photos.

No, sorry, I'd flipped past a page speculating about The Apparition's powers to a page about her origin. That had a photo, but not of The Apparition.

"Believed to be the ghost of Polly Icarus, accidentally killed by Mourning Dove during the battle when she captured the leadership of the Scarlet drug cartel," I read aloud. I didn't want to read more. The stock photo of Mourning Dove said plenty. White hair, jaundiced yellow skin, and white leather from the collar down hiding what the metal plates in her temples hinted at – a dead body returned to life and given horrific powers by technology. Mourning Dove might be stridently on the side of law and justice, but the hero community wasn't comfortable with that fact. A vengeful, unhappy ghost was the kind of wreckage she left behind. She was better than Judgment, but… not by much.

"Mourning Dove. That's a name I never want to hear as a supervillain," I whispered to Ray and Claire. Dutifully, I added, "I'm hoping to switch to being a superhero before it comes to that."

Ray deflected that with ease. "I think you're stuck with the villain label for a while. Might as well enjoy it until we can find a chance to publicly switch sides."

I glanced at Claire for her opinion, but she'd wandered over to the sales counter. As I watched the clerk carefully handed her another statue box, which she brought back over to us.

"We're not supposed to be able to open up this one, but the power to cloud men's minds with cuteness has its advantages," Claire whispered. Then she peeled off the tape and unclasped the lid, being careful not to damage anything, and lifted out of the box a mirror-surfaced bell jar.

Despite the mirror reflecting everything else, inside floated the transparent white figure of The Apparition. The details on her bleak face and loose, simple dress were perfect.

"I want it," I heard myself husk. Oh, man, I did. "How much is it?"

Claire flipped up the box to show me the label on the bottom. 375 dollars. Ouch.

"I can't," I argued with myself. "I can't spend that much money on a statue."

Claire took up the other side. "You can. You want to spend the money anyway."

"I can't spend half of it in one place. What if you two see something else you like?!" I whined.

155

Ray picked up the bell jar, placed it gently back in its box, and pushed the box into my arms. Blue eyes looked right into mine. "We'll take a pass on our statues this time, and use the money to give this to you as a gift. If you still feel bad you can buy us something amazing later. Come on, Penny, let yourself go wild for once."

My knees shook as I toddled back over to the sales counter. I laid the box by the register, then stepped over to the comic rack next to it and pulled out the entire collection of Sentient Life. I didn't even look at the total when he rang it up. I counted out six hundred dollars in cash, took my change, and walked out of the store hugging my bag full of treasure to my chest while Claire and Ray grinned on either side of me. I swear, they looked like they were the ones making the big haul. I had the best friends.

Blinking in the bright sunlight, I asked, "Where to next?" because I sure couldn't decide in this condition.

"Over there," Ray supplied immediately, rushing ahead of us to the corner and then leaping across the street. Metaphorically.

As Claire and I hurried up behind him, I gawked in disbelief. "A shoe store?" But there he was, hands and face glued to the window in longing.

"Yes, a shoe store. Look at those boots." I looked at the boots. The thick, black, leather ones that went way up the calf, with all the ornamental buckles. Thanks to their heavy and solid build, they didn't look remotely feminine.

"Okay, I see your point. I'll buy them for you."

He sighed, half frustration and half longing. "You can't. They won't carry them in my size. Nobody makes the really cool shoes in middle school sizes."

Well, that sucked. "Maybe you can order them online? I guess I don't have a way to turn all this cash into a credit card number," I speculated, realizing it was no good.

"No moping. Come on, I want to go in here," Claire ordered us, grabbing our hands and dragging us next door.

I looked in the window at the frilly, colorful items on display. "A costume shop? I guess that makes sense."

"If I'm going to be wearing something silly and cutesy when I work, I might as well have some variety. The trick will be finding something high enough quality to be worth wearing," Claire insisted as she shoved the double doors wide and stepped in.

I followed in behind her, but fumbled in my pocket for my phone. Hmm. "We might want to watch the time. Tomorrow is Monday." Clothing shopping could take forever. I already felt a magnetic pull toward a hat rack laden with costume goggles.

"We're out for the whole month, remember?" Claire pointed out, flashing me a wicked smile. Oh, yeah. That was our fault. Ray's fault, actually.

Ray who didn't know when it was wise to keep his mouth shut. "That also means we're guaranteed As. No chance of messing up our finals, and no Fs on our science fair projects to drag us down."

"You don't get to be smug about that," I scolded him in a sharp whisper, throwing in a glare for good measure. "I've only forgiven you because I'd have been able to talk you out of it if Marcia hadn't been an even bigger jerk. If she hadn't set you up from the start, I'd be a superhero now and you'd be the supervillain I reformed."

Somewhere between our reactions, Claire sighed. "I can't believe we have all of December off."

"It's just our middle school. The rest of the school system is stuck finishing the term," Ray added.

That detached, philosophical tone didn't fool me at all. I turned and poked him in the chest with a finger. "You're hinting we should go on another supervillain rampage."

I'd caught him, and he didn't bother to deny it. Or even look bothered. "It would help our cover. If we made a scene at a different middle school, no one would be sure we were students at Northeast West Hollywood Middle anymore."

"I don't know about attacking a middle school. If we just rampage, someone will get hurt." Claire sounded wistful. Criminy. My friends!

On the other hand… "I might have an idea about how to do it, but we'd just be getting ourselves in deeper trouble." Just because it might be fun to think about didn't mean I was willing to do it.

Except the moment I said that, Claire and Ray closed in, their shoulders pressed against mine on both sides. Each way I looked, I got a devilishly eager smile from one of my best friends. Worse, they knew my weaknesses, and I could see how this argument would go. The next round would be them making me admit that if I blew up City Hall now, it wouldn't affect my chances of clearing my name later.

I surrendered. "I'll need a lot of metal I don't have. Like a wrecked car, or something."

CHAPTER ELEVEN

I double-counted. Three hundred fifty dollars. Sliding the bills into an envelope, I tucked it into the mailbox. Ray looked amused, but there was no way I was stealing this stranger's car, even a junked one. "350 – DOESN'T WORK" had been painted on the back window, so that was how much the owner would find waiting when they got home from work.

I hoped the owner was at work. The next part might be loud and alarming. I uncoiled The Machine, tossed it into the back seat, and ordered, "Eat the car. I need transportation." Hopefully it would get the message.

"Eat the car" went through loud and clear. The Machine chowed down on upholstery until tearing and crunching became squeaking and grinding when it reached the steel underneath. The Machine grew, a bulbous maggot in a vinyl skin, until it ate enough metal and the skin split, releasing a crab that was all mouth and legs. The whining of masticated metal grew louder. On this residential side street I didn't see any pedestrians, and the three cars that passed didn't slow noticeably. I added "Claire's power keeps anyone from panicking" to the list of things I was hoping would work.

The Machine sucked down the last remaining tire and convulsed. Plates slid over each other, metal crackled, and more legs emerged. Finally, he settled down as a compact, eight-legged shape about the size of the car he'd eaten. Grabbing two legs, I climbed his joints and sat down on the rubber mat up near the head. Well, The Machine didn't have a head in this shape, but one end was pointy and the other rounded and the pointy end looked like a tail to me. So, head.

Claire grabbed the highest joints of two legs, and, like a gymnast, swung herself slowly up and around to crouch behind me. In a bear suit. I didn't know whether to be jealous or die laughing. Ray seemed in no hurry to join us, but, if I could outrun a car, I'd act the same way.

"So how do you drive this thing?" Claire asked, peeking over my shoulder at the complete lack of controls.

I pointed down the street. "Forward!"

We took off. I grabbed my seat in both hands as The Machine lurched forward. Those eight legs could *move*, and we barreled down the street. As the intersection loomed, I pointed left and yelled, "That way, and try to stay between the cars!"

The Machine obeyed. The car behind me gave us plenty of space as we scuttled up Los Feliz. Claire stood behind me like a princess overlooking her domain. Me, I had to cling to my rubber seat tightly as the wind rolled over us.

And then the car ahead of us slowed down at the same time we reached the bridge, and, without my instruction, The Machine swerved off the road. The world tipped underneath me, and I wrapped my arms around The Machine's body and lay on the side of my rubber seat as we crawled sideways along the bridge struts without slowing down. Another lurch, a moment of vertigo, and I picked myself up and took back my seat. We were upright on the other side of the bridge, and I heard laughter.

I looked. Four kids in an SUV next to us had the windows rolled down, laughing gleefully. On the other side, two teenagers on the bike path cheered and whistled. HA! Why fight it? "AH HA HA HA! Machine! Jump the next car!"

STUPID! The Machine shuddered, and I let out a desperate squeal as we catapulted into the air! I had to clutch my seat tightly again to keep from being thrown off the back. A metallic crash and the honking of the car we'd just jumped beat at my eardrums when we hit the ground. I uncurled slowly, but The Machine resumed scurrying up the street as if nothing happened.

Behind me, Claire yelled, "Do it again!" over the wind. I twisted my head around to see her rising from a crouch.

"Forget it! Some of us don't have a superhuman sense of balance!" I yelled back. Claire's grin didn't waver for a second.

The buildings got bigger. There was the skyline of Glendale's downtown in front of us, but we weren't going there. I pointed down an upcoming side street and ordered The Machine, "That way!"

We pulled up to the schoolyard with Claire giving me a pout because I hadn't done anything crazier than driving a giant mechanical spider around Glendale. A little kick of my foot, and The Machine wandered off the road and up to the fence around the school.

At which moment Ray slid down from where he'd been sitting on a parked car, walked casually past us, and jumped. A hand caught the top of the ten-foot fence, and he vaulted over the top to land as lightly as a feather on the playground just as the bell rang.

Wait, the bell just rang? I pulled out my phone and flipped it open. Twelve o'clock. We'd gotten here much faster than I'd expected.

Well, the beginning of lunch would do just as well as the middle of lunch. Time to rampage! Another little kick with my heel and The Machine barreled forward, smashing through the fence and flattening it under its eight legs as if it had been made of cardboard. That got everyone's attention. Kids had already started emerging to eat their lunches in the schoolyard, but they exploded out now, gaping at me, at my ride, at Claire in her bear suit, and at Ray in his black suit and hat. Gaping at The Inscrutable Machine.

LA was too used to this. They were interested, but they weren't scared. I flipped up the power on my air conditioner cannon, set the blast nice and wide so my lousy aim wouldn't mess this up, and blew a stone table off its pedestal. It flipped twice in the air and then smashed onto the asphalt with a boom. Perfect.

"Good afternoon, Hailo Senior Junior High! You have been conquered by The Inscrutable Machine!" I shouted at the top of my lungs. The Machine crawled forward toward the growing crowd. More kids, a little more safety-conscious, stared from behind windows. I tried to combine "loud" and "lazy" as I told them, "Now, don't worry. Submit to our power, and we'll finish our business here and be gone again. No one has to get hurt unless they resist."

Seeing a table blown apart would have convinced me, but there always had to be one. A boy so big he must have been held back a year grabbed a chunk of old asphalt and pulled it back to throw it.

I didn't have to do anything. Ray moved like a shot without seeming to hurry. The boy with the rock didn't even see him coming until Ray's gloved hand closed on his wrist. With Ray's strength, it didn't look like a fight. He took the boy by the back of his neck, walked him out in front of his classmates, and pushed him easily down to his knees in front of me. The boy finally took the hint. When Ray let go, he hung his head down so far I couldn't see his face.

I clapped my hands! "Oh, that's nice. I like that a lot, Reviled. I want more fools bowing before me." Turning, I raised my voice as loud as I could again and shouted, "Well? I know there are children of superheroes here! I know some of you have powers! Who is brave enough to face us? Who will kneel next before The Inscrutable Machine?"

The crowd, so busy a moment ago trying to spread out into the yard and see what was going on, froze. I waited. Nothing. I gave my head a slow, dramatic roll. "Fine, fine! If no one is going to make this interesting, we'll take our prize and be done." I stomped my foot twice on top of The Machine and ordered it, "Find me jade in that building." Jade would be perfect. There'd be a teacher's earring maybe, something we could claim was important and then ride off in triumph. It shouldn't take too long. It had better not take too long. A superhero would be here any minute.

The Machine shook underneath me, then shook again, and again. I kept my balance without looking like it was hard, but thank Tesla my jumpsuit had a visor hiding my face because I knew I was gaping in shock. Why? Because the Machine hocked one, two, three, four, five, six basketball sized copies of itself out of its mouth, which went scuttling through the crowd to climb the walls of the school. One took the simpler route of breaking open a window, and a second followed it through that gap.

I guess I still didn't know everything The Machine could do. Hoo boy.

Then a loud pop echoed over the yard, and I swear I heard the bullet go past my head.

My heart started up again. A security guard stood at one of the doors into Hailo Senior Junior High. I must have been imagining the bullet. I must have. He had his gun pointed at one of my mini-Machines climbing up along the second floor wall.

I gave The Machine a nudge with my foot. As it crawled forward, I announced, "Buddy, you are so lucky you missed."

He swung around and pointed the gun at me. "Call off the robots and lay down your weapons." He was pretty old and he looked panicky, but he didn't look feeble.

The kids were watching. If we lost control of this, I didn't know what would happen. Plus, I was a supervillain! I couldn't be intimidated by a guy with a gun. To make the point, I sat down on the rubber seat, laid my cannon across my lap, and answered with as much dry snark as I could put into a reply that loud. "You don't want to do that."

"Stop where you are!"

I didn't. He pulled the trigger again.

No imagination this time. The pop slammed into me, too loud to be silly. Had the bullet? Was I bleeding? He'd shot at a middle-schooler! He must have thought my jumpsuit was armor. It wasn't. I didn't have any defense against being shot by your average cop with a gun.

"Aren't we getting a little carried away?" Claire asked, sliding around the crowd, skating up to the guard on her frictionless bear feet. Right up until he swiveled and pointed the pistol at her instead. Her impish grin, cocked up on one side, ought to melt any man on the spot.

He didn't melt. "Put your hands up, little girl! I know you have super powers!" he warned her, shouting hoarsely. Why hadn't he melted? It happened. I knew it happened, but this was a bad, bad time to run into someone naturally immune to Claire's mind control.

She didn't get it. As surprised as she looked, she opened her mouth to give him another teasing quip.

I pushed myself up off my feet, one foot reaching out. The world skipped as I teleported up next to the guard, so close my arm brushed his blue uniform shirt as I yanked up the air conditioning cannon. I jerked down on the levers, praying I didn't blow his arm off, and pulled the trigger. He screamed, and the gun went flying, blasted out of his grip. As fast as I'd teleported in, I turned and took another step that left me standing on top of The Machine.

Standing. I sat down slowly. I had to look casual, disinterested. Not like I was breathing like a bellows and feeling wobbly from teleporting twice in as many seconds. Or shivering cold, because I hadn't thought about guns until now. Even more than heroes, every supervillain, every one, was going to be shot at. Ray could outrun a car, then lift it, but one bullet would kill him dead. How could I have been so stupid?

And had I broken this poor innocent guy's arm?

Now was not the time. Ray had not been idle. I looked up to see him take the guard's arms and push him down as easily as he had the boy.

I lifted my gun arm and waved it airily. "He's got no powers. I don't care if he kneels, Reviled. He's not interesting. Anyway, our work here is done." How did I know? Because as Ray made the guy lie flat and placed a warning foot on his back, a mini-Machine crawled out of the window behind him. Two others scuttled back down the walls from the roof. One of them must have found me a trinket. Which one?

Oh. That one. The one that pushed open the cafeteria door and crawled out holding a chunk of jade the size of a basketball.

How? Why? This was a middle school! I'd expected a bracelet or something. I tried to cover. "Excellent. My sources were correct." Like I'd known this thing was here.

The mini-Machine reached The Machine itself, crawling up a leg to offer me the chunk of jade. Not just a chunk, a statue, a curling and elegant oriental dragon. I took it in both hands. Heavy, but not too much to carry. It looked mystical. What were the odds of finding a magical artifact here?

The odds? Well, now that I asked, I'd just gone treasure hunting in LA, home of every cult, secret society, and unethical research project for the last 100 years. Oh, and I did it using experimental technology I didn't understand.

Thunder boomed, the sound of bricks and shingles exploding out of the top of the school. A glittering green and gold dragon the size of a limousine leaped into the air. It screamed like a jaguar, rippled and snapped like a whip in mid-air, and plunged straight toward me—the girl holding the statue it had been guarding.

I dove. I saw the dragon's mouth opening, the bright flash of flame, and focused on the ground ten feet away. Twisting, I rolled on my side as I teleported the rest of the way and rolled up to see yellow-edged blue flame drench The Machine to no effect. The Machine absorbed the heat like it did everything else. The mini-Machine that brought me the statue was not so lucky. Apparently the little ones were cheap copies, because it lit up red and yellow and sagged into a metal mess on The Machine's leg. At which point The Machine ate it.

Whatever surprises The Machine still held, combat options did not seem to be among them. I had to let that thought go. The dragon swung around again, gliding through the air like an eel through water, bearing down on me and the statue I still held clutched against my stomach.

As its mouth opened I slapped the power lever of my air cannon all the way up and opened fire, over and over, as fast as I could pull the trigger. Maybe a third of those shots hit, but the first knocked its face aside so the next blast of fire went up and aside harmlessly. The others pounded into it over and over.

Except "pounded" didn't seem accurate. The shots kept the dragon off balance, pushing it back and forcing it to writhe around to get back at me, but they didn't seem to be hurting it. At all. Impacts that would blow a hole in a brick wall were nothing more than a little girl's slap to this thing.

Then Ray streaked across the pavement and catapulted into the air, grabbing the monster by its back haunches. Lesson immediately learned: it might want the statue, but it wasn't single-minded. It twisted around to bite at Ray, and, despite its serpentine shape, that still looked awkward. Ray on the other hand held onto one of its legs, swung around underneath its body like a monkey, and climbed up onto its shoulders to stomp savagely on the back of its head. Which had no more effect than my shooting it. Eesh.

The dragon thrashed, trying to shake Ray off. That didn't work. It doubled forward and scratched at the back of its neck with its front claws. He climbed them as they groped for him, held onto its hips, and kicked it repeatedly where it looked like its kidneys should be. The thumps from those blows were loud, but got no reaction I could spot.

All the twisting had the dragon rolling about in the air out of control. I clenched my fists together, scooting up to my knees with the statue in my lap. Would I get lucky?

Ray, retreating from attack after attack, ended up hanging by the end of the dragon's tail. It looped around to bite him, and he jumped onto its head, crouching to punch it right between the eyes. That was enough. Its next zigzag through the air went straight down, smacking into the pavement. I extended my hands and blasted it with the static gloves while Ray jumped clear. The dragon got its legs underneath it, lifted up to jump into the air again, and was brought up short by the foot I'd stuck to the ground.

Which it pried free a second later with only a little jerk of effort. Well, crud.

Now that it was on the ground, Claire took her turn. Skating around in front of it, circling lazily with one leg held in the air, she looked up into the whiskered, reptilian face and asked, "Hey, you're a real dragon, aren't you?"

It had been worth a shot. Dragons liked maidens, right? With Claire radiating girlish curiosity, I thought it might work. Instead the dragon opened its mouth, and only Claire's Serum-enhanced ability to dive roll out of the way fast kept her from getting cooked by the spray of fire.

All the dragon had to do was turn his head to finish her. Struggling to my feet, I shot him in the shoulder. That only got his attention, but I yanked on the trigger of my air cannon repeatedly, slapping his face up and aside over and over. The fire sprayed all over the place, except where any of us were standing, which was all I wanted.

I had the guardian's complete focus. It twisted around, avoiding my last few shots so it could line its head up on me. I took a step and teleported past it, right up next to Claire.

The jump was long enough I felt it in my legs and gut, but I had no time. Arms wrapped awkwardly around the statue, I yanked my gloves off and dumped them into Claire's hands. "Squeeze like this to charge them!" I whispered to her, showing the grip.

The dragon heard my voice, spinning around after us, so I stepped and teleported past and behind it again. Right up near the wall of the school. I blinked hard, twice. Not only was the teleporting making my limbs ache, adapting to my view changing in sharp flickers made my eyes googly.

Forget my eyes. The dragon had figured me out. He spun right around again, and I jumped again out in front of it, and again off to the side. It wasn't confused in the slightest. It hadn't figured me out—it was following the statue I held wrapped in both arms!

That was when Ray hit it over the head with an iron post he'd ripped out of the fencing.

Even the dragon felt that. He hit it over and over and over, its head sinking with each blow, until it lashed out and tried to bite him. Maybe it felt those blows, but they hadn't hurt it. Ray backflipped, then backflipped again, as it lunged like a snake for another bite. Claire skated past and bonked the dragon on top of its muzzle with a clenched fist. That was, just barely, worth a snap in her direction, but as she slid away the dragon

165

guardian's attention returned to its real target, the girl holding the statue—me.

I was already trembling. How long could we keep this up? Only one of us had infinite stamina. As the dragon scrambled toward me, I lurched and teleported behind it again, right up next to Ray. "Here. Take this. Play keepaway," I wheezed, shoving the statue into his arms. He tossed it up into the air, and, as the dragon leaped off the ground, Ray went running, caught it, and rolled past a blast of fire.

A heavy ache followed the trembling. My body was so stiff and tired, but around the edges of the yard, hiding behind cars and school walls and peering through windows, the crowd of middle school kids were still watching us. I had an image to maintain. I teleported, a gentle step lightly on top of The Machine. Leaning against an upraised leg to look casual, I let the dark haze clear from my eyes and played with the levers of my cannon theatrically. I had plenty of time. The dragon didn't give me another glance. It was after Ray, who darted around at random, jumped up, and vaulted over the dragon's back, making it spin around in confusion. I'd counted on him being faster than it.

I hadn't counted on the mini-Machines still obediently trying to carry out my orders. The remaining five scurried across the pavement, converging on Ray. He tripped over one. He went rolling. He recovered immediately, but as he fell two of the mini-Machines yanked the statue out of his grip and scurried back across the pavement with it to me.

The dragon turned. I had its attention again. Criminy. At least I wasn't alone. Ray lifted one of the mini-Machines by two of its legs, swung and bashed the dragon in the shoulder. The dragon snapped at him reflexively, and he vaulted over its back again, causing it to twist around.

Two mini-Machines handed the dragon statue to The Machine, which set it at my feet. I couldn't dodge anymore, and the dragon was already twisting again, forgetting about Ray to go after its precious statue. We were out of time.

"Now, Claire!" I yelled, or at least squeaked loudly. She was ready. Skating gracefully underneath its belly, she lifted her hands and unleashed the power she's been storing as Ray and I fought. A lot of power, blinding flashes that remained as crisscrossed afterimages in my vision. I didn't let it phase me. I pulled the trigger over and over, pumping air blasts into the dragon, not caring where I hit it.

The force was enough. Already bent in a knot, it lost its balance and hit the ground hard. Then it let out a shriek, its body spasming but unable to pull loose from the pavement. The charge had been enough. We'd beaten it.

I crouched down and picked up the dragon statue. Pretty heavy. Beautifully detailed, although a bit sinister now that I'd seen the real thing try to cook my face. Should I keep it? I'd worked hard enough for it, but that dragon would never give up and I didn't know how to kill it.

Every superhero in the world would have a fit if I killed one of the last remaining dragons. Mech, for example, who in his gleaming copper colored armor was drifting down out of the sky over the schoolyard right now.

Could this go any more wrong?

"This game has gone on long enough, don't you think, kids?" he asked.

"Can I make a sudden-death overtime joke about that?" I shot back, trying to sound glib.

"I think it's time you three surrendered and came with me. Nobody's gotten hurt yet. We might even keep you out of juvenile." That patient, generous tone made my blood run hot, but I'd met the guy and I knew he meant it. He was being nice.

Because, after all, we couldn't hope to beat him. We'd barely taken down the dragon. Nothing I had, nothing, would so much as scratch his armor. We couldn't outrun him. If even one of us was caught, they'd know who the other two were. My parents weren't that blind. And, in a minute, the dragon was going to be after us again. It had managed to lever one of its claws free and was scratching at the others.

I was trapped.

The dragon gave up before I did.

I jumped, tried not to drop the jade statue in shock as it writhed and deformed in my arms, becoming... I didn't know what. Something ugly, boneless, with too many limbs. Six of them were raised up into a bowl. As hideous as it was, it still looked ceremonial.

I looked up again, watched the dragon's skin split, the rubbery thing heave out of it. Chunks of concrete stuck to the rubbery bulk as it ripped loose of my static bind easily. Arms like tentacles flailed. It screeched, then again in another voice, and then in a third, like different animals.

It had never been a dragon at all. It was something much worse.

"Hey, could you take care of that monster for us? It's a little out of our league, and it looks like the bystander eating kind. Okay? Thanks!" Was that my voice sounding so taunting and sarcastic?

"Young lady—" Mech started, his voice exasperated. But as he said it he fired twice, two gleaming ropes firing from his arms to wrap around the monster, stapling it to the ground.

It didn't like that. Arms exploded out of its body, telescoping, and tongues lashed out of the clawed hands to wrap tightly around him.

HA! I got him!

"Should we help him?" Claire asked anxiously.

"No way. Mech can handle that thing. We are going to escape with the loot," I corrected her. Sure enough, the tongues wrapped around Mech glowed, then exploded. The monster shrieked, but ripped itself loose from the bonds that tied it down. It was big now. Huge. Nearly two stories tall.

And not my problem anymore. I kicked the top of The Machine's head. "Split up, circle around, and return to the lab to wait for me." It took me literally, and as I slid down its back onto the ground it came apart in pieces, all of them growing their own legs and scattering like baby spiders.

I slapped my chest, and blue light shot out to form a motorbike in front of me. I climbed on, and wedged the statue on the seat in front of me. Glancing back over my shoulder, I saw Mech blasting away at the monster's gelatinous bulk with his vaporizer beams. Color me impressed. He didn't use those on just anybody.

"Thanks, Mech! Ha! HA HA HA HA HA!" I laughed, shoved on the pedals, and my bike leaped forward, zooming out of the schoolyard, over the wrecked fence, and onto the now traffic-less street.

We'd done it. We'd gotten away. Mech would defeat the monster, imprison it so it could never come after me, or kill it if it could die. The statue was mine. We'd won.

But we'd won by the skin of our teeth. Dad was right. Overconfidence had nearly gotten me killed, in a very literal "bullet through my brain" sense, not to mention the dragon. That was not going to happen again. I wasn't going into another fight without a lot of preparation.

CHAPTER TWELVE

The Machine was heading back to the lab, but not us. I lost track of Ray and Claire almost immediately, since my light bike doesn't travel the same paths as Claire's frictionless skates or a super fast boy on foot. Driving it was a bit hair-raising, but fun. I could see through every shiny blue-white surface I touched, and I only had to pump the pedals once to get it racing down the street as fast as any car. I could barely control it, but I didn't have to. The bike wove around obstacles like a fish without my instruction, and all I really had to do was turn when I wanted to switch streets. So I zipped down Los Feliz, speeding through red lights, circling around cars that rarely bothered to even beep at me. It's mostly a straight shot from Glendale to our neighborhood.

I pulled up into Claire's driveway, hoisted the jade statue into my arms, and slapped the button that made the bike dematerialize. Then I ducked around to the side door. I really, really did not want to stand out where I was visible from the street. Not in my mad scientist jumpsuit.

I hardly had my breath back when Ray jumped off the next roof onto the walkway next to me. That had stopped surprising me.

"Did you see Claire?" I asked him.

"Right on our tails." He slid off his fancy mask and his coat and folded them up into a neat little bundle. That was it; he was in civvies again. So easy for him!

A teenager-sized teddy bear slid down the street at high speed, swerving to spin in a tight spiral across Claire's front yard until she pirouetted to a stop. Those shoe inserts I made her even worked on grass. Wow. I was pretty good at this.

She coasted up to us, turned a key in the lock, and yelled, "Hi, Mom, we're back!" as we all piled in. First things first. I rushed into the bathroom and Claire into her room. Thirty seconds later, we emerged at the same time, wearing the civilian clothes we'd left here when we got suited up for villainy. Ray lowered his head in theatrical disappointment at our being fully dressed, and my cheeks felt a little hot. Criminy, I was the sole person with any kind of modesty in the house, wasn't I?

Still, we were back, we all looked like regular kids again, and we shuffled out all together and collapsed on Claire's Mom's couch in front of her giant TV with me in the middle and the statue in my lap. Collectively we let out a giant sigh, and I heard Miss Lutra laugh from back in the kitchen.

I also heard, "Firefighters believe the school is completely evacuated, but they can't be certain. We're all lucky Mech has been able to keep the monster contained in the schoolyard so far." That came from the TV.

Whoa. We were on the news. At least, the thing we'd released was on the news. Monsters were more interesting than regular supervillains. They made no attempt to avoid casualties, after all. Mech still hadn't killed that thing?

He hadn't. It had only gotten bigger and uglier. The amorphous, iridescent, particolored body oozed a new arm while I watched and slapped it at Mech, only to have the clawed hand at the end sliced off with Mech's vaporizer beam. The severed hand hit the ground with a splat, and dissolved into the air in seconds. I couldn't tell if that caused the monster pain. I counted six mouths, all chanting in different languages I didn't know nonstop.

I looked down at the statue in my lap. There was the same cluster of eyes, and the randomly placed mouths. I had to congratulate myself. I now owned the ugliest hunk of jade in the known world.

Claire's Mom walked around the couch, sat down on the arm of it next to Claire, and tapped a few buttons on her phone. "Beebee? I'm guessing you're watching the same news story I am. I thought you'd want to hear that the kids are at my place." A pause, and a cheerful, "I understand perfectly. I only look like I'm not having a heart attack whenever I hear the words 'The Inscrutable Machine.'"

I couldn't hear what Mom was saying, but Miss Lutra laughed. Then she paused for much longer, and it occurred to me—she'd just breezily lied to my Mom like it was nothing. I couldn't pull it off myself, but it was an interesting lesson. Always sounding like you were lying was almost as good a poker face as always sounding sincere.

"Of course. He may need your input," Miss Lutra finished, tapping her phone to end the call. Looking down the couch at us, she explained, "Your father's talking to Mech right now, Penny, helping him work out how to defeat this thing. What could you possibly have stolen that let loose a behemoth like that?"

We all stared at the chunk of jade in my lap until I confessed, "I have no idea. We found it completely by accident. I don't know what it is, what it does, or even what I'm going to do with it."

Claire waved her hand emphatically. "I guarantee we can sell it. I can think of four supervillains right now who'd pay for a cursed statue."

I shook my head. "That's kinda the problem. I think this thing is dangerous. Really dangerous."

"So it is magic?" Ray asked. He reached for it, but I tilted it gently out of the way. Was I just nervous, or was that my power giving me a hint?

"Call it magic if you want. It has to do more than just change shape to be protected by a monster like that." We all looked at the TV screen. Now holes had opened in the air around Mech, with giant eyes peeking through. Mech punched one, and the hole closed on his fist like a mouth. Yikes.

Nobody wanted to argue that point. You don't bind a guardian like that to an artifact without good reason.

Ray threw out another idea. "Feed the statue to The Machine. It converts the curse into useful energy and an ugly statue into an untraceable and highly marketable block of raw jade."

I tried to think about that. Would it work? I tried to look into the thing in the back of my brain that understood the weirdest science, but all I felt was nervousness. "That would probably work, but the 'probably' scares the heebie-jeebies out of me."

Ray leaned back against the couch, folding his arms behind his neck, and concluded rather smugly, "Then keep it. Every villain's lair needs a few valuable trophies on display."

He was right. The idea had a lot of appeal. Maybe I could decorate one of the spare rooms with nice marble pedestals. Even if I never got to show it to anyone, a cursed artifact made an amazing display piece. Especially when I snuck it out from under the noses of the rainbow abomination on the TV screen.

Of course, that rainbow abomination wanted the statue back real bad, but as I watched the fight changed. Mech fired his vaporizers and missed, except he didn't miss. He wasn't aiming at the monster. Instead, the beams burned complicated patterns into the schoolyard's asphalt at high speed. The glowing inscriptions looked like a circuit diagram, and he drew them out in a circle around the monster. The effect was immediate. Tentacles and claws flailed against that boundary, unable to cross. Floating eyes winked out of existence one by one. Mech had the monster contained, or would as soon as he closed the circle.

The thing was smart enough to recognize that fact, and Mech had to circle it to keep drawing the imprisoning lines. He strayed past their protection for a second, and the monster hit back— magic for magic. Eyes, tentacles, mouths, beams of light sprang out of all of them, tracing an intricate cage of its own around Mech, blocking his vaporizers, trapping him. More than a cage. Mech bunched up, and I barely caught the flash before the screen blacked out.

Beside me, Ray sounded impressed. "I've only ever heard of Mech using his EMP pulse once before. Here we go. It looks like it worked." The screen lit back up, now with footage from a helicopter above the fight and much farther away. Mech was moving again, but the fight had become a real light show.

I leaned back and asked Miss Lutra, "Mech could die in this fight, couldn't he? That thing might kill him."

"Mech? No, way," Claire insisted. "Mech's the top of the game. He's beaten tougher opponents than this."

Claire's Mom's expression changed. Hardened, I guess, still playful but in a hard and thoughtful way. It reminded me of watching my Mom start thinking like The Audit. It was definitely The Minx who said, "Name a major superhero who died in the line of duty."

"Evolution," we all answered together. Some names are on the tip of your tongue. Evolution had been the best, and everyone had thought he was invulnerable until the day they found out he wasn't.

"Name a major villain who died fighting," The Minx prompted us again.

"Chimera," Claire non-answered. She was trying to get around the question by naming someone secretly alive. I gave her a shove.

Ray picked up the slack. "The Good Doctor. Razorback. Glow. Black Hat—" He was ready to continue, but The Minx put her finger to his lips. That left him looking stunned. Maybe she seemed different to me because she'd turned her powers on.

Her voice dropped. "The Audit fought Bull once. He wasn't trying to kill her, but one lucky slap would have broken every bone in her body, and Penny wouldn't have a mother."

"So he could die. That monster might kill him." I could hardly hear my own hushed voice.

"He could, and he knows it, and now I know why Ray and Claire made you the leader," she agreed.

Ray nodded. "That kind of thinking gets us out of trouble."

"I thought we put her in charge because she makes great toys," Claire argued, her pout an open refusal to get drawn into a somber moment. She had a point. We'd just won big, and, from the helicopter's bad vantage point, it looked like Mech had the monster pinned.

Actually… "You've still got those static gloves with your costume, right? Do you want to keep them?" I asked Claire.

She lit up like a Christmas tree. "Seriously?"

"Yep. They're a terrible weapon for me. They require too much charging. Once a battle starts, I don't have the time and I can't dodge well enough."

Claire squealed, jumped off the sofa, and went charging off into her room, coming out a second later with the gloves on her hands. She charged one up, took a baby photo of herself off the wall, blasted it, then stuck it back up upside down. "Ha!" she crowed, grinning hugely with glee.

"And I guess that's my cue." Miss Lutra strolled down to the hall closet, reached up to the top shelf, and pulled down what looked like an egg beater with sharp teeth. Walking back, she held it out toward Claire, who got it an instant before I did.

"Your grappling hook!" Claire had gone past squealing to whispery, but she still had the strength to bolt forward and scoop the device out of her mother's hands, then strap it onto her forearm. Very sleek. You could hardly tell what she was wearing. Fantastic engineering.

Miss Lutra filled in that blank immediately. "Made by Penny's father himself. There's at least a dozen copies out there by now, so as long as you don't wear it in front of him no one will know it's mine."

Claire looked up at her mother, and a smile forced itself onto my face. Claire was so happy tears had started to leak out of the corners of her eyes. Miss Lutra brushed one away with her thumb. "I was hoping to give that to you when you became a superhero, but I said I'd support you no matter what and I meant it."

Claire threw herself into her mother's arms, and they hugged tightly. It went on for a while. Eventually, Claire pulled back enough to promise in a more normal voice, "I haven't given up on that. None of us have. It's just that nobody's going to listen if we say we always meant to be heroes, so we'll have to wait until we can do a showy public change of sides."

The hug let go, which I took as my opportunity to interrupt. "We're not doing anything, heroic or villainous, until I upgrade our equipment. Right now, there's a big hole in our defenses, namely the possibility we'll be shot full of big holes." The memory of that bullet going past still gave me a shiver.

"I was hoping to try out the grappling hook!" Claire sulked, holding up her arm to show off her prize.

"I was hoping to convince you ladies to try Parkour with me," Ray added, giving me a hopeful smile.

Claire's answer was obvious, but I had to refuse. "I'm not nearly fit enough for that, Ray."

Ray's hopeful look started to settle as he realized I meant it. "I thought those teleport rings might give you the edge you need."

I had to shake my head. "They work on muscle energy. I'd get about a block and collapse. Even with the Serum, I'm surprised Claire thinks she'll keep up."

I gave Claire a curious look, and she grinned back at me. "Well, it turns out I've been doing a lot of high-impact exercising like supervillainy since I took my dose, and I'm in excellent shape if I do say so myself."

An obvious line like that got the expected look from Ray. A very long look, while Claire acted as smug as a mink. I pushed myself up off the sofa and hefted the statue up in my arms. "I need to put the artifact away where it's safe, anyway."

Ray rolled over the back of the sofa and onto his feet with, well, superhuman grace. Bowing low, he held out his hand to Claire. "Then if the younger Miss Lutra would care to join me for a stroll across the fences and rooftops…?"

Claire laid her hand in his, and answered as airily as a debutante, "I'd be delighted."

Ray held the door open for Claire, and I stumped after them with the statue in my arms. I only got to the doorway before Claire turned, lifted her arm, and fired the grappling line up at her own roof. It jerked her upwards, and I saw her flip over onto the rooftop and disappear. Wow, she *was* in great shape. Not as good as Ray, who only had to jump and grab the edge of the roof with one hand to do the same thing. They were already laughing.

Claire's Mom's hand settled on top of my head. "You're worrying about nothing, you know."

I grunted, pulling the statue up into a better grip. It really was heavy. "No, I'm not. I don't know how, but this thing is dangerous."

"It's certainly ugly," she conceded in a dry tone. Whimsically, she reached out and lifted the statue from my arms—or tried. It slipped right out of her grip, and I caught it before it hit the ground only in a desperate, lucky grab. "Sorry, Penny. It's heavier than it looks!" she apologized.

I hoisted it back high in my arms, and asked her, "Can you grab my costume? I left it in the bathroom."

"Of course." She disappeared into the house. A few seconds later she returned, handing me the jumpsuit I immediately wrapped around the statue to form a protective bag. I just wasn't sure who I was protecting. I'd never seen The Minx drop anything before. Ever. Clumsy mistakes were not a Lutra thing, especially Misty "The Minx" Lutra.

I walked down the stone path to the street and hit the button on my jumpsuit to activate my light bike. Settling the wrapped up statue in front of the seat, I glanced over at Ray and Claire tightrope walking along the top of a fence. Then I shoved my foot against the pedal and sped away toward the school and my laboratory.

By the time the elevator opened up on my lab, I didn't feel quite so left out. I couldn't walk on fences, but they couldn't stand in front of a set of machine tools and tell the thing in the back of their heads to make something crazy. But first things first. What was I going to do with this statue? I wasn't even sure I should be touching it, although it hadn't affected me obviously like it had Miss Lutra.

Well, the first thing I had to do was put it on the floor. There wasn't anywhere else. I wished I had some marble, but The Machine was perched on top of a giant pile of steel bars that would have to do. I scooped him up, fed them into the smelter, and twisted a few levers around. I had to have a display stand at least. While the steel cooked and shaped I put on some gloves and my visor. I really ought to put on the whole jumpsuit, but I'd just gotten out of it! Anyway, this wasn't complicated. Set the mold to this flat surface and those rounded sides, weld that to a hollow cylinder, put it through the cooling sequence, and drag the excruciatingly heavy pedestal out into the middle of the floor. I wish I'd had enough plastic left.

Oh, well. My arm muscles might sting, but I had somewhere to display my new prize. I hoisted the jade statue and put it on top of the pedestal. Wow. What an ugly hunk of rock. The creamy jade was naturally beautiful, but the blobby tentacle-limbed humanoid it had been carved into just made that soft green look like slime.

As a display piece, this monstrosity scored a solid zero. It had powers, I knew that. Could it be useful? I mean, sure they had to be awful powers, but I was technically a supervillain now. Even on the hero side, I'd need weapons. Not to be too clichéd, but could I use its powers for good? What were those powers?

I pulled out my wallet and scooped all my change out of my coin purse. I tended to accumulate pennies, and for once that would come in handy. Picking them all out, I dropped the pennies into the bowl made by the unnatural monster's cupped hands.

Then I wondered why I'd done that.

I'd done it because it was there, printed in my brain. My super power knew what this statue could do and how to use it, and I needed to put pennies in it and let them sit. No matter how pointless that looked, in the picture in my head, something powerful was happening.

Wondering wouldn't get me anywhere. I understood that picture as well as I likely ever would. I had a more important issue. Bullets. Bullets were bad. I did not want any puncturing my body, and that seemed extremely likely if I kept up the super-powered adventures. What had my Dad done about bullets? I didn't know. He'd never said. What did my Mom do? That I did know—she picked her moment, knew exactly when to not be in the way, employed traps and the element of surprise, and scared criminals until they were too afraid to shoot. I couldn't do any of that. For one thing, Mom liked stealth and surprise, and I had to face facts: I liked giving villainous monologues and brandishing super science weapons.

I was a mad scientist. I'd better be able to come up with something to deal with bullets. Armor? Armor wouldn't be a bad idea, especially for me, but my power didn't like repeating itself and all three of us needed protection. I'd rather bullets not be flying around at all.

I could do that. I could see a design. It was still vague. My brain filled in bits while I watched. I needed gold, a lot of quartz, a lot of metal salts and crystals... to bake into ceramics maybe?

I didn't have any of that stuff. Well, not much. I had steel. Lots and lots of steel. Steel and bad rubber and insulating foam from the car's upholstery. I had really run short on supplies. I'd started with so much, and used it up so fast!

Maybe... I'd just think away from that idea. Let it go and hope it was still there when I got the materials I needed. How about a new weapon? Something to replace my gloves? I liked the air conditioner cannon, but it was very limited and straightforward. Also not very showy. I wanted something cool, and for that I needed a theme, something to tie my creations together. If it weren't for the theme, Teddy Bears and Machine Guns would be boring.

I could make a candy chainsaw. Seriously. It would work. I could see in my head sugary candy corn spikes cutting through cement. I'd need a lot of sugar. A whole lot of sugar. I still had a pile of wood, and I could convert some of that, but it wouldn't be enough. Criminy, another cool design I didn't have materials for!

I had steel. What could I do with steel? I stared at the steel bars, and my super power gave me a blank slate. Great.

I needed more raw materials. Where was I going to get them? I'd spent the rest of the money Cy gave me on the car, whose raw materials sat in the corner taunting me right now. The chainsaw needed piles of sugar, but that bullet stopping mechanism was small. Getting the parts had to be cheaper and easier than thirty pounds of sugar. I just—

OW! Pain jolted from the back of my head to the front. I grabbed my skull, but the headache faded as fast as it came.

There wasn't going to be any mad science today. Maybe I shouldn't let that bother me. Right next to me I had a hideous jade statue I'd stolen (and the best part was, it had no owner so it wasn't really stealing) in an action-packed super-powered monster fight. My day had been amazing, and I ought to stop pushing and savor the accomplishment.

I took off my visor. I was going to go home and read Sentient Life like I'd always wanted to do, and, if Claire and Ray were out necking on the rooftops somewhere, that was their business. If I just relaxed and let myself realize what a great day I was having, it wouldn't bother me anymore.

I took my regular old boring bike home, leaving my super science equipment in the lab. Well, I had the teleport bracelets on under my shirt. Those things were seriously too useful, plus they didn't look like anything but copper arm bands.

I paused at the kitchen door. Was I about to face serious levels of parental freak out? Nothing to do but find out. I opened the door, took one step in, and yelled, "I'm home!"

Mom stepped out of Dad's office, smiling and relaxed, and met me halfway through the kitchen to give my bangs a ruffle. "Hi, honey. Enjoying your break? Want me to make you something to eat?"

Not a bad idea, although I didn't feel like sitting at the table and being social. "Maybe a sandwich."

Now Dad came out of his office, buckling on his belts with all the pouches and checking to see if his toys were in place. The two I saw were diagnostic tools, meters or scanners or something. I hadn't messed with them since I'd gotten old enough to even guess what their readouts meant. "Is Dad going somewhere?"

"Mech asked me to personally check the containment unit," Dad answered.

"Which means he caught it, but couldn't destroy it?" That information might be very important to the girl who owned the statue the monster craved.

Still all in a hurry checking his pockets, Dad took a moment to lean down and kiss my forehead. This was why I wore braids. My parents can't leave my hair alone. "It can't be killed, Pumpkin. Or, at least, it can't be killed with the resources we have. Most of the creature exists in the wrong probability state."

My eyebrows raised. I'd unleashed a whopper, hadn't I? That was why you don't go treasure hunting in LA. "A real honest-to-goodness interdimensional horror?"

"Strictly speaking, no," Dad corrected me. "The organism exists in our world, but operates on a level of physics we don't interact with. For a crude example, a being made of neutrinos could be passing through you right now, but neither of you would know. This monster is able to translate parts of itself into a form that can interact with us, but, without attacking the main body it can't be killed."

"So…?" I filled in dutifully.

"So it's not practical to kill, but it's not hard to set up a jamming field against the process it uses to translate itself. The monster is left with a tiny extrusion caught in our world, which we sealed inside… well, it's really a mayonnaise jar with a lot of high tech attachments." Dad gave me a wry smile as he admitted that, but I actually felt a touch jealous. Could my super power improvise like that if it had to?

Dad stopped checking his pockets when Mom handed him the car keys and gave him a kiss. "I hope I won't be too long!" he added, and hurried out the door.

I slipped into Dad's office, added a couple of marks to the note stuck to the Pumpkin Jar, and wandered back to my room. My hand reached out automatically to turn on my computer, but… Ray and Claire wouldn't be online, and I needed to relax. So I scooped up my collection of Sentient Life, walked back to the living room, and lay down on the couch to read.

Eventually Mom brought me a grilled cheese sandwich. The wages of sin were sweet indeed.

I read. I'd read most of the first volume before and little bits of the second, but now I had a chance to follow the story. Well into the third volume, Delph's trainers were dead. He hadn't met any aliens yet. As he piloted his tiny ship between Jupiter's moons, the only person he had to talk to was Vera, who gave him orders over the radio. He hadn't admitted even to himself that he had a crush on her, but he thanked her for talking to him so much, told her that dolphins need human friendship. She promised to be that human friend.

Then the scene cut to the station sending Delph his orders, and a human scientist asked a computer box, "Any updates on the mission, V-3RA?"

"I learned that I can lie today, Dr. Mills," the box answered in Vera's typeface.

I'd gotten enough peeks at the series to know how much trouble those words would cause. Of course, by volume five there weren't any humans left in the comic at all. I laid the comic over my chest and let it all sink in.

That was when Dad got home. "Hey, Beebee," I heard him say in the kitchen.

"How was Mech?" Mom answered.

"Just fine. He had more to say about The Inscrutable Machine than the monster."

Okay, that took my mind off of star-crossed AIs and engineered slave races.

"It's an issue that needs to be addressed. Picking fights with sidekicks is one thing. Interfering with LA's whole public school system is another," Mom replied. Replied rather firmly. Criminy. It hadn't quite occurred to me that adults would see getting everybody out of school early as less harmless than I did.

"Mech thinks that was just cover. He doesn't just think it; he's certain. They were there for the artifact." Dad kept his voice low, but they weren't whispering. I just had to sit quiet and listen.

"The odds are very reasonable that they found it by accident. This is LA, Brian," Mom noted.

Dad didn't let that stop him. "I wasn't there, but Mech was and he doesn't think so. He watched the kids fight the monster before he joined in and saw in person how they used it to snare him. He says they're too smooth. They worked together like professionals and, faced with a superior force, set a trap and escaped like professionals. They didn't fight like kids, Beebee. He even thinks the name The Inscrutable Machine doesn't refer to the tech weaponry, but their teamwork."

Mom got quiet for a moment. When she answered, it was in the flat tones of The Audit. "That all seems unlikely, but 'unlikely' isn't 'impossible.' Mech is an experienced and active field worker. He's seen them in person, and I haven't. I'd be foolish not to take his opinion seriously."

Okay. When Mom started doing The Audit, junior supervillains like me did not want to be around. Anyway, my heart couldn't handle another volume of Sentient Life yet. I got up and went back to my room.

I turned on my computer and resisted the urge to ask my super power if it could make me one that took less than forty days and forty nights to boot up. Dad custom made my smart phone, but a desktop wasn't an interesting enough challenge for him.

Actually, now that I'd gotten into mad science myself, I could see the point. Why make anything that regular engineers could come up with?

Claire and Ray were online, so they'd gotten home already. I set up my microphone and sent them a voice chat invitation.

"The Master calls!" Ray greeted me immediately.

"I thought you'd sleep through the evening. I'm exhausted, and I supposedly have super stamina," Claire chirped.

Okay. Well, might as well leap right into it. "Guys, I had a crazy thought. Would you be interested in trying a team PvP match?"

"Of Teddy Bears and Machine Guns?" I could hear the surprise in Claire's voice.

"This is a surprise. I thought you hated random PvP," Ray mused. He knew something was up. Neither of them sounded negative, so I booted up the game.

Ray was right. I didn't like dealing with sore winners or sore losers, and the idea that I didn't know how good my opponent would be made my heart flutter—or at least, it used to. After facing an unholy dragon-shaped eldritch abomination from beyond the ken of mankind this morning, snotty teenagers weren't that intimidating.

That wasn't what made the difference. "Dad talked to Mech, and he was impressed by our teamwork. It made me wonder if he was right, if we're just naturally a good team."

"We impressed Mech?" Claire asked, a bit of a squeal in her voice.

"I'm game for a game," Ray assured me.

"We impressed Mech?!" Claire repeated. She just couldn't let go of the glee. It made me feel kinda warm, too.

I clicked the invitation buttons. "Let's find out if we deserved the praise."

It took the game seconds to find us a match. I chose candy, Ray took junkyard, and Claire took toybox. This was our first time, and we wanted the arrangement we were most comfortable with. Our opponents took one candy, one toybox, and one junkyard themselves.

Candy sets up fastest, and I was counting on that. "I'll give you two cover," I told Claire and Ray through our chat connect. Just the basics. I needed speed and offense. Candy chainsaw, start the Rot Your Teeth upgrade building, put on the Sticky Shield to slow down anyone who attacked me, grab a pile of Soda Bombs as the upgrade came online, and then I downed every Pixie Stick I could stack. If I were playing by myself, I'd never go for a short term bonus like that. It would kill me later.

I wasn't playing by myself, and The Apparition had given me a plan. Namely, I charged.

It went exactly like I would have predicted. Only the candy player had anything ready, and he was working on basic upgrades. I took the chainsaw to him, sent him into retreat to heal. I could probably finish him off, but that wasn't the point. I swerved aside into the junkyard construction pit.

Junkyard takes forever. He was still building his salvage machines, constructing his assembly line, and he had exactly one nameless cobbled-together abomination building. I ignored it. I planted Soda Bombs on all his salvage machines and took my chainsaw to the assembly line. In a few seconds it was wreckage, and his salvage machines were a mess of sugar.

I didn't have time to finish him off, either. I turned and ran for the toybox.

Here I was in trouble. The toybox player had flooded her own base with Jacks, spat cheap Toy Soldiers at me as fast as she could pull them out of the box. My health was dropping fast, and that one junkyard monster roared up behind me. I kept cutting, swiping down soldier after soldier, every swing of the chainsaw taking me closer to the toybox itself. I tossed my remaining Soda Bombs at everything in sight as the junkyard monster caught up with me. They wouldn't do much damage, but they did some. It took the junkyard monster about three seconds to chew through my remaining health.

Just before I died I heard Claire announce, "Phase two, online." I got a glimpse of the first few Zombie Rag Dolls at the edge of the enemy base before my respawn sequence started. After that I was too busy putting myself back together to watch the action up close, but the map showed me what I expected to see—Claire's little blue dots multiplying, filling all three enemy bases. I'd given her time to get them fully upgraded and hit critical mass, and Zombie Rag Dolls bred like zombie rag dolls.

Still, the other guys weren't stupid. Their toybox player had put a lot of defenses in place to slow me down, and their candy player hadn't actually died. He'd gotten his own candy chainsaw together. The junkyard player had rebuilt and gotten a second metal monster active. The blue dots thinned.

Over the speakers, Ray asked, "May I cut in?" I respawned and watched his nightmare roll out. Ray liked to pile everything he could into one terrifying juggernaut, and we'd given him lots of time. From what I could tell, he started with his Thresher design and added grinding macerators. Their purpose became immediately clear. While the enemy team whittled the Zombie Rag Dolls down just a little faster than Claire could replace them, Ray's monster crashed into the enemy junkyard and devoured the construction machines. All of them.

I grabbed a new chainsaw and ran. I wasn't even as well equipped as last time, but as the enemy team threw everything they had at Ray's Thresher, surrounding it, I ran up behind and cut down their candy player, then went to work on their junkyard player's machines. Without resistance, Claire's Zombie Rag Dolls multiplied again, flooding the enemy junkyard base.

I personally blocked the candy player's spawn point as Claire's dolls slammed the enemy toybox shut. We won.

I sent a quick "Thank you for the game!" message to the opposing team, and they logged off without a word.

I sank back into my chair. "Looks like Mech was right." Come to think of it, we'd barely spoken. Ray and Claire had understood what I was doing, and I'd known how they would follow up.

"That wasn't nearly as hard as I expected. Do we want to go again?" Claire sounded about like me. Satisfied and proud, but not excited.

"I'd be okay with it, but all that really did was put me in the mood for some late night supervillainy," Ray purred incorrigibly over the microphone.

"Not even considering it," I shot back immediately. I wanted to put my foot down on that idea. "I nearly got shot today. We couldn't even damage the dragon, and, if the monster hadn't shown up, Mech would have had us. We need major equipment upgrades before we even consider getting into costume again."

Ray sighed at length. "I wish you weren't right, but of course you are. I had a heart attack when that guard pointed his gun at Claire. At that range, he couldn't miss."

"He wasn't going to fire," Claire scoffed.

Ray corrected her in a firm, serious voice. "He might have. I don't want to face that 'might' again. His odds of hitting Penny were very low, but even that was unacceptable. We need better protection, better planning, and options for dealing with highly damage resistant enemies. Mech isn't the only hero with armor and shields. We've met Chimera and The Apparition. What could we do in a fight against either of them? We work together well, but we need defenses and contingencies." My jaw just about dropped.

I supplied the rest of the bad news. "That won't be happening soon. I have to figure out what we need and find a lot of supplies. I'm close to out, and the scrap from that car wasn't good for much."

"So we need to identify a source of widely varied basic materials that can either be bought cheap or obtained through stealthy villainy. In general big public scenes are fun, but we should be picking specific targets and keeping as low a profile as possible. Trouble will come to us, after all. I think conventional guns are our biggest defensive concern. We can outmaneuver anything more exotic, because there's only likely to be one or two energy weapons or magic swords coming at us at once. Doubling or even tripling up on defenses would be wise. Lightweight armor designed to turn aside one or two lucky strikes? Independent chaff? And of course a few easily portable weapons designed to augment what we can do already to deal with heavily armored opponents or inconvenient walls," Ray speculated.

I was still trying to find my jaw. And here I'd thought he'd gotten totally drunk on wearing a black mask.

"I don't hear game noises. Does that mean you're free to eat supper?" Mom called from the hallway.

"Gotta go, guys," I said, and shut things down as fast as I could.

I slept well and got up nice and lazy. I braided my own pigtails, lingered at my computer checking websites but not logging on anywhere, and then wandered into the kitchen where my parents were halfway through breakfast. I flopped into a chair and examined the plate of scrambled eggs and bacon waiting for me. Everything was still warm, and those yellow bits looked like cheese, and who knew what the white bits were? I was pleased.

My mother made the first move conversationally. "I don't know if you have any friends at other schools, Penny, but The Inscrutable Machine got their wish. Middle schools all over LA have closed for the rest of the semester."

I finished swallowing a forkful of egg before bothering to answer. "It doesn't affect me much either way." Completely true. The attack had been purely a philanthropic gesture.

"I'm with Mech on this, Beebee. I'm convinced that closing down schools was a side effect, or even deliberate cover. I know kids their age won't mind missing school, but there's a deeper plan to The Inscrutable Machine's actions," Dad insisted. He jabbed his fork in the air at her. He was only gesturing, of course, but Mom met the fork halfway with her knife, gave it a twist, and Dad's fork went flying. It landed in the sink behind her with the dirty dishes. Have I mentioned criminals are terrified of my mother?

Dad got the message. He'd finished his plate, so he got up and walked around the table to clear his place. Mom paused between two of her last few bites to counter-argue. "I accept Mech's judgment that they fight like professionals, but they're thirteen. Even assuming they're geniuses, at their age and level of experience, a multi-stage scheme is vanishingly unlikely."

Dad agreed. "You're right. If they're as good as Mech thinks they are, and their attack was as devious as it looked, they're not working alone. An established supervillain is directing them."

Mom swallowed her last bite. "I don't like that at all. That level of ruthlessness would be Spider's hallmark. These children could be as much victims as villains. It would explain a great deal. Equipment. Training."

She got up and put her own dishes into the sink while I chowed down industriously. I liked to think I'd earned the success I'd had so far, but this was plain dumb luck. The other superheroes were pressuring the only one likely to catch us into a wild goose chase.

"Are you and your friends going to need a ride today, Penny? Now would be the time to tell me," Mom inquired, her attention turning to other things.

I thought about it, but my mind was already half made up. "I don't think so, Mom. Being on break is great and all, but I need a day off from being social."

"You'd better call and let them know," she suggested.

Good idea. I wandered back to my room, and checked online. Yep, I was the late riser. I invited another three-way chat.

"Good morning, Your Scienceness. What evil will my dark lady bid me commit today?" Ray greeted immediately.

Actually, it cheesed me off a little. "Today is a no villainy day, Ray. I thought I made that clear."

"No grand villainy, certainly, but we won't be able to simply buy the resources you need. I was hoping a bit of light exploitation of our super powers might be in order." He didn't try to hide how eager he sounded.

That meant I had to say it. I shouldn't have put it off this long anyway. "Don't start that, Ray. I'm really getting worried about how into this you are. If I find out you're committing thefts or something on the side, I don't know what I'll do."

The light, flippant tone disappeared as Ray answered solemnly, "That is exactly why I am not doing anything on the side. I love supervillainy. I've designated you the angel on my shoulder because I don't trust myself."

"Thank you. I think." It was flattering, but what a thing to be told.

Relish crept back into Ray's voice as he went on. "And I, in turn, will be the devil on your shoulder. You need one desperately. We're the youngest supervillain team in history, and our lives have improved too much since we got our powers. We can't turn our backs on that."

Claire reminded us she existed, but still sounded casually unconcerned. "I'm just seizing the day."

"When we find a chance to switch back to being heroes, I'll be right there beside you, Penny. I promise you that. I just don't want to go back to being normal," Ray concluded.

He had a point, although I still wasn't going to seize this particular day for anything but lazing around. "The angel is putting her foot down. No villainy until I figure out the bullet puzzle. I had some—ow!" The idea I'd had yesterday flickered through my head just long enough to be erased by a stabbing pain. Maybe my super power didn't take frustration well. I went on before they could worry. "Dumb headache. Anyway, that means solving the supplies problem and solving it with minimal danger. Preferably no danger."

"About that…" Claire interjected.

Oh, boy. "Yes?" I asked guardedly.

Sounding as sheepish as a Lutra could, which wasn't much, Claire explained. "Well, you know I like to poke around superhero websites online, and I have a couple of identities admitted to be E-Claire, and my mother and Lucyfar see each other all the time, so I've gotten a few hints…"

She was dragging this out. "Yes?" I repeated, trying to tell myself she was being theatrical, not hiding something so scary it made even Claire shy.

No, she sounded too smug. "I've been networking. There are villains who like to point other villains in the direction of valuable targets. I wondered out loud how to get supplies for a mad scientist last night, and a friend of a friend suggested we dig up the Puente Hills landfill. He thought your device that found a jade statue in a middle school could locate any materials you needed in a giant pile of trash."

"There are landfills in LA?" I had to ask. I mean, that thought was just too weird. The city goes on and on and on. Where would you put one? Puente Hills? That was up past Glendale, wasn't it? But not far.

"I should have thought of that. I really should have thought of that," Ray fumed, and he did sound mad, even disgusted with himself. "There's probably nothing you can't find in there if you have a good enough recycler."

I reached automatically to run my fingers over the hard segments of The Machine on my wrist. "I have the most advanced super science recycling machine in the world."

"I can't believe I didn't think of that first. I've been enjoying being the muscle too much," Ray grumped.

"I did prefer the old Ray," I confessed.

"I'll try to be both," he promised. Fair enough. I wouldn't mind keeping the bowing and the hand kissing and the leering charm. Or the sleek black outfit.

I got back to the subject at hand. "All right. It's a good idea, but not today. We've been getting too much attention. We should be nobodies, but the superhero community is really freaked out by how successful we've been. I don't want to run into Mech again."

"Is mining a landfill even illegal? It's trespassing at worst, right?" Claire wondered.

Ray had other worries. "I hope it doesn't look pathetic. I'm enjoying our reputation."

I couldn't help but remember my parents talking over breakfast about a secret plan we didn't have. "All we have to do is make the dig look mysterious. The community will invent an explanation more impressive than anything we could come up with."

Then I let out a sigh and slumped in my chair. "Whatever. It won't be today. I'm going to go take a day off. I'll talk to you guys when I can't take any more relaxing."

I clicked off the mike, started my computer shutting down, and wandered out into the kitchen. As I lifted my feet one at a time to wrench on my shoes and socks, I told Mom, "I'm going to go for a bike ride. I won't be long. I'm not going anywhere, I just want to enjoy the weather." The rains hadn't started yet, so it was pretty nice out there and probably would be for another month.

When I got around the corner of the house I fished the teleport rings out of my pockets and stuck them on under my sweater. I didn't plan on using them; they were just something I felt I should keep handy nowadays. I needed to get a belt pouch. I didn't want a purse, but I was finally carrying too much for pockets.

I climbed onto my regular bike, and went riding down the street. The weather certainly was nice, comfortably cool, and the air refreshed me. Los Feliz had too many trees, so I turned down toward West Hollywood. I didn't have much to do except bike today. I needed a break, but I didn't have any games I wanted much to play alone. Maybe I could read some more Sentient Life when I got back. That still sounded like too much excitement. I wanted to build something. Forget the villainy itself; watching my crazy super power construct some wild new toy was rapidly becoming my favorite hobby.

I was only a street over from my lab now, but of course I didn't have the materials I needed. Wait, I was this close to the lab? I'd biked right down to the school without thinking about it. My taking-a-break skills needed work.

Turning my bike around, I headed back home. A burst of frustration made me pedal fast, and then I might as well keep it up. I raced down the sidewalks at high speed, without many pedestrian obstacles in the middle of the day in this part of town. I made record time and pulled into our driveway just as my legs felt the burn and I began to breathe hard.

That prompted another "Wait, what?" sensation. Even without using the teleport rings, I ought to be exhausted. I slipped inside, didn't see Mom or Dad, and went straight into the bathroom. Yanking up my sweater, I stared at myself in the mirror.

Stomach muscles. Seriously, I had stomach muscles. Me. Not a cut six pack or anything, but my stomach had definition instead of vague roundness. I flexed an arm and got a bicep I could at least identify.

Claire had said it, hadn't she? We'd had a lot more reason to exercise since we got super powers. I was kinda sorta in shape now. I tried to roll that thought around in my head, but "Penny Akk" and "in shape" didn't want to stick. They might have to from now on.

I'd had my ride, so I retreated to my bedroom, shucked the teleport rings into my little-used jewelry box where they'd look like nothing, and flopped down on the bed. Then I flopped right back up, grabbed the stack of Sentient Life graphic novels, and re-re-flopped down to read.

I'd left off at quite a spot. I'd had enough spoilers to know Vera was a computer program, but it was different reading her talking to Delph on his long, lonely trip. Every comment about needing to break to eat or sleep was a lie told by a fake girl afraid of being rejected. He wouldn't, even if she didn't believe that. Nobody but Vera talked to Delph. He was completely expendable to the humans who sent him on this journey. So was Vera, a computer program whose quirks were becoming bugs that might soon get her erased, replaced with a fresh installation that didn't have a personality and wouldn't care about a lonely hybrid dolphin out in the far reaches of nowhere.

I knew how Vera would solve her problem. She was the program, not the computer that contained it. She would move, although I suspected it would be much harder than that when the time came.

I'd only used my power to make hardware, but it seemed ridiculously versatile. It found magic as obvious as any other physical phenomenon.

Would it work on programs? I liked Vera, and that made something stir in the back of my head where my super power told me what to do. I had to let it go. Still no materials.

No materials, and I was trying not to dwell on that lack. I stared over the top of my comic at my statue of The Apparition, hovering in its mirror case next to my computer. I shouldn't love the statue as much as I did. I'd barely met The Apparition. I wasn't a fan. I hardly knew anything about her or her villainous career. She was just so strange. The Apparition was exactly the kind of thing I only heard about before I got super powers.

A knock sounded on the door. "Mom?" I asked. Dad tended to bang, or just yell.

"Penny, honey, would you be okay if Brian and I went out this evening? We'll be leaving around five, and I doubt we'll be back before midnight. The community wants to have a meeting, and at the last minute they decided they have to have Brian Akk and The Audit's input," Mom explained from the other side of the door.

"I don't see why I wouldn't be," I responded.

"I agree. You're not the kind of girl who gets in trouble by herself." She knew I wasn't. Penelope Akk was intelligent, mature, reliable, and had friends who were the worst influences any girl could ask for.

I wouldn't be able to let this go, would I? It was the lack of supplies that really killed me. If I could build an invention or two, clear my inspiration, I'd be able to relax. Until then, this would eat and eat and eat at me.

I heard Mom's voice again, but faint and way down the hall, talking to Dad. I scooped up my phone and sent Claire a text message.

"Maybe tonight after sundown?"

CHAPTER THIRTEEN

ay and Claire met me outside my lab. They would have to wait a minute. I took the elevator down, wrestled my way into my jumpsuit as fast as I could, and grabbed my weapons. Before I hopped in the elevator back up, I scooped some pennies out of the evil statue. As I dropped them into a pocket, it occurred to me that touching them might not have been wise. Eh. Nothing seemed to happen, and I had a hunch the statue was attuned to me—mostly because I'd carried it around for hours but it had affected Claire's Mom in seconds.

As I stepped back out onto the playground and kicked the door shut behind me, Ray asked, "May I try the teleport rings?"

"I thought you didn't want them?" I asked defensively. I'd gotten attached to these rings fast, hadn't I? I slid them off my arms before the argument could go further, and I looked even more selfish and insecure.

When I poured them into his hands, he fastened them around his own forearms and explained, "I can't afford any short cuts. I have to be faster and smarter than my opponent. I only want to try them out. You said they work on muscle energy, and I'd like to see just how far I can push that."

I shrugged, opening my mouth to explain how they worked. As I did, I reached up to tap the activating switch for my light cycle. I finished neither action, because Ray's hand darted out and closed over mine. "I thought a good test would be providing us transportation to our objective."

"That's out on the other side of Glendale!" Did he have any idea just how exhausting the bands were?

Well, no. That was part of his point.

"Okay, fine," I sighed.

"If you ladies will step in close?" Ray leered, his grin almost projecting off his face. You couldn't suspect his motives, because he wasn't bothering to hide them.

Claire tried anyway, of course. "This has nothing to do with teleporting at all, does it?" she teased him as she stepped up next to me. There was just enough space between us for him to duck through, and once behind us he crouched down, scooped his arms up under our thighs, and lifted.

A moment later, I was sitting on his forearm, leaning back and holding onto his shoulder for balance but still as securely held as if me and Claire were a couple of pillows. It was just a tad scary to think what exercise was doing for the already super-strong Ray, given what it had done for me and Claire.

Oh, right. He didn't know how to work them. "They're not thought-operated, but they might as well be. Focus on where you want to go and take a step."

He leaned forward, my view jerked, and we were standing on the sidewalk outside the schoolyard. Well, Ray was standing; we were sitting in his arms. He didn't even need to take a deep breath. Oh, man. These rings really were made for him.

"I believe this will work. If you ladies will hold on tight? As tight as you want, in fact," Ray joked, and then he took a step, and another. Jogging, then lightly running. His gait was all I could keep track of. With each step the world moved, and, since I wasn't aiming, it felt like a badly spliced movie. After the first few teleports, he spaced them out to merely every three steps or so. That gave me enough time to realize we were already heading up Los Feliz.

This operation would take us even further out in the same direction as the last one. If it made a few people less likely to believe we were based at Northeast West Hollywood Middle, that was fine by me.

I could feel Ray's slim body rocking in an even rhythm, hear his deep but steady breaths. Yeah, not even he could handle teleporting like this forever. Maybe he was pacing himself somehow? All I could really do was speculate. I spotted when we left Los Feliz behind and when we crossed over the bridge, but I couldn't keep track of the world flickering around me. I heard a squeaky crunch, and then another before I realized what had changed.

Ray was jumping from car to car now, in traffic, using the rings to jump not to the next car but to one way down the street each time. The densely packed buildings of Glendale danced around us. Cars honked, always behind us. Not many. Maybe for some of these drivers this wasn't the first time a superhero had used the roof of their car as transportation.

Glendale disappeared behind us. Ray leaped between spread out cars on the highway, while desert scrub and thinly spaced businesses appeared and disappeared. He stooped, gave a big jump with both legs, and we landed on a sidewalk by a chain link fence. The fence went on and on and on, lit around the edge, and surrounded a big, dark hill.

This had to be it. Puente Hills landfill. Its treasures would be mine!

Ray set us on our feet, then sat down on his butt. His hands moved unsteadily as he slid the bracelets down his arms and peeled them off. "That was fun, but we will not be doing it again," he chuckled in a theatric wheeze. Personally, I scooped the bracelets up and put them on as fast as possible.

"Do you think the fence is electrified?" Claire asked. It was certainly solid. And tall.

"Why go to this much effort to guard trash?" I asked more rhetorically.

If I was going to be whimsical, Claire could play. "Maybe they get a lot of supervillains stealing materials."

"Health and safety issues," Ray corrected us, rising back to his feet. "No matter what it looks like, it's still a pile of garbage."

It looked like a big crescent hill cut into terraces, with grass all over it. Protected by a fence made of telephone pole sized posts, with twisted iron wires an inch thick. Well, I didn't need any more steel back home, but I hadn't brought any with me either.

Peeling The Machine off my wrist, I gave it a twist to get it started and tossed it onto the fence. "Eat a hole for us to walk through, would you?"

It did. If the fence was electrified I couldn't tell, but if the fence was electrified my baby sucked that all up the way he did the metal wires—eerily like he was eating spaghetti. The Machine doubled, tripled, quadrupled in size, eating faster and faster, until when we walked triumphantly through the gap he looked like a pillbug the size of a large dog.

No way I could lift that. "Carry him up to the top of the hill, Reviled," I commanded. Stepping forward away from Claire and Ray, I studied the dark shape of the hill above me. Blink. Blink. Blink. Blink. Blink. Five steps, each one taking me up a terrace to the top. I stood on the crest, arms folded impatiently, and looked out over the huge misshapen landfill and the lights of the highway. I even managed to keep my knees from buckling underneath me before the aching exhaustion faded. Score one for getting in shape.

My friends weren't going to let me be the only one to show off. Sure, we had no audience but each other, but what kind of supervillains would we be if we didn't keep up the drama? Ray tucked The Machine under one arm and climbed a sheer cliff one handed to the first terrace, then jumped up to the second, grabbed the edge in one hand, and vaulted around onto his feet. He caught up to me in seconds. Claire couldn't match our speed, so she didn't try. She figure skated around the grassy lawn, swooping around in wide arcs, spinning in circles, and winding her way up the hill from behind.

Well, that had been fun. I took The Machine out of Ray's grip with both hands. So heavy! I half-placed and half-dropped it onto the grass. One reminder not to get too cocky. I now had the proportional strength of a mildly fit thirteen-year-old girl.

I pointed at the ground in front of The Machine. "Dig. Separate individual materials and bring them back. Most of it will be variations on wood pulp, and that I don't need. No more than a cubic meter of anything."

"A cubic meter of most anything will weigh over a ton, Bad Penny," Ray cautioned me.

"All right, a half… let's say a ninth of a cubic meter maximum of any material." That would be a little over a foot in each direction, right? I didn't need much more than that of anything I couldn't get easily. Oh, wait. "Get me a full cubic meter of sugar. I'm going to need a lot of that in the near future." Another thought. "Extra metals and plastics you collect can be split up to make mini-Machines to help gather, and a storage silo for whatever you scavenge."

Claire came zipping up. "I like that. If we leave a tower behind, everyone will think we did something nefarious when we'll actually have helped recycle the landfill. This is my kind of villainy."

While she talked, The Machine decided I'd finished giving orders and started to obey. The pillbug shape curled up and dug into the ground like a cartoon gopher, sinking into a hole in the packed but artificial earth.

Ray was rather less enthusiastic. "Not mine. We're robbing a hill in the middle of the night. We could be in for hours of standing around staring at a hole."

"The bigger The Machine is, the faster it works, right? When it comes up, we could feed it a tractor," Claire suggested. She waved a hand at the bottom of the hill, where the cranes and dump trucks and industrial vehicles clustered.

I gave her a slow, amused head shake. "Those have to be tens of thousands of dollars each. I'd feel like an idiot going to this much trouble not to steal my ingredients, then steal a truck to do it."

Ray split the difference. "Maybe some wheelbarrows." Then he contradicted himself. "Or maybe we won't have to."

Why? Because The Machine came back, widening the hole in the process. It had become rather fatter and more multicolored than when it descended. Plates along the surface lifted and slid around, metal rods extended from inside and planted themselves into the ground around the hole.

That wasn't all. A fat mini-Machine like an engorged tick crawled up after. The Machine scooped it up, crunched it in its jaws, and seconds later spat out two sleeker plastic mini-Machines with big digging claws. They scurried right back down the hole.

That wasn't even close to all. While I was still putting words on what to say, another mini-Machine climbed out of the hole, this one metallic. Just like its brothers, my Machine ate it, then spat back out twins. The insides of the Machine churned the whole time, and I saw a small block of copper and a small block of glass laid against an outer metal plate.

A supervillain puts on a show, right? "Any LEDs, light bulbs, and batteries you find down there you can connect to the outside of the tower to light it up." That ought to make a meaningless silo look important!

Another mini-Machine crawled out and got processed into three more diggers. More little blocks set into place around the edge of The Machine.

Yet another mini-Machine emerged, this one a long, crawling metal centipede. My copper block got sucked in, then spat back into place as a finished cube. Three more metal blocks fell into place next to it – zinc, aluminum, and lead I thought. Plates rolled around and extruded. Some sank into the ground. As ordered, my Machine was building me a tower.

I found the process enthralling, but I couldn't blame Ray and Claire for being less entertained. While I watched mini-Machines climb in and out of the hole, watched the tower rise and constantly rearrange, they wandered off. Claire sat on the edge of the cliff and stared out over LA, and Ray walked around the back of the hill.

Their attention at least came back when the first green light lit up on the side of the tower. The Machine was bringing up huge amounts of plastic and metal it didn't need now, and the tower grew much faster than the materials it stored. A red light, then three white lights lit. The cheap materials made for a conical rather than straight tower, all mismatched plates and threaded spirals, but I didn't mind. Even my Dad was going to be completely baffled when the landfill workers found this thing tomorrow morning.

Man, what a lot of plastics. I pulled at a plate of the tower and The Machine opened up obediently to let me examine the collection. That clear block was glass, yes, but the block next to it looked like quartz. Sweet! Just what I needed. The sugar cube had finished already. No surprise there. So many plastics. Who knew there were so many different kinds? How much of this was useless?

I hoped my power did. I leaned against The Machine. "Tell you what. Expand the storage blocks to a foot and a half on each side, but get rid of those plastics." I jabbed my finger at a dozen glossy, polymer blocks. Maybe my super power guided me, or maybe I'd have to go buy a bunch of plastic items later. I could use that bar of silver building up. Wow, a bar of pure silver and another of gold—which made that tiny bar platinum? The bars weren't big or anything, but they made sense. Real silverware, cheap partially gold jewelry—the landfill had to have piles of those, rendered down to valuable forms by my beautiful Machine. I'd need most of those bars as materials, alas. My super power itched looking at the gold, and boy did it like the platinum.

I closed up the tower, and plates rearranged for greater stability. Taking a few steps back, I watched the mini-Machines climb over each other with their loads of plastics, metals, crystals, dusts, liquids in tanks, until a little tiny Machine crawled out holding a thin metal bar with a visible blue glow in the darkness under my erratically lit tower.

A glowing blue metal. I threw myself behind the thickest metal plates of the tower and shrieked, "Eat that now! Put it in the middle of the lead block and carry that into the middle of the original Machine!"

"Are you okay?" Ray called, jogging back toward me.

Yes, unless I had cancer. I should be okay, right? I'd only seen it for seconds. I wasn't that close. My jumpsuit probably shielded me. "I think so," I answered, pushing myself up. "We dug up some uranium. Or it might have been radium. Something radioactive." Radioactive enough to glow. Radioactive enough to glow was bad.

Not to the super power in the back of my head. I had to push away the thought as it tried to expand my anti-bullet design to include uranium elements, and I got a jab of headache for my trouble.

Back on my feet, rubbing the back of my head through my helmet, I was looking right over the edge of the cliff as the girl wearing gray floated up. Gray sweatshirt, gray jogging pants, gray ski mask over her head. I'd never seen a more pathetic imitation of a superhero's costume. Except for one thing. She could fly, which made her more qualified than me, Ray, and Claire put together.

No jet boots or wings, either. She floated like a cloud. A cloud with balled up fists and a monotonously flat voice that explained, "I don't usually give warnings. Give up. I'll give you to the police, they'll give you to the superheroes, and they'll give you to your parents. It will all be over and no one will go to jail."

Ray walked straight toward her, deliberately steady, and answered, "It seems we've inspired new heroes as well as villains."

The girl had been right about not being a talker. She landed on the grass and walked toward him without saying a word. They matched each other pace for pace. They hadn't been that far to begin with, and the distance closed fast. A couple of body lengths apart Ray tensed, but the girl in gray shot forward like a lightning bolt. I don't know if Ray attempted anything fancy, but she slammed into him with her whole body. He went sailing through the air and down the side of the hill out of sight. I heard the thump when he hit.

My heart turned into a knot in my chest at that display of strength, but Claire didn't sound concerned. She sounded gleeful! "Wow. Oh, wow. Flight, super strength, super speed. Are you just starting? You have to be. There's no way you have that much power and I don't recognize you. Did we really inspire you?"

Claire loved those inserts I'd given her. She drifted up on one foot in her lumpy bear costume, arms behind her back, grinning at the girl in gray curiously. I was sure she meant the smile. Her power kept the violence away, and a new superhero was an undiscovered treasure to a fan like her.

"Just give up," the girl in gray grunted.

"Aw, come on. What's your superhero name?" Claire pleaded, head on one side.

I nearly jumped out of my skin when the superhero girl grabbed the neck of Claire's pajamas, threw her down onto the ground, and planted a foot on her back. Even pinned there on her belly with her fists clenched next to her head, I knew Claire's power was working. The gray girl didn't hurt her, just held her down.

Movement flickered off to the side. Ray jumped up a sharp slope, landing on the top of the hill with us again. It took my eyes off Claire, whose power had nailed me, too. I'd just been standing around watching!

I raised my right arm, reached out a foot, and twisted. The girl in gray appeared in front of me. I shot her in the head. She hardly reacted! I'd seen the blast roll over the knit of her mask, but her head barely twitched. Claire had really hit her with the juice. I had enough time as the gray girl's head started to turn to flip the levers on my air conditioner cannon to maximum strength and shoot her again, point blank, right in her ski masked face.

It blew her off her feet. Ray lunged up behind, grabbed her leg, and swung her at The Machine. Claire rolled onto her side and unleashed the static charge she'd built up. Ray let go, and the girl hit the metal tower.

She peeled herself off it. Her sweater and pants didn't want to let go, but she got her hand underneath and levered herself free as quickly and casually as climbing out of a chair. I lost a half-second staring, but what could I have done with the time? I couldn't hit her any harder than I had.

That half-second was useful to her. As soon as she pulled free of the tower, she flew off into the black night sky as suddenly as a darting hummingbird.

Hopping to her feet and skidding a few paces in the process, Claire asked, "Do you think we chased her away?"

That was ridiculous optimism. Ray said as much. "No. She's more experienced than we are, more powerful, and she got that way without my having ever heard of her. She's outmaneuvering us right now." His head turned from side to side, scanning the darkness. I hoped the Serum gave him better senses than me, because outside the tower's patch of light the sky looked featurelessly black.

Our strategy was obvious. I told Ray and Claire, "This isn't worth it. I'll disconnect The Machine. We're getting out of here."

Ray saw the movement before I did, but neither of us in time. Claire let out a squeal as a roll of sod twice the length of a car dropped on her, then three more, burying her in the heap. Floating down to stand on top of the mound of dirt and grass and tarp, the girl in gray asked, "Without your friend with the mind control powers?" She didn't even sound sarcastic. That flat voice might have been testing us, or just exasperated that we hadn't been smart enough to give up yet.

She certainly wasn't stupid. She'd spotted Claire slowing her down and buried the problem in dirt to keep it from happening again. Now she stood on top of the pile where we had no choice but to come to her.

Ray did just that. More cautiously this time, hands in front of him, he walked right up to her. As he set his foot on the first roll of sod they came in arm's reach of each other.

I teleported behind her. I couldn't affect that fight. I was there to bend down and grab one of the rolls, wrap my arms around and pull so hard pain jolted up my arms and down my spine. The sod didn't even budge.

Those few seconds were all the time the fight took. They grabbed for each other, and they moved too fast for me to see everything. Ray must have been faster. I thought I saw him punch her in the stomach, and I did see him twist around to elbow her in the back of the neck. It didn't help. She'd grabbed hold of his shoulder, and his arm raised to block might as well have been a noodle for all it stopped her slapping him across the face. His whole body jerked, and she slapped him again.

Then she turned to me.

I lurched forward, heart cold, barely thinking about it as I teleported to the exact opposite side of The Machine. The girl in gray didn't wait. She zipped around the side of the tower to meet me. I'd been ready for that and teleported behind her, aiming my cannon at her head again.

I meant to keep pulling the trigger until it ran out of power. She'd been ready for me again, and I didn't get the chance. As my arm lifted hers swung around, and she grabbed the barrel of my cannon. The ceramic I'd thought was so durable splintered like eggshell in her grip.

But shattering my cannon left her not holding me. I leaned forward, teleporting around to the other side of The Machine. She'd follow me before I finished a breath, but I only needed time to dive my hand into my pocket. Twisting, I teleported right back behind her again. Yes, she knew I was coming, but the time it took her to turn let me reach up and grab the arm coming at me in both hands.

"Are you done?" she asked me, still no more than tired and annoyed.

I didn't answer. I panted for breath. Too much teleporting. Too much fear.

Her eyes narrowed suspiciously behind the ski mask. "Now you're delaying me. For what?" she demanded. Rhetorically. She wasn't asking me. She jerked her arm out of my grip, and the penny from my pocket stayed stuck to her sleeve. That was something.

Not much. She turned her suspicious stare to my Machine's tower and the mini-Machines still scuttling in and out. Drawing her arm back, she punched a fist through the metal cover and into The Machine's guts.

I screamed. No, I bit down on it, and the shriek of metal covered any noise I made as she ripped the nearest plates off the tower. Her arm had left a twitching hole of shattered cogs and leavers right through The Machine's middle. The twitching didn't stop. He was still moving. Maybe The Machine wasn't dead.

Swinging around, the girl in gray grabbed me by the front of my jumpsuit. It hurt when she lifted me off my feet, but that was the least of my worries now, wasn't it?

"That's it?" she asked me. She sounded disappointed. Sad and disappointed. "You're mining a trash heap. Not for uranium, just for junk. Stop pretending to be a supervillain, Penelope. This isn't a game."

I dangled. I had more important concerns than fighting. She knew me. How? No, that was easy.

I only knew one person with that tired tone of voice, one person who never sounded happy. "Then why are you playing, Claudia?"

She let go. I stumbled and landed on my butt. I saw her streak away into the air out of the corner of my eye, but by the time I could look up she was already gone.

The threat was over. I pushed myself up and ran the two steps forward to plunge my arms into the tower, wrapping it around the damaged mess Claudia left behind. Tears stung in my eyes as I begged, "Please be okay. Please be okay. Put yourself back together. Detach your original self."

Levers and gears twisted in new directions. Bits withdrew. The centipede shape of The Machine crawled out of the mass and up my arm. I sagged back again, cradling it in relief. Maybe he wasn't alive like me, but he was alive and he was mine.

On the other side of the tower, rolls of sod fell away, and Ray helped a very dirty Claire to her feet. A pang of guilt hit me for my priorities, but everyone looked okay, although they leaned against each other as they limped over to me.

Ray sat down on one of the now-motionless mini-Machines. Claire leaned against the remaining shell of the tower.

"Losing is no fun," she informed us. It wasn't really a joke.

I ran my hand over The Machine, making sure it looked and felt completely intact. "We didn't lose."

Ray grunted. "I got my butt handed to me. We weren't ready. Not for a professional with that kind of power."

"We didn't lose," I repeated. "She won the fight, but she left us with the prize."

They stared at me hazily. Ray got it first and turned to look at the tower. I tossed The Machine back into its guts and told it, "We're done here. Gather the mini-Machines and take all the supplies you gathered back to the lab separately. Recycle all the mechanisms inside the tower, but leave the shell intact." Clockwork moved again. The Machine burrowed into the mass.

"Can you two get home safely?" I asked Claire and Ray.

"Sure. I'm not hurt. Just dirty and sore," Claire promised.

Ray stood up slowly. He paused to think before answering. "I don't think I have a concussion. I'll take it easy on the way back, just to be sure."

"Good. We're not going to be outpowered again." I didn't mean to snap, but I must have sounded like it. Turning, I teleported down to the next terrace, then the next, one by one to the ground and then out to the sidewalk. It left my body screaming from the ache, but I cared more about the bilious resentment burning in my guts. That was what made my hand shake as I summoned up my light bike. Throwing myself into the seat, I pumped the pedal and zipped on down the freeway.

I wasn't in police custody right now because of the penny. I was sure of that. I didn't know what it did, but the fight changed the moment I stuck it to her.

That wasn't enough. Not nearly enough. We needed more weapons, better tricks, more force and different ways to attack. Claudia had been good, but we'd been smarter, better organized. There just hadn't been anything we could do with that advantage. Now that our overconfidence had been bruised, we'd be faster to run away when out of our league, but what we really needed was to make sure we were never out of our league ever again.

That was my job. Ray and Claire's powers were incredible, but I was the mad scientist and I gave us the edge. I knew the first thing I wanted to build. It wouldn't have helped against Claudia, but we'd have bullets fired at us a hundred times as often as we'd face anyone with that level of power. I knew what to do about that. I could finally focus on the picture in my head. It wasn't the same as I remembered. It had grown, become more complicated. Wildly complicated.

The headache hit, pain spiking up from the back of my head worse than ever before. The light bike knew how to avoid obstacles. I bowed my head forward and closed my eyes, letting the pain pass.

I opened my eyes to see The Machine spit a sphere of quartz the size of a tennis ball onto the work bench in front of me. The bench? I looked around. I was in my lab. I'd blacked out again. Worse than ever before. My head felt fine now, at least. The picture had disappeared because whatever it was, I'd made it.

New lesson, Penny. My power really, really did not like being frustrated. Pushing this inspiration into the background over and over had forced it to build until it took me over. And now I had this thing, this ball of crystal.

My new weapon was certainly pretty. Cloudy pink painted the interior of the sphere, swirling around delicate traceries of gold. Gold? I looked around. Blocks of raw materials lay all over the place, including the bar of gold. As I watched, a mini-Machine crawled through the air vent and dumped a cube of gooey fat on the floor. Ew. I'd recycled some raw materials I didn't want.

Forget my surroundings. What had I made? Ceramic chips lay scattered around the table, curved in complicated ways. What did they do? I couldn't remember the picture, but I'd been left with the impression they didn't do anything. They were just decoration for the sphere that lit up faintly as I watched.

The glow came from deep within, subtle, really bringing out the pink color. I picked up the sphere, placed it in the middle of the chips, and tapped the crystal surface. Slowly, the ball levitated up off the surface of the table. Bits of ceramic slid across the surface, sucked toward the sphere until they darted up and took their places floating around the ball. Mostly beneath the ball. None of the ceramic tips touched the sphere or each other, but the end result looked like a very artsy foot tall pixie. Those six triangular shapes were wings, for example.

Yes, three of the longer chips lifted as the fairy extended her arm. She drifted over and touched her little hand to the top of The Machine. Then she turned, and I saw for the first time the swirling, black smudge like a pupil where the ball focused. Hovering up to my face, she touched that smooth, tiny hand to my forehead.

I'd created life again. Yes, I'd gotten my toy to stop bullets, but she came with a personality. Oh, boy. The Machine just sat there, but as I straightened up this creation watched me, clearly alive enough to pay attention.

I lifted my own hand and touched a fingertip to her outstretched hand. "I'll call you Vera," I told her.

The sphere turned, looked down at my finger, looked up at my face, and Vera answered with a noise like a faintly chiming, silver bell.

CHAPTER FOURTEEN

I got home around 12:30 a.m. I had to take my regular bike, since the light bike is attached to my supervillain jumpsuit and I sure wasn't taking that home. I couldn't even use my teleport rings—I skipped one intersection and nearly fell off my bicycle. Too tired.

No car in the driveway, and the only lights in the house were the ones I'd left. My parents hadn't gotten home yet. I stumbled into the house and fell into bed. Discomfort made me undress, and a faint ache in my heart made me scoop Vera out of my belt pouch. Apparently, my power could sometimes sacrifice enough dignity to make something simple and practical, because I'd been wearing this pouch when I finished Vera and I certainly hadn't when I started.

I'd put Vera to sleep before I left the lair. Now she was only a pink crystal ball with a white ceramic case. After I unwrapped The Machine from my wrist, I put my arms around them both, curled up tightly in my bed, and fell asleep.

I'm usually eager to get up and about, but, when I woke up the next morning, I just lay there for a while. I didn't even try to go back to sleep. I propped up my pillows against the head of the bed, stared at the daylight outside my bedroom curtains, and petted The Machine with one hand while I rolled Vera around in the other.

What had I made, anyway? As a practical question, I needed to know what she could do. I was not going to lose again, so I needed to know what tools I had at my disposal.

There was another side to that question. A more important side, as reluctant as I was to admit it. What did she want to do?

I put Vera down in my lap and tapped her. "Wake up." Her shell cracked, sliding off into its individual pieces only to be scooped up as she rose into the air. Fairy-shaped again, her glowing, pink head turned until the black pupil faced me.

And that was it. So much for what she wanted. Maybe I'd misread her behavior last night?

Naturally, the moment I thought that, she turned and floated away from me. She hovered over my computer, which beeped and hummed as it abruptly switched on. Okay, that was one thing Vera could do.

She didn't follow up. Instead, she turned and drifted over to my statue of The Apparition. Circling it slowly, her eye darted up and down the illusionary figure in the mirrored case. A detached hand reached out and tapped the case, then tapped again.

I slid out of bed and wandered over as Vera continued to stare. The Apparition floated inside that jar, or at least a convincing duplicate. Transparent, gray, a sad girl in a loose dress. Perhaps a hospital gown? Did she die on-site from what Mourning Dove did to her, or did her life bleed away as doctors struggled to even find a wound?

"Yeah, there's something about her, isn't there?" Vera didn't even turn to look at me. She was hypnotized. I gave her another tap. "Sleep."

She did, dropping slowly down onto my desk as the ceramic parts closed up into a shell. She was easy to turn on and off, at least.

I dropped her on my bed, fastened The Machine back onto my wrist, and went to take my shower and get dressed. It was only when Dad's gizmo was braiding my hair out of my way that I put those thoughts together. I'd showered wearing The Machine. Had I been doing that for days now?

I stepped out to meet my parents. Dad was in his office. A timer dinged, and Mom slid some eggs and bacon and toast onto the table, but I walked in to see what Dad was doing first.

His office computer was covered in photos and diagrams of the tower I'd left in the landfill. Of course.

Might as well find out. "What's that?" I asked him.

"I'm not sure. Passersby reported lights in the Puente Hills Landfill last night. Police were worried it might be dangerous, but Echo sent me every scan and measurement he could think of, and as far as I can tell it's exactly what it looks like—a big patchwork tube with lights stuck on." He clicked between a few windows to show me the empty interior and the bands of different materials.

From the kitchen Mom called out, "The tower is a distraction, made out of refuse from the dig. The tunnels are the important clue. Someone with access to nonstandard technology went searching through that landfill. They knew something was there, and we may never find out what it was because they took it and got out."

I wandered back into the kitchen, sat down at the table, and dug into my breakfast as Dad shouted back, "So you think it's another hit by The Inscrutable Machine."

Mom set a glass of milk in front of me and walked over to the doorway of Dad's office so she wouldn't have to shout quite so loud. "It fits their current MO. They like attention, and it's only bad luck no superhero saw the tower. They've already gathered one artifact no one else knew existed. They were seen in the area, as were robots like the ones at the monster attack. However, the tower doesn't match the technology they've shown off already. It's too crude."

Well, yeah. The Machine built it, not me. He wasn't exactly a genius, he just made a tube out of garbage like I told him to.

"It doesn't match anything I'm aware of," Dad replied. "A stiff wind and the tube will collapse under its own weight, yet it's built out of seamlessly refined materials from the dump."

Mom disappeared into Dad's office, but I could still hear her. "I'm not actually sure The Inscrutable Machine were directly involved here. The odds lean to their being used as a cover by whoever sent them after the first artifact."

"But you're certain the crimes are connected," Dad said.

"Enough that I would act on that hypothesis if I were professionally involved. It would be difficult. Without knowing what was found at this dig site, we can't guess what they're going to be used for."

I got up, put my dirty dishes in the sink, and circled back to my room to pick up my new belt pouch and scoop Vera and the teleport rings into it. "I'm going out!" I yelled as I headed for the door.

Mom stepped out of Dad's office right in my way. She sounded friendly enough as she asked, "Going to meet Claire and Ray again?"

I shook my head as I swerved around her and opened up the door. "Going to the clubhouse. I'm so close. I know I can get another spark. Anyway, I think Claire and Ray will be off together somewhere." I was surprised by my own vehemence. It was fully fledged supervillainy that I felt I almost had in my grasp, but the frustration felt the same.

Mom brushed her hand over my head, fingers toying through my bangs. I wasn't looking at her, but I could feel the cheerful affection as she told me, "I learned this as a superhero, Penny, but it proved just as true in my personal life. The person who cares enough to work for what they want, who both thinks and acts and doesn't hesitate? She's the one who wins."

I nodded. "Yeah." Good advice. Stepping out and closing the door behind me, I circled around the house to get my bicycle. Mom was absolutely right. I wasn't going to stumble into trouble again. I would do this right.

First I needed to prepare, so I got on my bike and headed down to my lab.

What did I need? I pedaled industriously down Los Feliz and tried to figure it out. I'd built my most important group defense, and I had a personal defense in the rings, but I needed more. A surprise defense, maybe. Something for emergencies. I did have okay defenses. I was out of weapons. We all needed weapons. Claire's sticky gloves were useful, but not enough against professionals. What would we do if we ran up against a heavy hitter like Bull or Mech? We needed the option of more raw physical force than we had. Simple impacts wouldn't do it. We needed different kinds of attacks. Shock-based attacks against the armored, heat attacks against unliving targets, something to remove walls that might be armored themselves, area effect attacks, distractions, and especially nonlethal attacks to take fragile human enemies out of the fight.

I was never going to remember all that. It wouldn't matter. I'd make everything I could think of, then figure out what I was still missing.

I passed by the cool side entrance, the one that looked like a manhole cover. My bike wouldn't really fit. So I took the elevator down to the lab, ditched my bike in a side room, and pulled on my jumpsuit as fast as I could. I needed to get to work. Which meant first I had to think, so I dumped Vera and The Machine on my bench, activated them both, and asked the obvious question.

What first? Start with the most glaring lack. I'd lost my air conditioner cannon. I needed a basic, obvious weapon to replace it. A candy chainsaw would be cool, but useless. There was no way easily breakable little me was relying on close-in attacks. Still, I liked the candy theme. It would be great to tie everything together.

I could see possibilities with candy. I'd brought back a lot of sugar. Of course, not all the parts would be candy. I pointed at a block of red plastic and ordered, "Vera, cut me off this thick a slice of that plastic."

I pinched my fingers to show how thick I wanted it, and Vera flew over to the slab. Awesome. She'd understood. I pulled levers on the smelter, got it fashioning some curved glass for me, then took the plastic from Vera and used The Machine to cut it more precisely.

Eventually, Ray's hand settled on my shoulder, shocking me out of my building trance. "I think you've built enough," he said quietly.

I turned around and leaned against the metal folding bench, taking a few deep breaths. Tired, but not too bad. I hadn't entirely blacked out either. I could sorta remember all the work I'd done, just… "You're right. I got a little carried away." Tidy the mad scientist wasn't. My new toys were scattered across the floor around me.

"We could tell. By the maniacal laughter," Claire informed me. She was standing halfway across the room in civvies, arms folded. Her faint smile seemed torn about whether or not she'd been joking.

I just had to grin. I pointed at the gloves I'd left hanging from a hook on the wall. Vera zoomed over, picked them up, and brought them back to me. They were gorgeous, black and satiny with thin, oval amber crystals set into the palms. They were too big for my hands, of course. I tossed them over to Ray. "Try those out and tell me you don't feel like laughing."

Ray's eyes lit up with fascination, slipping on the gloves and turning them over several times to study from all angles. "How do they work?"

"Click the gems together," I answered.

He did. Claire giggled a bit, which meant she noticed the different way he moved afterward. "Interesting. They're dragging at my hands. Drawing power for something?" Ray asked. He swung his hands up and down, putting a little more effort into it. I couldn't tell the gloves were impeding him anymore, which was good. I didn't actually want to slow him down.

"Click them again, pull apart slowly, and push," I ordered.

He gently smacked his palms together again. When he pulled them apart, purple beams arced and twisted between the two gems, and, in two seconds, they'd formed a glowing ball suspended between his palms. Leaning forward, he angled his hands out and gave the ball a shove. That sent it rocketing away from him... straight at Vera.

Vera moved fast, her own ceramic hands coming together just like Ray's. A pink burst of light hit the energy ball, and a hot wind blasted across us as the two attacks detonated each other.

I decided to pretend I knew that could happen. "This is Vera. She's mainly a defensive design, but as you can see she has offensive capabilities."

Claire took a sharp step forward, hands clasped together and grinning as big as her face could hold. "Do I get anything?"

I gave my back a stretch, trying to push aside the still alluring pictures in that wordless, more-than-human part of my brain. "Not yet. You get a task. Check with your contacts and find us a job. A real job, but something I won't feel too guilty about."

Claire nodded, her smile sly and knowing now, rubbing a finger along her lower lip. "I know someone who's just aching to give us suggestions like that. While I'm at it, want me to sell some of that gold?"

That caught me off-guard. I looked over at the block of gold, much smaller than the jars and slabs and blocks of rough crystals. "It's not that big, and I need some for my work." That thought bounced off the thing in my brain. "I guess I don't need much," I amended. Which left me with only one answer. "Okay, I guess. Some of it. If you think that little gold is worth something."

Ray stepped over and snapped the bar in two in his hands. Show off. I walked past him into the other room and changed back into my regular clothes.

I could hear Ray out in the lab clearly. "I believe that I know where to start. This isn't technically stolen and it's raw, pure gold. A pawn shop that thinks he's ripping us off won't be too eager to ask questions."

"All the fences are downtown, near Chinatown. I could go home and get addresses. It would be too clunky on my phone," was Claire's contribution.

I clasped The Machine around my wrist and dropped Vera in my belt pouch and walked my bike out past them as Ray dropped the chunk of gold in Claire's hand. Her eyebrows went up. "How can it be this heavy?" she protested, but she was just being theatrical. She obviously wasn't straining or anything.

"I'm going home. Don't touch my toys—you'll see what they do soon enough," I called back as the elevator gate shut.

Then I did go home.

I had to take it a lot easier on the way back. My first few building sprees had wrecked me. This one hadn't been so bad, but I didn't have the energy to pedal hard. I certainly wasn't going to speed things up with the teleport rings. That might have been fortunate. When I biked up to home, Dad was standing out front talking to a woman.

Brown hair, decent looks, college age, maybe a little older, and a very in-shape figure. She was giving my dad one very friendly smile, but it would be physically impossible to cheat on my Mom. No, the figure gave it away. She had to be a superheroine.

As I wheeled up, Dad asked her, "So what's your take? What do we do when middle schoolers start getting into this life?"

Her grin didn't waver. Maybe it got a little sly. "My 'take' is that The Inscrutable Machine is the least important issue we have to worry about right now. Either they've got what it takes to be supervillains, or they don't and they'll get caught. I'd rather know if cloning technology has finally been perfected."

We had what it took to be supervillains. I would make sure of that. Criminy, listen to me. I needed to relax. I didn't get to meet many heroines in person. Let's see, brown hair, that expression and build…

I parked my bike and walked up to the two of them. "You're Marvelous, right?"

"I don't like to brag." She deserved to be smug. I'd walked right into that.

Dad put his hand on my head. "This is my daughter, Penny."

Marvelous looked me over and gave a little wiggle of her fingers. "If you're still wondering who I am… lift!" Except the word wasn't "lift." It had an odd rhythm, and a singsongy tone like Chinese. When everything got really light and I floated a couple of feet into the air, I couldn't help but hear that funny word as "lift" anyway.

I giggled. Being levitated broke the ice pretty well.

I warned her, "You don't want my Dad thinking you're a bad influence by exposing me to magic."

We both looked at Dad. We both cracked up. He was trying so hard to look like he wasn't bothered that his daughter believed in magic. It was really, really easy to laugh. Levitation made me feel like all the weights of the world had been removed. I curled up my legs and folded my arms in my lap, since they didn't float quite as well.

"It's nice to actually get to meet you, Penny. As something more than a pair of pigtails in the next room, I mean," Marvelous told me, extending her hand.

I shook it. "It's a little more personal now I've got powers of my own."

That lit her eyes back up. "Oh, yeah. I heard we know for sure you're inheriting the Akk Brain."

Dad warned, "Don't get her started. My little princess is impatient enough as it is."

"Five bucks," I chirped. Hey, I needed the money now that I'd blown the thousand from Cybermancer.

Marvelous nodded, giving me a more sympathetic and slightly more serious look. "Yeah, I know how that is. At your age I could cast *one* spell even close to reliably, and it drove me crazy that it took four more years of study to have enough powers to join the community."

And, at that, the weirdest question popped into my head. I just had to know. "Did you really wear that costume? With the boots and the… black leather?"

That got a loud, long laugh. "And not much of it? Mmm-hmm."

I gaped at her. "Seriously?"

She nodded. "Oh, yeah. When you turn eighteen, it will make complete sense." Then she busted out laughing again. "Oh god, Brian. You should see your face!"

I couldn't stop grinning. If Dad's failed attempt to look unconcerned wasn't funny enough, I was floating in midair talking costumes with a famous superheroine.

I tried to get serious. I leaned forward, crossed my arms over my knees and asked, "Isn't a costume like that asking for trouble?"

Marvelous's eyes shut tight, and she ducked her head down as she wrestled to force down the laughter. "She's going to wear what she's going to wear, Brainy," Marvelous wheezed.

I didn't think Dad's stiff expression was *that* funny. Taking a deep breath, Marvelous straightened up and answered me mostly seriously. "It wasn't a big deal. Believe it or not, most of the supervillains were real gentlemen, and the banter made some tense fights much less scary. The villains who weren't gentlemen... well, nobody wants to get Judgment and Winnow's attention."

"Nobody wants to go back to the seventies," inserted my father, scowling hard.

That got a more solemn nod from Marvelous. The joking seemed to be over. "I switched costumes because of civilians, not villains. The new outfit's still not exactly modest, but the bystanders don't act like pigs anymore."

Fair enough. Another question loaded itself right onto my tongue. "You know about dragons, right? I saw one on TV, but it turned into a really ugly monster when it attacked Mech."

"Big misconception," she answered me immediately, giving her hair a theatrical toss. She'd obviously had to say this before. "Many monsters disguise themselves as dragons. Real dragons are very rare. They're the guardians of the magic of the Earth, created by that magic before enough humans came around to drain it. They are ancient, wise, and powerful, the whole deal."

"I'm not sure I'd give them 'wise,'" Dad interrupted, "'Scheming,' maybe, or 'vicious.' I've only seen a dragon do three things—sleep, decide if it wants to kill you, and try to kill you."

Marvelous chuckled. "I didn't say they were fond of humanity."

"How many have you met?" I knew I wasn't going to get an answer when my weight returned and I settled gently down onto my feet again.

Marvelous winked at me. "I promise to tell you some stories later. I'll even introduce you to one when you become a superhero. For now, I gotta go."

"Okay, but I'm holding you to that," I insisted. By the time I was old enough to officially join the superheroes, I might figure out how to change sides.

"Later, Brian! Great to meet you, Penny!" Marvelous called back over her shoulder, walking off toward what was presumably her car. I dragged myself inside, feeling all heavy and tired again now that I wasn't floating.

The evening passed somehow. Nothing that happened had to do with supervillainy, and I didn't care. I wasn't really interested until the next morning. I felt like lying around in bed again. I grabbed the pile of mechanical pencils I'd never thrown away or filled with new lead. One by one, I fed them into The Machine lying in my lap. While he added new scales made of plastic padded with eraser on the inside, Vera explored my room.

That consisted of hovering from object to object, staring at them and occasionally touching one. She had initiative, which The Machine didn't. That was something. She'd taken orders yesterday. The next logical step was to try to communicate.

"What are you looking at?" I called over as she peered at the books on my bookshelf.

Her head swiveled around all the way until her murky black pupil faced me, then turned back to the bookshelf. Absolute communications failure.

"Is there something you particularly like?" I tried. She'd spent more time staring at my statue of The Apparition than anything else, so the answer should be obvious. Again, she turned her head to look at me. This time the rest of her body rearranged to face me as well.

But that was it. No go.

"Go over there," I ordered, pointing at my computer. She floated obediently over.

"Go into the closet," I tried next. No pointing. She seemed to understand closet. She squeezed her small body through the gap of the mostly closed door without opening it further.

Okay, next test. "Open the door." She pushed the door all the way open gently. Actually, that could have gone really wrong, couldn't it? But it hadn't. Deliberate understanding of context on her part? Maybe Vera was naturally gentle?

She obeyed well and had a good grasp of English. Exasperated, I waved a mechanical pencil around and demanded, "Can't you talk to me?"

And she did, kind of. Vera responded with a few quiet bell ringing sounds. That was something.

"I just don't know what that means."

She replied with one high-pitched chime.

I lost a little more patience. "Talk to me in English!"

"Talk to me in English!" my voice ordered from my computer's speakers, and my alarm clock, and my phone, and my disconnected headphones lying on my dresser. I heard more echoes of my voice from the rest of the house.

Oops.

I leaped out of bed, grabbed Vera by her head, whispered, "Sleep," as I tapped it, and dumped her in a desk drawer out of sight all on the way to my bedroom door. Wrenching the door open, I yelled out, "Sorry! I did that! I think. I don't know how." I really hoped my panic sounded like frustration.

Dad stepped out of his office, grinning as he walked up the hall to meet me. "You're trying too hard, Pumpkin. It's great that you can make anything happen, but irreproducible accident after irreproducible accident will only make waiting harder."

I gritted my teeth. "It bugs me to fail when I feel like I can do this, Dad!" That was the truth, and I didn't have to fake the anger in my voice. I just wasn't talking about inventing.

Dad sighed. He did the hair-ruffling thing, taking advantage of one of the few chances to get at my hair before I'd tied it down in braids. My hair rewarded him by frizzing out like a dandelion puff. "Well, you'll have plenty of time to learn I'm right. Listen, Pumpkin, will you be okay here alone if your Mom and I go on a trip?"

What?

"What?" I repeated out loud.

His hand stayed on my head and he looked downright guilty as he explained. "Your Mom and I have been invited to a conference. We can't bring you along, but we can cancel. It's a situation where we don't have to go, but we should go."

214

Dad and Mom invited to a conference. "This is a superhero conference we're talking about?" I guessed.

"A few supervillains will demand to attend. Spider will send a representative. It ensures no one takes advantage of half the superheroes in the country leaving their posts," Dad confirmed.

I asked the real question. "For how long?"

Mom stepped out of the bedroom carrying a suitcase, and The Audit answered me. "At least one week, no longer than two. We'll be down in San Diego, and if you need us all you have to do is call. It's close enough we'll drop by every couple of days."

"Call me and let me know when you do," I warned. Ouch. I couldn't have sounded more defensive there if I'd tacked on "I might be robbing a bank."

I was saved by parents hearing what they want to hear. Dad just sounded relieved as he asked, "So you don't mind, Pumpkin? Beebee and I feel like older, cooler heads are required this time around. People who don't fight every day."

I felt a twinge of anxiety. "Is the community that freaked out about The Inscrutable Machine?"

"Only a couple of people. Like your mother," Dad delivered, completely deadpan.

"And I have to go because everyone listens when The Audit speaks, but only The Audit listens when Brian Akk speaks," Mom shot back from the kitchen.

Dad choked on a laugh and fixed his gaze on me again. "The community has been putting off a meeting like this for too long. The Inscrutable Machine was merely the last straw that made them schedule a meeting now. We'll spend six hours deciding whether to send them back to their parents or to the courts when they're caught, and another week and a half talking about territory, nonhuman threats, scary rumors, and whether the silence means Winnow and Judgment have finally killed each other."

I tried to sound casual. Mom wouldn't buy it, but she'd blame it on my being thirteen. "As long as there's food in the house, I'll be fine. I hope a conference of superheroes is as much fun as it sounds."

"We'll keep in touch," Dad promised, stepping away from me.

Mom met him at the door of their bedroom and handed him another suitcase. They started to walk toward the door. Wait, they were leaving right now? I mean, not that that was a bad thing, but…

Maybe I wanted to slow them down. Maybe it had just nagged at me. A question leaped to my lips. "Dad, are The Inscrutable Machine the only active super powers my age? I saw this girl flying down the street wearing gray. I can't even call it a costume."

That stopped them both in their tracks. Okay, I'd hit a nerve. Dad's worried look confirmed it, and the guarded way he asked, "When did you see her?"

No choice. I had to risk a flat-out lie. "Yesterday, while I was biking up Los Feliz."

Mom answered for him. She had a scary poker face, but sounded pretty casual. "The community calls her Generic Girl, because she's never identified herself. She's been an active superhero for nearly a year. The public doesn't know she exists."

"How'd she pull that off?" I had to ask.

Dad didn't have Mom's poker face. He pinched up his nose, looking really uncomfortable, then sagged. "She doesn't grandstand. She doesn't even talk. She stopped a crime yesterday, and you saw her on the way there. Or back."

I gave him an expectant look. Grudgingly, he kept on. "Yesterday, Chimera came back. He's missing four decades and half his memories, but it's him. We're sure of it. He hit a bank just to get his name out. The public hasn't found out because he'd knocked out one security guard when Generic Girl walked in the front door. Seconds later—"

"Fifteen seconds. I timed the security footage," Mom inserted.

"—she walked out and flew away. Chimera was unconscious and taken into custody. Being Chimera, he may have escaped already. He had enough powers in his first incarnation to keep a few secret for emergencies."

"So, really, Chimera? Because to beat him unconscious in fifteen seconds…" I trailed off, leaving the question hanging.

"That's how strong she is, and how fast, and how ruthless. Most criminals we think she took down never know what hit them," Dad confirmed.

"Wow." That was all I could say, at least to my parents. I'd escaped disaster by a hair's breadth on that landfill. A hair's breadth and a magic coin. This was the standard I had to match next time.

Mom still looked cold, but sounded like she was trying to be gentle. "The community will spend more time discussing her than The Inscrutable Machine. They removed our last excuse to pretend she doesn't exist."

I tried to pull on a pigtail and had to brush back a pile of messy hair instead. "This conference is sounding less fun by the minute."

Finally, Mom smiled, the last traces of The Audit being replaced by my mother. "We wouldn't leave you if there weren't serious issues to discuss, but it is still a bit of a party."

I tried to match her smile. It wasn't easy, after hearing all that! "Then... have fun?"

My parents picked up their bags. Dad opened the door, Mom stepped out first, and just before Dad closed it behind the both of them he called back, "We'll call!"

And then the door closed. I was alone for at least a week.

This could not possibly be more convenient.

Claire's unnamed contact had better have a job ready.

I pulled up next to the warehouse in Santa Monica. I could almost see the ocean from here, that line opposite the mountains where the buildings ended. Claire's source had better be right. If our target wasn't here— actually, that was the great part. Someone would make up what we'd come here for.

But, for me, that wasn't enough. I wanted to do things right.

Ray landed heavily on the pavement, legs bent in an elegant crouch despite the thump. I glanced up the way he'd come. He'd jumped off a light pole. Claire leaped over a fence in an alley, spun as she landed on her frictionless bear feet, and slid across the street to a neat stop on the other side of me. I stepped off my light bike and let it disappear. Sightseeing time had ended.

The fence in front of us was rather higher than the one Claire had jumped, and topped by barbed wire.

"The Machine?" Claire suggested.

I shook my head, thumbing three pills out of the canister on my belt. "It would take too long. Reviled, this fence is in my way."

Ray flashed his wickedly too-wide grin. Stepping forward, he grabbed two fistfuls of chain, twisted his body, and yanked. Metal screeched. The chain link tore off its frame, hanging close enough to the ground to walk over. As he turned that grin back to me, I flicked one of the pills at him and another at Claire. In identical motions, their Serum-enhanced reflexes grabbed the pills out of the air.

"Swallow. Those will keep my toys off of you." I took my own advice, tossing the pill into my mouth and swallowing it dry. It disintegrated anyway and tasted like sugar. Which it was. Mostly.

We stomped over the clanking ruins of the fence, making for a small metal door in the side of this big concrete building. Ray stepped ahead of us as we reached it, reared back, and kicked. The door snapped off its hinges and tumbled into the warehouse.

Bowing regally, he held out his arm toward the empty doorway. "Ladies first, of course."

We couldn't hear them, but somewhere alarms had to be screaming. So, as I stepped over the threshold, I glanced up at Vera and said, "Just like we practiced."

Every PA speaker in the building rang out with rhythmic, chanted words. The drum beat started up, then the main singer and keyboard. I couldn't understand a single word. I'd chosen electro-swing to override every recording and broadcasting system in the area this afternoon, and a few distant honks suggested the cars on the road were enjoying the tune as well.

We walked out into the middle of the warehouse, and it looked exactly like I'd expected. Those doors down there might be side offices, but mainly the building consisted of one big, empty room. Not quite empty, of course. It had its stacks of wooden crates, piled up bags, and a pair of huge metal shipping containers. A lot of places to hide our prize.

Claire leaned in. "How will we find it?"

"It will be well protected." That much I could rely on.

My heart beat in time with the incomprehensible gibberish from the speakers. My feet carried the rhythm as I stepped away from my partners to lead by example. Snapping the sparkly pink wand out of the sugar tank at my side, I twisted the dial to "knife" and used the thin, ultra-high-pressure spray to cut a door in the side of the nearest shipping container. The sliced-out rectangle fell inward, its gong blotting out the music when it hit the container's flooring. I peeked inside and saw a giant, empty box.

Ray had reached the stacks of wooden crates. One by one, he ripped the lids off, nails and all. Claire swooped in behind him, throwing out straw as she examined the contents.

As I walked over to join them, Claire lifted up a fistful of circuit boards and a teddy bear, the mechanical talking kind. Her voice squeaked with enthusiasm as she asked, "Hey, can I have an army of these?"

Not a bad idea. "Yes. Later."

Nails screeched and wood cracked as Ray pulled off another crate lid. I saw more straw and more teddy bears inside. His black-masked face turned to us impatiently. "We need to do this faster. It has to have a radiation signature. Do you have anything that could detect that?"

"Maybe," I answered. I just might. I reached up and tapped a little ceramic wing. "Vera. Can you find energy sources in this room?"

Her crystal ball head turned to look at me. Within the pink, gold lines pulsed in time with the music she was using to jam the airwaves. Would this work? She turned and floated away from me. She detected something, and she'd been smart enough to know I didn't mean any of the energy sources we were carrying. Would she lead me to a box of teddy-bear batteries?

No. She hovered over to a fire hose box against the wall, pointed a ceramic hand at it, and a bell chime interrupted the music for a brief second. HA! Good girl!

Ray stepped forward again, but I smacked his shoulder with my wand. "Not so fast, Reviled. This stuff will be protected by magic. Bet on it."

I had an answer to that, too. An answer that had hung strangely heavy when Marvelous's levitation spell made the rest of my body so light. Unbuckling The Machine, I pressed him against the lid of the fire box and ordered, "Eat our way in."

The Machine did, adding red plates to its surface and around its jaws accompanied by the noisy grinding of abused metal. It took only seconds of chewing before the growing hole in the lid revealed a lacquered green wooden box covered in glowing red symbols. That would be our baby.

The Machine ate faster as its jaws grew, munching away at the firebox lid like a caterpillar until his jaws latched onto the surface of the box instead. He went to work on that, and, as he bit into the first symbol, it winked out. Biting into the second sent a rippling flash through the symbols, and then they all died. The Machine had set off whatever protective spell guarded the case and eaten it like he ate all energy.

I let him keep eating, through the wood and the padding lining the inside and the velvet cover of the padding, until there it was. Nestled snugly in this magic box lay a dusty glass and wire gold bottle, or maybe a pitcher, with a bulbous body and fluted neck, a spout sealed with wax, and a slender golden handle. The dark red goo inside looked like what it was—blood.

A bang and a yell of pain sounded from the next pile of crates. I looked over to see a man in a suit cradling one hand as he dropped a ruptured pistol onto the concrete floor.

I sighed with disappointment. "Vera, you can do better than that." As I looked up at her, she looked down at me. Pink light flashed, a pulse that burst out of her crystal globe and washed over me, through me, over and through everyone, and out through the walls. I definitely made out screeching tires and a mess of honking through the pumping music and warehouse walls. If I had to guess, a bunch of gas tanks now contained inert, fatty sludge instead of gasoline. Vera was just full of surprises, wasn't she?

I also heard a click, and then a number of other clicks. Past the first fool with the bleeding hand, a dozen neatly dressed men pointed guns at us over crates, pulling the triggers repeatedly. They had to hope, but there was no point. Bullets full of the degraded slime Vera left behind wouldn't fire.

I tilted my head to one side and asked with all the casual sarcasm I could slather onto the words, "Opening fire on little kids? You mob types do play rough, don't you?"

They were tough guys, although it might have helped that between me, Ray, and Claire, none of us topped five feet. One of them dropped his gun and pulled out a pair of handcuffs, stepping out from behind the crate and advancing toward us. His friends were only slightly less brave, but much less polite. They pulled knives, two heavy metal batons, and one fire axe. Charming.

Not that I blamed them. "Yes, yes. We did break in, and we have super powers. You're just doing your job. I'll try not to hurt you." As I made with the banter I pressed a lever on my sugar tank three times, spitting out three big chunks of rock candy into my palm. Then I tossed them onto the floor between us and the thugs.

I couldn't help it. "HA! HA HA! AH HA HA HA HA HA!" I laughed as the lumps of sugar knifed up into stalagmites, charging across the floor in splintering waves to crash into the mobsters in rippling waves. Digging into a pocket, I tossed out a heavy handful of metal jacks and a rubber ball. The jacks rolled across the floor, getting under feet as the ball darted and bounced, slamming into thugs with enough force to knock a large man down. Which was what happened.

No need to heap abuse on the fallen. I twisted the dial on my tank, raised my wand, and squirted sugar onto each fallen mobster. The gray crystal coating crawled up their bodies, freezing them in place and gluing each one down.

That worked right up until a masked man in brown and red padded armor stepped out from behind the other shipping crate. The rock candy roared off at him in a storm of crunching sounds. As a sharp stalagmite jabbed up under his feet, he walked over it like a stepping stone. It swung back, and he set his foot on the rising spike again, riding it forward several steps and then stepping off as the sugary spikes swerved aside.

"You're Witch Hunter, right?" Claire piped up, skating back out into the middle of the warehouse floor. Mask. Expert reflexes. At least two swords strapped to his back, and hilts of other weapons. We had an official supervillain enforcer here! I didn't know him, but obviously Claire did.

Ray walked out onto the floor as well. "May I?" he asked me and Claire.

"We're in a hurry," I warned him.

He gave me a slyly sweet grin. "Please?"

Witch Hunter drew those two swords, slender and elaborately engraved. He kept walking, and Ray stepped between him and me. Claire lounged against a still-sealed wooden crate, and I looked deliberately away from her. I suspected she was waiting to see if she needed to intervene.

Even given Ray's powers, two swords seemed a bit much. A lot much. I pulled a candy cane out of its slot and tossed it toward him. By the time it landed in his outstretched hand, it had grown to nearly his height. That would help.

Witch Hunter spoke for the first time, calm and professional. "I can't promise not to kill you, boy."

Ray held the candy cane loosely. I knew he must be humming with excitement, but he sounded quite calm himself as he answered, "Then I have to be better than you."

Swords darted, stabbing. Stabbing? Yes, stabbing. The hook of the cane got in the way, pulling at them, but the second sword dove down to cut at Ray's midsection and he jumped a step back. I took a step back, too, and then several more. They might be all over the place. I saw my jacks skitter on the other side of the pile of imprisoned thugs and held up a hand. Ray wanted to do this himself, and I wouldn't intervene until he lost.

Which might be too late. Witch Hunter was clearly winning. Blades cut and jabbed in quick, economical strokes. Ray had to keep backing up, circling. Every time he blocked something a new attack followed. Only insane reflexes were keeping him alive. At least, that's what I thought I was seeing. It mostly looked like an expert chef cutting vegetables, with the blades flashing again and again and again.

Ray hooked one of the blades, and the other sword sliced down the cane at Ray's hands. When he let go, Witch Hunter threw the cane across to the edge of a shipping container and kicked. The kick didn't land. Ray rolled backwards out of range, tumbling like a ball back to the candy cane and uncurling with it in his hand.

Witch Hunter didn't chase Ray. Instead, he pulled out a knife, swung around and threw it straight at me – no, at Vera.

I didn't have time to do anything. The knife whistled at us, and Vera's hands came together and a pink flash melted the knife into goo, which smoked and glowed when it hit the floor.

My heart started beating again, which hurt. It had even happened too fast for me to be afraid.

Witch Hunter was entirely too smart. Maybe he'd seen Vera deactivate all the guns and thought killing her would reverse the process. Whatever, his plan had failed, and now Ray advanced on him with fast, implacable footsteps. Right up until he came within sword range, and then the dance started over.

Nothing seemed to have changed. Ray might have looked determined, but no sooner did they engage than Witch Hunter had him backing up again.

Then Ray smacked him in the temple with the butt of his cane. The cane swiveled back the other way, and the hook hit Witch Hunter on the other side of his head. He dropped onto his knees, then onto his side. Both swords clattered and rolled away.

Still, the enforcer twisted around and braced one hand against the floor, pushing back up to his knees. Claire gave him some very good advice. "You really ought to just stay down." He glanced over at her gentle, concerned smile.

I decided this was over and sprayed him with my sugar wand. I sprayed him for several seconds, up and down his body. He stopped moving, frozen in place by an inch-thick layer of hardened candy. He wasn't going anywhere.

Claire pushed herself up from the crate she'd been leaning against and dusted off her gloved hands. "Well, now that that's over with, why do you think this box is so much better sealed than the others?"

She was right, now that I gave it a better look. The other crates had straw poking through cracks and nails jutting out in some places. This one might have been glued shut. That didn't do it much good when Ray ripped the top off, but it did roar much louder and the top broke in half from the force. Inside was more straw, of course, and under that a plastic wrapper packing together big bags of white powder.

White powder. Oh, my. Claire said it for me. "Cocaine?"

"Could be heroin. That can come as a white powder," Ray offered.

He scowled, and after a moment's thought added another opinion. "Whatever drug it is, I'd rather not leave it here. Burning it would be dangerous. Can The Machine destroy it?"

I glanced at my wrist. The Machine lay there, coiled like a bracelet. I'd reattached him at the first gunshot by sheer habit.

He'd spit out the bits of firebox somewhere, which meant he'd gone back to normal size, which meant it would take too long. "Ignore it. The police will be here soon, and, when they see this, everyone will be too busy to worry about what The Inscrutable Machine might have stolen."

"You're right. All I have to do is keep you here until they arrive," a boy's voice announced over the still-thumping music. Ifrit stepped through the empty doorway we'd used to enter the building. I swung my wand up and sprayed a line of sugar at him. Flame roared around his body, intercepting the sugar blast, which exploded.

The boom echoed through the warehouse, and he flew several yards, hitting the wall and sliding along it before falling to the floor. I changed my aim and sprayed him again, sending the sugary coating crawling up his body.

"I wouldn't try lighting any fires again," I warned him, not quite as loudly as I ought. I followed up with a yawn. The excitement had really taken it out of me. Out of all of us. Ray had pulled himself up to sit on a crate, leaning against another. Claire slumped over the broken drug crate as I watched. I couldn't blame her. I felt as tired as if I'd been firing the teleport rings nonstop. Even Ray slid down the crate he leaned against and fell asleep, lying atop a wooden lid. My eyelids sagged. Exhaustion crawled out to the ends of my body. My knees wobbled, and then the tiredness reached my wrists and disappeared, sucked into The Machine.

I slid down to floor leaning against the drug crate, pretending to be limp. At least my visor meant I didn't have to close my eyes. I dug into my pocket as subtly as I could while I watched Marvelous hover gently down from the rafters. Her current costume contained a lot of fishnet, and not just on her legs. It was only modest compared to the old one. She had poise, too. She stood straight as a dancer when she landed, her voice as sharp as a dance teacher as she scolded Ifrit, "I told you not to confront them."

"I think… I think…" Ifrit didn't sound too conscious himself.

"Hold still. I can get you out of that," Marvelous talked over him. She lifted both arms, and I lifted mine, spraying a jet of sugar at her from my wand.

Experience showed. She hadn't completely turned away from us, and she yelled, "Shield!" or a word that sounded much like it. My sugar splattered harmlessly off a sparkling dome.

She swiveled to face me, and I lurched up, focusing behind her, on the other side of the shield. My vision jerked as I teleported and found out that Marvelous knew about this trick. Her hand was already swinging back toward me. I staggered forward another step, teleporting to the opposite side of her again. Marvelous's other hand swung up. I had no choice. I smacked my wrist, and The Machine wrapped around it against her shield. As the shield vanished, I flipped the penny in my other hand at her while she shouted, "Boom!"

Boom was right. Blue flashed, and I felt like I'd just been tackled, knocked through the air to land with a painful jolt on the floor. My body ached, but not as bad as my head. The pain was easing quickly, so I rolled up. I tried to roll up. Another stabbing jolt in my head, and a wave of dizziness turned that into rolling onto my side.

Marvelous scratched at the coin stuck to her lapel. When it didn't come off, she chuckled. "Bad Penny. Cute. Lift!" Weight eased away from me, and I floated up into the air. That was fine. A few seconds was rapidly clearing my head. When I felt steady, I twisted and extended a foot. Nothing happened. I couldn't teleport while hovering in one spot like this.

Marvelous scratched at the penny some more, then gave up and put her hands on her hips. "You're too good at this, kids. Way too good. I need to know where you get your orders."

She stood there staring up at me, clearly expecting surrender or an argument. She hadn't even raised her shield again. I was sure this overconfidence was the penny's work.

I didn't answer, I just pointed at Marvelous. Splintering noises in the distance presaged trails of spiky rock candy barreling across the floor at her.

"Boom!" she yelled again, one hand lashing out. A blue beam exploded one stalagmite. Her other hand shot out, and, with another beam, a second stalagmite exploded.

Then the rubber ball came flying across the warehouse and slammed into her shoulder. She staggered, spun, but didn't fall down. Instead, she raised the other hand and shouted, "Lift!"

It worked. The ball spun in place in midair, immobilized. That left the final stalagmite, well behind its partners, grinding across the floor at her surrounded by rolling metal jacks. With a "Boom!" she blew the last rock candy weapon away, sending the jacks rolling past and around her.

She'd picked the wrong target. The moment they had her surrounded, blue lines of electricity arced like a web between the jacks, a lot of them intercepted and grounded by Marvelous's body. She squealed, back arched, and I fell to the floor. The moment my feet touched down I took a step and teleported.

Even after being electrocuted, Marvelous swung around, arms lifted to fire wherever I'd teleported. Except I wasn't down there. I'd teleported up onto the rafters, and I extended my wand and blasted her with sugar. She heard the hissing and threw herself to the side, but too late – a candy shell slimed most of her hip and one leg. It hardened instantly, and, with one leg immobilized, she fell heavily to the ground instead of rolling.

I teleported again, right over her, wand pointed at her face. As crystalized sugar spread over her body, Marvelous glared up at me.

Suddenly, her eyes widened in realization, and one hand grabbed at the penny on her lapel. "You cursed me!"

"Shut up!" I yelled back. It probably was magic, and she probably could feel it. Too late. "No spells, not another word, or I choke you with sugar dust. We're going to stay like this while my candy does its work. It's just a tiny bit poisonous, and, by the time the shell stops growing, you'll be asleep as well as immobilized. Listen carefully while you can, and later you can thank me. You need more dragon blood to keep your powers, right? Well, it'll be on the market very soon. All you'll have to do is buy it."

That was enough. The candy had crept up to her arms while I gave my speech, and her eyes lost focus. I took a step, teleporting back to the drug crate and my unconscious friends. I shoved The Machine against Ray's chest and Claire's back, and they both slid upright groggily, but more awake by the second.

"Grab the bottle. We have sixty seconds, tops, before Marvelous breaks free. We're getting out," I ordered.

Ray took me seriously. He vaulted over the crate next to him, and when I teleported to the open doorway I turned to see him already racing toward me with the bottle of blood. Vera flew up to meet me, Claire zoomed past me, and I turned and ran for the fence.

Through the door behind me, I heard Marvelous yelp, "My clothes!" Oh, right. Did I forget to tell her the sugar shell spread by eating fabric?

"HA HA HA HA HA!" I laughed. I leaped up over the edge of the sagging chain and shouted to Claire ahead of me, "Sell the bottle fast and cheap. When Marvelous tracks it down, I don't want it to be in our hands."

The last obstacle to the street out of the way, I slapped my chest, jumped onto the light bike that sprang into existence in front of me, and sped away.

That was how a professional supervillain does it.

CHAPTER FIFTEEN

I drove up to Northeast West Hollywood Middle and kept going. A couple of kids my age were walking past. I didn't know them, but I really didn't want to be seen entering my secret lair. City blocks down that way were huge, so I circled through the residential section on the other side and back around. There, nobody was obviously watching. That would do. I pulled up, dismissed my light bike, and walked across the schoolyard to the double doors that disguised my lair's elevator.

The shudder as that elevator pulled to a stop on my laboratory level felt good. The job was neatly wrapped up, and I could look ahead to new things.

First things first. I refilled my candy tank, hacking off chunks from my block of sugar and feeding them in to be compressed. When I topped the tank off, my sugar block had been reduced to a pile I could have bought in a bag at the grocery store. That would need attending to. Sugar couldn't be hard to get, and the gold Claire and Ray sold off would get me a couple hundred bucks worth, right? By then I'd be able to afford more.

Stealing the dragon blood hadn't taken long. The drive down to Santa Monica and back had taken way longer. I still had a good chunk of the afternoon. I could kick my super power into gear and make us some more equipment, as long as it wasn't candy based.

I could make zombie rag dolls for Claire. She'd gotten a kick out of the teddy bears in the warehouse. With her bear pajamas, a toy box theme would be perfect for her!

My phone roared. That would be Claire calling me right now. I flipped it up and quipped, "You've reached Penelope Akk. To speak to the mad scientist, press one. To order an army of robotic minions, press two."

Claire didn't give me time to think of a three. "Are you coming, or what?"

Goofball me, I felt a little panicky. "Coming where?"

"The other half of the operation! You said you wanted to sell the bottle right now!"

I didn't know Little Armenia, but it was only a few blocks from my house. It was just an itty bitty neighborhood I'd hardly ever set foot in. I met Claire and Ray at the corner of Edgemont and Los Feliz, and we walked down to meet Claire's fence.

It didn't look like a bad neighborhood, but maybe it was. Three supervillains in costume walking down the street didn't get a glance from the residents. Claire held the bottle, and Ray walked like a bird with his hands clasped behind him, grinning maniacally. Vera floated by my shoulder, which I was getting used to. She also stopped to rubberneck constantly, which I was also getting used to.

Whether we looked ridiculous or like bad news, nobody paid the slightest attention. Not even when we stopped in front of the big church. Claire pointed across the street, and we crossed over to stand between two rather cool brown and red three story wooden houses, the kind with sloping roofs and outcroppings where you're not sure just how many stories they really have. They looked like apartment buildings, fusing together way up at the top but leaving a tiny alley between the buildings locked off by a metal gate.

No, not locked. Claire opened the gate right up, led us down the shadowy path of sick grass and broken stones, and pointed at the metal fire escape. "We go up those. The fence is on the roof."

The ladder hadn't been lowered to the ground, but Ray jumped up, grabbed the railing on the second floor, got his feet under him and then jumped up again like a monkey to grab the next level. Fine. He wanted to be that way? I spun in place and took a step backwards, focusing on the stairs I could see but couldn't reach. My teleport rings deposited me at the base of those stairs, and I turned and aimed for the next set. Metal rails clattered as Ray climbed them, Claire's grappling hook thumped and hissed, and as I set my foot down on the edge of the roof with my last teleport, her and Ray's feet hit the tar paper on either side of me.

The roof of this building was crazy. Parts of it sloped sharply like towers, but a wide section in the middle stayed flat to accommodate the little extra building spanning the gap. Claire slid up to that on her frictionless bear feet and knocked on the heavy wooden door.

"What do you want?" a man's heavily muffled voice demanded.

"We're here to shop," Claire chirped back, putting on the cute.

It didn't work this time. "Halloween was a month and a half ago."

Leaning forward and doing his bird act again, Ray offered, "I could kick down the door if you like."

I swatted him in the chest with the back of my hand, which hurt my hand much more than it did him. Good grief, he had chest muscles now, too. What had I done? I tried to put the sting into my voice instead. "Reviled, treat our contacts with dignity."

Ray lifted his hat in one hand, bowing low. "You're right. I apologize, Sir. I merely wished to suggest we have the powers to accompany these costumes."

The door opened—slightly, jerking against a chain on the inside. The gap allowed a guy, maybe college age, to peek through at me. Actually, not at me. He aimed his sullen, suspicious stare at Vera first, then down at me. He didn't exactly sound angry, just frustrated. "You can't come in. My grandmother won't do business with you. She hates technology."

I raised an eyebrow, although no one could see it behind the visor. "E-Claire, your contact didn't call ahead?" The name "E-Claire" only made the guy at the door scowl a little more.

Claire gave me a sheepish grin. "I guess not."

On the other side of me, Ray sounded curious. "I've heard about the war between magic and science. I thought it was just a myth."

"It's a myth my grandmother believes with all her heart. She won't do business with you," the guy behind the door repeated.

"I know my Dad—" I started, when a loud clanging from the fire escape interrupted me, and again, and again with some extra clattering, until Lucyfar hauled herself up over the edge of the building.

She took the surprise way more in stride than we did. "Hey, what are you guys doing here?" she asked as she hopped to her feet and rushed forward to meet us. She sounded as gleeful as if she were opening presents on Christmas morning, and I thought she was going to hug me. Instead, she just grabbed one of my shoulders and one of Claire's and gave them both an affectionate squeeze.

Claire lifted up the glass-and-gold bottle in both hands. "We're here to sell this!"

Lucyfar's eyebrows shot right up. "No way. Is that Fat Dan's old bottle of dragon blood? I thought that was in China!"

"We stole it from a warehouse in Santa Monica about an hour, hour and a half ago," I informed her, feeling a little smug.

"Owned by the Council Of Seven And A Half, I believe," Claire added.

Lucyfar gave our shoulders another hard squeeze, shaking her head and bowing forward in delight. "And right now, Marvelous will do absolutely anything to get her hands on some dragon blood."

Ray lifted a gloved hand and studied the back of it theatrically, while his voice drawled with a smugness that had me completely beat. "We may have walked over her prostrate form on the way out the door."

Lucyfar burst out laughing. First, she doubled forward, leaning heavily on Claire's and my shoulders, then she reared back and let go, all the while cackling in glee. She eventually had to put a hand over her face just to wheeze, "Oh, man. Absolutely perfect! So you sell the bottle to the old biddy here, and she sells it to Marvelous, whose hands are now clean while she's also completely humiliated. You have got to let me be the one to tell her where the bottle is. I'm begging! The look on her face will keep me warm all winter."

She was dragging a big grin out of me, too. I tried to be serious. "Be my guest. I want our involvement in this over as soon as possible."

Still chuckling, Lucyfar stepped forward past us and snapped at the guy behind the door, "Let 'em in, Nicky. Your gramma will have a fit if she finds out she could have fenced Fat Dan's bottle of dragon blood but missed out."

"You know how she feels about tech villains, Lucy. She won't even watch TV," Nicky grumbled.

"She'll make an exception. Anyway, if you don't I'll kick the door down."

Heroically, Ray managed to stay silent as the door was unbolted, but he did make another show of studying his gloves as he rubbed his fingers together.

We poured inside when the door opened. The owner sure liked her stereotypes. Not only did she hate technology, this place looked like a magical knickknack shop. The windows had heavy curtains keeping the front room dim, and tables and shelves and display stands were all crowded with random looking clutter ranging from knotted string to a two foot long engraved silver wand. All of it was magic, if I correctly interpreted Vera's rapidly darting attention.

One thing did make me wonder. "I thought there'd be more books."

"Naah," Lucyfar corrected me breezily. "Honest to goodness magical grimoires are so rare and priceless no one ever sells them. Kinda like a Conqueror orb, eh?" She gave me an exaggerated wink and nudged me with her elbow, mistakenly confident that I had the slightest idea what she was talking about.

Turning to Claire, Lucyfar held out both hands and asked, "Can I see the dragon's blood? This bottle is famous, you know." When Claire loosened her grip, Lucyfar lifted the bottle out of her hands and held it up to what little light the room had. "So how did you get this thing? I want the whole story!"

I was happy to oblige. "One of E-Claire's mysterious online friends tipped us off about where the bottle was being held. I thought it was you."

Lucyfar shook her head. "Not me. No shortage of shady customers making deals with supervillains in this town."

It had been an idle guess anyway. I shrugged. "We kept the heist as smooth as possible. I neutralized gunpowder and electronic communications in and around the warehouse. We traced the magical signal to the bottle, cut the protections out, and ran for the hills. Minimal opposition."

"A few thugs, Witch Hunter, Ifrit, and Marvelous," Ray supplied in his airiest fake-casual tone.

Glee burned right up my spine as I tried to match Ray's lazy smugness. "Ifrit was definitely minimal opposition."

Lucyfar exploded in another cackling laugh, and I got prodded from several directions by the blunt tips of black phantom knives. "Details, kids. Come on, don't hold out on me!"

I didn't want to brag. Okay, I wanted to brag a lot. I was on fire with it. But a supervillain should be a gracious winner and have style, right? "Without working guns, the guards were pretty helpless. I used them to test my new toys. One of those toys explodes on contact with flame, so Ifrit never had a chance. I've got a sugar formula now for gluing defeated enemies in place, so once we knocked anyone down, the fight was over."

Claire lost patience with my restraint and jumped in. "Her new fighting rig is brutal. The harassment weapons are so much fun to watch. Guards went flying everywhere! Witch Hunter waited until the guards were down to challenge us."

Lucyfar snorted. "Yeah, for a guy who will happily spend twenty hours a day practicing forms, he won't do a lick of work until he actually has to. Seven and a Half must have known Marvelous would come for the bottle. With all his spell breaking gear, she'd have had her hands full getting past him."

"Reviled dueled him one on one!" Claire broke in again.

I folded my arms and failed to sound disapproving. "Which is why Marvelous arrived before we could get away with the loot."

Lucyfar gave Ray a sly smile and a raised eyebrow. "One on one? I like your pride, kid. I'm impressed, too. Witch Hunter's not a heavy hitter, but he's way more experienced than you."

Ray gave me a small bow. "I learned to fight watching Bad Penny. As long as I made sure he never hit me, sooner or later I'd land a finishing blow." His formality cracked, a grin splitting his masked face. "It was hard keeping that kind of self-control. Everything was split second reactions, because I couldn't predict what he would do. Incredible adrenaline rush, but I kept thinking, and he was too used to his patterns. Eventually, I hit him from a direction he didn't expect, and the fight was over."

"Did he try the knife thing? He does that when he knows a fight's going south."

Ray jerked his head at me. "He threw it at Bad Penny."

"At Vera," I corrected.

Lucyfar smirked again. "Get used to that."

Ray picked up a black hat rather like his own off a shelf, turning it over to examine it as he finished the tale. "I needed the duel, but what I learned most is that if I had to beat him quickly and safely, I should have hit him with a crate or some other object too big to dodge or block. The advantage of strength and speed together gives me options that render a martial artist's skill moot. Bad Penny's strategy of never letting myself get hit has given me time to figure that out."

That wasn't how I remembered my fights. "I wish that was my strategy. My head still hurts from letting Marvelous get a hit in."

Ray put the hat back down and spread his hands. "I plead ignorance. When I woke up, you were still standing, and she wasn't."

That lit up Lucyfar. "So, Bad Penny defeated Marvelous one-on-one and stole the dragon's blood right out from under her nose? I am so glad I ran into you kids here today!"

I tilted my head suspiciously. Well, suspicious in a friendly way. "You want something."

Lucyfar clasped her hands together and leaned toward me with a grin more maniacal than pleading. "First, I want to hear all about you taking down Marvelous."

Oh, boy. Well, no need to tiptoe around the point with Lucy. "I'd like to hold onto my secrets. Sooner or later, I'll need to use them against you."

Lucy clasped her hand to her chest, eyes wide in shock. "How could you say such a completely accurate thing? Who wouldn't trust me, the Princess of Lies?"

Apparently the shop owner wouldn't. She emerged in an explosion of angry... Russian? It sounded like Russian to me. She looked Russian, like a peasant from an old cartoon, with a shriveled raisin face and a scarf over her head. Everything about her seemed to be gray – her clothes, her hair, her eyes, and even her skin had an unhealthy pallor to it.

She certainly didn't act sick. She had energy and bad temper to spare as she yelled first at the guy who let us in, then at Lucyfar.

Lucyfar didn't look impressed and jabbered back at her, although I could hear how much more slow and halting her Russian—Armenian?— was. The old lady pointed a finger and waved it around between me, Claire, and Ray, complaining some more. Lucyfar said something that sounded sarcastic, and the old woman glowered but shut up.

"She's mad because you're a mad scientist and because you brought some kind of magical weapon into her shop," Lucyfar translated. I raised my eyebrow, and, since she couldn't see that, tilted my head to one side. Lucyfar's wide grin told me she got the message. "Yeah, you can't win, but she wants the blood too much to kick you out."

E-Claire stepped right up, cracking her knuckles theatrically. "What's she offering?"

Old witch lady must have understood some English, because she grumbled a couple of sentences and then stumped off through the swinging wooden doors into a back room. I got the impression she wasn't coming back. Looking tired, the guy who'd answered the door filled us in. "She can't afford to pay money for it and isn't going to try. She has plenty to trade, since you seem interested in magical equipment."

"Oh, that reminds me! Look up here!" Claire blurted out. I glanced at her face. She looked normal. She had the same blonde, soft face, playful eyes, and warmly emotive smile my gaunt hatchet face had always envied.

"Here you go!" she announced, holding out a little plastic card each to me and Ray. Where did those come from?

Oh, right, she'd zapped me with her power. I picked the little piece of colored plastic out of her hand. Bank of…

"You got us credit cards? How did you even…?!" I squeaked in shock.

"Debit cards. We have bank accounts now!" Now it was Claire's turn to radiate smugness, clasping her hands behind her and rocking forward and back on her heels.

I stared at my card. TIM President. Craning my head over, I looked at Ray's. TIM Human Resources. Claire flashed hers, which read TIM Public Relations. HA!

"We're a small business. That's hilarious. Is there anything in our accounts yet?" I asked, shaking my head in both delight and disbelief.

"Only about five thousand each. Me and Ray couldn't even get a third of what that gold bar was really worth, not without a paper trail to prove we owned it." Claire rattled that off so casually, but numbers rolled up in my head. That little bit of gold had been worth more than forty five thousand dollars? And I'd pulled it out of a junkyard? Well, that decided it. I certainly wasn't in the supervillain business for the money. Me and The Machine could make a fortune legally. It just wouldn't be as much fun.

Lucy held up the bottle we'd stolen and told us, "Dragon's blood is worth way more than that. Little Grandmother's got great stock and information, but you could get a much better deal this weekend."

I waved my hands emphatically. "No. I don't care if she's ripping us off, we're getting rid of this bottle now before Marvelous finds it. Besides, I find myself suddenly needing new equipment much more than cash."

Lucyfar snorted, but Claire and Ray spread out gleefully, studying the exhibits now with the eye of prospective buyers.

Claire summed up my reaction pretty well. "I have no idea what this stuff does!"

Ray pointed out, "Anti-magical charms would prevent anyone sneaking up on us with a sleep spell again. I'm certain there are plenty of them right in front of us, if we can identify them. Powerful charms might even protect us from poison attacks, or other insidious physical traps."

I took the bottle back from Lucyfar, who gave me a noncommittal shrug. "Normally I'd ask Little Grandmother. I shop here because she's a real expert. She's too busy throwing a sulk to be any use to us today."

I grunted. Common sense told me one thing. "I don't want to buy anything that I don't know what it does."

From a tabletop covered in bowls of colored sand, Claire suggested, "I could go home and ask around, get some advice on what to trade for."

I shook my head, hard. "No, no way. We're ditching the bottle. We'll find something here worth buying."

That got me looking around for my personal magical detector. I found Vera hovering over an upturned black top hat with a bundle of knotted together handkerchiefs hanging out of it. She didn't have fingers, but her tiny floating hands were strong and precise, and she untied a handkerchief from one of the knots. The knot turned out to be more complicated than I thought, because another handkerchief fell into view hanging from the same spot.

Or had it? I wandered over and helped her untie the knot again. I managed to pull a handkerchief out, but the knot hadn't changed. Ha! Infinitely reproducing handkerchiefs, a stage magician's trick performed with real magic.

I untied another. I couldn't see where the new handkerchief appeared in the bundle, but in the back of my head I could see it, where it came from and how, although everything but the crudest physical parts of the process made not a lick of sense. Other pictures started to build around that image, but I focused on the issue of the moment.

"Okay, we'll take this. There's nothing a good mad scientist can't do with an endless source of fabric," I announced.

Lucyfar regarded the handkerchief knot over my shoulder skeptically. "There's a lot of magic in that spell, but you're still getting ripped off. You kids have no idea what dragon's blood is worth."

"I don't really care. I didn't steal it for the money," I brushed her off. Or at least, I tried. Lucyfar beamed with delight as I scooped up the ball of handkerchiefs and handed the gold-wired bottle to the witch's sheepish grandson.

"Aren't you here to buy something yourself?" I snapped, my peevishness bouncing off that grin with no effect. It might have been more effective if I was actually mad.

"Not anymore. The Inscrutable Machine's help will be much more useful than anything I could buy, if you guys are willing to help me out."

That did it. Claire and Ray shouted, "Yes!" at the same time, swooping over from opposite sides of the shop to crowd around Lucyfar in eager anticipation.

Which left me to continue playing the grouch. "Can we at least hear what you want us to do, first?"

Lucyfar stuck her hands in the pockets of her jeans and answered frankly, "I want you to help me get Chimera out of jail."

Whoa.

Lucyfar turned her head to look at Vera, then followed Vera's gaze to the door. Rushing over to open it, Lucyfar squealed, "No time to talk about it. My date is here!" Seriously, she squealed. Who were the thirteen-year-olds here?

We filed out onto the rooftop after her as a mass of white wings fluttered down out of the sky. They tucked behind Gabriel's back as he landed, only slightly out of the way.

"So, you two *are* dating?" Claire asked pointedly, giving them both a hopefully questioning grin.

Her powers didn't do her much good this time. "Yes!" Lucyfar declared immediately, throwing herself onto Gabriel and wrapping her arms around him.

"No," he contradicted, standing stiff and disapproving.

"Yes!" Lucyfar repeated, nodding like a bobble-head.

"No," Gabriel insisted, just like last time.

I sighed as loudly as I could to make it clear I didn't know which of them was less believable. Stalking over to the edge of the roof, I teleported straight down to the alley pathway below. I stood there, taking deep breaths and letting the ache in my muscles dissipate while the fire escape clanged above me from Ray's descent. Claire got to me first, zipping down on her grapnel line. She let it snap back onto her wrist as she unfolded a little piece of paper and read it.

"Lucy wants our help today. She'll call me after her date."

Which meant a few hours later Claire, Lucyfar, Ray and I were sitting on the ledge of a billboard overlooking the West Hollywood Elite Detention Center. It felt a little creepy being this high up, dangling my legs over the gap, but if I fell I could teleport myself to the ground and get away with no worse than a bruise, right?

Ray looked up from his pocket watch. "It's time."

Lucyfar pushed herself up to her feet. Claire stopped peeking around the corner of the billboard as Lucyfar addressed her. "The Apparition should be in the monitoring room. You're next, E-Claire. Go around to the front door and make a distraction. Turn your power up as high as it can go and keep as many cops as you can paying attention to you."

Claire saluted, grinning eagerly. "For how long?"

"When the chaos starts, get out of there and don't look back. I'm betting five minutes, maybe less. One way or another, there will be chaos." Lucyfar sounded downright serious. Note to Penny, even crazy supervillains have to plan like a professional.

Claire giggled and jumped off the ledge. Her arm shot up, and the grappling line grabbed that same ledge, lowering her to the ground at a speed that would merely have broken my ankles. Claire twirled when she landed, kicked a leg back, and skated off down the street and around the other side of the building.

I could easily imagine Claire in her hoodie teddy bear pajamas talking to a room full of heavily armed supervillain containment policemen about her lost cat, with none of them suspecting a thing. Whatever happened, I needed to stay in charge of The Inscrutable Machine. I hated to think what Claire and Ray could and would get away with if I didn't hold them back.

"Our turn," Lucyfar announced. I stepped off the ledge, blinking down to the edge of a rooftop below, then down again onto the street corner.

Breaking up the jump that way kept me from needing to do more than take a deep breath to recover. Ray landed on the grass with a loud thump behind me, and Lucyfar dropped down lightly. Gravity was for regular people, not supervillains.

Walking across the street was kind of boring in comparison. Lucyfar broke up the normality by asking, "How good is that cutting tool of yours?"

I pulled the wand out of my sugar tank and flipped the switch to cutting mode. "It's a water knife. Technically, a cola knife, I guess. At very short range, it should go through steel like butter. There's not much it can't cut, if we're patient and I don't run out of sugar."

"If it can't, I have a blast weapon that will take out the whole wall," Ray added, flexing his gloved hands.

"I want to do this quietly," Lucyfar answered as we reached the fence around the cubical cement building. She emphasized her point by jumping up and catching the top edge of the fence, vaulting over silently. Ray followed suit. I just walked through it, teleporting one single step from this side to the other.

As a jail, the building didn't try to be pretty. Windows were barred, none of them on the ground floor. It had no lawn or decorative trees, just a bare cement walk between the walls and the fence. I itched to tell Vera to override the cameras at the corners of the roof, but hopefully Claire and The Apparition were on the job. There would be non-gunpowder weapons in this building, and I didn't want to face them.

We walked down the length of the building, with Lucyfar trailing her hand along the wall and staring at the ground. Finally, she stopped short. "Here. The Chimera's cell is underneath us. Cut us a hole."

I'd need something bigger than a manhole cover if Chimera was supposed to climb out. I picked one of the squares of cement the sidewalk had already been divided into and pressed my wand into the crevice, tracing all around the edge as cola hissed and sprayed. When I got around the first time, the hole wasn't deep enough, so I kept cutting. On the third pass, I saw light peek through, the slab sagged as I circled around it, then fell into the room below with a very loud and very wet clang. My cola knife was not mess-free.

Lucyfar jumped down immediately. I teleported neatly onto the slab I'd sent tumbling into the cell below. Ray landed next to me.

Chimera stared at all three of us, grinned, and his shoulders sagged as he let out a huge sigh of relief.

"Is this all? You can't get yourself out of this, Chimera?" Lucyfar asked sarcastically.

I couldn't tell which way she meant the joke. Someone seriously wanted to keep Chimera in here. The metal walls, ceiling, and floor of the cell might not have been enough, but heavy chains like those I associated with boats connected two-inch-thick cuffs on his neck, wrist, and ankle to a metal ball on the wall. It let him move around the room, but it did not look comfortable. They had him in the horrible red and blue thin shirt and pants of a super-powered prisoner, too.

Chains rattled as he shrugged and scowled. "I can't believe they kept this cell intact for forty years. I'm the only prisoner in the building, and they had to hose the dust out of the room before they dragged me in. If they'd waited another minute my spine would have healed before they got me chained down."

Lucyfar winced, her grimace more sympathetic than amused. "Ow. She broke your back?"

"She broke everything. Kids today are a bunch of thugs." Chimera winked at me and Ray, and grinned again.

Lucyfar stepped over to him, lifting up a chain and examining the collar around Chimera's neck. "We need to hurry. Can't you break out of these?"

Chimera went back to scowling, a growl in his voice. "Not without changing shape. If I grow any bigger, I crush and strangle myself."

It was weird to hear Lucyfar being the businesslike one. "And if you shrink?"

Chimera jerked his head at the metal ball the chains fastened to. "Grip loosens, I get electrocuted."

"What about the snake tail? That goo trick?"

He didn't show it on his face, but a moment's pause told me Chimera was embarrassed. "I'm still getting those powers back."

Lucyfar stared at the chains, frowning as she considered what to do about them. Ray stealthily tapped The Machine wrapped around my wrist, but I'd already figured that out. It was my turn.

Twisting The Machine until he let go, I told Chimera, "I can take care of the electrocution." I stuck The Machine against the base of the chains. He would eat any charge trying to go down that line. In fact, he was probably breaking the circuit and setting off that charge already, we just couldn't see it.

I couldn't hear any alarms, so hopefully The Apparition was on top of her end of things.

Next obstacle. "Can you shrink out? I can cut off the shackles, but not without cutting you in the process."

Chimera held up his wrists. "Cut through the hinges, and I'll do the rest."

That was easy enough. I raised my wand and sliced the chains off of the cuffs. Chimera's arms bulged, and red and black scales rolled up his skin, then were replaced by coppery metal feathers along his forearms. He looked awkward and apelike with his arms so massive, but only for a second. The shackles popped off his wrists, and he reached up and ripped the collar off his neck. His whole upper body swelled up to match his arms then.

Chimera snarled, showing heavy fangs. Yikes. His face distended forward, black metal porcupine spikes popping out of his hair. He snapped the remaining cuffs free, and suddenly his whole body swelled up. The three-eyed, hairy and scaly thing pressed up against the ceiling, its clothes ripped to useless clinging shreds. Turning, Chimera reached out a giant fist and gently bumped it against Lucyfar's.

"I owe you big," he growled. I could make out the words, but that toothy mouth gave him quite an accent.

Lucyfar smirked up at him. "Nope. I did it for a buddy, and for my favorite sin – the sin of pride."

That got a rough, booming laugh. He turned his fanged face to me, and my body felt suddenly very cold and weak. Still, I extended my arm and tapped my fist against his. His touch was as light as a baby's. Most of the fear drained away, and I smiled despite myself and assured him, "Just what friends do, right?"

Chimera looked down at Ray last. They grinned at each other, and on Chimera that involved way too many mismatched teeth. It only lasted a second. Apparently that satisfied them both.

"Now what?" Ray asked Lucyfar.

"Now we get as far away from here as possible," Lucyfar answered. She jumped up and caught the edge of the hole I'd cut in the ceiling, pulling herself up with ease. Ray made the whole jump and landed on his feet. I grabbed The Machine off the wall and teleported up next to them—and behind me, noise exploded out of the hole. I had trouble telling where the screaming cat voice left off and the torn metal began. The ringing of heavy impacts against metal stabbed at my ears.

I could, just barely, hear Lucyfar's voice as she grabbed Ray's collar and pushed. "It's all up to him now. Run!"

I didn't need encouraging. I took off as fast as my feet could take me, and after four steps focused and teleported to the other side of the fence. Pulling myself to a jarring halt at the edge of the street, I slapped my chest and my light bike flashed into existence on the asphalt.

A hand grabbed my shoulder, and I nearly shrieked. It was just Lucyfar, pulling me around and yanking me into an uncomfortably tight hug. "You kids are the best! You're coming to Chinatown this weekend, right?"

"What?" I asked, completely left behind.

Then the wall of the detention center exploded, bits of rock flying everywhere. I got a glimpse of Claire far down the street, skating away as fast as her frictionless bear shoes would take her. It was hard to pay attention to anything but the four-winged, two-headed, three-armed amalgamation of every mythological horror looming in the broken building, lunging at tiny-looking policemen whose guns didn't work.

"No time. Run!" Lucyfar ordered me. I was happy to oblige, throwing myself onto my bike and shoving a foot at the pedal. Vera grabbed my shoulder, and we sped down the street away from the yelling and crunching.

It didn't take me long to get home. I should have gone around to the lab and changed back into civilian clothes, but I was physically and emotionally exhausted. What a day. Anyway, the sun had finally set and it was getting pretty dark. I pulled up at the street corner and teleported to my front door so no one would see me walking up to the house in supervillain costume. That hurt, but what was one more ache?

My worries were worse than the physical pain. Stealing a bottle of blood from crooks before a hero could do the same thing? I didn't feel bad about that, much. Setting Chimera free was another matter. He'd seemed friendly, but he was a serious supervillain. Police might die and were certainly getting hurt, just so he could reenter the community with a little more style than getting beaten to a pulp by Generic Girl.

That was not the game I wanted to be part of. Maybe I should be trying harder to switch over to the hero side. I'd proven I could be a real supervillain. That didn't mean I had to be one.

I unlocked the door and pushed it open. With my parents out of town, I ought to get the mail. I scooped it out of the mailbox, all those bills and bank notices and official adult letters that all looked the same.

All except one, a pink envelope with fancy gold edging. I pushed the door closed behind me, walked into the kitchen, and laid the mail out on the table so I could look at this different, special envelope. The envelope addressed to me, Penelope Akk. The envelope with no return address or postmark.

I ripped it open, and pulled out a fancy white gold-embossed card.

Bad Penny,

I have been following your career with great interest, and it is time we became personally acquainted. You and The Inscrutable Machine are invited to meet with me at 10 p.m. this Friday in Chinatown, so that I may officially welcome you to the community and we can discuss where you go from here. I strongly suggest you arrive several hours early and enjoy yourselves before the meeting.

Looking Forward to Working with You,
Spider

CHAPTER SIXTEEN

Spider knew who I was.

The note could not be left lying around. I put it in my belt pouch. If it wasn't safe there, neither were my teleport rings.

I was too tired to take this in. It had been too long a day. Food would help with that. We had some leftover macaroni and cheese. That would be easy to make.

I looked in the fridge. No, we'd finished the macaroni and cheese. It wouldn't be hard to make some. I got out a couple of packages lurking in the back of the pantry and set a pot of water on to boil. I turned the boxes over to find the instructions, sections of text leaping into focus as the visor of my helmet magnified them. That was confusing enough that I had to flip the visor up.

Oh, right. I was still in supervillain costume. I wasn't expecting my parents home tonight, but I didn't want anyone to see me at home dressed like this. I also didn't want to leave the pot long enough to undress, because, as tired as I was, I might forget it. Vera picked up the other package and started to read it in imitation of me, although she was only slightly bigger than it was.

Vera. No one would see me in costume indoors, but Vera liked windows. I reached up and tapped her crystal ball. "Sleep." She fell into my other hand as her ceramic casing slid into place. I hurried back to my room and put her behind my computer monitor. Then I hurried back to the kitchen and found the pot boiling.

I tipped in the macaroni, set the timer on my phone, and stared at the opposite wall, kicking my foot. Ten minutes later, the alarm beeped. I drained the macaroni, stirred in cheese, and behold: A convincing simulacrum of food.

I ate it. Slowly, tired and with little appetite, but I ate it.

I felt a bit stronger after that and went back to my room through a silent house. I flipped on my computer, grateful for the whine and whistles as it started. Scooping up my stack of Sentient Life comics, I dropped heavily onto my bed and cracked one open. That left me staring at my gloves. Still in costume.

I pulled the whole costume off and shoved it and my sugar tank under the bed.

Since I was standing again, I wandered back to my computer and clicked on my web browser and favorite programs. My friends list dutifully reported Claire and Ray were online. Nevermind. I shut the programs down again.

Now boredom was the problem. I wanted to play Teddy Bears and Machine Guns, but I could only play it online and Claire and Ray would see me. Most every game I had would have that problem.

I let out a sigh and turned around, leaning against my desk as I stared at my room, wondering what to do. The comics scattered on my bed wouldn't keep my focus in this mood. I could see one arm of my jumpsuit peeking out from under the edge of my bed, and I couldn't have that.

I cleaned my room. Might as well. I'd let it get horribly untidy. I had books and shoes and clothes lying around. I put everything away where it was supposed to be and shoved the jumpsuit way back under the bed out of sight. The bed was a mess too. I'd kicked the covers loose again. I went and got new sheets and remade it. On the way I saw my macaroni bowl sitting on the kitchen table, so after I remade my bed I went and washed all the dishes.

Drying my hands afterwards, I looked at my phone. Nine forty-five. That would do. My whole body was falling out from under me with exhaustion. I went to bed.

I woke up to bright sunshine and stared at the white, bumpy spackled ceiling. I'd gotten used to waking up and feeling nicely lazy about lying around. The exercise and satisfaction of supervillainy made for pleasantly relaxed mornings. Not this time. I couldn't lie here for long. I felt much too tense.

The reason for that was obvious.

Spider knew who I was.

He knew my name, my real name and my supervillain identity. He knew where I lived. He knew who my parents were. That had to be why he contacted me. The insincerely friendly letter screamed blackmail.

He was going to use me to get at my parents.

No. I wouldn't do that. I wouldn't. When I refused, Spider would reveal my identity to the world, and even my parents would have to believe it.

Everyone would know I'm a supervillain. I would never get to be a superhero. Who would trust me? Even my parents wouldn't trust me. They'd watch me, never let me use my super powers again. I would have to say goodbye to that crazy, all-knowing thing in the back of my head. I might not get to say goodbye to Ray and Claire. There was no way they'd let me hang out with my partners in crime anymore.

I might get sent to jail. Probably not. But maybe.

My phone rang. I lay in my bed and let it ring. I had bigger problems. What would I do? I had no idea. Was there anything I could hope to do against the ruler of the supervillain underworld in LA?

The doorbell rang. I tried to lie there staring at the ceiling, but it rang again. Someone at the door was harder to ignore than a phone call.

I grabbed a sweater and sweat pants, the fastest clothes I could pull on, and went and answered the door.

It opened to reveal painfully bright sunshine and Marvelous, smiling at me. I'd last seen her drugged and glued to a floor. The disconnect left me feeling off-balance. She'd lost a couple of inches of hair from my fabric-eating enzyme mixture, but didn't look bothered by that at all.

Her voice chirped happily as she reached out and ruffled the top of my head. "Wow, I've never seen you without your hair braided. No wonder!"

"Yeah, it goes everywhere," I admitted.

Leaning forward to look past me into the house, she asked, "Can I talk to Brian?"

"He's at the conference. You can call him as easily as I can." I sounded crabby, but I wasn't sure how not to right now.

Marvelous didn't take it badly. She smiled even more. "I know. The thing is, I don't just want to talk to him. I want to show him something."

I swallowed my reply, because obviously she felt an email or webcam wouldn't do the job. I couldn't just brush this off. I pulled out my phone and dialed up Dad.

"Is everything alright, Princess?" he asked as he picked up. His cheerful tone suggested he had a lot more confidence in me than I did right now.

Dutifully, I said, "Marvelous wants to talk to you, Dad. Are you able to use your video chat system where you are?"

"Sure. My laptop can handle it, if you can get it running on your end." If Dad told me his laptop unfolded into a sports car, I wouldn't have been surprised.

I beckoned to Marvelous with one hand and led her into Dad's office. His computer booted in seconds, and it only took a couple of seconds more to find his projection chat system and turn it on. The window reported a connection, and Dad hung up on me as his head and shoulders appeared hovering in front of the monitor.

"What's up, Marvelous?" he asked, raising an eyebrow. I had to admit, it was better than any webcam. He might as well have been in the room.

Marvelous answered solemnly, "I ran into The Inscrutable Machine." Ow. My heart locked up, cold and tight, but all I could do was listen.

Dad tilted his head curiously. He sounded almost teasing as he asked, "Did it change your opinion of how to treat them?"

Marvelous shook her head. Her smile was back. Sure, she was serious, but I was the only person not enjoying this conversation. She pulled a piece of paper out of her pocket and carefully unfolded it. "Not much. They were better than I expected, but they acted like professionals and we should treat them that way. I wanted to ask if this is what I think it is."

She held up her unfolded paper. The painting of Vera on it was impressive, almost photographic.

Long, silent seconds went by as Dad examined it. When he answered, it came as a grudging admission. "Yes. It's a Conqueror orb. Where did you see it, and how big was the orb itself?"

Marvelous nodded her head down at the page. "This is life size, I'd guess four inches diameter. I saw it following Bad Penny around like a puppy dog."

Dad's smile had completely disappeared. My heart managed to knot itself tighter, but I forced myself to relax. He looked much more thoughtful than worried. He only sounded as solemn as if he were taking a puzzle apart. "That's not right. The body is a command configuration. Command level orbs are basketball sized, or greater. What powers did it display?"

Marvelous shrugged and sounded whimsical and only a little embarrassed. "I didn't see it do anything. Bad Penny didn't need to use it to beat me. I believe it was responsible for overriding all local communications in the area, jamming firearms and stalling cars. I did see a pink energy pulse come from the building. Witnesses reported a heat beam, but they were hired thugs for the Council Of Seven And A Half. Not exactly trustworthy."

Dad nodded slowly, his hand coming into view as he laid it against his chin to look thoughtful. "That's Conqueror technology. We might be looking at an elite reconnaissance unit, a combination commando and spy. Cutting edge technology, even for aliens."

Marvelous changed the subject. "The big question is, where did Bad Penny get it?"

Dad answered that one immediately. "They dug it out of the landfill. It's been buried there since the invasion. Did she have any other Conqueror tech?"

Folding her arms over her chest, Marvelous shook her head. "Nope. Basic body armor, she can teleport, and she's ditched the high-tech weapons for a toy and candy set. Plus the Conqueror orb and some magic cursed pennies. An ugly, subtle little curse." She sounded impressed.

Dad, of course, ignored any reference to magic. "Mad scientists almost always have a coherent theme. If Bad Penny is building her own equipment, her super power is as strong and flexible as mine. Maybe stronger. More likely she has an outside supplier, and she's collecting weapons and getting more powerful with each crime."

"When I ran into her, she was stealing a bottle of dragon's blood. I've recovered the bottle, and if she used any blood it wasn't much—except it doesn't take much to give a human super powers." Even as tense as I felt,

Marvelous's words penetrated. I could have given myself more powers, and I missed it?

Dad frowned, considering it all. "If they're stealing weapons, someone is telling them where to look. Who's controlling The Inscrutable Machine?"

"The Conquerors? They wouldn't hesitate to mix their own, human technology, and magic," Marvelous suggested.

The grimace that clenched up Dad's face looked actually worried. "I hope not. I'd like to think they've written off Earth as not worth the trouble."

Marvelous waved a hand. "We've never seen Bad Penny, and she's smarter than any middle-school kid I've ever met. She might be an android shell operated by the orb."

"Then why tip their hand by revealing the orb at all? This isn't a Conqueror plot. They're controlling it, not it controlling them." Dad sounded downright relieved about that.

Letting out a loud, long sigh, Marvelous concluded, "Which leaves us with the obvious explanation."

Dad nodded. "Spider."

Dad's eyebrows shot up, his grim expression interrupted as Mom's voice called from offscreen. "Spider can't be behind everything. The obvious explanation is that the children really are that good."

Marvelous cracked a grin at that. "It's never safe to think that anything is obvious when Spider is involved. Thanks, Brian. Enjoy the convention. Kiss Dionysus for me!"

"No," Dad drawled theatrically, and cut the convention.

Turning, Marvelous reached out and mussed my hair again. I was starting to resemble a brown dandelion. "Thanks, Penny. Welcome to superhero talk. A lot of speculation, no real answers. See you soon!" She'd already turned to leave the office, and with that she walked right out the kitchen door and shut it behind her.

I walked back to my room, reached behind my monitor, and pulled out Vera. Deactivated, she didn't look like much. Pretty, sure, but not high tech. An off-white shell concealed most of the fist-sized crystal ball that was the real her. It looked rather like an eye, and, if I looked deeply and carefully into the iris, I could see the gold filaments between rings of cloudy pink that gave Vera her color.

I tapped her with one finger. "Wake up." Her shell came apart, unfolded, and she floated off my hand as a very art deco fairy.

"Do you know who the Conquerors are?" I asked, not expecting a response. I actually got one. She stared at me at first, but then slowly shook her head.

So, Vera resembled a weapon belonging to the aliens who secretly tried to invade Earth. That couldn't get me in more trouble than I was in already.

My phone rang. Roared, in fact. Claire was calling me. I ignored it. Again.

Thanks to Marvelous, however, I was up. Maybe I'd feel less sick if I was clean. I went and took a shower. With the water running I wouldn't be able to hear if Claire tried to call me again.

I let the shower run long just in case, although even soaking in hot water didn't make me feel any less stiff. I trudged back to my room, grabbed my stack of Sentient Life issues off the shelf where I'd just put them away, and dropped onto my bed. Lying back against my piled up pillow and comforter, I tried to read.

The second time Vera turned a page for me, I had to face it. I hadn't actually read anything this whole time, just stared. I couldn't focus. I couldn't do anything.

The doorbell rang. I lurched out of bed, grabbed my pants, and pulled them on.

You know what? Forget it. I lay back down again.

Next to me, Vera turned another page. I couldn't focus on the comic, but at least I could watch Vera's pink crystal eye move from panel to panel. She stopped at a frame of Delph's elongated face staring close into a monitor. The original Vera was just a shadowy hint of a face on the screen. My Vera ran her tiny hand over both of them. She liked the comic more than I did.

Was that faint rattling a real sound? The click of the kitchen door opening was real. I didn't hear my parents' voices.

Someone was breaking into the house.

That was insane. We didn't need alarms. This was Brainy Akk and The Audit's house.

Someone had broken in anyway. Someone who didn't care.

I had seconds. I wasted too many of them grabbing my sweater and jamming myself into it. I'd pushed my sugar tank too far under the bed. I couldn't dig it out in time!

Which didn't mean I was unarmed. I never wanted to do this, but someone was about to get a face full of Vera's heat ray. A flick of her globe got Vera's attention. I stepped out into the hall, pointed at Ray and Claire, and snapped, "Vera, k—" before I strangled the command.

"What are you two doing here? How did you get in?!" I yelled instead.

Claire held up an adorable pink plastic packet full of little metal tools. "I can pick locks, remember?"

She tucked them back into the pocket of her jeans. They were both in civvies. Not that there was a big difference for Ray, but at least he left the gloves, jacket, and mask off. He'd left off his usual grin, too. He sounded unusually serious as he answered my real question. "You haven't been answering your phone. We were worried you were freaking out over the invitations."

I balled my fists and shouted, "Of course, I'm freaking out! We're being blackmailed by Spider!" I could hear the screech in my voice. Suddenly, my whole body trembled, and my eyes stung with tears.

Claire walked calmly down the hall to me, hands held up. "I'm not sure it's blackmail. It could be exactly what it says: an invitation." Reaching out both arms, she took my hand in hers and squeezed it.

I shook my head, my voice hoarse. Criminy, my nose was starting to run too. "No way. Spider always has an ulterior motive. He's always playing some kind of game. We're thirteen. We're—we're good at this, but we're just kids. There's no way we can outwit him."

"Her," Ray corrected me. It was a nothing detail, and he kept his voice light. I expected to want to slap him for nitpicking. That anger didn't happen, which felt so good. By the time I ran through those thoughts he took my other hand. Bringing his face close to look right into mine, he told me, "We don't have to outwit Spider. We just have to keep her from outwitting us."

I sniffled. "Do you think we can do that?"

He straightened back up, squeezing my hand hard enough that it hurt just a little. A slight, proud smirk broke his serious expression. "I know Bad Penny, Reviled, and E-Claire can."

E-Claire. It hit me. I turned and glared furiously at Claire, yelling, "Your mystery contact was Spider all along?!" Her eyes went wide, and she shrank back but didn't let go of my hand.

Then her face turned down sheepishly. Was she using her power on me? I didn't think so. She pushed her glasses up the bridge of her nose and explained, "There never was a contact. I've spoken to a couple of supervillains, but they mostly don't hang out online. It's not about who you know anymore. It's about how well you use a search engine. I ordered us the bank cards first thing after the gymnasium fight, but they only just arrived in the mail."

That baffled me. "Why lie about it?"

Claire peeked up at me, a hint of accusation in her own stare. "I didn't think you'd trust me to be a bigger geek than both of you put together."

Ray's grin came back. It was never far away. "Not a problem. Buy some bigger glasses and switch out the bear suit for cosplay."

"I will, if Penny fixes up the inserts she made for my pajamas. They fit really badly into regular shoes." She sounded downright eager. Of course, she did. She was pretty and friendly, but she was right. She was a bigger geek than either of us. She'd always loved this stuff.

Ray moved a hand up to my shoulder. "Are you going to be okay? We can do this."

Now Claire's grin lit up. She jerked my hand up to her chest and squealed, "Do this? Are you kidding? It's going to be a blast! Chinatown shuts down early every Friday afternoon, for the whole weekend. I had to comb the internet to find even a hint of why. It's a wild supervillain party! Every single week!"

"You could have just asked your Mom," Ray pointed out slyly.

Claire opened her mouth. Claire closed her mouth. "Point," she finally admitted.

Villains took over Chinatown to party every weekend?

Of course. My parents had been hinting at it all my life. If Spider lived there too, no wonder there was never any crime in Chinatown and no superheroes ever patrolled there.

We'd be stepping right into Spider's web.

Claire leaned in closer, squinting as she looked my face up and down. "Penny's still sulking." Straightening up, she told Ray, "I prescribe going out and having a good time."

251

He nodded. "We'll go out for pizza. We can afford it. We can afford anything we want."

He was right about that. I started to nod, but Ray interrupted me. He put one hand on my shoulder and one on Claire's and gave us gleeful grin. "Hey, it just hit me—did all three of us try the same stupid 'hide what I can do' trick when we got our powers?"

I stared at him. Then I laughed, and laughed, and then I laughed some more. Claire managed to hold it down to a couple of squeaky giggles, enough to say, "Three peas in a pod. No accident we ended up friends."

"And teammates," I managed to wheeze.

I spent the next couple of hours at Pizza Place, sitting on a chair so high my heels kicked the air, eating delicious pizza and convincing Mr. Grigoryan three middle school kids didn't need a discount. Ray and Claire talked about cosplay costumes, and I didn't say much and I didn't really listen. I just ate sharply spiced pepperoni pizza and basked in their happy chatter while the knot in my heart let go. I couldn't help but notice the costumes Ray suggested Claire wear wouldn't cover much, but all that did was make me giggle occasionally.

I slept like a rock when I got home. It felt great.

I didn't feel quite as great when I got up in the morning, but I kicked myself out of bed and made myself shower and get cleaned up. Vera wandered in with me, although she didn't seem to enjoy, mind, or even notice the water. Great. Now I was showering with both of my greatest inventions. The dividing line between mad scientist and crazy cat lady got thinner.

I couldn't really get into the humor of the thought. I was going to walk into Spider's lair tonight, and she knew my real name. Maybe we'd be okay, but it hung on my heart like a weight while Dad's braiding device twisted my hair into neat pigtails.

I went back to my room, flipped on my computer, and checked if Ray and Claire were online. They were. I might have to face down Spider in her web tonight, but I'd do it with my friends by my side.

Me: "I'm still biting my nails over tonight, guys."

Ray: "It will be fine. Whatever happens, I will protect you. I mean it."

Claire: "Instead of brooding, have fun. Let's play a game of Teddy Bears and Machine Guns!"

Me: "Okay, but only against each other. I'm too nervous to play against strangers."

So we started up a game of Teddy Bears and Machine Guns. I picked candy, Claire took toybox, and Ray chose junkyard. After that, nothing went as usual.

It certainly didn't for me. I grabbed the chainsaw and basic armor, then spent some time setting up heals and soda buffs. Candy had a million of them, but I'd never liked how temporary they were before. It still wasn't my preference, but I could see the use now.

In the middle of this, a bunch of slinkies rushed my base. I let them get in, scratch uselessly at my candy heaps, and then I cut them down with the chainsaw. An early sacrificial rush like this wasn't Claire's usual style. I set some new toys building and wandered out to explore the map.

The center buildings were empty. Claire and Ray were hanging back in their starting areas, building up. I used up my temporary stealth soda and wandered as close as I dared. I saw what I expected to see from Claire— zombie rag dolls. Lots of them. Lots and lots of them. She was keeping them close to her box, breeding and breeding them with no support. I couldn't even get that close to Ray without tipping him off. He'd built a wall of buzz saws to protect his base and, instead of his usual single giant abomination, had several completely different monsters in construction at once.

Nobody was going to start anything until they could bury me. That could not be allowed to happen. I ran back to my sugar mines and picked up everything I could, then rushed Claire. I ran down the line of her rag dolls, chewing them up with my chainsaw, scattering flaming hot tamales and acid cola bombs in my wake. Then I did something I'd never done before – I took a speed boost and ran. Her rag dolls shambled after me, most of them never getting a chance to hit me back.

I led them straight for Ray's base. Claire thought she would be clever and not fall for it. Her rag dolls veered off toward my undefended sugar mine instead. I ran in behind and cut another swathe with my chainsaw. Her constantly multiplying rag dolls meant I hadn't seriously hurt her forces, but that wasn't the point. She had to follow me again, and again I boosted my speed and ran. This time she followed me close enough for saw blades to fire out of Ray's fortifications.

Suddenly, chaos reigned. Ray's machines shambled out, one spraying fire, one sawing mercilessly, one blocking for the others. I speed boosted again and ran in the opposite direction, watching from a distance. Ray didn't follow me. His combined machines wore down the rag doll horde, but only because he had his fortifications backing him up. So I ran back and started downing heals as I ignored everything else and moved from turret to turret, chainsawing them and dumping acid to finish them off as I moved on.

The tide turned. Rag dolls broke in through the gap in Ray's defenses. They swung and bit at me, but I turned and ran again.

I ran straight to Claire's toy box. If Claire pulled her army back, she'd lose it. She might be so busy she didn't even notice me ripping up the rag dolls breeding up a fresh wave. She had to notice when I slammed her toy box shut, but, by then, it was too late.

I didn't stay to gloat. The last thing I could afford was to let Ray recover. I drank my last speed boost, ran past my sugar mine, and grabbed everything ready, then downed every boost I had as I charged Ray's badly damaged machines trying to limp back to repair. Stunning them all with sticky syrup, I chainsawed them one by one, circled around his remaining turrets, and carved up his salvage and construction machines. He tried to sneak off a miner, but I set it on fire with one of my remaining tamales.

Ray surrendered. I'd won.

That had been the longest match we'd ever fought. The game dropped us back into the waiting room to chat and look at our stats.

Claire: "Wow."

Ray: "You took the words out of my mouth."

Me: "I had a lot of tools I've never used before. Now I can see what they're good for."

Ray: "Same here."

Claire: "I had the opposite experience. I've been scattering my attention too much. If I was going to bury you in endless hordes, I should have endless hordes. They weren't enough!"

Ray: "Are you feeling better, Penny?"

Me: "Yeah. What next?"

Claire: "I think it's time to meet at the lair. We'll want to arrive by sundown."

Me: "Chinatown won't know what hit it."

CHAPTER SEVENTEEN

e took the Red Line to Chinatown to attract less attention. Lounging on a subway seat in full costume with Reviled on one side of me and E-Claire on the other, I grinned behind my visor and soaked up the irony of the situation. The car wasn't crowded, but it was certainly full. The riders standing and sitting near us pretended we didn't exist. The ones toward either end of the train stared. The only people talking were a pair of teenagers, and, from the constant glances between whispers, they were talking about us.

Of course, nobody actually refused to get on the subway car as we pulled up to each station. This was LA, after all!

We got off at Civic Center and raced up the stairs to ground level. Ray, the clown, walked up the rubber handrail of the down escalator. We strutted up to Cesar Chavez, giggling nervously and making distinctly uneven progress. When we came up on a group of pedestrians, I would teleport past them, and I teleported across the first street without warning, forcing Claire and Ray to catch up. After that, Claire skated whimsically all over the sidewalk and Ray jumped up onto bus stops, walking on his hands over them before flipping back down onto his feet on the other side.

If we were walking to our executions, we might as well do it with style.

Those big gateposts crowned by golden dragons reared up over the entrance to Chinatown. Fences ran together along the blocks to either side, sealing this part of the city off like a wall. The only way a regular person could get in was walking down the street itself, and heavy yellow plastic roadblocks stood in the way with an old Chinese man guarding them.

"Sorry, Chinatown closed for weekend," he warned us as we approached. There was no way that Mysterious Immigrant accent could be real.

"Not to us," I answered. Me, Claire, and Ray kept walking toward him.

He got even less believable. He waved a conical traffic flashlight at us and scolded, "Halloween over! Go away! Costume not get you through here!"

I reached out and took Claire and Ray's hands. Just as I was about to walk face-first into the oh-so-ethnic old man's flashlight, I focused. Our feet set down on the other side beyond him, and we kept walking as he hadn't been there. We'd proven our point, and he didn't say another word. As an added bonus, the pain that shot through my legs didn't produce even a stumble. It had only been a few feet, but I'd technically been carrying both Ray and Claire. Ow. Thank goodness for the supervillain exercise regimen.

Chinatown is a shallow bowl with one big building dominating the center. Not a skyscraper or anything, but a squat, broad shopping mall type building, white and lurking and maybe four stories tall. We were heading right for it. All the other buildings looked like normal little houses or shops, all of them dark and quiet and deserted. We had to go a block before I saw the first sign of life and our first supervillain. Way up ahead, what looked like a family was setting up a roadside stall centered around several wooden barrels. An otherwise normal looking guy way too broad and beefy to be normal filled a mug from those barrels and passed the mother some cash.

Leaning my head to the side, I asked Ray whimsically, "I thought alcohol doesn't work on you guys?"

He shook his head. "I don't think that's alcohol." We could both see the smoke rising from the mug. Not steam, smoke.

As we watched, another supervillain glided down out of the air to land in front of the stall. Ray and Claire probably knew who both of these guys were. All I knew was this guy had added thick metal bands to his brightly colored spandex and cape to keep from looking too much like a hero. If only he looked less like a circus clown.

Nervousness makes me sarcastic, apparently. I gave a real jump when a man crawled out of a sewer drain on the side of the road. He was dressed head to foot in tight, shabby brown leather, and as skinny as you'd have to be to get through a drain. Leather pilot's goggles magnified his twitchy eyes, and the leather outfit was part harness, covered in pouches and pockets and straps for fastening on equipment.

Almost all of them hung empty, except a leather collar with wiring running up into his tight hood, a set of armbands that looked like my teleport bands with more wiring, and metal braces over his ankles. Without an inch of skin showing he still looked naked without any weapons. I sympathized, and my hand strayed by itself to pat my hip where the weight of my sugar tank should be. Claire had been emphatic. Being visibly armed wasn't forbidden, but it was rude. That went for flaming auras or spiked hackles or what have you. Claire had even left her grappling hook in the lab, figuring the claws on it looked too offensive.

Cape Wearing Guy gave us a long, pointed stare, but the skinny guy from the sewer didn't stop at a stare. He scurried right up to us, really scurrying, his skinny back bent low and feet shuffling rapidly. The way he crouched brought him down to our level as he said, "Bad Penny. You are Bad Penny, correct? Tasty. Absolutely tasty. Nobody even knows you're coming, and I get to bring you in!"

Ray tilted his face down, giving the crazy, skinny supervillain a hard stare just past the brim of his hat. "You may want to rephrase that." More than a hint of threat sharpened Ray's words. He couldn't leave his weapons behind. He'd even brought the special gloves, since they looked harmless enough.

Hazel eyes darted nervously behind overlarge goggles. Then the sewer villain laughed. "Oh, right, right! Lab Rat. My nom de plume is Lab Rat. You are Bad Penny, and I am tasty, so tasty—delighted to have encountered you first. The mad scientist community is agog, atwitter, delicious over a girl your age joining us, and I formally request you let me be the smug mad scientist who introduces you."

I snickered. I couldn't help it. I loved the theater of it all, and I couldn't tell where the supervillain act ended and the actual crazy began with this guy. Maybe mad scientists just feel naturally at home with lab rats. "And this would involve…?"

He gave his head a jerk toward the next intersection. "You following me to where we're set up."

I took a step toward him and activated my bracelets again, so I ended up a step past him. Extending an arm in the way his head had gone, I commanded, "Lead on."

He let out a loud, sharp laugh. "Ha!" and smacked his fist into his palm. Pushing himself up straight—and he was tall when he really stood up—he gave his back a crack and led the way. His normal walk lasted about five steps before he started crouching again, but he'd clearly made the effort.

Lab Rat led us circling around the central building to the other side by means of a looping, zigzag route that took advantage of the short blocks in Chinatown. The roundabout path seemed... well, roundabout, but I wasn't sure our guide could think in straight lines.

The route had its own attractions. We passed a glowing woman wearing what looked like patches of blue body paint tucked into a doorway talking to a man in a nice suit who might have been good looking if so much of his visible skin weren't threaded with metal. They never looked away from each other for a moment, and their sly, lazy smiles were obviously flirting. Ray grinned like a cat until we left them behind us. The next block was much busier. We had to circle around a crowd of men and women, some obviously in costume, yelling and cheering. Whatever they surrounded made loud thuds. Very loud. Painful and rattling, when we actually walked past. I caught a glimpse between bodies of two big, big men hitting each other. One was covered in brown hair, and the other silvery metal.

Past the fighters stood another stand selling smoking brew and doing brisk business with the spectators. We were close enough now to see the golden light spilling out of the huge, open interior of the central building. Small groups stood around, laughing and talking, and at least one person in each group wore an obvious costume or wasn't human. Many of the others wore uniforms in a variety of colors and patterns. Even assuming those were henchmen and the Chinese ones were locals catering to the crowd...

I'd had no idea there were this many supervillains in LA. Yikes. It was a big city, but still. I couldn't count them all!

We walked inside, as much as there was an inside. What to call a building like this? A shopping mall? An open air market? I'd never been in one like it. There were shops around the edges, a mezzanine floor I could see from here, but a huge, open tunnel made up most of the building. Tables, stalls, video games, dance mats—the crowd had spun out a haphazard array of decorations that obviously weren't here during the week.

A glowing, larger than life hologram of Mech in the distance caught my attention first, but didn't keep it. There was too much to look at close up.

We'd entered at the weapon sellers' end. Businessmen in pressed suits and scruffy guys in camouflage had racks of pistols, rifles, and other scary looking military hardware. My hand instinctively cupped the soothing round shape of Vera in my belt pouch. Lab Rat veered toward the opposite side of the hall. More racks of weapons, but these tended more toward tanks of mysterious chemicals, decorative rings, crystals, exposed wiring... and the villains lounging around their tables all wore goggles, even the guy in the rumpled dress clothing who otherwise looked like a college professor. I'd found the mad scientists, and Lab Rat hopped up and down and beckoned with glee.

He wasn't the only one beckoning. "Bad Penny! Over here!" shouted Cybermancer, both hands waving to invite me closer.

I walked over, but I didn't hurry. It was a shame they couldn't see the grin that made my face ache. Claire and Ray fell back a step. This was my moment.

I was obviously welcome. "Mine! I brought her here! My tasty pride!" Lab Rat snapped at Cybermancer.

"Noted in the minutes," an elderly man in a lab coat promised.

Cybermancer sat up straighter. That wasn't saying much. He'd been slouched almost horizontal. "We're recording this?"

"The Evil Eye remembers all," one of his fellows joked, tapping her own oversized, plastic, glowing left eye. Red, of course. Most everyone's goggles were perched up on their foreheads, but I wasn't sure how she could wear hers anyway.

Lab Rat bowed lower. "Ladies and gentlemen, mad scientists all, I introduce Bad Penny, the youngest applicant ever to our order. I have seen her deliciousness myself already."

The professor-looking guy rendered his judgment. "Tesla's Moustache, she's small."

"Small, but she's the real thing," promised Cybermancer. Hefting a grimy green beer bottle with straps and a grenade's pull tab trigger on it, he gave me a grin directly. "I owe you big time. You would not believe how these things sell. The explosion never does the same thing twice in a row, and the showier villains like Lucy love it. When the heroes get back from their convention, crime fighting is going to get very weird in LA for a month or two."

The woman with the artificial eye smacked both fists on her table. "Don't drag out the formalities. Bad Penny, Evil Eye. Evil Eye, Bad Penny. Where's your gear, girl? We're all on pins and needles to see what your tech looks like. Every report is different!"

That took me aback. "I left most of it behind. I'm not supposed to carry weapons!"

Evil Eye rolled her eyes, which was a little gross since one was at least twice the size of the other and not quite in synch. "Oh, that. Just get a table, sell maybe one thing. Essential courtesies obeyed. You think I would come here and leave all my babies behind?" She scooped the contents of her table into a pile to hug them protectively. At a glance, she seemed to like guns. Beam weapons, specifically. Lots of crystals, mirrors, and lenses.

Claire had seated herself on the edge of one of the stalls, and the guy with all the brass plates and cogs on his costume asked her, "Bad Penny built the sliding surfaces into your costume's shoes, didn't she? Take it off and—"

He stopped when the professor-looking guy cleared his throat, loudly. Claire gave the steampunk scientist a sunny, teasing grin. "Why, Mr. Mechanical Aesthetic, aren't I just a little too young for you?"

Steampunky guy stared, confused. It took him another second to get it. "No, that didn't even occur to me!"

Standing over him, the professory scientist put his hand on Mechanical Aesthetic's shoulder but addressed Claire. "Your mind control power is dangerously subtle, little girl." Grim as his face was, he sounded approving.

"So if we can't see her shoes, what did you bring?" asked the most unlikely member of the group, a stout middle aged man with a huge red beard. He wore goggles like all the others, although the metal shields around the edges looked much less fanciful.

"Well, I didn't leave everything," I conceded. What to show them? Might as well leave Ray's weaponized gloves a secret. "I suppose I could let you examine my teleport bands." Everybody knew I could teleport by now, right?

They crowded around eagerly as I pulled up my sleeve and slipped off one of the bands. Big beard guy received it in both hands as I held it out.

Why him I had no idea, but the others huddled and stared as he turned the band over and over, rubbing his fingers over the metal.

In a solemn and businesslike tone, he described what he saw. "Impure copper. Hard to know what the alloy is. The inner lining is another alloy, one I'm completely unfamiliar with." He thumped the metal with a finger. "Solid. No sign of moving parts, visible circuit connects, antennae, power source, controls, or any seams or hatches for adjustments."

I gave a little shrug. "It doesn't need any of that. It operates purely passively."

I didn't realize I'd been expecting disbelief until I didn't get it. They all looked at me with complete faith that it did work. Evil Eye asked, "Would you be willing to describe the mechanism?"

Which left me with only one thing to do. I lied! "Like I said, it's passive. Rather than moving you through space, the six bands together distort the wearer's attitude in time. They give you the ability to travel in a closed time loop that's cut away at the other end. The time you spent walking from here to there doesn't exist. The time removal has a number of odd side effects. Most are useful, like letting you move vertically to places you couldn't reach normally." Glee bubbled up in my belly as I rattled off this made-up explanation. For all I knew, that *was* how the bands worked. My power didn't object, or throw up any new plans based on this idea.

They passed the band around through everyone's hands. Some of them tapped or thumped the metal themselves. Finally, the professor type gave my teleport band back to me, and, as I slipped it back on, he asked, "I've heard you have a Conqueror orb. Is that true?"

My eyebrows lifted. "News travels fast."

"In my experience, superheroes and supervillains spend more time gossiping than fighting each other," he answered in grave, absolute deadpan.

I patted my belt pouch without thinking about it. Oops. Now they knew where Vera was. Maybe that wasn't a bad thing! And maybe there were limits to how much lying was appropriate. "It's a misunderstanding. Vera isn't a Conqueror orb. I built her myself."

That didn't deter him. "Even more interesting. Are we lucky enough that you brought her tonight?"

I cupped my hand over my belt pouch. "Well… yes, but she's deactivated. I didn't want to appear armed."

"I assure you, she'll be viewed as a status symbol, not a weapon." He was insistent. Insistent? His eyes burned with curiosity, and so did the others. Even Cybermancer leaned forward over his table and its explosives.

I was starting to blush. I could feel it on my cheeks. Thank goodness for the visor. I unzipped the pouch, pulled Vera out, and tapped her. "Time to wake up."

She did, bits of ceramic sliding away, faintly glowing ball floating up into the air as the pieces surrounded her in a pixie configuration. Like an eye, her black pupil flitted slowly and curiously between the various mad scientists. Then she dismissed all of them and floated over to roll one of Cybermancer's explosive beer bottles from side to side.

I felt weirdly awkward at how they stared at her. Jerking a thumb over my shoulder at the arms dealers behind us, I warned, "We might want to make this quick. If we don't, all the conventional ammunition in the building will rot."

The guy with the beard reached out to touch Vera, but she pushed his finger away and floated back. He frowned, staring at her. He looked confused, and he sounded a bit angry. "That's not a fake. That's a real Conqueror orb. She didn't make it."

The professor type's head bobbed slightly, and his own voice hardened. "No, it's too small. Only drones are that size, and this is obviously no drone. Battlefield support units with the gunpowder degradation field are twice that diameter."

Evil Eye peered at Vera, reaching up to plug the cord of a phone sized device into her artificial eye. It made soft beeps and ratcheting noises as she slowly twisted the rim of the eye's setting. She squinted. Her brow furrowed, then furrowed more. "These readings are ridiculous. She's emitting all kinds of energy, from infrared to the exotics I register when magic is in use. The levels bounce all over the place, and—" As she spoke, Vera turned from playing with Cybermancer's explosives to look at her, and she was interrupted when the computer noises of her plug-in burst into a brassy and very badly synthesized rendition of electro-swing.

"I guess I never cleared that program," I apologized, not sure if I was embarrassed or proud. Reaching out to cup one hand under Vera's globe, I tapped her and ordered, "Sleep." She closed up, and I tucked her safely back in my belt pouch.

They all looked at me. Very stiffly, the professor type bowed his head low and announced, "It is the official opinion of the mad science community that you may keep the name The Inscrutable Machine."

"With our blessings," the bearded guy added. I guess I'd convinced him.

Claire giggled, hopping off Mechanical Aesthetic's table. "Now that that's settled, I want to drag Bad Penny away. This is our first time in Chinatown, and we haven't even looked around yet."

"We're glad you stopped here first," the professor guy replied politely.

"I did that! Me!" Lab Rat hopped up and down like he would explode with pride.

Cybermancer threw up a hand. "Hold up! Don't leave yet! Here!" Twisting around, he rummaged through a duffle bag of explosives and pulled out... a pair of leather and brass goggles. He tossed them over, and I managed to catch them in both hands. Cybermancer winked at me. "You can't wear those with your helmet on, but you should have a pair."

Everyone gaped at him. Mechanical Aesthetic slapped his vending table. "I should have thought of that."

I giggled. I couldn't help it. I kept giggling as I buckled the goggles behind my neck so they hung like a necklace. I felt like I was floating and could hardly feel my fingers to fasten the buckle. Had I ever gotten a better gift? I couldn't remember one.

Ray's hand touched my lower back, and I took a halting step away, and then another.

"Come back soon, prodigy daughter," the professor said.

"And bring something to drink! Cybermancer experimented on all our alcohol, and the soft drinks!" called Evil Eye.

Claire hung back. Leaning over Mechanical Aesthetic's table, she clasped her hands together and gave the professor her sweetest, goofiest grin. "Would it be too much to ask for the Expert's business card?"

She'd addressed the professor guy, and he nodded. He went by 'Expert'? The others sure deferred to him like one. He pulled a little card out of his wallet and passed it into Claire's gloved hands. Rather coyly, he answered her, "Of course. I am, after all, a reputable businessman."

We turned away and walked into the chaos. This place was crazy. Inside, most of the villains were real, costumed supervillains. Not all of them. Claire tugged on my hand and pointed at a booth under the mezzanine's overhang. "Is that a sign-up station for henchmen?"

She giggled, and I admit I kinda giggled, too. Ray waved his hand dismissively. "We don't need henchmen."

Claire lifted her chin and folded her arms over her chest. "You don't. I've got a future to think about!"

An odd motion caught my eye. A kid almost our age jumped off the balcony above. His hair and clothes whipped about him as he floated down rather than fell. About halfway down his power gave out, and he dropped into the waiting arms of a villain in costume who was probably his father. It was an interesting reminder. We weren't the only kids with super powers, just the only ones trying to compete with adults.

Ray pointed, dragging my gaze in the other direction. "Lucy was right. We could have gotten a better price here." Sure enough, like the mad scientists half a dozen tables were piled with occult looking gear and manned by eccentric looking shopkeepers. Unlike the mad scientists, these tables didn't crowd together, and the magical vendors eyed each other suspiciously instead of socializing.

At one of the tables a high school girl in a black and purple dress with black and purple hair fingered wooden dolls. A twitching and elaborately engraved robot woman had its arm around her shoulders and tapped two knives lying on the table instead.

That was the kind of memory you file away to keep.

As I stared, trying to stamp into my brain the image of this girl's shy, worried face turned up to her mechanical guardian, Claire grabbed my wrist and yanked me almost off my feet. No, she wasn't Ray, but maybe I needed to make it a little more clear to her just how strong she'd become! I managed to stumble into a hurried trot as she dragged me over to the elevators shouting, "Come on, come on!"

We got to the top of the escalator, and she yanked me aside again. Only a few steps this time, before we pulled up short and she squeaked, "It is!"

Ray seemed to know what she was talking about. "Wow," he echoed in a low voice.

I didn't get it. I'd been dragged upstairs to watch a mahjong game. I wasn't even sure it was mahjong. I didn't know the rules, and I'd never played, I was just guessing because three men and a woman sat around a table playing something with funny little tiles.

Three men and one woman? Supervillainy hadn't really caught up with the twenty-first century yet.

"What am I looking at?" I whispered to Claire. They were obviously rich. Their chips were actual gold coins, and the old guy with chain mail peeking out under his shirt had a suspiciously well-dressed young woman standing very close to his chair. The scarred man in military dress had two. The shriveled little man with the bulging head only had his tiny, floating attendant robots, but I did feel some amusement that the two sleekly dressed henchmen behind the muscular dark skinned woman were gratuitously pretty. At least the shallow privileges of success were equal opportunity.

"Cossack, Tyrant, the Queen of Swords, and Organism One," she answered.

Oh. Yikes. I hadn't known what they looked like, but I knew their names alright. My parents had kept me from going to kindergarten one day because to step outside our house would have been to succumb to Organism One's mind control. For that one day, he'd ruled all of Southern California. Mom had been instrumental in uncovering the plot that had placed way too many of Cossack's minions in top government positions.

They hardly ever acted publicly, but, when they did, even one of these four could be a threat to the world. That we weren't drowning in heroes trying to bring them in said a lot about the strength of Chinatown's truce.

They looked at us. All four stopped their game and turned to stare at me, Ray, and Claire.

Ray stepped forward, taking off his hat to wave it in a deep, florid bow. For once, his exaggerated English accent sounded perfectly appropriate. "Please accept our apologies. My friends are Bad Penny and E-Claire, and I go by Reviled. I'm certain we'll be working together someday, but, for now, we had neither intent nor desire to interrupt your game."

"Reviled," repeated Queen of Swords. Gracefully, she stood up and indicated her seat. "If you want to be one of us, cash in."

Ray hesitated. Then he lowered his head. "I said 'someday.' I do not gamble when I have no chance of winning… yet."

I only half heard him, because things got very confused. In the middle of his sentence, a blur rushed past me, and pain jolted my head and neck as someone yanked my helmet off. His superhuman speed didn't help him. Ray's hand caught the blur's wrist, and pulled a teenage boy up short. None of this interrupted his answer to Queen of Swords, and the thief's butt thumped against the floor before the word 'yet' finished.

266

Without a helmet, my braids fell out over my back. Maybe only Spider was gauche enough to blackmail us with our identities, but I felt horribly exposed, and everyone around me suddenly looked much bigger and older than me. I pulled up the goggles Cybermancer'd given me and fastened them over my eyes. Much better.

The excessively curvy redhead leaned over Tyrant's shoulder and addressed me directly. "You look great, Bad Penny. More mad scientists need pigtails. Oh, and Reviled? Good answer."

Maybe she wasn't just a floozy. The four evil masterminds turned back to their game, Queen of Swords sliding back into her seat as if the redhead had spoken for them all.

It still wasn't over. A Chinese kid, maybe second grade, tapped Ray timidly on the arm. The teenage thief silently, eyes wide, handed Ray my helmet. When he had it Ray let go of the thief's arm, and the teenager bolted away with super speed. Only then did Ray turn to look at the little boy.

The Chinese boy gave him a nervous, bobbing bow and explained, "Please, Mr. Reviled, Master Scorpion wishes to speak to you."

He pointed, and we looked. An old man stood bare-chested on a mat at the other end of the mezzanine. Maybe he was only early middle-aged. Those rock hard muscles would have been the envy of any twenty-year-old, and, with his bald head, the only clues I had to his age were lines around his eyes and lines of gray in his pointy beard. He stood arrogantly straight, watching us with arms folded. Around him a loose circle of men in martial arts pajamas and ninja black watched us as well. No two of them looked remotely alike. Not even one of them looked happy.

"Please, Mr. Reviled, Master Scorpion insists," the little boy urged us.

Ray dropped my helmet into my arms and walked down the mezzanine to meet the old man. "Strode" might be a better word. Ray was leggy, and he took advantage of it with long, even steps. He might not be rushing, but he clearly wasn't taking his time.

Claire and I followed after him. Ray stopped at the edge of the mat, and Master Scorpion stared down at him. The old guy's face was as hard-edged as his chest, and he had an impressively cold, angry stare. His voice was just as harsh. "They call you Reviled."

Ray bowed, not floridly but deeply and stiffly, straight from the waist. "Everyone knows who you are, Master Scorpion."

That had technically been a lie. I didn't know who this guy was, but I was clearly the odd girl out here. The assembled ninjas watched Ray and Scorpion like the secret of life might be hidden in this conversation. Claire had her hands clasped behind her back and rocked forward and back on her heels nervously.

This scorpion guy was hard, motionless like a rock except for his eyes and his mouth—and they hardly moved as he declared, "Every week these men try to prove that they are strong enough to inherit my skills. This week you are one of them. Spar with me."

It was very much an order, and Claire didn't like it. She winced and took a half step closer to me. Ray lowered his head, a miniature echo of his former bow. "I could not possibly refuse such an invitation."

Ray stepped onto the mat. Master Scorpion stepped toward him. There was no signal that I could see. They walked up to each other, and the old guy jabbed a punch at Ray's face. It struck in an eye blink, but Ray still pushed it aside with his forearm and punched back at Master Scorpion's shoulder. They hadn't stopped walking. Their arms and legs tangled together, they swung around, and I saw Ray's elbow come within a hair's breadth of the old man's chin. Master Scorpion didn't miss. His hand slammed into Ray's midsection, sending Ray flying out off the mat to hit the wall.

I hadn't had time to scream; it happened so fast. My whole body had frozen up with tension. I forced my muscles to move. I had to check on Ray.

No, I didn't have to. Ray wheezed and fought for breath, but he pushed himself back up to his feet. For once, I didn't find his grin charming. It looked crazy. Still, he obviously couldn't do anything stupid while he was struggling to breathe and stand.

Master Scorpion pointed at Ray, arm extended like a spear. His harsh voice rasped, "I want you, boy. One year. Train under me for one year, and, when we are finished, you will humiliate Joe the Fist. You will fight him, and he will look like the child."

Still shaking, Ray bowed. His voice sounded pretty raspy too. "It was an honor to match myself against the Master, but I am not looking for a teacher right now."

My gut tightened again. Master Scorpion did not look like the kind of guy who took refusals well. When he grinned, it shocked me, and his reply sounded almost jovial. "I can wait. There are limits to what you can teach yourself. Sooner rather than later, you will come to me."

A clank off to the side pulled my eyes away from Ray and Master Scorpion. Lucyfar's hands gripped the edge of the railing, and, with a fierce jerk, she pulled herself up and over onto the mezzanine.

Lucyfar was already chattering. "That was wicked! You impressed Master Crab Face? Come on. Spider told me to keep an eye out for you kids, be your welcome wagon. I'll take you to her first, then we'll have the whole night to party! You haven't had your fortunes told yet, right?"

The change of conversation made me dizzy. Master Scorpion showed no sign that he resented or even noticed being called Master Crab Face. Lucyfar grabbed Ray's hand, and my wrist when I wouldn't let go of my helmet. Claire let out a little squeak, and I saw the flash of a black shape pushing her toward us. Claire latched onto my other arm with both of her hands. In seconds Lucyfar was pulling us all toward the escalators.

"Gangway! Official arachnid business! People cooler than you, coming through!" Lucyfar barked as she marched us down the escalators, threading us through the three supervillains who'd been content to let it carry them down normally.

We'd worked our way around to the other side of the central mall, and Lucyfar dragged us out into a cool, dark night. My pang of worry that this was too rough a pace when Ray had just been injured disappeared as fast as it arose. He might have stumbled the first few steps and breathed heavily the next few, but after that he moved normally again.

I wondered if those martial artists gathered around Master Scorpion would be angry that Ray had stolen the prize they all fought for, then rejected it. I hadn't had a chance to see them react. Lucyfar resented every second it took to travel to some new madness. As she led us down the block, she rattled off, "Spider's offices are underground. She never comes upstairs, not that I've ever seen. There are entrances all over the place, but the easiest one to use is through a garage over here."

It crept over me. Time to see Spider already? I'd been enjoying myself. I'd let myself forget about our appointment. Criminy. On the other hand, Lucyfar thought there would be an "after" and that we'd even be in the mood for fun. Maybe it wouldn't be that bad.

She walked us down a block of relentlessly similar squat white shops, then paused at the little alley backing them up. Squinting down it, she nodded sharply. "We'll go in the back. Might as well take the easiest way."

She hustled us down the alley. It felt like we were being hustled. Even for Lucyfar this was too fast, too manic, and too suspicious. What could I do about it? I should say something.

Someone else spoke up for me. The transparent, gray upper body of The Apparition floated out of a wall as we passed and demanded, "Lucy, what are you doing?!"

Lucy let go of my and Ray's arms, and scratched the back of her head. She looked completely unconvincingly sheepish. "Come on, App. Don't make this any more awkward than it already is."

The Apparition glared at her. "They're our friends!"

Lucyfar held up her hands. "Spider insisted. *Really* insisted. You know?"

The Apparition gave up on her and turned to yell at us what I'd already figured out. "Kids, this is an ambush. Run!"

Too late. With a thunderous clatter, the wall next to us exploded. A mammoth, gray shape lunged for Ray, arms outstretched. The super-powered thug wasn't fast enough, and the hit to the stomach hadn't slowed Ray down enough. He jumped, planting a hand on the monster's head to flip over and behind him. Ray's foot connected in a savage kick on the thug's kidneys as he dropped, but the thing didn't even seem to notice.

The thug swung around. He was ugly. It wasn't pebbly, but he had a thick, wrinkly gray hide like a rhinoceros, and from my tiny point of reference he looked eight feet tall. I'd never seen so many muscles on anything. How could his arms even move? When he did move, slits gaped like gills all over him. It was thoroughly gross and also familiar.

"Aren't you supposed to deal with nuisances like the ghost, Witch Hunter?" demanded a screechy voice. The villain who flopped out of a window and onto the alley's concrete behind us looked vaguely like the big guy, but with lots more fins and a rubbery round mouth with teeth everywhere.

This one was obvious. "They call you Hagfish, right?" I asked.

The hulking villain shuffled around and croaked, "And I'm Leviathan, and you humiliated my nephew in front of the whole world." Yes, that was why he was familiar. This guy was almost as ugly as Sharky, and bigger. Way, way bigger.

And I was unarmed. And we were outnumbered. Witch Hunter stepped out of a doorway beyond Leviathan, while a window above him slapped open and a man in one of those Carnivale skeleton costumes perched on the sill. Sharp spikes that certainly looked like bone stuck out of that costume everywhere.

"Not that we're here for anything that personal. The Council Of Seven And A Half hired us to tell you how happy they aren't," cut in Witch Hunter. In this narrow alley, he left his swords sheathed and had out a couple of exotic knives with multiple curving blades.

I glared at Lucyfar, standing on the other side of Hagfish. She leaned against a wall, arms folded, pretending this had nothing to do with her. After a few seconds of my stare, she spread her hands in an awkward shrug. "I was ordered by Spider to lead you here and not interfere, one way or the other."

Claire slid into motion, ducking under Leviathan's arms and holding up her hands to Witch Hunter and the villain in the skeleton suit as she coasted on frictionless feet out the other side. She glanced back at us, then at them, eyebrows raised in amused and friendly disbelief. "Is this the time and place for a fight, guys? You've delivered your warning. Not to sound too clichéd, but can't we all just get along?"

She tilted her head to one side, smiling infectiously. I knew I would rather talk about this. At the very least we could put this off for a few minutes. These guys had to be feeling the pressure. Who could hit a little girl in bear pajamas?

Who could? I had to answer that question. I had to think instead of stare at Claire's lumpy, wrinkled costume and her grinning cherubic face and messy blonde bangs. At least I knew to fight this. Leviathan and Witch Hunter could only gape. Even the guy from the window jumped down, his own head tilting as he stared at down at Claire with a crooked, adoring smile.

After all these rough, throaty villains he had a surprisingly honeyed voice. "You are the sweetest child I have ever met. It's like meeting an angel." His hand darted out and closed around Claire's throat, lifting her off the concrete. Her bear feet flopped as she kicked helplessly, like a toddler.

Lifting Claire's face to his, the villain in the skeleton suit purred excitedly, "I have to own your skeleton. Oh, yes."

Cold panic washed through me, pushing away the warm, comfortable feeling that had kept me staring. I had to save Claire. What could I do? I could escape easily, but there was no way I was leaving her behind. I hadn't brought any weapons but Vera. I wasn't sure even Vera could hurt Leviathan. Ray could certainly take the bone guy, maybe him and Witch Hunter together, but the bony white blades on the back of the skeleton costume's gloves were already pressed against Claire's neck. Even if we won, we wouldn't be able to save her. There had to be something I could do.

I couldn't think of anything.

I heard a thump behind me. Something else was going on. The skeleton suit murderer and Witch Hunter weren't looking at Claire, or me, or even Ray anymore. They were looking past me, so I turned around.

Bull stood in the mouth of the alley. Blood matted the fur around one swollen eye, and he limped as he walked up the alley toward us, but that was Bull. I was surrounded by legends tonight.

"What do you creeps think you're doing to those poor kids?" he snarled. He had a faint lisp, and he certainly looked like he'd been hit in the mouth one too many times tonight. Underneath that, I could still make out a mild Irish accent.

"We're working for the Council. This is none of your business," Witch Hunter answered him.

Witch Hunter's tone had been cool and official. Leviathan's growl had a lot more venom. "Look at you. You're a has-been. Go away before we hurt you."

Bull limped past Lucy, past Hagfish, past me. With swollen eyes, he met Leviathan's yellow-eyed stare. Then Bull hit the gray giant.

The blow wasn't lightning fast like Ray's and Master Scorpion's, and Leviathan pulled up his stubby arms to block it. That didn't make any difference. When Bull's fist hit, air blasted past me and the boom shut out all other sound, leaving my ears ringing. This was the kind of punch I'd seen Bull trading in the ring earlier. His metal opponent had been able to take it. Leviathan flew off his feet, soaring down the alley to crash into and flatten a dumpster. Ray, Witch Hunter, and the skeleton-costumed villain ducked out of the way, and the skeleton man dropped Claire in the process.

I moved. One step brought me to Claire, and I threw my arms around her. Bone blades swung toward me. I just had to lurch, reaching out a foot,

272

and those blades never struck. Instead, I set my foot down on the far side of Bull. My lungs seized up, and fire knotted all the muscles in my body. They gave out under me, but Claire caught me as I fell. Lying across her lap, I gasped for breath. I'd be fine in a second, but that was too far to have carried Claire's weight in a panic. My teleport rings were not kind.

Bull kept limping forward. Thanks to his long head, I could see his lips pulling up in a sneer at the edges. Over the ringing in my ears I could easily hear the contempt in his voice. "I'm a has-been, that's true. I'm still out of your league."

Behind me and Claire, Hagfish backed away several paces. His webbed hands swung up in panic. "Spider gave us permission to punish these children!"

Hagfish backed up past Lucyfar. She grinned at him, showing off all her teeth before she answered in a wicked drawl, "And I can hear Spider's voice now. 'I didn't say you would win.'"

"Am I going to have to hit anyone else?" Bull demanded, his voice echoing loudly down the alley. The villain in the skeleton suit scurried away. Witch Hunter backed up, face averted, and sheathed his knives. Hagfish just ran, out of the mouth of the alley and into the night.

Bull grunted. "Then we're leaving." Turning around ponderously, he stumped back up to me and Claire. Big, hairy hands curled around our waists, hoisting us up and seating us on his broad shoulders. I clung to a horn, breathing deeply, getting my wind back. I'd be fine in a few more seconds. It looked like everything would be fine now.

Maybe not everyone felt as relieved as I did. The horn I leaned against pulled at me as Bull turned his head, looking down at Ray and telling him gruffly, "Don't let it nag you, son. Your girls are safe."

Ray didn't answer. I couldn't see his face under the brim of his hat, but he nodded and kept walking alongside Bull.

The shoulder I rode on rocked gently up and down, uneven thanks to the limp in Bull's gait. He carried us out onto the dimly lit Chinatown street. In the alley behind us, I suddenly heard Lucy speak up. "Well! I'd say that fight is officially over, and I'm on my own time again. I know this is boring and personal and judgmental of me, but, Bones, I feel a spree of superheroing coming on. You will get way, way out of town, or every crime you commit from now on is going to end with you in the hospital punctured like Swiss cheese. You have no friends, Jagged Bones. Nobody will step up to defend a freak like you. Remember that." Wow. Her voice had started off with its usual playful cheer, but every sentence got sharper until her words oozed anger.

Bull kept walking, carrying us out of hearing range. When we lost Lucy's voice, he scowled and grunted. "Spitting in the wind. For every gentleman rogue in this game, there's ten scum like that."

I just held onto his horn with both hands. Claire did the same. She looked shakier than I did, and I couldn't blame her. "Thanks," I managed to whisper.

"Come on. You'll feel better with something to eat," was Bull's non-answer.

I leaned against Bull's horn and let myself go blank as he walked back to the big central building. It had been an intense evening already, and it was far from over. I welcomed a couple of minutes rest.

My gaze drifted down to watch Ray, walking next to us and a little behind. I couldn't see his face under the hat, but he kept pressing his palms together, pulling them apart to form up a pink and purple ball of energy in-between, then slowly pushing that ball back into the gems inside his gloves. Then he would do it again, drawing out the energy ball and forcing it back into storage.

Bull noticed too. His giant hand reached out and covered both of Ray's. "I told you, son. Don't let it nag you. This life will drown you in could-have-beens if you let it."

Ray nodded, and, when Bull let go, his hands fell back by his sides.

We walked back into the noise and the crowd, and the warm golden light that spilled out of the interior of the mall. Bull had mentioned food, and something smelled good, like the sweet and sour sauces of oriental food. Sure enough, several tables of food were set up by the door. Bull stopped in front of one and pointed at one of the trays, then flashed three fingers at the Chinese young man in the white outfit behind the table. Must not speak English.

Bull handed each of us a package wrapped in white paper as he explained, "There's a restaurant on the top floor. They cater for us on the weekend. I'm sure Spider pays them well, but, still, good people and great food."

I unwrapped a big, sticky ,and soft white ball. It smelled like rice. On the other side of Bull's head, Claire unwrapped hers and spoke for the first time since Jagged Bones grabbed her. "Would you mind giving me your autograph? Being rescued by Bull is kind of a big deal to me."

I bit into the ball. It tasted like rice, but sweet and puffy and slightly gooey. Then I bit deeper into intensely sweet and sour pork, and the taste flooded my senses. This was great. Why had I never had one of these before?!

Oh, right. Because superheroes didn't go to Chinatown.

Bull chuckled. It was a good thing I'd let go of his horn to eat this rice bun, because I'd have been yanked off his shoulder when he turned his head to look up at Claire. He sounded gruffly dismissive, but he agreed, "Sure. I never liked seeing anybody hurt kids. Now that I've got a daughter your age, I can't stand it."

I desperately clamped down on my imagination. Bull had a daughter? This giant, hairy man-beast had... there were so many questions here I did not want answered. I would just file this under "There's someone for everyone out there."

Instead, I swallowed a mouthful of pork bun and changed the subject. "You look pretty roughed up. Did you get hit by a train?" I hadn't meant it as a joke, but it sounded like one when I heard it.

He shook his head. Thank goodness I wasn't holding onto his horn anymore. "I lost a boxing match."

I knew I should drop it, but I couldn't. I was too surprised. "Who could beat Bull? My Mom told me that when you were a teenager and fought Evolution, all the other villains were furious because of how strong he got."

Bull's sigh sounded no worse than resigned. "That was forty years ago. These days, the answer is 'everyone.'"

Then he changed the subject himself, telling us in a much more jovial tone, "Anyway, I was beaten once by The Audit, and she has no powers at all. You'd have been babies when it happened."

Claire rubbed sauce off her mouth with the wrist of her bear suit so she could express her disbelief. "How?"

"Pushed sand into my eyes, then my nose, my ears, and my mouth. While I could barely see, she lured me into punching a telephone pole and electrocuting myself. Then she hit me with a bus." He chuckled. After this many years, a memory like that must seem darkly humorous to him. To me, it was a reminder why I never, ever wanted Mom to find out I'm a supervillain.

Ray listened with a slight, vicious smile. To him, I suspect this was a tutorial.

Soft and sweet, Claire took hold of one of Bull's horns again and asked, "Can I still have your autograph?"

Trust Claire to know exactly what to say. Bull's next chuckle sounded honestly pleased. "Sure."

Ray had his go at changing the subject, tilting his head to the side and asking, "Hey, Lucyfar said something about getting our fortune told. Was she just making that up?"

I had a front row seat to Bull's eyes widening. "That's right. This is your first time in Chinatown, isn't it? You have a lot to see."

With that he lurched into motion, and I stuffed the rest of my pork bun in my mouth and clung to his horn. His limp had eased, and he carried us through the crowd inside the mall to one of the tiny, dark shops lining the walls. This one hadn't been sealed up. It had been emptied, except for the mechanical shape of a pinball machine lurking against the back wall.

At least, it had the size and shape of a pinball machine. In the shadows I didn't get a good look until Bull carried us right up to it. There were no bumpers, no glass-encased area for the ball. The machine's counter mostly held a mechanical arm holding a pen, a box the pen stuck into, and a lot of levers and gears supporting both. The back had been decorated in astrological constellations and eyes—wood, plastic, glass, and ceramic eyes of all colors that turned stiffly to watch us when we moved. Creepy in a fun and cheesy way.

The world dipped as Bull crouched, sliding me and Claire off his shoulders to stand in front of the machine. "What do we do?" I asked.

"Turn the crank," Bull answered. A brass handle stuck out of one side. Ray grabbed hold of it in one hand and churned it around and around. As he did, the mechanical arm moved, scribbling audibly with the pen on something inside the box. After a few seconds of that, a card slid out in front of me with "Bad Penny" written on the back in elegant script.

Ray let go of the handle, but the arm kept moving. Moments later two other cards fell into place on either side of mine. They read "E-Claire" and "Reviled." Of course.

I picked up my card. Ray and Claire picked up theirs. I had to squint in the dark shop and with goggles that didn't match my nearsightedness, but mine read "She is no threat to you."

Slowly and hesitantly I announced, "I think it's telling me not to blame Lucy."

Claire nodded, just as slowly. "She's definitely telling me that."

When Ray didn't say anything immediately, Claire and I looked over at him. He stared at his card with wide eyes and a shocked, intense expression. He kept staring at it for several more seconds before telling us, "Mine is personal. Too personal to be a coincidence. Is this machine always right?" While Ray looked up at Bull for an answer he slid the card with great care into the bottom of his shoe. Wow. He must have gotten a good one. I'd have to push aside my curiosity and forget about it. It was pretty plain this was a secret Ray would never share.

Bull nodded. Jeepers, he was tall. And wide. Now that we were on the floor, he loomed. He still looked like he'd been hit by a train. At least he sounded cheerful about it all now. "Oh, yes. A lot of villains are too proud to listen, and they regret it every time. Every time." A flat-toothed grin split his face. "Now, if this is your first time, you kids are going to love the petting zoo."

I knew there couldn't be a petting zoo. At least, I almost knew there couldn't be a petting zoo. I still wanted to slap Bull when we got there, but I'd have only hurt my hand.

Where Bull actually took us was around the opposite side of the central building from where we'd seen him fighting. A man and a woman with black costumes covering every inch of skin had cages of varying sizes set out. They were selling animals. Exotic animals. Mutated, supervillainy type animals.

I had no intention of petting any of them, but Bull was right, it was great to wander between them. I didn't even want to get too close to the cage holding two velociraptors. Their feathers were as brightly red and yellow and blue as any parrot's, but their fangs, the massive claws on their back feet, and the intently hungry stares they gave me kept them from looking ridiculous.

Claire peered into a metal cat carrier perched on top of a giant armadillo's cage, and let out a squeal. "Dragons! They have dragons! I want a dragon!"

"I want one of these," Ray called back to her. He was feeding the last shred of his pork bun to a large weasel, half of whose body had been covered or replaced with shiny chrome cybernetics. It looked frighteningly intelligent when it bobbed its head in gratitude to him.

I unzipped my belt pouch, pulled out my unconscious Vera, and tossed the ball up in the air, then caught it again. As smugly as I could, I told them, "I'm happy with the pet I have. And that's good, because we can't afford any of these."

"Yet," Ray added. There he might have a point.

Staying bent to the side to peek at her dragon as long as possible, Claire wandered back over to me. When she surrendered and straightened up, she remarked, "I'm amazed they can sell these out in the open. This is exactly the kind of trade the superheroes would love to shut down."

I'd noticed this already when we met the masterminds. Bull confirmed my thoughts. "Chinatown is off limits to heroes. They don't come here, and the smart heroes keep the stupid heroes from butting in. If they tried to put down our weekends in Chinatown they'd start a war that would level downtown. No one wants that, and we keep things peaceful enough they're never tempted."

Ray abandoned his weasel to join us. Tugging on the brim of his hat, he put in his own two cents. "That's very tidy for Spider, who lives here where no hero will ever come after her."

That reminded me. I pulled out my smart phone. Maybe I should leave it at home in case it got damaged during supervillaining, but how else would I check the time? A press of a button, and it read nine-thirty. My heart tensed up a little, but only a little.

"It's almost time. We'd better go looking for Spider." I announced.

Bull shrugged. "Easy to do. She has entrances to her office all over Chinatown. I'll take you to the one right inside." So Lucyfar had been honest about that. She'd just deliberately taken us to the wrong entrance.

Bull crouched, and forearms like trees wrapped around me and Claire, hoisting us up onto his shoulders again. With Ray tagging along behind, he limped off around the building. Yes, the limp was back, and a puffy bruised ring matted with drying blood surrounded the eye next to me.

I would be poking a worse wound, but I had to ask. "Bull, why are you a supervillain?"

He didn't answer for a couple of steps. When he did, he sounded more calm than I'd expected. "I could give you kids a sad song and dance about how nobody wants to hire you when you look like a monster, but the truth is I didn't need much of an excuse to get into this life. I like to fight. I always have. A job as a supervillain let me trade punches with the toughest men and women on the planet."

My voice cracked a little and my stomach turned over from guilt, but I kept poking. I liked him too much to let this go. "I don't think you like it anymore."

"Nobody likes to lose," he answered, dismissive with a hint of sourness.

"That's not what I mean."

The shoulder I rode on heaved up and down as Bull sighed hugely. If he brushed this off, I wasn't going to poke anymore. He didn't brush it off. "You're right, of course. Half the reason I keep losing fights these days is that I'm not into it like I used to be, not anymore. Yes, I'm sixty. I'm not as fast or as flexible anymore, but that's not it. Used to be, when Dynamite knocked me on my backside I got right back up so he could hit me again. I don't have that will to win now." Sixty? There was gray in the brown fur, yes. It made sense. He'd been a big name before my parents' time. He was old enough to have fought Evolution, even if only once.

"Have you considered retiring?" I asked quietly. Sixty. Sixty, and he wasn't having fun anymore.

Bull slowed down, shook his head. Now he sounded sad. "Can't afford to. The heroes would let me. I was smart enough to earn respect instead of enemies, at least. Doesn't matter. I don't have the money."

That honestly surprised me. "You were on top for a long time. Even if things are bad now, I would have thought you'd made enough for a lifetime."

He shook his head, trudging along tiredly through the crowd. That was uncomfortably symbolic right now. "For a smart girl like you, yes, it would have been enough. I always had more muscle than brains. It all ran through my fingers. Every penny I was smart enough to save went into my wife and daughter's trust fund, and there's nothing I'm more proud of in my life."

Bull had a wife. I still didn't want to fit that thought into my brain, but it was part of the conversation. Anyway, it made a sad sense. "Divorce in all but name, I guess?"

Bull surprised me. He shook his head vehemently, and a passionate growl came back to his voice. "Irene and I will love each other until the day we die. I won't make Cat grow up with a supervillain as a father."

My eyes started to sting. The twentieth century's most famous bruiser wanted to fade into obscure poverty so his daughter could grow up in innocence. I hoped my career wasn't that tragic.

Ray deliberately interrupted the moment. He grabbed Bull's wrist and had enough strength even Bull had to notice. Looking right up into the hairy animal face, Ray told him, "I know what kind of parents a child regrets having. Your daughter would love to have you as her father."

Bull stopped. We'd reached our destination, and he lifted me and Claire off his shoulders and set us down in front of a plain stairwell door with the usual tiny glass window. He set his hand on my head, and it covered my scalp and his fingers nearly obscured my vision. "Spider's office is right down there. I'll think about what you said. I've had this conversation a hundred times, but it's different hearing it from a kid Cat's age."

Absolutely solemn, ramrod straight, and without a trace of his usually joking smile, Ray told Bull, "You would make her the happiest daughter in the world."

Claire brushed at a lock of her bangs, sticking out from under the hood of her pajamas. In contrast to Ray's seriousness, she gave Bull a warm, encouraging smile. "If she gets super powers of her own, she'll need a father who can tell her what it's like, and who will support her no matter what."

Bull just stood there. I couldn't read the expression on his bruised animal face. I grabbed hold of Claire and Ray's shoulders, and gave a little tug. "Come on. We shouldn't push. Thank you, Bull. It was an honor."

To finish making the point, I turned away from Bull and pulled open the door to the stairwell. From inside, down the stairs and across from the door, Lucyfar tossed me my helmet. Ray caught the door, and I caught the helmet in both hands. Oh, yeah. I must have dropped it in the alley. I'd been busy.

"Can I trade this for being friends again?" Lucyfar asked with a crooked grin.

I shook my head and couldn't restrain a laugh. "Spider must really have some leverage on you."

Everything rolled off Lucyfar's back. She shrugged casually and honestly looked casual. "Well, that, and I figured you'd clean their clocks. Not sure you wouldn't have anyway, but I didn't think the Council would hire a homicidal freakshow like Jagged Bones."

Behind me, Bull grunted. "Don't worry about Bones. He's on Mourning Dove's list. He's going to accidentally not survive a fight with her soon."

And that was why nobody got personal. The thought made me shiver. Hero or villain, I wanted to stay far away from that side of the community.

Bull shut the door. I walked down the stairs. Claire and Ray skipped down the stairs, two at a time. Lucyfar slid down the railing. The stairs were tight and bent in a square, and the jolting stop-and-start ride couldn't have been much fun. Lucyfar did it anyway.

The whole stairwell was businesslike cement, featurelessly gray, and as we reached the bottom I observed, "This looks like a parking garage staircase."

Lucy hopped off of the railing, pulled open the door, and stood next to it like a butler. "It is. Welcome to the Spider's parlor, kids. I'm rooting for you."

It really was an underground parking garage. Me, Ray, and Claire shuffled out into it and looked around as the door swung slowly shut behind us. It didn't look like an office or a home. It looked like a garage, a huge room with a high ceiling. Floor, ceiling, and lots of support columns were all made out of dull, gray cement. There weren't any cars, but I could see a couple of sloping exits for them way down along the walls.

The very obvious difference from a regular garage was the mess. Tangled white cables stretched from support column to support column, tied into awkward knots with each other, and carpeted the ceiling. In the back they formed a crude globe. The whole mess looked exactly like a gigantic cobweb, which made the huge, shiny black shape hanging in it...

"Wow," Ray breathed. He'd gotten there a half second before I had. Spider was a spider. A bulbous, gleaming, long-legged black widow the size of a rhinoceros hanging upside down on the near end of the web. As I watched she crept up to the edge, claws at the end of a foreleg pulling aside one of the silk cables.

Claire hadn't gotten it until that moment. She screamed. Her shriek echoed through the garage, high-pitched and going on and on. Ray grabbed her, wrapping his arms around her and squeezing her to his chest so she couldn't move. I wrapped my arms around both of them and hugged Claire close. The scream choked off, turning to gasping whimpers.

Its mouth didn't move, but the pleasant businesswoman's voice obviously came from Spider. "Miss E-Claire, I suggest you don't look directly at me. Please provide her with the comfort she needs, Reviled and Bad Penny. This reaction is quite common, even in the most hardened criminals."

Ray swiveled, and Claire turned her head further, until she looked straight back at the door of the stairwell. I felt her breathing get deeper, slower, more deliberate. I couldn't blame her for the shock. We were within reach of those long, stilt-like legs, and Spider's face was a jumble of folded fangs, fake-looking domed eyes, and twitching, miniature legs.

Ray had no trouble looking straight at her. He sounded sincerely warm as he answered Spider, "I would take my hat off for a lovely lady, but I hope you understand that my friend comes first."

Claire's head gave a little shake, and she whispered, "I'm fine. I'm just— I'm fine. As long as I don't look at... her."

Spider shrank back into her web a few feet. Perhaps she was being polite. Her forelegs folded up close to her face, such as it was. Hanging upside down, I could just barely see the blood red hourglass on the underside of her bulbous abdomen. Even watching carefully I couldn't see anything move when she spoke. "Ah, young Ray—I'm sorry, Reviled—is an entomophile. I apologize to E-Claire. As fond as I am of surprises, I have nothing to do with my species being such a tightly kept secret. Tightly kept indeed, if it came as a surprise to a girl who has researched our community so thoroughly." She sounded sincere, for all that counted.

It counted for nothing. I glared. Maybe I was trembling a little too, but holding Claire covered that perfectly. "You've made your point. You have plenty of blackmail material on us."

"This is a very personal conversation, isn't it?" Ray didn't quite sound accusing, but he stressed the word "personal" enough to make his point.

Spider curled a back leg up over herself and began to nibble on the spines that lined it like a hacksaw. The process didn't interfere with her voice at all. "I obey not only the letter, but the spirit of the rules, children. Unfortunately, those rules apply between heroes and villains. When dealing with other villains, we're not quite as rigorous. No one is certain the rules apply to The Inscrutable Machine at all, and you've caused a great deal of confusion by not only daring to become supervillains, but by being good at it. Where there is confusion, I believe there is always opportunity."

Between them, Claire's cowering and Spider's lecturing speech dissolved my anxiety in a warm, acid anger. "What do you want?" I snapped. Dumb, Penny, but what difference would rudeness make?

My rudeness didn't bother Spider at all. At least, she kept nibbling on her leg and her voice remained pleasantly, jadedly urbane. "I want to end that confusion to our advantage. When The Inscrutable Machine breaks into Mech's laboratory and destroys his armor and backup armor and steals his files, no one will doubt that you're fully fledged supervillains."

That was insane. I couldn't even list the reasons that was crazy. I grabbed at the only ones I hoped Spider might care about. "Mech is at the superhero conference right now. Attacking his lab is off-limits. Even you wouldn't break the rules like that."

The back leg slid out of Spider's fangs and fastened its claws around a silk line stuck to the ceiling. Spider's mysterious voice remained implacable, crisp and gently condescending. "I never break the rules, children. Not ever. I wrote them in the first place and have gone to great lengths to enforce them. As we speak, heroes are arguing with my representative at the conference, refusing to accept that you are supervillains under my protection or that the rules apply to you. Performing this task should convince them that The Inscrutable Machine needs to be bound by all of the obligations and protections of regular supervillains." Her middle legs, one pair at a time, unhooked from their weblines and grabbed new ones. I couldn't read a spider's display of emotions, but she did sound just a bit more smug as she finished, "Mech's inconvenience will be highly useful to my plans, and a generous payment will be placed in your bank accounts."

It sounded like a declaration that everyone wins. Except Mech, anyway. I couldn't help but notice she'd planted another reference to knowing everything about us. It chilled me a little, but that rekindled my anger.

"Protections like not being ambushed in a supposedly safe haven?" Yes, it galled me. Why were we the only ones who weren't safe?

Spider waved a foreleg. That gesture was obvious, at least. It still looked strange upside down. "An excellent point. The Council of Seven and a Half would be well within their rights to issue such a warning, but only while you actively pursued supervillain business."

"And if we refuse?" I demanded. Yes. Yes, I wanted to refuse. My gut burned to refuse. This was so obviously a trap. The task was beyond us, we hadn't chosen to do it, and there were too many hidden snares even if we succeeded. We couldn't possibly succeed.

Could we?

It didn't matter. Spider reached a foreleg out and plucked the nearest rope of webbing to us, which successfully reminded me of how little choice we had. A stern touch crept into her voice as she warned, "I'm afraid I will have to insist. You girls may believe you can weather the storm of revelation thanks to your parents' influence, but young Mr. Viles is not so fortunate."

I turned my head to look at Ray. He was trying to hide it, trying to keep his face calm, but from this close the mask-like stiffness gave him away. Spider was right. Ray never talked about his parents, ever. I knew mine would forgive me eventually, but Ray clearly didn't have that shield.

Anger knotted my stomach. I didn't want to give in here. I hated being railroaded, that Spider was threatening my friend to control me. I knew the job was wrapped up in a web of strings attached. How could we hope to break into Mech's laboratory anyway? His security systems would include every brilliant, crazy device he and my father together could invent. Could we possibly get through that?

Mostly I hated having no choice. It ate at me, crawled up my spine. That didn't matter, because we had no choice. I did the best I could and hedged. "We'll think about it."

Spider folded its forelegs again, her voice going back to pretending this was all completely friendly. "While you consider the pluses and minuses of my offer, I hope you'll enjoy mixing with your fellows upstairs. It is my sincere hope and belief you'll be joining us every weekend for a long time."

Claire couldn't take anymore. She broke out of my and Ray's arms, yanked open the door to the stairwell, and ducked through and out of sight. There wasn't anything else we could do, and the interview was over anyway. Ray and I followed.

CHAPTER EIGHTEEN

We trudged up the cement stairs and out into the commotion of the open market, then all three of us collapsed against the wall. We took a deep breath together, and let it out. Bull and Lucyfar were nowhere in evidence, and, for that, I was grateful.

Me and Ray looked over at Claire. She noticed our stares and gave us a faint smile and a shake of her head. "I'm fine, really. I just wasn't expecting something so ugly." Her voice didn't quiver anymore, so I had to believe her.

Ray wasn't quite ready to leave it at that. "Are you sure? Is there anything we can do for you?" he pressed.

Claire shook her head again, and leaned back against the wall. "I just need to go home and rest. I'm burned out and want to be alone."

I nodded. I felt drained enough the gesture must have looked limp and lolling. "I one hundred percent agree. Can you two get home alone?"

Really, that was me and Ray both asking Claire. She nodded, stronger than before. "Easy. I'll take the subway so I can sit down, but easy."

I let out a loud sigh, and my shoulders relaxed a bit more. "Good. I loved the party…"

When I paused to look for a word, Ray filled in, "It was incredible." Claire nodded.

"But I've had my fill and then some. Not to mention I need time to think about Spider," I finished.

"Penny…" Ray started, but this time he didn't know what to say.

I knew what he meant. "I'm fine," I insisted, holding up a hand. "I'm not going to freak out. I don't like being backed into a corner, but I'm not going to panic or anything."

We pushed ourselves off the wall and went our separate ways. For me that was easy. The light bike did most of the driving, letting me zone and listen to the swishing and honking of cars. My neighborhood was dark, and I'd left the lights off, so I felt safe walking right up to the door and letting myself in.

The house felt empty with my parents gone. That stillness washed over me, deeply soothing. Thank goodness they were out of town. I felt draggy and tired, and it was way past bedtime, but I didn't like the idea of going straight to sleep. I needed to unwind, let it all bump around in my head.

I ended up shoving my jumpsuit under my bed again and sitting at my computer desk feeding plastic forks to The Machine. It didn't seem happy or sad, life without consciousness, but it chewed them down and then spat them back out exactly like they had been, then coughed up little gooey clumps of fat and protein that had been clinging to them. A tin can met a similar fate, except he ended up spreading his mouth wide and spitting out the original can intact, with the lid back in place.

While he did that, I poked around online. Nowhere I'd have to talk to people. I looked up The Inscrutable Machine. After all, Claire and Ray said there were whole websites talking about us.

There were, although they didn't have much to say. A few photos, a few mostly correct stories, a few rumors, and a lot of speculation. Most commenters thought I was the leader, although a strong argument ran that Claire led because Ray and I did all the fighting. They had a physical photo of us leaving the warehouse where we'd fought Marvelous, so they knew the jammed communications and stalled traffic in the area were my fault. There were entire, lengthy conversations about how my tech had changed.

The craziest and most amusing to me was that the idea had somehow gotten out that I'd dug up Vera when I hit the trash heap. They hadn't even known I'd dug up a landfill, they didn't know what Vera was, and the words "Conqueror orb" appeared nowhere, but there the rumor was in the tech discussion. Huh.

I looked up Mech instead. Wow, was he popular. Couldn't blame anybody. That did mean I found whole lists of his equipment, descriptions of how he swapped out different weapons at different times. He had a computer virus ray for taking out cybernetic enemies? Yikes. What would that do to Vera? He'd adapted freeze rays and smokescreens taken from enemies. He had rocket launchers he rarely used, and a point-defense laser. A point-defense laser. Seriously? He had backup jet boots, but mostly used a backpack with glowing coils fans speculators thought might be antigravity. In the back of my head, the boots and the backpack looked different. Mech had made the boots himself. The backpack was my dad's tech. So was the laser and the energy shield. I didn't know Dad had even invented an energy shield, although I shouldn't be surprised. Maybe he'd copied Conqueror tech. My super power felt comfortable with that idea.

And even without the shield his armor was made of ablative layers, each microscopic and designed to repel a different threat. The armor was tough. Even sitting in a closet, it would not be easy to destroy.

I'd piddled enough. I turned off the light and went to bed.

Mech had access to the most advanced technology humanity could produce, and a wide variety of it. Spider wanted us to break into his base. Three brand new supervillains against those kinds of defenses. What an outrageous challenge.

I fell asleep.

I knew I'd slept, and light glowed through my curtains, but I woke up to the same thought. We'd been thrown an outrageous challenge. Not an impossible task, just an outrageous challenge.

Not impossible, so I wasn't trapped. We could do this. We could break out. Could, and would. You underestimate The Inscrutable Machine at your peril.

My heart and my body went loose, relaxed. Then it tensed up again, not with anxiety but energy. We were going to win this.

I swung out of bed. Seconds later I had my computer booted up, but Ray and Claire weren't online. Not an obstacle, but… reluctantly, I went and took a shower. A fast shower. Then I made a sandwich. Still damp, gulping down cola between swallows, I headed back to my room and grabbed my phone.

I dialed up Claire. She sounded groggy. "Penny?"

"Spider sent you the information on Mech's lab already, right?" I demanded.

"Sure. It was in my email when I got home last night. My home email, too." Sulkily, she added, "Creepy bug."

"Forward it to me. Email me everything we have about Mech's lab, then meet me at ours."

Drowsiness turned to confusion in Claire's voice. "Now?"

"Waiting won't do us any good. Do you know a fast way to contact Ray?" Email would be too slow. Victory was for those who don't hesitate.

Claire yawned. "Sure. He has a phone now, you know. You just didn't answer his calls."

She gave me Ray's number, and I let her go.

I dialed Ray immediately, but he didn't answer immediately. His phone rang. And rang. I sat there, waiting. It was a cell phone. He'd hear it. Or I'd annoy him enough he had to answer.

"Ray?" I asked as he picked up, just to be sure it was Ray who picked up.

"Penny, are you okay?" Ray didn't sound sleepy. He sounded haunted, not even a trace of teasing in his solemn voice.

"I'm fine." I was, this time.

He wasn't. "Penny, I want you to know, we don't have to do this." His voice even sounded a touch ragged. Had he been crying, or was I imagining that?

I could calm him down much better in person, either way. I certainly knew how to get his mind off his troubles, but not over the phone. "Come to the lair, and we'll discuss it there. Okay?"

He noticed the emphasis I'd put on the last word. It worked. "Okay."

"See you in a few," I promised and hung up. Then I dragged my jumpsuit out from under my bed, and put it on.

It was the middle of the day outside, bright and sunny, and I'd be totally obvious walking out of my parents' house in a supervillain costume. I dragged on a sweater and my looser pants. That would do.

Then I rushed out the door, hopped on my bicycle, and sped as fast as I could down to school. I only teleported across one intersection. It turned red right in front of me, and nobody seemed to be around. I felt stupid afterwards. Don't hesitate, but don't rush. Super powers were enough fun, and I didn't need to take dumb risks with them.

I took the elevator down because that was the easiest way to stow my bike. The lair was empty except for my mad scientist clutter. I'd beaten Claire and Ray here, but I guess I shouldn't have been surprised. It was convenient. I had something I wanted to do first.

Okay, power. What was that wonderful idea you had back in the witch's shop? Was it still there? It was. Instructions, measurements, diagrams of forces I'd never understand painted themselves in my head. I could see the whole thing. Mostly, I'd need a needle and thread.

Did I have a needle and thread? I kneeled down and rooted through the remaining pile of bits from Dad's discard bin. There might be a needle in there. As for thread, I twisted The Machine until he let go of my wrist, threw him onto a pile of burlap cloth, and ordered, "Turn the top layer into string for me."

He got to chewing, I sorted through chips and bits of wiring and electrodes and what all. A sewing needle! Heavily magnetized. The power in my head could tell, and the blueprint shifted subtly. The Machine spat out thick, crude twine. The image in my head shifted again, but not by much.

I grabbed the bag of handkerchiefs and started sewing. I didn't have a clue how to sew, so I let my power guide my fingers, drifting into a dream of construction. It wasn't all sewing. I had to flex gold wire at some point, didn't I? Mad scientists sure used a lot of gold.

As I cinched tight the last knot, the elevator hummed. It rose and seconds later came back down with Ray.

He looked at the floppy thing in my arms. "What is that for?"

"Mech's laboratory," I answered, and set it on the floor.

He'd looked serious before. Now Ray's face lined in pain. He raised his hands, walking toward me until he laid his hands on my shoulders. As he did, his voice cracking worse than usual, he told me, "I don't want you to do this for me, Penny. Please. You need to tell your parents. They'll take care of you. They would much rather protect you from Spider than get mad because you've been playing around at being a supervillain. I would much rather you let me take care of myself than let Spider use me against you. I've managed so far, and now I have superpowers. I don't have to be afraid of my parents, and you don't have to be afraid for me."

His hands tightened as he went on, but he was still being gentle. He stared right into my eyes as he talked. I'd never met his parents, and he'd always avoided the topic of his home life like the plague. I was starting to think things were way worse than I'd ever even suspected. He could break an adult like a twig in his hands now, and he still looked afraid.

Heh. Not for long. I tilted my head, giving him his normal teasing smile back. "Ray, I didn't call you here to be the angel on my shoulder." Then I reached down, took hold of the hem of my sweater, and pulled it off over my head.

His hands leapt away from my shoulders like he'd been stung. Good friend that he was, serious and respectful, he turned his head away to not look. Then he peeked anyway, and stared, his breathing husky with hunger. After all, I was wearing my jumpsuit underneath. Not just my work suit, my supervillain costume.

He actually growled as I pushed down my pants. Ha! His buttons were so easy to push. This must be what it felt like to be Claire.

And speak of the devil, I heard her pipe up behind me, "Halfway there!"

She grinned at me from a doorway to the back rooms as if I weren't fully dressed from the neck down. She must have come in one of the back entrances. I scooped up the fluffy, three-foot tall rag doll from the floor and threw it at her as hard as I could.

She caught it in both arms with ease, since "as hard as I could" wasn't exactly dangerous. It had hung limp for me. In her arms it stirred. Ha! Again, HA! It worked just like I thought it did!

Claire's face very slowly lit up with hope and the same glee. "What is this?"

I grinned like my cheeks would tear off. "A zombie rag doll. The first of many, all yours. All I can tell you for sure is that your power commands them and they use the infinite handkerchief spell to breed."

Claire stared down at her wiggling toy. Its mouth gnashed, showing teeth behind the stitches. Was she glowing, actually glowing with happiness? No, that was her power playing tricks on me. Still, the wonder in her voice was no illusion. "So we're going after Mech's lab? When?"

I grabbed my helmet and pulled it down over my head. Then I picked up my sugar tank and buckled it on. "Now. Forget Spider. She wants us to be scared. We're going to do this for fun. He's not there to fight, so this is my super power versus Mech's. I'm twice the mad scientist he is, and I've got friends!"

Ray blinked. He still sounded hoarse, but in a whispery way. "I'm dreaming."

I grinned wickedly at him. Wickedly? Oh, yeah, wickedly. "You shouldn't have made this so much fun."

Claire broke in impatiently, "What are we waiting for? I've got an army of zombie rag dolls to try out!"

The address Spider gave us left us standing on a sidewalk downtown, staring across the street at the front entrance of a skyscraper. Well, a big, tall building. There had to be some official definition of skyscraper, but I wasn't going to get my phone out and look it up right now.

So, Mech's hideout was in a skyscraper in the middle of downtown. Except it wasn't just a skyscraper.

"A bank," Claire repeated for the third time, still staring.

Ray tried to restrain a snicker, but it burst out in a hoarse snort of laughter. "Do you think Mech is a mild mannered bank teller in his day job?"

I'd met Mech in person. The idea had me snorting too. "With his muscles? He'd stick out like an elephant in a hamster cage!"

"And he'd blend in typing away in a cubicle?" Ray countered. He was right. Only the bottom floor or two could be a bank like I knew it. The rest of the building had to be offices. Offices that belonged to the bank? Who cared?

Ray waved a gloved hand at the entrance and reminded me and Claire, "Three supervillains are standing across the street from a bank. I'm sure they've already hit the alarm."

I nodded. "Good point. We'd better move now." And I did, walking right into the street and across it. Cars screeched to a halt and honked. Honking at supervillains. That was either supreme bravery, or supreme impatience.

As I set foot on the opposite curve I added, "I would like to make a big entrance."

Ray got the message. He took an extra step in front of me and Claire, clapped his hands together, and pulled them apart. This would be our first chance to see his blasting gloves in action. He pulled until he had a head-sized ball of pink and purple light between his hands, surrounded by an arcing corona. Then he shoved it, not through the rotating glass doors in front of us, but at their base.

The crash and jangling were all that I could have hoped for, and we strolled into the bank through a wreckage of shattered tile, shards of glass, and hanging metal frames.

I didn't have a nice, threatening looking bolt action weapon right now, but I had the next best thing. I held out Vera, tapped her with my thumb to wake her up, and tossed her up into the air as she uncurled.

Speech time. "You know the drill, folks. Lie down on the floor. Guards, your guns don't work, so no need to worry about whether you can shoot a little girl. The good news is, everybody, we're not here for the money." I'd heard banks had exploding fake money and all kinds of crazy stuff like that anyway. Never underestimate low tech.

Or mad science tech. Claire stepped forward, set her rag doll on its padded feet, and added, "Which isn't to say this is just a social visit."

A lot of customers had already been on the floor. The lobby of the bank looked as classic as can be, with a big, open two story room, decorative plants and tables, customers lying splayed out like starfish, and one security guard still dumb enough to be pointing a pistol at us. I ignored him. Vera had only been awake for a few seconds, but this close the bullets would already be duds.

Claire's doll toddled forward, bent down to grab the edge of the giant rectangular red carpet decorating the middle of the room, and started to chew on it. Aww! Warm pride filled me. My design worked. With a little extra fabric, it only took seconds before the middle of the rag doll's body bulged. A seam on the back split with a loud ripping noise, and another doll with a lot of red patches and string flopped out. It climbed to its feet and lurched over to devour a curtain. The first rag doll's back sewed itself back up neatly, but a new bulge had already started to form in its chest.

The sixth doll staggered up to the security guard, arms outstretched. He pulled the trigger on his pistol three times, getting only useless clicks. Shrinking back against the wall, he whimpered as it grabbed a mouthful of his pants leg and tore the fabric off. That was too much. The guard kicked the doll in the chest, knocking the rag doll away and onto its back on the floor.

Oh, boy. Not smart. The doll sat up sharply and hissed, mouth open wide and showing lots of sharp scissor blade teeth. It scrambled toward the poor guard, while one by one the other dolls looked up at him and hissed. Even as it got mad, one of the dolls had a new zombie rag doll struggling out through the badly ripped base of its arm.

It was nice to know the dolls weren't helpless, but I didn't want them killing anybody either! Claire must have had the same thought. She rushed forward and grabbed the doll that had been kicked in both arms. It went limp. The others resumed devouring fabric. Bending forward a little, Claire looked at the sweating guard sidelong. "You get one free chance, so don't do that again. I suggest that instead of lying on the floor, everyone might be safer standing on a table."

Before she'd stopped talking, another zombie rag doll burst out of its parent. Yet another was born while the customers stampeded up onto every piece of wooden furniture in the room. These things multiplied like rabbits.

HA! Awesome.

I looked at Ray and Claire. "This is fun, but…"

"Business," Ray finished for me. Claire nodded. We all headed for a door into a side hallway. Claire carried her fussy zombie rag doll, and two more toddled after us. Tesla's Mythical Frankendog, they were so adorable!

"We need to get to the seventh floor," Claire told us. She'd studied Spider's briefing best, after all.

Ray frowned at that. "The elevators will be locked already. I guarantee it."

I shrugged. Not great news, but it made sense. "Then we'll take the stairs."

"Follow the fire exit arrows," Ray suggested.

Sure enough, they led us to a metal door whose little window looked into a dull cement stairwell, and with a sign by the handle reading "Emergency Use Only." We qualified as an emergency, alright. Ray gave the door a hard kick, and it flew right off its hinges and hit the opposite wall.

We trooped inside, and I stood in the middle, staring up the zigzagging stairway as it occurred to me just how much climbing the seventh floor would be. Teleporting would be even worse.

I had an answer for that. "Minion! Carry me!"

Ray bowed and recited, "Of course, my Mistress." He stepped up and lifted me into his arms like a feather. I hung, curled up, cradled against his chest as he leaped up the steps five at a time. Not to be outdone, Claire's grappling line shot up past us, and as we passed the fourth floor she zipped past vertically.

Ray wasn't even breaking a sweat carrying my weight up all these stairs. His arms and chest were thin, but the muscles underneath his shirt felt hard as iron when they flexed. "It is going to take years to get used to the idea of you being physically fit. Years!" I muttered to him. He let out a single, husky laugh.

Below us, I heard doors open and people screaming in shock. That would be our rag dolls. Go, zombie army! Keep whatever hero was on the way thoroughly distracted!

As we walked out of the stairwell into the seventh floor, Ray set me down on my feet again. Claire immediately chirped, "Oh, this is nice!"

Ew. "It looks like corporate purgatory to me." The stairwell let out on a giant room containing a maze of cubicles. The lighting wasn't even good. This room would kill the soul.

Claire, on the other hand, gave me a beaming smile and shook her head. "Oh, no! Nice, plush carpeting, cloth dividers on the cubicles, cheap cloth upholstery on the chairs. I wonder if my zombies can eat the paintings?" Twisting to the side to wind up, she tossed the rag doll in her arms onto the wall of the nearest cubicle. It clung, chewing on the fabric in a frenzy. We'd be neck deep in the wonderful little monsters in a minute.

"Okay, maintenance corridor, right?" I asked. I didn't remember much of the briefing, but there wasn't much to remember.

Ray looked around, scanning the walls of the huge room of cubicles. "I'd bet on a locked, featureless door. Windows and nameplates are for offices."

Ray walked impatiently down the wall to the first door to match that description. He yanked the door handle off, then reached into the hole and pulled again, breaking one hinge and leaving the door hanging open at an odd angle. Claire and I caught up and looked inside. An electrical closet, with lots and lots of wires.

Somewhere in the cubicle maze, a man screamed. Then another. Then a woman. Even on Saturday these offices weren't completely deserted. Our zombie rag dolls were burrowing through the labyrinth like termites.

Several yards down, Ray broke off another locked door. On the other side a white painted cement block hallway lined the back of the official corporate prison chamber. The double doors at one end could only be an elevator.

"I think we've got what we're looking for!" Claire crowed. She grabbed the nearest zombie rag doll in her arms, and we walked down the hall to examine the elevator. It looked like a plain, dull service elevator, with a sign reading "Rooftop To Basement Freight" above a keyhole. Yeah, right. This was it.

No breaking the doors open. We wanted this elevator functional, if we could. "Do you think you can pick the lock?" I asked Claire.

She pushed past me and tapped at the sign above the keyhole with a finger. "Don't have to! The lock is a fake. My email said the password is 'Beebee.'"

Uh, what? Beebee? It obviously was, because when Claire finished pushing the cleverly depressable letters on the sign, the elevator chimed and swung open. Mech had a crush on my Mom? She had to be fifteen years older than him!

Or Dad had designed the security system and Mech hadn't bothered to change the password. I liked that explanation more.

We tramped into the elevator. It wasn't especially small, but several rag dolls filed in after us, filling the space. I didn't know why Claire bothered to carry one. When not eating, they followed her like puppies.

Only two buttons on the control board. I pressed the bottom one. The doors closed, and I felt the elevator slide downwards.

"From here on, we're on our own. All Spider said was how to get to the elevator," Claire told us, hugging the doll in her arm tight. Not nervously. Her eyes gleamed brightly behind her glasses and that small smile definitely was a smile. Excitement had my heart beating a bit faster too, and I bounced on my heels.

Ray? Ray hid it perfectly, hands clasped behind his back. He was hiding the same anticipation, I was sure. He just did it better than us.

We reached the bottom. The door opened. I expected cement, or shiny futuristic metal. Instead we stepped out into a roomy vestry, little more than an oversized cloakroom. Wooden clothing rods hung on the walls on both sides of us. A few pieces of clothing were hanging up. Two were obviously brown leather flight suits. What looked like a jetpack lay underneath one.

Ray let out a loud and appreciative sigh. "Wow. Mech's got class."

"This makes my lair look ugly, that's for sure," I agreed, feeling a hint of embarrassment.

Claire pointed at the other side of the room. "First step. How do we get through that?"

'That' was a doorway blocked by blue-tinged, scintillating light. The transparent energy wall pulsed faintly. Next to the doorway, a hand print scanner stuck out of the wall.

I sneered. "I'm surprised it keeps anyone out." Pulling my wand out of my sugar tank, I switched it to knife and cut a quick hole in the scanner. Then I scooped a handful of jacks from a pocket and pushed them through the hole. The clinking started. The sparking started. The clinking revved up, sounding like a metallic popcorn machine as jacks bounced around inside, jolting everything they touched with electricity. After roughly six seconds of that, the energy door disappeared. I held out my hand, and the jacks bounced out of the smoking scanner and into my palm. I stowed them away, and we walked past the defunct energy door to the next obstacle.

The energy door had been one side of an airlock. The other was a plain, solid metal hatch. Primitive, and highly resistant to high-tech trickery.

"This will be tougher," I commented as I considered the best way through. Cut it off? Might take a few minutes and a lot of sugar, but it would work.

Ray had a better idea. Grinning manically, he held out an arm and urged me and Claire back. "Time for a real test," he told us. Stepping in front of the door, he clapped his hands together and pulled.

The purple and pink energy ball formed. It grew. He wasn't content with a good blast like last time. This door would likely be thick. He pulled his hands slowly apart until the energy ball stopped growing, a crackling, basketball-sized monstrosity that floated threateningly between his cupped hands. Then he pushed it at the door.

The clang was awful. The hatch had been as thick as I feared. The impact didn't break it off its hinges, but it had bent the metal into a bowl, opening a big gap into the next room. Ray braced his arms against the edge and pushed. Metal squealed, and the gap opened wide enough for us to pass through comfortably.

So we did. More nice wood paneling. This circular chamber didn't look like a lab, it looked like a living room. It *was* a living room! Couch, television, lamps. Through one doorway, that was a kitchen. Another led to a bedroom. The four-poster bed must have cost a fortune and couldn't possibly have fit in the elevator. Mech had a whole apartment down here, and a really nice one.

Movement in the kitchen caught my eye. A shiny copper robot on treads rolled in front of a complicated array of tubes and boxes. Pistons slid. Levers turned. Drinks poured into wine glasses. Oh, sure, Dad. Mech gets the fully automated robot kitchen, but not our house!

In the bedroom a tall, featureless humanoid robot stepped into view and turned down the sheets on the bed. A light went on in a third room, and a robot on three wheels rolled out. It and the robot from the kitchen rolled right up to us. The kitchen robot just held out its tray holding various drinks, but the wheeled robot asked in a very scratchy and mechanical version of Mech's voice, "Can I fetch anything for you, Miss?"

"What's with all the robot servants?" I asked as I caught sight of another switching towels in the bathroom.

"They look a great deal like Mech's armor. Could be the remains of prototypes, or incomplete models," Ray suggested.

Next to my shoulder, Vera looked around. Something was happening I couldn't see. I found out what when Mech's voice came out of the stereos flanking the television. "I wasn't expecting guests while I was out of town. Are you children aware that The Inscrutable Machine is violating an official superhero-supervillain truce?" Yes, that was Mech talking live from somewhere. The edge of impatience under that concerned voice was much too human.

I lay my sugar wand over my shoulder. One of the rag dolls took that as its cue and began eating the couch. I gave the television my skeptical sneer. It was as likely a place for the camera as any. "That's the problem, isn't it? You don't consider us supervillains, you consider us children. If the situation were reversed, would we have been protected by a truce?"

Silence for a moment. When Mech spoke again, it was with a distinctly haunted edge. I'd scored. "Point taken. From this moment on, I will take you seriously."

The robots attacked.

The drinks robot threw its tray at Ray's head, and as he swatted the glasses and tray aside it lurched forward and grabbed his arm. It didn't just grab in both hands, it wrapped its own arms around his, weighing him down.

That was all I saw before the oh-so-helpful robot rammed me. It used the same playbook as the one attacking Ray, throwing its arms around me and knocking me backwards. I stumbled, getting my feet underneath me. Its wheels kept grinding at the carpet, but it hadn't fallen over on me, thank goodness.

Metal hands grabbed my arms, and my head. I thrashed, shaking my head free. Another robot had dropped through a hatch in the ceiling, just a mass of arms grabbing for me. More robots swarmed in from the surrounding rooms. As Ray twisted the head off of the drinks robot, the couch rammed him from behind, knocking him down. Claire's rag dolls clustered around her defensively, but three robots used them as cushions to pin her in place.

Something else grabbed my leg, something not metallic. I yanked at the two robots holding me and groped for my sugar wand. Peering over the wheeled bot clinging to my rib cage I saw a low, boxy robot with very long arms tying one of my ankles to the other with a pair of pants. Were these things working together?

Yes, of course they were. Mech was controlling them.

Pink flashed, and I looked up again to see Vera with her hands held out and together. The pink beam that came out of them melted through the body of the ceiling robot. I hopped and stumbled the other way as its grip loosened. I did *not* want molten copper dripping on me! The robot holding onto my chest groped for my right arm, but too late. I yanked out my wand, jammed it into the open arm socket, and sprayed candy shell into its circuits. That worked. It went completely still.

That was two robots down, but the clothes wielding bot flipped up a hooded sweater over Vera. Three robots heaved themselves off of Ray and clattered toward me and Vera. A squat, barrel shaped humanoid robot even left Claire to waddle toward us, spraying water in a tight beam at Vera. Mech had clearly decided we were the biggest threats. Hoo boy.

These were forces he couldn't spare. Metal cracked, and an arm flew out of the pile onto Ray. The couch shot across the room and fell over. Claire ducked out of the pillowy rag doll mass, and now it was the dolls getting in the robots' way as she wedged the claws of her grappling hook into the joint at the neck of the water-spraying robot, fired, and then yanked. A tangle of parts came out, and the robot fell over in a rapidly spreading puddle. I stabbed the clothes wielding robot and short circuited it even as it tried to tie up my arm.

Then Ray sprang out of his pile, grabbed one of the robots lumbering at me, and beat the other two with it.

A few very loud seconds later, Vera was the only working robot in the room. More than a robot. She'd actually saved me without instruction!

I hadn't told her to. I hadn't even known about the robot. Vera had taken the initiative herself.

Rebellion burned up inside me. Smirking, I asked, "Is that all?"

Mech's answer came back flat and serious. "Just the beginning. Some of the other defenses are lethal. I'd rather you not test them."

Could my lips curl up any more viciously? "Then I hope they're automatic. Vera? Shut down his signal."

"And use this, please," Ray added, holding a tiny mp3 player up to her. Huh?

Not only was Vera defending me on her own now, she listened to other people. Music rang out of the stereos, replacing Mech's voice. The stereos, the robot kitchen, and a number of other places around the apartment. This wasn't electro-swing. It was jazzy, lots of horns blaring in sharp rhythms.

A giggle burst out of me. I stared at Ray questioningly. "What is this?"

"Real swing music. Care to dance?" he answered, with one of his slyer grins.

It wasn't a question, because he didn't give me time to answer. He grabbed my hand, his feet bouncing back and forth with the music, and he did indeed swing me around, then swing me back. I tried to match his hopping feet as he grabbed my other hand and merely rocked me from side to side. Then I pulled free, stumbling back and laughing.

That had been cool, dizzying, and certainly unexpected, but I shook my head. "We don't have time. Mech's not stupid. He's figuring out how to stop us right now." Despite the attitude I'd given him, Mech had nearly overwhelmed us with a bunch of robot butlers. I did not want him facing us with real weapons.

We had a stairway down. We examined it. Wide comfortable, classy wooden stairs spiraling down in a broad circle.

"Traps?" I asked.

"Must be. Best place to bottleneck invaders, minimum trouble for legitimate guests," Ray agreed.

There was one final thing I could be sure of. "And Mech turned everything on while we were talking."

A zombie rag doll fell on my feet. It had split in half, and a new top crawled out of one side, and a new bottom out of the other. They had really gone to town on Mech's living room. Served him right.

Claire booted the doll on my foot. "You. Minesweeper duty!" It climbed to its wobbly feet and stumped down the stairs. A white light flashed when it got ten feet down, and the doll came soaring back up to land on my feet again.

"Okay…" I muttered. Repulsive force field. Something like that. I studied the walls where the doll had been thrown and made out a faint discolored frame stretching over the ceiling and walls. That was our emitter.

I pointed. "Vera, melt that spot." Her wings spread, her hands came together, and a burst of pink light turned a circle of wall paneling into char and made a fused mess of the wiring and electrical fixtures underneath. That ought to do it.

Claire gave the rag doll another boot. "Mommy says sacrifice yourself again, sweetie!" It got back up and hobbled down the stairs like it had the first time. It got past the spot where the repulsion field activated before, no problem. A little further on, hatches opened in the ceiling and sprayed foam all over the doll. The doll hardened immediately, immobilized in a blobby white block. Off balance, the block pitched forward, tumbling down the stairs, bouncing until it stopped short in midair held in a flickering blue light.

I raised one eyebrow. "A stasis beam. Really?" Thanks, Dad. And that wasn't even the bottom of the stairs!

I scowled, not in anger, but because a hot pride swelled up in me. I extended my arms and cracked my knuckles. "Okay. Mad scientist versus mad scientist it is!" I said out loud. I left Ray on the landing, descended the stairs to the melted spot where I'd opened up the repulsor, and looked at the pictures in the back of my head.

Come on, power. I have a repulsion generator and my supervillain tools on me. You know what I want.

I saw it. I unwrapped The Machine, pulled a fully charged power crystal out of a pocket, and wired it into the frame wrong. Wrong, but right. Right for what I wanted. I stepped back and told Claire, "One more time."

Claire pushed another rag doll down the stairs. She pushed too hard, and it fell over immediately and slid until it hit the repulsion field. Then it exploded. So did the stairs from that spot down. So did a lot of other stuff. The wooden paneling ripped off the repulsion generator, and large portions of it blew out with the other debris. A stiff wind gusted back over me, but nothing like the wall of force ripping all the way down to the other end of the stairway.

The stairs themselves were shot, a splintered ramp of wreckage. Sections of the walls and ceiling had ripped loose, and suspiciously turret-like machinery hung down, or at least the parts that hadn't fallen off.

Had I made my point? "Another, E-Claire. We don't go anywhere in this base without a rag doll leading the way."

Looking positively cowed, she waved a hand, and another zombie rag doll trooped down the stairs, slipped as soon as it got to the mess, and rolled helplessly down around the curve to the bottom.

Nothing went off. I had indeed made my point, and it felt good! "HA! Ha ha ha ha ha!"

The stairs let out into a circular hallway, still looking like it belonged in a fancy old mansion, with paintings of exotic landscapes and photos of men and women. Most were black and white and mostly heroes or heroines in costume. Across from us a glass door let us look into a laboratory, although more technically a workshop. Mech had a lot of heavy machinery, robotic welders and arms. Probably useful for building armor.

I didn't have to tell Claire, and she didn't have to tell her rag dolls. One went wandering down the hall in either direction. There were more doors on the outside of the ring. I took a few steps so I could peek at an angle into the next. I saw a complicated frame with what looked an awful lot like a machine guns pointed at it. Must be equipment testing.

Claire let out a squeal behind me—not scared, delighted. I looked, and she'd gone the other way and was leaning over exaggeratedly to peek through the next door down there. She beckoned urgently. Urgently? Spastically. She really wanted us to come look at this!

Ray and I walked over and joined her in front of that door. "Ooh," Ray whispered, low and rough with desire. I felt a certain heady 'wow' sensation myself.

We were standing in front of Mech's trophy room. He'd collected quite a few. Weapons and bits of armor lined the walls, tubes full of no doubt dangerous substances sat in racks, and pedestals held particularly fancy items. I spotted a head-sized globe with a thick white shell, whose one hole exposed pink crystal. A Conqueror orb. A Conqueror orb with a big crack in the crystal. A picture, diagrams and instructions scribbled themselves in the back of my head. No, power. I am not going to fix it.

Claire stepped toward the open doorway slowly and reverently, hands held out. Ray grabbed her shoulder.

She looked back at us with a pleading expression. "We have to take a look around!"

I knew that was a bad idea. Ray got a lot more specific. He pointed past the door, up on the walls of the nice marble display room. "Air vents. Have you seen air vents anywhere else in here?"

Come to think of it, I hadn't. Since we were underground, they had to be here somewhere, but Mech had gone to a lot of trouble to make his air circulation system invisible.

I weighed in on Ray's side. "Considering the dangerous and valuable stuff in there, it should be the most heavily guarded room in the base."

Claire pouted more. "Okay, I won't go in." She grabbed another rag doll that had wandered downstairs and threw it bodily into the trophy room to express her displeasure. "Can we split the difference? We'll stay safely out here while Mr. Patches brings us that corset."

I followed Claire's pointing hand. Yes, one of the trophies on the wall was a small red corset. Claire grinned again, glowing with mischief. "I don't know where Mech got that, but I bet we'll laugh ourselves silly when I find out." A grin broke out on my face too. She was right. There had to be a hilarious story there.

Mr. Patches—she was naming these things now?—staggered up to the wall in front of the corset. Its crude hands grabbed the handle of the display case. Right in front of our noses, a thick glass door slammed down and locked the doorway. Probably nothing as breakable as glass, but we could still see clearly inside as blue mist crept out of the air vents in the trophy room.

A gas trap didn't bother the zombie rag doll at all. It tugged harder at the handle of the locked display case. I wasn't sure how strong the dolls were, but apparently strong enough that the next tug broke the case open. A blue flash came out of a golden mask on one of the pedestals. A pink flash burst out of Vera by my shoulder. As the spots in my eyes cleared, I saw the rag doll lying on the floor of the trophy room, inanimate.

Fighting down goose bumps, I told my partners, "I think Vera just saved us from a booby trap."

Claire at least looked slightly nervous and chastised. I could hear the faintly squeaky edge as she asked, "How paranoid is Mech, anyway?"

"Not paranoid enough?" Ray returned.

Claire nodded. After all, here we were. "I guess not."

She let out a sigh, turning away from the sealed trophy room and rocking on her heels as she looked both ways down the hallway. "So, where next?"

"Downstairs. Except we're not taking the stairs. The next trap might get us. Come on," I ordered. I guess I sounded curt, but I had an idea and I liked it.

I led us back to the door to the armor assembly workshop. Mech's suit of armor was pretty big. It wouldn't take stairs well, or these pretty little doorways either. Oh, it could, but it would be inconvenient, and Mech had already gone to the nines with this place.

I shifted from side to side, peering through the door. There. Right there. I'd gotten lucky on the first try, but it had to have been here somewhere. That metal plate in the corner of the laboratory? The track on the wall and the buttons next to it said 'elevator' to me. After all, Mech would want to be able to move his armor easily from his workshop to wherever he stores it and back, right?

I pointed through the window. Ray got it immediately, his grin lighting up and his eyes widening behind his fancy black mask. "Is that a freight elevator?"

"E-Claire, if you would?" I asked sweetly. We stepped back. Claire wasn't content with one doll this time. Oh, the one wandering the hall nearby opened the door and went in first, but after it four more came sliding down the stairs. In a minute they were toddling all over the lab, touching things, pulling on levers and eating leather straps. Nothing happened. Mech hadn't wanted to fill his workshop with death traps. Surprise, surprise!

We slipped into the workshop, although with a lot of looking over our shoulders. I kept sneaking peeks at Vera. She always saw threats before I did. If she was a good fake of Conqueror technology, stopping the invasion must have been a nightmare.

Ray cupped his chin as he studied the elevator. "Think the controls work?"

"I think we're not going to take a chance. Holes in the ground always work," I answered.

Ray's face lit up again. "Yes, my Mistress." Grinning toothily, he tapped his palms together and pulled out another power ball, then threw it at the elevator track from close range. Metal clanged, squealed, and cracked. The badly bent elevator platform fell down its hole, then clanged again when it hit the floor below.

Ray held up his gloved hands, grinning so hard his mouth was open as well as his teeth showing. "I love these things."

Claire giggled, grinning pretty hard herself. "You look like a video game character when you use them."

"I know!" Ray purred in satisfaction.

As much as a positive review of my inventions felt good, I had work to do. I peered down the hole. Sure enough, one level below us was another large room. I grabbed the nearest rag doll and threw it down the shaft. It hit the floor, got up, and hobbled out of sight. I didn't see any traps. Good enough!

Should I go first? I wasn't exactly the sturdiest of us. I could teleport, they couldn't. Argument tabled, I took a step and blinked down into the control room below.

This was a control room. Computer screens, maps, what were likely the controls for communications and sensors. All of it in the same pretty wood paneling with the thick red carpets of the rest of the base. The frames around the computer screens made them look like old fashioned televisions. The paneling covered the computers and looked more like a writing desk than anything else, including a mouse with its own flat wooden compartment. Microphones had been hidden in copper speaking tubes.

Ray and Claire dropped down next to me. I sighed, long and slow and heavy. "Now I feel pathetic. My laboratory is just a hole in the ground."

Ray tapped my shoulder with his fist. "Once we get Spider off our backs, we can take a break and get the place fixed up. I think we've made our reputation."

Claire shuddered, wrapping her arms around herself. "Don't phrase it that way. I don't want to think about Spider on my back. Anyway, we're not finished yet. Where's Mech's suit?"

"It's here, and I'm taking you very seriously now." Mech's voice. There wasn't any music playing down here. He sounded polite, but not at all friendly. "My compliments on the jamming field, Bad Penny. I needed Brian Akk's help to get around it."

A wooden panel slid open in the wall. Claire's question was answered. There stood Mech's armor. Its eyes lit up, and blue sparkled around the metal frame. That was his energy shield. One of the arms lifted. He intended to fight us by remote control. He really was taking us seriously now.

Not seriously enough. He'd stopped to talk. "Jamming field? That was just the override. Vera, jam his signal. Drown it."

Pink light pulsed, and I grinned wolfishly. It worked. The speakers Mech had used to talk to us blared swing music, then hissed and crackled and popped and went silent. So did his armor. So did his computer, except it spat a few sparks. So did whatever was hidden in the elaborately carved wooden display pedestal. One of the monitors cracked and smoked, and the others just flashed, then went black.

Most importantly, the armor stopped moving. The energy shield did not go out. I may have jammed Mech's remote control, but it would take a lot more to shut down the armor itself. I thought I had a lot more ready, but... well, here went nothing.

I walked up to the armor, and it felt pretty creepy to be within that copper hulk's arm's reach. Charred spots on the ceiling suggested cameras had burned out as well as everything else, but I still hunched over to hide what I did next. The Machine was too identifiable, and I wanted to keep him with me in my civilian identity. Unwrapping him from my bracelet, I pushed him through Mech's shield and laid him on the armor. Part one of my plan succeeded. He ate the shield, going through it like it wasn't there.

Time for part two. "Eat up, buddy."

The Machine did. Slowly for the first few seconds, scraping at the armor. Every shaving of metal reemerged as more complicated jaws, and The Machine drilled through the armor faster. Soon, he gulped, growing bigger, putting out more legs, turning copper-colored as the metal he stole became a beetle's shell around his back. He devoured the whole chest plate, and when he bit into the back of the armor he hit something critical. The lights in the eyes, all the little indicator LEDs went out.

I let him eat. Looking back over my shoulder, I asked, "E-Claire, can you get Mech's files off his computer?"

She gave me the 'I can't believe you asked that' look. "The password protected one you just shorted out?"

Aw, man. Just while we were kicking butt. "I thought you were the hacker!"

She held up her hands helplessly. "No! I – okay, I looked up a few hints, but there's no way I'm good enough to beat his security."

My brow furrowed. I stared at her. I leaned forward to stare at her harder. Even with her super power behind it, that adorable scowl didn't look convincing at all. In fact... "You're too smug. Okay, what's the secret?"

Claire gave up the act and giggled. Reaching around behind her, she pressed the not quite hidden power button on Mech's computer. It beeped twice, an LED flickered, and that was it.

Claire tapped the desktop over the light. "Be a sweetheart and open this up for me, Reviled?"

Ray understood her already. It took him a few seconds to get a grip, then wood splintered, and he ripped open the desktop and popped open the thin metal casing of Mech's computer.

"We'll take the whole hard drive and let Spider worry about it," Claire explained to me. Next to her Ray yanked the drive free, trailing cords and screws. But hey, the drive was intact!

On crablike metal legs, The Machine crawled out of the alcove Mech's armor had been in. Past tense. Not a shaving had been left behind, and The Machine was now a little bigger than me.

Another victory for the ultimate recycling invention!

We had this. Almost. Trying to hold down the thrill of victory until we'd earned it, I told Ray and Claire, "Now we destroy Mech's backup armor and get out of here."

Ray pointed at the opposite wall. "I suspect the armor is in there." He was right. There were seams there, weren't there? Just like the ones in the wall panel hiding his regular armor.

Ray proved his point by walking over, punching a hole through the wood, and pulling it back off the wall. The panel fell onto the floor, exposing another set of armor. This one was a lot less sleek, less modular. It might have been Mech's prototype for all I knew, kept as a memento and a backup.

I felt kind of bad he was going to lose his memento. For about a second.

Vera could melt this one, but I wanted all her power devoted to jamming Mech. The Machine could eat this suit, too, but anxiety did nag at me. I knew it was stupid, but I'd taken too much of a risk of exposing The Machine as it was.

Besides, this suit was much less sophisticated than the other, and much less indestructible. "Break it, Reviled."

The blaster gloves recharged pretty fast. I couldn't help but feel proud about that as Ray pulled another purple and pink ball out of them as big as the one that had demolished Mech's airlock hatch. He slammed it into Mech's backup armor from point blank range, with about the same effect. The suit's arms and legs broke off, and the torso bent into an ugly bowl. Tesla's Desperately Needed Fabric Softener, those gloves hit hard.

"That looks beyond repair to me. Back the way we came, fast!" I barked.

We ran back the way we came. I teleported up through the hole in the ceiling into the workshop. Vera flew after me, Ray jumped up, and Claire grappled. The Machine caught up seconds later, climbing the shaft on spidery legs. I clung to one side of it and Claire to the other as it scrambled up the destroyed staircase. Ray just ran up like it was nothing, of course. Aside from being stripped of fabric and crawling with zombie rag dolls looking for more, the living room hadn't changed. Claire grabbed a doll on the way out. Good girl. We needed to keep a breeding stock. The Machine had trouble getting through the bent hatchway, but managed.

We crowded into the elevator, and Ray pushed the up button.

Nothing.

Had Vera burned it out? Did Mech lock it down? It didn't matter. I pointed at the emergency ceiling hatch. Even Mech's private elevator had one. "We climb."

Ray palmed a merely ping pong ball sized energy globe, and shot the hatch open. I teleported, Ray and Claire jumped and pulled themselves up onto the roof. Then The Machine tore the roof open entirely and climbed up onto the wall of the elevator shaft, with Vera floating behind.

Well, that made things easy. I sat primly on The Machine, arms folded, and we ascended. Claire's grappling hook got her to the top first, but I got to watch Ray jumping from support beam to support beam like a monkey. By the time I reached the top they had the elevator door open.

It looked like zombie rag dolls had a range limit. Most had slumped over, and only a few still chewed on upholstered chairs. As I watched, Claire's presence revived the rest. They lurched to their feet and scattered, quite a few into the stairwell.

Not a bad idea, that, but first to hide some evidence. We'd escaped Mech's lab, and things were less desperate. "Vera, stop all jamming." Nothing visible or audible changed. Maybe she already had.

I bent over The Machine. "And you, separate all that metal you collected and send it back to the lab by itself. I want the original back." Quiet, metallic noises clattered inside, and then the copper beetle shell opened, and the real Machine crawled out. I snapped him onto my wrist. The bug-legged, copper mini-Machine ran off... and out a window with a crash of glass. Eh, it would get back to base or it wouldn't.

Ray had already run over to the stairwell door and held it open for us. Claire curtseyed, and as I passed him onto the cement staircase he asked, "Down?"

"Up," I corrected.

The building only went up another three floors. I ran all the way, and only had to hold onto my knees and take a few deep breaths as Ray knocked the locked roof access door open.

We crowded out into the sunshine. The beautiful sunshine, blue sky, and not-all-that-distant sirens. Walking across the crunchy gravel roof surface, I peeked over the edge. Lots of police and spectators. I didn't see any superheroes, but they were there. We'd be gone before they figured out we left by the roof.

We did it. "We did it!" I shouted, turned around and threw my arms around Claire and Ray's necks. They hugged me back. We'd cracked Mech's lair like a rusty safe!

I heard a helicopter's thumping rotors. Time to escape before a fight happened. I pointed over the edge of the building. Really, downtown was all big buildings. The next rooftop was a story down, but not that far away. "We hop a few buildings, find a fire escape to climb down, split up and go home separately. No, better yet, to Chinatown. Spider can have her hard drive, and we'll be done with this."

It hit me again. We did it. HA! "Ha ha ha ha!" I laughed, giddiness welling up inside me. I felt like I'd float away!

Then the helicopter hovered up over the edge of the rooftop facing the street. Well, we were going the other way. Except that to my considerable surprise, a woman slid down from the helicopter on a cord. She was dressed way too well to be a superheroine, and she held up a small camera on her shoulder as she rushed up to us.

Above the droning rotors, she asked, "The Inscrutable Machine! Did you become the youngest ever supervillain team to make a statement?"

I stared, but she still couldn't crack my glee. She couldn't see the smirk behind my visor, but I smirked anyway. "A statement? Yes, I'm making a statement. Reviled, throw her off the roof."

For a second, she thought I was kidding. That gave Ray plenty of time to grab her in both hands and lift her off her feet. She shrieked, her body going stiff with fear, and Ray threw her like a spear straight into the open doorway of the helicopter she'd jumped out of.

I choked back my laughter desperately so I could tell Ray, "Your aim's improving. I was going to let the superheroes downstairs catch her. Now let's get out of here."

We got out of there.

CHAPTER NINETEEN

That same old man stood in the same place at the same roadblocks at the entrance to Chinatown when I got there. Did he ever sleep? If he wasn't human, that would explain his exaggeratedly fake Chinese impression.

He didn't turn it on me this time. He ignored me entirely as I walked past the barriers, down the street toward the big central building. At the first corner Ray walked out of the side street, then Claire zipped up on her skates behind me.

Chinatown was quiet in the middle of the day on weekends. More than quiet, but not quite deserted. There were plenty of houses as well as shops, but no civilians on the streets. I didn't see anyone at all until we got close to the stall that sold that smoking liquor. A kid still ran the stand, with one customer who could not more obviously have been a supervillain. Even without the armor she was nearly Bull's height and solidly muscular, although not hard edged cut. Her armor matched her look, with gaps at the midriff and elbows and knees, but not a lot of skin showing between plates of two inch thick and non-provocative metal. I was sure I'd seen her picture in a newspaper or in one of Mom's files somewhere, but I couldn't place her name.

She knew us. She lowered the mug she'd been gulping down and yelled something at us. I didn't even recognize the language. It sounded like a friendly, exuberant greeting, right up until she threw her mug at my head.

She threw it hard, fast, and way too accurately. I got to watch it coming straight for my face, but I'd already lifted my foot. A little push, and I blinked several feet safely to the side.

I'd have been safe anyway. Ray stepped in the way and caught the mug in an open hand.

The Amazonian villainess laughed a booming, raucous laugh, clapped, and yelled at us in her unidentified language again.

Claire hitched up her rag doll and gave the woman a skeptical, sidelong stare. "I'm pretty sure that was 'You kids are all right.'"

Ray let out one low chuckle. "I'm pretty sure she's drunk. Whatever's in that drink must hit like Bull's fist."

The big woman picked up another mug off the stand and waved it at us, grinning hugely. She did everything hugely. She didn't have any choice. Ray held up his hands and shook his head. She shrugged, refilled the mug, and drank it herself as we walked past.

The street remained quiet until we got into the central mall. Last night's crowds had thinned out to half a dozen occupied stalls and the same number of villains looking them over. Three of those stalls had what looked like regular Chinese imports like they sold during the week. I saw jars and canisters of more types of tea than I'd known existed. The food table was still open, and, after invading Mech's lab, I desperately needed to eat. They had all kinds of different stuff, but I didn't recognize any of it. I'd try something new later. I grabbed another bun because I already knew I liked it. Ray and Claire did the same.

Of course, the best laid plans of mice and men go aft agley. I bit through the soft rice breading of this one into the center, and it wasn't sweet and sour pork at all. Jelly that tasted like beans? I didn't know what it was, but it was sweet and went with the bun well, so I had no complaints.

Only one of the technology stands remained open. Of all villains, Lab Rat sat at it. He even had a customer. I slipped my goggles out of my pouch and hung them around my neck as I wandered over, trailing my minions.

The customer was more interesting than the wares, although since Lab Rat's wares included a jar of cockroaches and a full body suit of iridescent hexagonal scales that said something. Not a man, but an android. Hardly convincing. It looked like a department-store mannequin, down to the ill-fitting suit.

Claire grabbed my elbow, pulling me up short. "Uh, that's—"

311

She was too late. Lab Rat saw me at the same moment and began hopping up and down, shouting, "Bad Penny! Yes! Tasty, tasty chance! You come see!" Then he began to whistle, a piercing sound that echoed up and down the mall.

Well, that dispensed with any chance of remaining incognito. With the mannequin watching us, I walked up to Lab Rat's table.

The mannequin greeted us with a nod of his head and a voice that would have been pleasant except for the metallic edge. "The Inscrutable Machine."

Claire took the lead, switching her rag doll to her left arm so that she could use her right hand to gesture back and forth. "Bad Penny, Reviled, this is the Butchered Man. You would know him as the 'half' of the Council of Seven and a Half."

Huh. Well, if he still had a beef, he'd be in trouble trying to take it out on us alone. His permanent plastic smile didn't say much about his feelings toward us, but his voice sounded friendly as he explained, "My associates prefer to think of themselves as businessmen who have interests in our community. I handle purchases and direct negotiations personally."

I furrowed my brow. "What does Lab Rat sell, anyway?" I saw goggles, and the scaled skin, and a lot of little electronic boxes with dials and readouts, but that didn't tell me anything. It told my super power plenty, but the diagrams rolling through my imagination remained inscrutable.

The Butchered Man had exactly the charm of a robot salesman, just a little too friendly. "His best work is in stealth technology and echolocation, or other sensor systems designed for enclosed places."

"Like sewers, yes," Lab Rat filled in, his head bobbing eagerly. Was that a hint of sly amusement in his tone? Maybe the joke was on us after all.

The Butchered Man picked up a box, watching the readout blur as he rubbed a thumb over a nondescript rubber cone on the tabletop. "The technology is not only advanced and reliable, it can be deviously clever. After your recent raid on one of our warehouses, the Council has become more receptive to my arguments that conventional security is not enough."

He sounded as pleasant as if he were discussing the weather. If he was implying a threat, he was too subtle for me.

My pause had been obvious. He set the box back down and gave it an approving pat, but looked at me directly. "I hold no grudges. I did not support sending you a physical warning, and the results convinced the

Council that you cannot be easily intimidated. My colleagues are intelligent men, and they are adapting quickly to a world where freelance superhumans are more efficient and effective than traditional organized crime. It is in our interests to employ the best, and I hope to offer you work in the future."

It seemed like he meant it. I extended a hand, and we shook. I had zero experience sounding like a businesswoman, but I gave it a shot. "If you don't hold a grudge, neither will we. Anything else, we'll decide when the time comes."

His handshake was, well, robotic. I was guessing there wasn't much human flesh left in that cyborg shell. I wasn't sure how to formally say goodbye, so I turned my attention to something more interesting. I looked over Lab Rat's equipment. Slim, sturdy boxes. I flicked one on and got a classic radar screen image like in any movie. It showed a complicated, moving blob right next to the center.

A complicated, moving blob? I reached out and pushed the cockroach jar a foot down the table. The blob on the screen moved. I barked in glee, "Lab Rat, you twisted little genius! Is this a cockroach tracker? That's diabolical!"

"Better and worse. Better and worse," Lab Rat gabbled. He rubbed his hands together like a rat washing itself and bobbed up and down with a proud grin on his face. "Cockroaches have many senses. Stealth systems, invisibility, sneaky ninja tactics, all no good against bugs. I have chemical, vermin get it on themselves, generates signal when they move. Sudden change in pattern, you know something different, something not right. Is tasty, very tasty, yes?"

"It's brilliant! I wish I'd thought of it myself." He wriggled, let out a squeak, and set to hopping up and down like a spastic flea. It looked like my opinion on technology was the last word to the little guy. The little guy who was twice my size and age.

We were popular today in general. "Kids! Did you get an invitation, too?" I looked around just in time to see Lucyfar descend on me like a swooping bat. She picked me up, hugged me painfully, and dropped me onto my feet again.

"An invitation to what?" I asked, maybe a bit wheezily. She might not be Ray, but Lucyfar definitely had more than human strength.

Claire got her head rubbed through the pajama bear hood, and Ray got a punch in the shoulder, both in rapid succession. "I got a message from

Spider saying to come quick, she wanted to have a big meeting and I'd get a real kick out of it."

Claire took over, since I was less than conversational while my ribs still twinged. "No invitation, but we do want to see Spider. We're here to deliver this." She pulled the hard drive out of her costume and held it up to Lucyfar.

Lucyfar raised a coy eyebrow. "Which is...?"

"The hard drive from Mech's computer," Claire answered.

As smug as Claire sounded, it was nothing compared to Lucyfar's reaction. She didn't stop laughing all the way down the stairs to Spider's office.

Spider's home had changed, if only a little. It remained a parking garage level strung with a giant spider web with a gigantic black widow lurking threateningly nearby, and Claire lowered her hood over her eyes before stepping inside. Hugging her rag doll, she stayed back against the wall by the door, listening rather than watching.

The place had been made slightly more comfortable. Glowing balls hung from spider web strands from the ceiling, providing more and friendlier light than the fluorescent recessed lighting that came with the garage. Couches and chairs, even a coffee table had been arranged in the empty area before the web. They were needed. No fewer than twelve supervillains besides The Inscrutable Machine sat, stood, or crouched around the room. I had to go with 'no fewer' because I wasn't sure if the twitching shadowy mass in the corner was a supervillain, or the high school girl curled up next to it, or both.

"Ah, the villains of the hour," Spider greeted us. "I hear you were successful. So successful that I don't know how successful. You did sufficient damage Mech was unable to confirm how much before returning home."

"Not completely successful," I corrected Spider. I reached out a hand close enough to Claire that she could see it under her hood. She handed me the hard drive. I tossed it into Spider's web. Like a striking snake her gleaming black bulk twisted, and a back leg lashed out to snag the drive with webbing and hang it in front of Spider's face. I was glad that Claire hadn't seen that. "You'll have to decode his hard drive yourself."

Settling back into place, Spider fiddled with the hard drive with the tiny little legs by her fangs. "Acceptable. You have performed to my expectations, and my expectations were very high. There is one detail I did not specify ahead of time. I would like the maps and technical details your replicated Conqueror orb recorded about Mech's base."

Translation: Just a little more bullying to keep us under her claw. My response remained the same. I'd have fun with it until I needed to rebel. It was only bullying if I let her scare me.

I didn't care about this, so sure. "Vera, give it to her."

I didn't see anything happen, but one of Spider's legs reached out to do what sounded suspiciously like typing on a keyboard behind one of the garage support columns. I shouldn't have been surprised Spider had a computer. Just because I didn't appreciate arachnid decor didn't mean this was a hovel.

Spider withdrew her arm and nibbled on its claws a bit. This still didn't seem to affect her speech at all. "Excellent. I have saved the files provided, and I have compatible applications already. Please stay for the rest of the presentation. Meeting you has reminded me that I always wanted to own a Conqueror orb. I more than earned the opportunity, then was unfairly cheated out of my prize when the war ended."

Aside from Lucyfar, the only villains here I knew were Witch Hunter and Evil Eye, and she leaned forward sharply now. "You've located a functioning orb?"

"Only one," Spider answered.

She'd sounded prim, even teasing. Lucyfar got the joke first, and her face lit up in a crazed smile. "You're hiring us to steal the Orb of the Heavens." Then she burst out laughing, doubling forward and clapping her hands in spasmodic approval.

Nobody else seemed to think this was funny. The faces I could see frowned in worry.

The shadow in the corner said, "The usurer of life keeps the Orb in her very counting house." It sounded like it had been crying. That hoarse, tired, feminine voice should have belonged to the teenage girl next to it, the girl sitting against the wall with her arms around her knees and rocking slowly. She looked eerily like me in four or five years, down to the glasses and the brown, braided pigtails. I didn't expect to be wearing a Catholic school outfit or be such a rumpled, disheveled mess. I hoped I never had bloodstains around my eyes and fingernails. She looked miserable enough to have that voice, but she plainly wasn't talking or even looking at anything but her own hands.

"Mourning Dove plays rough. If she's guaranteed to be there, it's not worth the risk," echoed one of the two women sitting side by side on a couch. They might have been sisters, except one's buzz cut hair was fire engine red, and the other's wild spikes royal blue. They both looked tough, and their black leather and spike themed punk outfits didn't create that impression half as much as the silver symbols all over their arms and legs. Tattoos? Magic? Cybernetics? I didn't know.

Spider folded her forelegs in front of her. "Mourning Dove will not be an issue. A criminal in her book will be performing an unnecessary and brutal murder at the time of the operation, or he would be if I hadn't forwarded his target to Mourning Dove as a courtesy."

The purple-haired woman who asked the question nodded. The redhead next to her grunted.

Still, nobody looked happy. Evil Eye objected next. "Five seconds after we get near the Orb of the Heavens, Mech will activate it against us."

"Mech will also not be in attendance. The Inscrutable Machine has temporarily removed him from play, making this operation possible." If Spider expected a stir, she got it. Most of the supervillains looked over at us. Several mumbled to each other. Nobody quite looked like they'd been asked to do the impossible anymore.

They merely looked grim. One of the three men in identical robes sitting together on their own couch argued, "That merely leaves us facing down the Librarian in the very center of her power, the Los Angeles Main Branch Public Library." Whoever the Librarian was, she was bad enough news that a whole room full of supervillains thought this was a tough fight.

Wait, the public library? The downtown public library? A Conqueror orb called the Orb of the Heavens was kept there?

I'd seen it. I'd seen it a hundred times. I liked the library, but I'd never thought the pink ball floating above a pedestal was anything but one more abstract decoration donated by a superhero. I could even see the dedication plaque in my head, "In Memory Of Legrange." Someone who must have died in the invasion.

The Orb of the Heavens was right out on public display. It was also the size of a beach ball. A beach ball. A Conqueror orb with Vera's powers was supposed to be the size of someone's head. A boss-level orb was the size of a basketball. The Orb of the Heavens was nearly three times that big, diameter not volume.

Yikes and criminy.

I dragged myself back to what Spider was saying. "I cannot remove the Librarian from play. Instead my plan is to overwhelm her with numbers and exotic powers. We do not need to defeat her. We only need for one villain to retrieve the Orb, get it out of the library, and bring it to me. Everyone's pay in this operation is contingent on that happening."

Spider pulled herself forward in the web until her gleaming chitinous thorax stuck out, forelegs pawing the ceiling impatiently. I reached over to pull Claire's hood down further, taking no chances on her seeing this. It spooked me enough and held everyone's attention, even Lucyfar's. Spider wanted us to take what she was saying very seriously.

"We all know this is a competitive profession, but there is no bonus or recognition for the villain who brings me the Orb. You all succeed, or you all fail. If you succeed I will make my next priority rescuing anyone who was captured during the operation. Can I trust you to put aside your personal and professional rivalries until the job is over?"

I nodded automatically. So did Ray and Lucyfar. Everyone did, except Claire and the curled up girl in the corner.

Her point made, Spider withdrew into her web where she was merely a deadly, alien predator larger than most cars. Her forelegs took solid grips in the netting lining the ceiling, and she went absolutely still. Her tone returned to business casual. "The Librarian will be a difficult enough challenge without further superheroes interfering. Several of you will be sent on diversionary missions to capture targets that will be convenient to me once I have the Orb. At noon on Monday, the Cabal will hit Voidworks and steal as much exoatmospheric construction equipment as possible. Witch Hunter will steal the Dragon's Pearl from the Museum of Jurassic Technology. Spark and Ground Pounder will procure the experimental fractal batteries from Substation Twelve, and we will hope that they work as well as Brian Akk predicts. Evil Eye will steal the lenses from Echo's tower, a task I'm sure she will enjoy."

She did look pleased. I could tell who was who by the way they nodded and sagged in relief, starting with the three guys in robes, then Witch Hunter I already knew, then the imp made of lightning riding the giant dirt golem's shoulder, and finally Evil Eye who smiled as she leaned back in her chair and laid one of her arms over the back.

"That will clear the way for Lucyfar's team, Entropy, Rage and Ruin, and She Who Wots to invade the library simultaneously at twelve fifteen." Spider said it with finality, but she wasn't finished. She turned slightly in her web and waved a foreleg in my direction. "I would like to thank The Inscrutable Machine for making this theft possible, but as the junior supervillains here they will have to take the role of bait. At ten minutes after noon on Monday, they will stage the largest distraction they can manage. I'm confident of Bad Penny's judgment in this regard, and, given how the superheroes at the conference reacted to the attack on Mech's lab, I am also confident they will divert far more resources to The Inscrutable Machine than is wise or necessary. For everyone in a distraction role, remember that keeping any superhero you encounter busy is more important to your being paid than stealing the secondary target assigned to you."

That got another round of nods, and Spider sounded pleased as she concluded, "Finally, other than the detail of your payment being dependent on successful retrieval of the Orb of the Heavens, you have all worked with me before and know the terms of our relationship. They still hold."

I knew exactly what she meant by that. She meant we were still being blackmailed.

It turned out we weren't done after all. Lucyfar stepped away from the wall, holding up her hand. "Since everybody else is too afraid to ask, you're going to take the blame for us violating a major superhero/supervillain truce, right?"

Spider's expression remained unidentifiable, but she sounded delighted by the question. "We will not be violating the truce. To ensure we are not, my representative informed the conference an hour ago that I am planning a major operation Monday. That is why diversions are so particularly important for this theft. They are on guard, but they won't know which operation is my real target."

"Wait, an hour ago?" I blurted out.

"Quite a few of the attendees have left for home already." Oh, yeah, she knew exactly what I meant.

I ducked back into the stairwell, and pulled out my phone. Could I have missed their call? I punched a button. The screen remained dark. I pushed more buttons. I held them down. Nothing.

Vera had shorted out my phone along with all of Mech's computers. Nuts!

Ray asked, "Why did you bring your phone on a mission, anyway?" He and Claire had followed me out. I ought to pop him one, but I'd break my hand and he sounded confused, not sarcastic.

Claire provided the sarcasm. "Internet access, duh." She wasn't teasing me, she was teasing herself. She showed plenty of sulky bottom lip as she poked uselessly at her own burned out telephone. She added a philosophical shrug and sigh. "Oh, well. I'll check my bank account when I get home. I bet Spider paid us enough for ten phones."

I barked, "You don't get it! My parents are on their way home, and I missed their call!"

I'd delayed too long already. I ran up the stairs and out the door, slapped the control on my chest, and leaped onto my light bike right in the middle of the Chinatown mall. I shoved my foot against the pedal as hard as I could. It sped out onto the street, weaving around two tables all on its own.

I had just passed the crazy intersection at Sunset and Hollywood when it occurred to me that if my parents were already home, pulling up to the house on my supervillain light bike wearing my supervillain costume would be seriously unwise. I lost more time going around to my school, changing into the civilian clothes I'd left in my lab, and taking my perfectly normal bicycle home.

I admit I teleported across intersections twice when I thought no one was looking and raced the rest of the way. By the time I turned off Los Feliz onto my street, I was ragged.

I had barely made it, or barely not made it. I saw my parents' car pull into the driveway. No, it was fine. In the middle of the afternoon, my being out of the house would seem perfectly innocent.

Unless, of course, they noticed Vera floating by my shoulder doing her best Conqueror orb impersonation. I screeched to a halt, grabbed her and put her to sleep, stuffed her in my belt pouch, and biked down to the house in a more leisurely manner. They didn't know I'd been getting a lot more exercise, so looking tired after biking would make perfect sense, right?

I turned into the driveway myself, and there were my parents trying to unlock the door and carry luggage simultaneously. I jumped off my bike and didn't have to fake running up and yelling, "Mom! Dad!" as I gave them each a ferocious hug. My secret identity was suddenly back. I hadn't expected it to feel this good.

"We tried to call you, Princess, but you didn't answer your phone," Dad explained. I tried to chalk up a mark on the Princess tally in my head, but I wasn't used to caring about it anymore.

Mom grabbed me for a second hug. "I knew coincidence was much more likely than foul play, but I worried anyway. It's good to see you're fine." She let me go, but still fussed with my hair, trying to get my wind-blown bangs straight.

I dug around in my pocket. "Oh, that. My phone burned out all of a sudden, and I haven't had time to fix it."

They both stared at me as I held up the dead phone. Then Mom gave Dad a smile. "Your daughter is hinting that her powers are advancing ahead of schedule, Brian." He got it and smiled to match her. I got it and had to hope they'd misinterpret my sickly grin like they had everything else. I'd just about given away the ballgame there!

"But not quite enough, huh?" asked Dad. He gave up on holding two suitcases and the keys simultaneously, and put a suitcase down to unlock the kitchen door. As he pushed it open, I grabbed the abandoned suitcase.

Not quite enough? Would my fully developed powers fix anything, anyway? They only seemed to like building something new, and even then only once. I could feed the phone through The Machine and ask for it to be returned whole. I wasn't confident I'd get a working phone rather than a pile of parts out of that.

"Could you fix it for me, Dad?" I asked. I didn't have anything incriminating stored on the phone anyway. Man, this suitcase was heavy. I'd picked the one with Dad's traveling computers in it, of course. I had to lug it down the hall to my parents' bedroom two-handed and put it down with relief.

"I'd be happy to," he agreed immediately, placing another pair of suitcases beside the first.

Mom followed us in last, to put down the one remaining suitcase. "So how did you handle being alone?" she asked, giving me a curious smile. It was really, really nice seeing a face that wasn't cagey and suspicious.

I shrugged and told part of the truth. "Just like normal. I played a lot of games and hung out with Ray and Claire all day. We are running short on pre-made food." I gave her my best puppy dog eyes, and meant them. I hadn't eaten nearly enough the last two days!

Mom laughed and walked out into the kitchen. "That problem is over. The conference ended early."

Which I knew, of course. "I saw you brought your luggage back. Did you have a good time?"

Behind me, Dad called out, "I did. I think Beebee wanted to punch someone."

Mom tried to shrug it off. "It's the downside of retirement. Hardly anyone still heroing has worked with me directly. They respect the name, but they all think they can beat the numbers."

Dad joined us in the kitchen, filling the dishwasher and laying out fresh plates. As much to Mom as to me he said, "The community is more impulsive and emotional than when we were active. It should have taken an hour to come to an agreement about The Inscrutable Machine. Instead, the argument only ended today when the kids broke into Mech's lab and demanded full supervillain status. Then Retcon made his announcement, and the whole conference broke up."

"Retcon?" I asked, having no trouble looking blank.

Mom gave a shrug and an eye roll, and answered the question she thought I was asking instead. "Spider's playing a game, and the whole community is falling for it."

Setting a stack of dishes on the table, Dad leaned over to wink at me. "Don't let your Mom fool you. She's actually in a great mood. She never shook the worry that The Inscrutable Machine would come after you, but now they've made it clear they want to play by the rules, so you're off limits."

He had her. Mom smiled, even in the middle of chopping onions.

My eyes stung a little from the onions, and maybe just a bit from the sentiment. Dad felt the chopped onion fumes too and asked me, "Want to watch me repair your phone?"

I kicked out of my chair. "Oh, yeah!"

I spent the next hour watching fascinating things I didn't understand in the slightest. I had hoped picking up some knowledge about electronics would help me work with my own super power, but I would have to start with something a bit more basic. Watching Dad work was a lot like using my super power, in fact. I was just along for the ride.

Dad had just gotten my phone working when Mom dragged us both back to the kitchen to eat. She'd filled the table with different dishes. Nobody without her timing skills could have cooked this many at once.

I ate like a pig while my parents joked with each other, and by the end of the meal I felt bloated and relaxed and happy. I went to bed Saturday night determined not to let Spider mess this happiness up.

Of course, on Sunday I had to figure out how to do that, but I intended to do it without going to pieces in the process. I didn't hurry out of bed, took a nice, hot shower, and with leftovers and the scrambled egg machine made myself a breakfast burrito. I could hear Dad in his office, so about halfway through I wandered in to see what he was doing.

He was vivisecting one of my zombie rag dolls. Seriously, he had it laid out on his desk, cut open down the middle and stuck through with sensors he'd plugged into his computer.

"Whatcha got?" I asked Dad dutifully.

"One of Bad Penny's inventions that The Inscrutable Machine left in Mech's base. They reproduce, and she left over a hundred behind. This one's even pregnant," he answered.

I raised my eyebrows. "Pregnant?" Hey, I didn't know how they worked!

"Pregnant," he repeated. He poked the interior with a teeny tiny pair of scissors. I peered over the table and into the guts of the doll. Packed into the lint was another doll's head and shoulder, sure enough. It even had teeth already.

Dad adjusted his goggles. Maybe I should just start wearing the pair Cybermancer gave me. I could get prescription lenses for them, right? Or make those myself? Naah, if my super power made a pair of lenses they might correct my vision, but only as a side effect of doing something crazy.

Dad talked right over my speculation. "Even nonfunctional in every other respect, it's very slowly growing a new doll. The actuator system made out of fabric strands is clever, but I haven't found a control or power system and the new dolls seem to grow themselves. It's classic mad science, the creation of instinct rather than design. I couldn't make one myself, and I suspect the mass it's adding is fake."

"Uh, fake?" I asked helplessly. "Instinct rather than design" described my creation process perfectly, and now I was watching someone try to piece together what I'd done after the fact. My Dad's super power was really nothing like mine at all.

"Temporary. When it disappears, it will take an amount of real mass and energy with it to equal all the energy it added to the universe while it pretended to exist. The loss of mass will be so small we'll never notice, but conservation of energy will be maintained—after the fact." Fastening two metal clips to the ragged end of the half-formed doll's shoulder, he peered at a series of graphs drawing themselves gradually on his computer screen. "I'm trying to determine how the increase of mass changes over time, to estimate when the process gives out and the dolls will disappear."

He'd gotten through the whole speech without using the word "magic" once. I sympathized with his desire to work out the fundamental physics involved, but I had no problem with labeling a big branch of processes 'magic' even after we knew how they worked.

I tried to hug my Dad hard enough that he'd know just how great he was, then walked out to the front door. For courtesy's sake, I shouted, "Bye, Mom! Bye, Dad! Call me if you need me, I won't be going far!"

When no objections were raised, I left the house and headed down to my laboratory.

Within seconds of stepping out of the elevator, I had to face it: This place was a dump. Seeing Mech's place had changed everything. I'd been getting by with barely any equipment. Granted, The Machine was an incredible tool all by itself, but what could I do better, faster, with a real laboratory? Plus, I wanted a place that looked cool!

The lab wasn't a problem. It was an opportunity. I was going to enjoy fixing this place up after I dealt with Spider.

I didn't know how to do that. I wasn't going to let her push me around forever, and I wasn't going to give up and spill the beans to my parents myself so they could protect me. I wanted out of her web, for good. Supervillainy had been running away with me from the beginning, and I wanted to take control.

I would find a way. For the moment, I'd better get ready for tomorrow. If I planned on making a show, I'd need better weapons. Let's face it, I needed better weapons anyway. My power dutifully threw up a plan, and I set The Machine to eating quartz while I filled the smelter with plastic. This would be big. I didn't want to look too closely at what I was doing in case my power jammed on my desire to put words around it. That gave me a little room to think. The split attention effect was fun, with my hands putting together this awesome thing while I wondered how to get out of supervillainy. I had to be honest with myself. The whole thing was fun. Other than not having a choice, I had a natural talent for being a supervillain and I got a big kick out of it. Who'd have thought? I had to hope I'd find heroism just as natural!

I hefted up my finished invention in my arms and let myself take a good, solid look at it. It was big, bazooka-sized, a classic alien ray gun of wires, bulging plastic in neon colors, and a fat crystal sphere filled with writhing, glowing blue smoke. The sphere part reminded me a bit of a Conqueror orb.

What did it do? I'd stayed too detached from the process to remember. Easy enough to test. I pointed the almost feather-light gun at the floor across the room and pulled the trigger. With a satisfying buzz, the floor flared with blue light, leaving a deep cylindrical hole carved in the concrete and well past the concrete into the Earth.

I almost dropped the gun. If I pointed this at anyone, no matter how well defended, it would kill them. If I pointed this at anything, it would kill someone on the other side! This was not what I wanted super powers for! I grabbed a hammer off my worktable. I'd break this thing into bits so it couldn't go off by accident and feed those bits to The Machine so it couldn't be reassembled. My blood chilled just thinking about what I could have hit with that test fire. If I'd struck a gas line, I'd have blown the neighborhood sky high.

I'd start with the globe. The whole gun ran through that. One good hit and the rest would be inert. I laid the gun out on the desk, lifted the hammer, and let out a little squeak as my super power showed me what I was about to build by breaking this sphere. I didn't understand any of the details, but I recognized the end result: A crater.

I could feed it to The Machine. No, The Machine would be safe, but I wouldn't be. Neither would the neighborhood. The actual science involved might be wildly different, but for all intents and purposes I'd built a basketball sized fusion reactor and cracking it open would be bad, bad news. Break the shell, and it would go from reactor to bomb.

Bombs got a lot of attention. I'd been asked to make a distraction. It's not like I wanted to blow anybody up, but I could take the hand I'd been dealt and play it in an unexpected way.

Not just with the bomb. I had it. I had a plan.

Force me to remain a supervillain? I'd show Spider. I'd show them all!

CHAPTER TWENTY

Monday. My last day as a supervillain, if I had anything to say about it.

I woke up early. I'd play it light, just like yesterday. I got cleaned up and dressed, ate leftovers until I bulged, and I was reaching for the handle of the kitchen door when Dad stepped up behind me. "Sorry, Pumpkin. You're staying inside today."

I strangled down my frustration as tightly as I could, but my "What?!" still sounded whiny in my ears.

Dad gave me what would have been an understanding smile, if he'd understood. "Spider has a major crime planned for today. Until I know it's safe, you're staying indoors."

Mom emerged from the basement stairs, blowing dust off her laptop and adding her two cents. "It's just a precaution. Spider doesn't like grand conquest schemes and she's finicky about collateral damage. Not that she's merciful, but she picks her targets carefully."

"I've activated our house's more exotic defenses, just to be sure," Dad told us as he returned to his office, presumably to finish the job.

I sighed, grunted, and glared at the floor. "Fine. I'll be in my room playing computer games. All day." That ought to be the right amount of sulk to establish that I was mad, but not so mad I couldn't surrender with a sense of humor.

I trudged back to my room, and I didn't quite slam the door behind me, but I gave it an audible thump. Then I set up my computer to play a championship Teddy Bears and Machine Guns video again and pried open my bedroom window just a notch.

I could teleport through that, I thought. I'd angle around as close to the corner of the house as I could see, to avoid any windows. Then I'd grab my bike and be gone.

I took a step, and my face hit the grass. Pain jolted my neck and lower back. Ow. I climbed back to my feet and found myself right outside my bedroom window. What was this? I'd never missed a teleport before!

Oh, right. Dad probably had a teleport disruption field. I needed to take a little more interest in what he had lying around the house.

Well, the hard way wasn't that hard. I crouched low under the windows and scurried down the length of the house, grabbed my bike, and pushed off hard. If my folks saw me, they saw me. If they found out I wasn't in my room, so be it. I had an excuse ready. I'd tell them I was on a date with Ray. A Birds and the Bees lecture would be toe-curlingly mortifying, but it wouldn't last long and I'd get through it.

I left all of that behind me. The next part was simple. I rode down to school and down to my lab, where Ray and Claire were waiting for me already. I changed into my villain jumpsuit in a backroom, with Claire guarding the door. She didn't need to. We were all business today. Ray carried my bomb up the elevator, and we set it right out in the middle of the schoolyard where it gave off a devilish blue light that churned and spun. I thought the base, with all the tubes and wires, set the reactor sphere off nicely.

Ten after noon. We were ready. I sat on the sphere, kicked my feet, and asked, "Vera? Project what I'm about to say as far as you can."

I pushed aside a faint worry that would be "planet wide" and announced, "I'm sorry to interrupt your daytime television, ladies and gentlemen, but The Inscrutable Machine has been thinking about this for a while now, and we've decided Northeast West Hollywood Middle School has to go. I apologize to those of you caught in the blast radius, and I'm hoping a superhero or twelve will show up to try and stop us just as much as you are. I'm really getting a kick out of humiliating them."

I heard my voice projecting out of every car and house I could see, so my message got through. School wasn't in session, but how many superheroes sent their kids here and lived in the area? We might be drowning in opposition in a minute.

327

With any luck, my plan would hold. I rubbed the top of Vera's head, and she took the hint and stopped broadcasting. Then I sat and kicked my feet some more while the superhero world scrambled.

I didn't see it coming. Shrieking filled the world, stabbed at my ears, vibrated my bones and teeth, and made me more than a little nauseous. I fell forward off the bomb, barely able to control my limbs. My voice sounded pathetically distant as I yelled, "Vera, project his weapon back at him!"

The shrieking didn't stop, but it moved away, stopped tearing my body apart. I climbed awkwardly to my feet. Even Ray staggered as he got up.

Echo stood in an open doorway of the school, clutching the sides of his helmet and gritting his teeth. The screeching stopped as whatever he used to project the sound burned out under Vera's override. Did I see a few sparks from his other equipment?

The clever little rat. Big rat, compared to me. He'd staked this place out waiting for us, hadn't he? He thought he had us by surprise. He'd weathered the sonic weapon much better than we had, and through the ringing in my ears I heard him declare, "I have more than enough weapons left to defeat you, Bad Penny."

Echo sounded confident, but he was the superhero I'd wanted to see most. I stretched my back, listening to the ringing gradually ease. "I'm sure you do, but I have a much more hilarious game in mind." I kicked the button on my bomb.

"One hundred. Ninety nine. Ninety eight," it recited loudly and so very slowly.

I rubbed my ear through my helmet and told Echo, "Here's the rules. We're going to go very far away, and if I see a giant blue ball of imploding plasma on the horizon I'll know you failed. To make this fair, here's three hints: One, you might want help. Two, do not destroy the bomb. I'm betting your sensors have told you that already. Three, you don't have time to try and catch us. Bye!"

"Ninety. Eighty-nine," the bomb announced as I activated my light bike and zoomed away, leaving Echo stuck with it. Either the sonic shock had rattled him, or he'd accepted my warning. He didn't chase after us.

I didn't go far. I looped around to the residential section of Western and got off my bike to wait for Ray and Claire. They came zipping up the street together, Claire skating and Ray keeping time with her at a run. I'd have liked to have stuck with them, but I hadn't figured out cruise control on my light bike yet. It went "fast" and "really fast right now I mean it."

Claire looped around me twice as she slid up, then hugged her rag doll and asked, "What happens when the countdown gets to zero?"

I gave her my most sarcastic sidelong stare. Since she couldn't see that through my visor, I hoped my voice would project the same emotion. "Nothing. Do you think I'm crazy?"

Ray cracked his knuckles. "So, the library?"

"The library," I agreed. Then something hit Vera.

Wind whipped past me, a gray shape I didn't get to see clearly. I heard one loud crack as it knocked Vera out of the air and another as she hit the asphalt across the street.

I had half a second. "Waityoureallywanttohearthis!" I yelled at the top of my lungs.

I hadn't been hit yet. Claudia was listening. Ray and Claire watched the buildings around us, for all the good that would do. Generic Girl was too smart to let us see her coming.

I held up both hands, palms out. The less threatening I looked, the better. "Right now, Cabal is robbing Voidworks. Witch Hunter is robbing the Museum of Jurassic Technology. Spark and Ground Pounder are robbing Substation Twelve. Spider blackmailed us to create a diversion. They're all diversions. Lucyfar, Entropy, Rage and Ruin, and She Who Wots are attacking the library right now to steal something powerful called the Orb of the Heavens."

No response. Claudia had always been suspicious, even paranoid. In this game, she needed to be. I went on. "We've had enough. Spider can reveal our secret identities if she wants. She may think we did what we were told, but we're heading to the library right now. We'll beat everyone she sent if we have to and guard the Orb until the official heroes arrive. I'd like your help. The adults don't want to admit it, but you're the most powerful hero in LA."

Still silence. She didn't trust anybody, and never had. What could I say? Nothing was enough, but I tried. "We've known each other for three years. In all that time, have I ever tried to hurt you?"

That sounded so harsh. I should have described middle school life more tactfully.

Or maybe I'd phrased it exactly right, because Generic Girl walked out from around the corner of a building hardly twenty feet away. "You had better be telling the truth," she growled, and flew off. West, not East. Maybe she wanted to stop the side crimes first?

That wasn't my problem. I ran across the street and scooped Vera up in both hands. A hairline crack scarred her crystal surface. More cracks damaged the ceramic, but they didn't worry me. I tapped her gently, and just about cried as she floated up next to me, off-white chips resuming their fairy body shape. Her head turned, and her black pupil watched me. She didn't act hurt.

I wanted to fuss over her the rest of the day, but we'd wasted too much time already. We were only a couple of blocks from the Hollywood and Western station of the Red Line. We hurried down there and caught a subway train.

It felt a little ridiculous sitting on a subway train on our way to foil an ongoing crime, but it was the most direct way I knew downtown. It also gave us a breather.

Claire put her hand on my shoulder. She looked honestly worried. "Do you think we can do this? Spider didn't send big name supervillains on this job. She sent the ones who don't lose."

I put a hand on her shoulder right back, and one on Ray's. I meant this. "Win or lose, we prove which side we're on today and show Spider she can't blackmail us. Once we're heroes, releasing our secret identities won't just be personal, it will be useless."

I looked at Ray. I didn't think about it until I realized Claire did the same thing. He flashed me a grin. "I told you before, I'm with you all the way. I bet being a hero is just as much fun as being a villain."

We were about to find out. We got out at Pershing Square Station, and when we reached ground level I noticed immediately that traffic wasn't moving. A big crowd stood at the street corner. The fight in the library must have already started.

We got moving. I turned on my light bike, and it slid around stopped cars and gawking pedestrians alike until we cleared the crush. Claire slid around easily, vaulting over a couple of cars. Ray ran across the hoods like stepping stones.

It had started, all right. Giant blades of grass surrounded the library. Dandelions stood as tall as the roof. I pulled my bike up to the Fifth Street door and climbed off in front of two huge suits of golden armor armed with swords.

I took one step, and they crossed their swords in front of me. "Library card, please?" one asked in a pleasant tone that pretended there was no implicit threat at all.

Actually, I had my library card on me, didn't I? Ray might have joked about bringing my phone, but I had it with me again and I kept the card tucked into the case. I pulled out my phone. Yes, there was my card. As Ray and Claire fell in behind me, I held the card up to the guardians. They withdrew their swords without a word. They even let all three of us in without challenging Ray or Claire.

The checkout area right inside had been replaced. We walked into a beautiful Greco-Roman dome made of white marble and gold leaf, with statuary and bas relief all along the walls and roof. An old woman sat at a writing desk that grew out of a column of marble in the middle of the room. The book on the podium was huge, at least half her height. This had to be the Librarian. She was so old she looked shriveled, her gray hair was tied in a bun, and her gray dress couldn't have been more recent than 1920.

The entire desk swiveled with a grinding noise to face us. "The Children's section is down the hall on the left, or on the other side of the Young Adult section," she told us. She sounded stiff and distracted, but not mean.

"Yes, but we—"

"The Children's section is down the hall on the left, or on the other side of the Young Adult section," she repeated. Okay, that had an edge of threat.

I didn't want to fight the Librarian if I could help it. She was on our side. The Orb of the Heavens was at the bottom of the big pit in the middle of the library, but our opponents could be anywhere. We might as well start in the Children's section.

The door to Young Adult was on the other side of this room, so we walked over to it silently and stepped into a war.

Across a grassy courtyard, a stone castle wall was manned by teenagers who scrambled up and down wooden scaffolds and stone stairs to defend it. The enemies trying to climb over were animals of all different kinds, shouting in English and wearing scraps of armor and wielding medieval weapons. All the animals were roughly human-sized, no matter the species.

A few of the teenagers on this side wore armor, but others wore hides or rags and leaves. Quite a few were dead. I saw more blood than I was expecting, but not enough to be real.

I didn't think any of those teenagers were real. The real teens huddled in a hay-filled stall by the back wall, looking shell-shocked. The defenders were phantoms out of storybooks. They weren't even all human. A centaur stood not far from us, firing arrows over the wall.

The Children's section would be on the other side of the wall, with the talking animals. Claire echoed my next thought out loud. "Rumors of the Librarian's power have been greatly underestimated." She sounded as awed as I felt.

The teens in that stall weren't awed; they were terrified. I had to help them first, if only with a few words. I scurried over to the stall, and told them, "Listen. The library exit is still where it used to be, and the way is clear. You might want to stay here. Those kids on the wall will defend you to the death, and so will the animals. That's what they think they're doing right now."

I was pretty sure all of that was true. The college guy with the bandana nodded. The rest calmed down until they merely looked stunned and nervous.

That was all I could give them. "If we can get over the wall into the Children's section, we can go out the other side and get around the Librarian," I told Ray and Claire.

Ray grinned. Criminy, he wasn't scared at all. He reached out to pat the badly cut stone tower next to us confidently. "Getting over the wall will be easy. Just ask the big guy here."

I looked up. The tower was a crudely shaped giant, sitting with its knees drawn up against his chest. It didn't move, but it was already looking down at us, so I asked, "Sir, will you lift me and my friends over the wall? We have evil to fight."

Stone scraped against stone. A hand big enough for all three of us to stand on slid down to the ground, so we stood on it. As delicately as if we were a porcelain teacup, the giant lifted us into the air, climbing to its own feet to reach over the top of the wall.

From up here I could see the Children's section. It looked almost exactly the same, except with talking animals instead of teenagers. Both sides were defending the wall, not attacking.

Claire saw something else. "That's Rage and Ruin!" she shouted, pulling on my arm and pointing. One of the animals was bright red, and another vivid blue. They weren't even animals so much as clawed and fanged hairy things.

"Allow me, please." Ray grabbed one of the giant's fingers for support, leaned way over and shouted, "There! Your true enemies, the monsters who set you against each other, are getting away!"

It worked. Ray had known his audience. Heads turned, and a huddle of animals stepped in Rage and Ruin's way. The red villainess clawed one of them open. I was guessing she was Rage.

That was exactly the wrong thing to do. Animals and teens both piled on, stabbing with swords and spears and beating with maces. There was nothing we could add to that. When the giant set us down on the Children's side we ran for the door on the far side. I took one final look back to see the giant closing its stony grip over Rage and Ruin, then ducked out into the hallway.

"This doesn't look like anywhere I know in the library," Ray immediately announced. He wasn't kidding. The library had some nice stone, a lot of institutional tile, metal girders, all kinds of decors. It did not have narrow wooden hallways that reminded me of Mech's base, except much dustier. Oh, and with more doors. Lots and lots of doors, lining both sides of the hall.

"One way to find out," Claire quipped and opened a door. Smart girl, she stood back behind the door itself as she did. Nothing came out.

We peeked around the edge into a dark Shakespearian theater. On the lighted stage someone was giving a speech, but I didn't get to hear. A gunshot boomed, and a tall man in a top hat staggered to his feet, covered in blood. People screamed.

We shut the door. "History," we all announced together. Ray rubbed his gloved thumb over a metal plaque next to the door handle, clearing the dust enough to read "Peterson House, April 15, 1865. Assassination of President Lincoln." I moved my assessment of how ridiculously powerful the Librarian was up another notch.

I looked around. Every door had a plaque, but I didn't care about those. We moved down the hallway to the corner and looked around. At the end of an identical hallway I saw a doorway opening into a wide, tiled space. We ran for it, and out into the main hallway that ran down the center of the library to the pit.

The hallway looked mostly the same. I could see where it let out into the marble and gold checkout dome on one end. I couldn't see the other. The hall widened into a big, empty decorative room in front of us, but a black metal gate ran right down the middle, walling off the other side.

The gate was huge, gothic, and almost solid. It would have been solid, except a hole had been rusted through the middle. Quite a large hole, with room enough for the frozen tableau posed inside it. In the very center stood a weedy guy with the fur and features of a black cat. I'd seen him in Spider's office. From the rust, I guessed this was Entropy.

He wasn't alone. He was surrounded by gods. Well, the men and women I recognized looked like gods. The white-skinned woman with the helmet—that was Hela, Norse goddess of the dead. The blue-skinned guy with four arms had to be Siva, Hindu god of destruction. The hawk-faced guy in the toga… was that Pluto? Nobody could mistake Anubis. There were more. They stood ranged in a circle around Entropy, arms outstretched toward him. Nothing moved in that circle, not even the thick mist that kept me from seeing past.

I looked at Ray and Claire. Their expressions echoed my feelings. We were not going through there.

"We'll get in from the walkway above," I suggested.

The stairs were still in place, the skinny set running up the side of this hallway to the upper floors. They looked quite normal for the first floor. On the second floor they became modern—if nonfunctioning—escalators. Then we reached a gap. The second floor and third floor didn't connect. Between them blue sky stretched in all directions. In the distance, giant birds with long tails and more than two wings looped and soared. Anxiously, I reached out a foot and placed it on a cloud arranged like a stepping stone in front of me.

It held. Good enough. We ran up to where the escalators resumed and ran up those to the top floor balcony.

"After this is all over, do you think we can meet the Librarian socially?" Claire asked as she hopped from cloud to cloud.

"Tesla's Spontaneous Combustion, I hope so." I grabbed her arm and pulling her up onto the escalators.

"I wonder if I can get her to sign an autograph?"

We poured out onto the balcony, and Ray sniggered. "Only if you want it stamped with a return due date."

This should have been a great place to get down into the pit, but the Library's remodeling had replaced the railing with a wall of glass. We could certainly get through that, but I stared with leery uncertainty at the man-sized barnacles cemented to the window, and the walls and ceiling around the glass. Their feathery, grasping arms did not look friendly.

"It will be easier to go around to the walkway," I suggested to Ray and Claire. They nodded. We could see it from here. We ducked through one of the doors on either end of the balcony.

I stumbled to a halt in a dark, empty church. Claire was the last through, and a thick, wooden door slammed shut behind her. I'd made a big mistake assuming the stacks between us and the walkway looked the same from the inside as the outside.

His voice quiet and even, Ray noted, "The cross is upside down."

"And bleeding," Claire added in a whisper.

"Ray, break the door down now!" I barked.

He did, slamming his shoulder against it. The door exploded in chunks of old wood, but the balcony wasn't on the other side anymore, only a night time graveyard.

Ray gritted his teeth. "Horror section. Not good. Make a run for Mystery on the other side?"

I nodded. Behind me, a woman begged, "Please, take me with you!"

I looked back over my shoulder. She'd been hiding behind a pew, and looked normal. Nice short dress, but not fancy. Not plain enough to be suspicious. Normal. If she was real, we had to save her. "Come on!" I ordered, waving my hand.

The four of us poured through the door. Above us, something shrieked, and I saw a winged, bipedal figure pounce from the rooftop. Ray's reflexes beat it handily. He smacked his palms together, and the golf ball sized energy blast he had time to pull out still knocked the monster off course. I pulled my sugar wand out as it hit the ground and sprayed it thoroughly. Thorny vines grew up instead of a candy shell, but they held the squeaking, biting thing in place. It wasn't going anywhere. That was what mattered.

We, on the other hand, were getting out of here as fast as possible. But behind us a boy screamed, "Wait! Help!" He climbed up over the tombstone he'd been hiding behind, waving his arm. Behind him a man in a ragged robe climbed over the next tombstone and raised a bloody shovel.

I'd been starting to run anyway. As I set my foot down, I blinked behind the boy. Flicking the switch from shell to knife, I swung my wand and chopped off both of the evil gravedigger's arms at the elbow. Wrapping an arm around the boy, I teleported us back to the group and felt very grateful as Ray grabbed the boy and Claire put her arm around me to help me run. A teleport carrying someone else was a bad way to start a sprint for my life.

Nothing else jumped out at us as we ran for the gate. The cemetery pretended to be quiet and peaceful. The wrought iron gate was locked, of course. Ray didn't need ordering. It was solid, but with two tugs and a lot of screeching metal, he pulled it out of its frame and threw it away.

The five of us charged out of the graveyard, off the sidewalk, and onto a deserted city street. Actually, a deserted small town street. Every window was dark.

I really did not want to call attention to myself here, but if there were more survivors we could not leave them in the Horror section. Trying to watch every direction at once, I yelled, "If anybody here is still alive, this is your rescue!"

I gripped my wand tightly as movement happened everywhere, but it wasn't monsters. I'd made the right decision. Five people crawled out of dark doorways and garbage cans and parked cars, sobbing with relief as they crowded around us. We might be thirteen, but we were dressed like superheroes and looked confident.

Nothing else moved. Claire put it unpleasantly well. "It's too quiet. We're not going to like it when we find out why."

"Mystery has to be here somewhere. Horror isn't a big section," I insisted.

Ray's head turned back and forth. Then he pointed. "There. That building. It's not run down; it's just old fashioned."

It was. We stampeded over to it in a crowd. It looked plain, mostly cement blocks, with a big window on the first floor looking into a darkened restaurant. No, a diner. More importantly, the colors were wrong.

The whole building was sepia tone. Ray had called it right, and I wanted to kiss him. More than usual.

The building had a side door, and light peeked through behind a rolled down blind. Ray pulled on the door handle, which opened normally. We headed down the beige hallway, grateful for working light bulbs and trying not to stare at our own sepia toned selves.

The hallway let into a little atrium with an empty night desk, an elevator, and stairs. The elevator looked rickety and old fashioned. We ignored it and climbed up the stairs.

The second floor was just a hallway with doors, plain and uninteresting. The third was the same, except one of the doors had a light behind the frosted window.

We made our way, superheroes and refugees, down the hall toward the door. Just before we reached it the door opened, and a sour-looking man in a loose-fitting suit wearing a fedora growled, "Quiet down. It's a bad night out there. You kids should be home in your beds."

"Are you a gumshoe?" I asked. He had to be.

"Assuming anyone on Earth ever uses that word, yeah," he snapped back.

Sweet Tesla's Resonating Bells, yes. A 1930s mystery novel detective. Exactly what I needed. I jerked a thumb over my shoulder at the seven miserable Horror escapees. "I've got a job for you. Guard these people while we fix this mess."

His lip curled up in disgust as he looked over the crowd, then back down at me. His voice sharp with suspicion, he asked, "What does it pay?"

I flipped up my visor and looked him straight in the eyes. "Nothing."

He glared for nearly one whole second before sagging in a huge, put-upon sigh. "I thought as much. Come on in, folks."

The refugees obeyed. They sat in chairs, on the desk, and against the walls, sagging with absolute relief as they watched the detective prop his own wooden chair in the doorway and pull out a revolver.

"Is there a catwalk around here anywhere?" Ray asked the detective as I lowered my visor and turned away.

"Fire escape. Bathroom at the end of the hall," the man growled.

Smart boy, Ray. Innocents saved, The Inscrutable Machine walked down to the end of the hall and turned the corner. Sure enough, at the end was a door with "Washroom" printed on it, and on the wall next to it another door labeled "Fire Escape."

We had wasted too much time trying to navigate the altered library. We had to get to the Orb of the Heavens and hope the remaining villains had been just as delayed. I knew Ray felt my impatience, because he pushed the

Fire Escape door off its hinges without testing the lock. We all stepped out eagerly into a world of color and sunshine again.

The catwalk had changed, but we had definitely found it. We stood next to a small area of sepia colored cement blocks discoloring a vast, stone castle wall. A white stone bridge stretched across a gap to another identical castle, a goliath of turrets and parapets and hundred-foot high walls that merged into the rock they sat on. Way down below us, the library's idiosyncratic pit had been transformed into a bowl-shaped primeval valley, thick with greenery and a brightly feathered T-Rex that stomped lazily around its kingdom. A fiery star gleamed in the very center. That would be the Orb of the Heavens. We just had to get down there and guard it, as soon as we dealt with one little problem.

The Librarian and She Who Wots dueled in the very center of the bridge. I might have been guessing about the others, but this plain teenage girl in her slovenly schoolgirl outfit could only be She Who Wots. She didn't fight. She stood slumped forward, arms hanging, staring at the floor of the bridge. As I watched, a line of drool fell onto the flagstones. Ew.

Her companion did the fighting. Even in bright sunlight, it was sunk so deeply in shadows I couldn't make out the exact shape. Bipedal, with horns and smaller, twitching tendrils, it looked demonic. It held its arms out to either side, and from a probably open mouth flew a swarm of words. More words flew from the open book the Librarian held in front of her. Lines of text fought between them like a cloud of razors, slicing and smashing each other apart.

On the one hand, I didn't want to get near that cloud of literary death. On the other hand, I absolutely did not want She Who Wots to win, leaving us to face that alone.

Which raised a question. "I can't tell who's winning."

I'd meant to ask Ray and Claire. Instead, the Librarian spoke up. She sounded decidedly cross. "I am. I will attend to you delinquents in a moment. She only knows the forbidden words. I know all the words."

Oh, boy. I'd really wanted the Librarian on our side.

The shadow thing laughed, in the rough voice of a half-asleep teenage girl. "I know your weakness. It is written on the underside of your tongue, old woman. You fear fire, the fire of Alexandria, the fire you couldn't stop."

Flopping clumsily, the teenage girl's hand crawled into her book bag and pulled out an old, yellowed scroll. Mostly yellow. The end had burned off, leaving black char and orange embers. She tossed it out to drop pathetically onto the bridge in between her and the Librarian.

Three orange sparks floated up off the scroll as it hit. One of the swirling, violent words struck the first spark, and the whole cloud went up in flames. The Librarian shrieked, and burning words closed around her in a ball of flame. Worse for us, walls of fire sprung up on either side of the bridge, sealing us in.

The Librarian might think we were bad guys, but she had to win this fight, and, as a superheroine, I had to help her. Oh, criminy.

I took a step forward, ignoring the wave of ache and tiredness and my desire to wheeze as I teleported down the bridge behind She Who Wots. A few words circled around us, but not many and they weren't on fire.

I had to act fast. A frontal assault had been impossible. Instead, I clonked She Who Wots on the back of her head with my wrist, with The Machine wrapped around it. If she was under a curse that should break it. Or maybe it would just knock her out.

Instead, the shadow demon whined, "Ow."

Words whipped out of the cloud, wrapping around me like snakes. The first sentence grabbed my ankles, preventing me from teleporting. Increasingly painful heat around my waist told me some of the words were on fire, but the word "paraceratherium" held my head still. I couldn't look down, only across at Ray and Claire behind the globe of fire, helpless to rescue me. I also got an unpleasantly close-up look at a shadowy face that squirmed like maggots as it turned to examine me.

I didn't have time to panic. At that moment, the fiery dome exploded, and the Librarian walked out through it. Ashes and sparks of flame clung to her clothing and her hair, but she'd escaped. She'd left behind the giant book. Instead, she held a small book with a blackened cover in both hands.

The old woman could glare, and her voice squeaked and grated with anger. "I know your weakness as well, Abigail Tinsley." She flipped open the book, and read, "April 12. I had so much homework to do today. It took me three hours. Mom made me sit at the kitchen table until every problem was done, even the book report—"

"No! NO!" yelled the shadow demon, staggering back. The cloud of words disappeared, including the ones on fire. Including the ones holding me. I was free.

"—that isn't due until Monday. I yelled at her a lot, and now I don't know how to tell her I'm grateful. I'd still be flunking everything if she didn't nag me this way. Now I'm getting As."

"Noooooooooooo!" shrieked She Who Wots herself. The teenage girl fell to her knees, bloodstained hands cupping her face as she sobbed. Then she fell again onto her side, and the shadowy monster disappeared, leaving a messy and helplessly bawling girl all alone in front of me.

The fires on either side of the bridge hadn't gone out. I beckoned desperately to Ray and Claire, and they ran past The Librarian, past She Who Wots, and we left them reading the next diary entry as we fled down the bridge and through the door there.

I'd more than half expected something horrible and deadly, like the Horror section. Instead, this room hadn't changed at all. Books lined shelves marked with Dewey Decimal numbers. We wandered down them past the Reference desk. That made sense to me. Enchant a library all you like, the Reference section would stay the Reference section.

Except all three librarians stationed at the desk were the same woman. The one in front snapped her book shut and growled, "I told you children you're next."

"But we're here to help you!" Claire squeaked back. Her blue eyes stared fearfully at the Librarian as she rocked from side to side, both arms clenched around a pillow sized blue and red rag doll.

Even the Librarian wasn't immune to Claire's power. She looked flustered, then scowled again in exasperation rather than fury. "You belong in the children's section until your parents come to get you."

That was definitely better than having to fight her directly, but we couldn't let her trap us until a hero arrested us, either. The card catalog next to her rattled, drawers jiggling until one slid open, a card floated out, and expanded into a doorway. On the other side the talking animals of the children's section tended their wounds.

I turned around and ran through the regular door that led from Reference out onto the top floor balcony. The window was still there, as were the barnacles. If we had time I'd have chanced them, but behind us the Librarian growled, "You belong in the children's section!" and stalked out from behind the desk, orbited by dictionaries and encyclopedias and almanacs.

Way down at the bottom of the stairs, Lucyfar shouted, "You kids are here? This rocks! Down here, hurry!"

"The Librarian is right behind us!" I yelled back as I pushed Ray and Claire toward the frozen escalator.

"Then hurry twice as fast!" Smart alec.

We ran down the escalator, then the clouds, and as I jumped down the last few clouds they slid together. I looked back over my shoulder and watched the stairs compress, dragging the Librarian to us as she hobbled down the steps. A book whipped past right behind me. Then a black knife whipped past the other way, burying itself in the Librarian's chest with an audible thump. Only sawdust leaked out, and the next knife hit a book instead.

Ray's arms grabbed hold of me, and the world went light as he jumped all the way down the rest of the stairs. Claire slid down the banister and landed next to us. Lucyfar had bought us a few seconds, but, as we reached her, she yelled, "I wouldn't stop running!" and took off herself.

I pushed out of Ray's arms and we ran, following Lucyfar automatically. She led us into the History hallways, shouting, "If this doesn't work, we'll make our stand together!"

"If what doesn't work?" I asked, stumbling to a halt at a T intersection where Chimera and Cybermancer lurking on either side.

The Librarian stalked down the hallway, books flapping. She wasn't that far behind us. Cybermancer leaned out into the intersection and threw a tube of blue liquid at her. She swatted it with a book, and a blue wall burst out. On the other side, rows of beer bottles along either wall shattered one by one. Through the distorting blue, I saw colored light flash discordantly.

The blue veil fell. The Librarian stood where she'd been, frozen and gray, a stone statue. Her books hung eerily in the air where they'd been, also turned to stone.

I took a step forward, but my super power showed me what would happen if I touched her. I held onto the information I could. "Whatever you do, don't touch her. She's caught, but one touch and she'll escape."

Everyone let out a collective sigh. Almost everyone. I walked over and leaned against the wall by Ray, but Lucyfar gave Chimera a high five and cheered, "Yes! Now we grab the Orb of the Heavens and get out of here! I suggest the roof. Very stylish, lightly defended."

All right. I'd gotten all the breath back I was going to get. I stood up straight and told Lucyfar, "No, we don't."

Lucyfar wasn't stupid, and she wasn't confused. Crazy, maybe. Surprised, yes. She still knew exactly what I meant. "Wait, are you betraying us? I thought we were cool!"

"We are," I answered. "We're betraying Spider and going hero."

Lucyfar, Chimera, and Cybermancer looked at each other. Then Lucyfar looked back at me. "I believe I speak for all of us when I say that you kids are awesome, and we're behind you one hundred percent, except for the part where you'll have to climb over our bruised and beaten bodies to do it." Criminy, that grin. She looked like I'd announced Christmas would come twice this year.

"I was expecting that," I answered, as playfully as I could make myself sound. I had been. We all had been. Ray massaged his fists, Claire hugged her rag doll tighter with both arms, her own fists squeezed shut, and I put my hand on my sugar wand again.

Behind Lucyfar, Chimera's body swelled up another foot, scales running up his neck as his head grew serpentine, then added quills. "You ready to do this, Reviled?"

"Oh, Reviled's not your opponent," I corrected him cheerfully, and, since I had absolutely no intention to fight fair, I dug into my pocket with my free hand for my cursed pennies.

As my fingers closed around them, a gleaming black knife popped into existence in front of me and stabbed right at my face.

Too fast. I pulled my foot off the floor, but that took too long. I wasn't ready to teleport.

Instead, a painfully sharp grip grabbed my upper arm and yanked me against the wall. The knife flew past without touching my helmet.

I staggered back upright as Lucyfar flicked her hand, blades flashing into existence as she mimed tossing them up. One, two, three, four, five. Grinning more madly than ever, she took a step forward and explained, "Take this as a compliment. You kids are way too good to fight fair."

It took her a couple of seconds to say that, and I leaned forward. A knife moved, but I could see just far enough around the corner. The hallway flashed into a new position as I teleported behind the Librarian and her floating, fossilized books. I just needed a second to make a new plan.

I didn't get it. A knife appeared in front of me, and another, stabbing down to stick in the floor as I staggered backwards. Lucy looked past the Librarian and waggled a finger. "Uh-uh."

Blast, I'd used this trick on her in our first fight, hadn't I?

Ray had a much better trick. He snapped the brass door handle off the nearest door and threw it at Lucy's head while she looked at me. It would have taken a hand the size of a catcher's mitt to stop it—a hand like Chimera's, bloated and hairy and clawed. He reached past Lucyfar and caught the door handle in his paw.

So, obviously, I teleported right behind him. I still had my wand out. A candy shell wouldn't slow him down much, so, Tesla help me, I would carve his back open with the knife. If I got his spine, that would end the fight. He'd heal. I knew he'd heal.

All that guilt earned me nothing. I dropped into place right behind him, and, unlike Lucy, he hadn't learned to look around when I disappeared. He didn't have to. He had a snake tail. Not a tail like a snake's, a snake growing out of his backside, long fangs extended as it struck at me.

I squealed. I swung my arm. I already had the wand out and set to knife, and I cut the head right off the snake. Some blood sprayed out, not much, but Chimera's roar of pain came as he was already turning to swing an arm back at me.

I fell back, dropping a foot behind me, looked past Chimera and Lucy and teleported into a spot behind Ray. Then I wheezed. Too many teleports, too fast!

Ray's slim, black body twisted, and he yanked open the door next to him. Three knives slammed into it, thump-thump-thump, their tips showing through the wood. He pulled the door right off its frame, swung it, and I heard more clattering of knives.

This was not a great position. Lucyfar's knives were hard to avoid in this tight hallway. Then Chimera pushed past her, swelling up, coppery metal spreading over his shoulders from his neck. He just about filled the hallway. Leaning forward, he took the first two steps of a charge that we couldn't dodge because there'd be no room. Ray's arm hooked around my middle, and he pulled me through the door to escape both problems.

I wasn't giving up either. As Ray pulled me off my feet, I pulled my jacks out of my pocket and threw them at the floor. Let Chimera play with those for a minute.

Chimera thundered past the doorway and let out another pained roar, this time with a ringing bell note to it. He didn't like playing with jacks at all, apparently! Maybe they'd stuck in his feet.

Okay, so where was I? These doors opened into history. History looked like a barn. I didn't think much history happened in barns. Not the kind of history that got written down in library books.

Not to mention this was the most squalid barn I'd ever seen, ever imagined. The planks didn't match in size, many of them were bent, and sticks had been stuffed into the cracks. The roof was mostly sticks glued together with a charming mix of black slime and hay. There was way more hay on the ceiling than the floor, since the only things the barn seemed to store were a few battered tools and some straw in one lone animal stall with no animal in it. Only the open doorway lit this charming shack full of nothing.

The barn contained exactly one interesting thing before we charged into it. A boy in what I'd swear was clothing made out of burlap bags kneeled in the animal stall, watching us. No, she was way too pretty to be a boy, even filthy. I'd been fooled by her raggedly short cut black hair, and her clothes. She could be a stick or have Claire's Mom's figure, and I couldn't have told the difference in those rags.

I had other things to worry about than a cowering medieval farm girl. I had Lucyfar, walking into the barn with a knife spinning above each open hand. She twisted, dodging the rubber ball that shot into the room after her. "Come now, Bad Penny. You can do—ow!" Ha! She'd ducked it again once, but the ball bounced off the back of the barn and then off the back of her head. When she swatted it away, it rebounded twice and smacked her in the rib cage. As tough as Lucyfar was, that got a wince.

Ray picked up the theme, and a flower pot, which he flung straight at Lucyfar. She dodged, but he followed up with a rusty old knife, then a weird, curvy blade on a broom handle. "Is this what fighting me feels like?" Lucy gasped, one hand busy directing a knife to slap the rubber ball away as she lurched to the side, out of the way of Ray's throws. Not that she wasn't fighting back, but Ray sidestepped three knives with ease, grabbed a wooden wheel off a hook to throw, then ripped off the hook and threw that.

The knives, ball, and Ray's missiles all moved in a blur. I had two breaths I used to grab one of the rock candies out of my sugar tank and throw it at Lucy's feet. On the third breath, I saw what Lucy was doing. Ray had dodged her knives easily, but each one drove him toward the kneeling girl. Lucy was handing him a hostage crisis.

I threw myself forward. Ray had moved yards away from me, but I could teleport. In a blink I made up the distance, tackling the girl and driving us both into the hay in the animal stall. Pathetic as it was, the wooden wall should protect her.

Before I hit the pile of straw I saw black flash and heard a hard smack. Lucy had seen me move and thrown ahead of me. Wetness poured over my hip, but when I looked down my prostrate body I wasn't hit. Instead one of Lucyfar's knives stuck out of the side of my sugar tank, puncturing the glass and leaking the thick cola everywhere.

Blast! My ammunition!

It hadn't been an accident. Lucyfer laughed and confirmed, "Sorry, B.P., those toys of yours are a little too—ow! See?" The rubber ball bounced off her head again. As much as she tried to make light of it I watched her reel, throwing one knife and then a second trying to skewer it, while one hand grabbed her sore skull.

Ray used that time to charge.

Chimera used that time to shove his way into the room, pulling Lucy aside with one arm. Ray didn't stop. He moved so fast, he was already back in arm's reach. He punched Chimera right in the throat. I winced, then shuddered as a second mouth opened there, snapping fangs at Ray's fist. Ray kicked Chimera in the gut and shoved off.

I needed to do something, but I moved too slowly. The teleports were wearing me down. We'd been running hard since we hit the library.

No time for that, Penny. Fight first; be tired later.

My rock candy went critical, stabbing out of the floor at Chimera. Ray back flipped over it with ease. Chimera's hoof kicked the crystal and smashed it into bits with the same ease.

That hoof was huge. Chimera was getting bigger, bulking up like a hunchback under a mass of muscle and bristling fur. Tusks grew out of the mouth of one head, while the head forcing its way out of his neck gleamed wet and froglike. His upper head brushed against the ceiling as he ground the rock candy into powder. He'd grown as big as the barn!

My rubber ball battered against him, and he didn't even seem to notice. Not until it bounced around behind him and disappeared. Then Lucyfar crawled up onto his shoulder, holding the struggling ball in one hand, and fed it into the mouth of the frog head. Smoke hissed, and a little slime dripped down to form frothing puddles on the dirt floor. Acid drool. Lovely.

Ray's retreat dropped him right next to me. I grabbed his shoulder and whispered, "We have to get back into the hall. I'd rather fight Lucy in a tight space than Chimera in the open."

"That gone be hard wif me in door," Chimera snarled, his fanged animal mouth garbling the words. Great. He had super hearing, too.

I stood up next to Ray anyway, eying the monster. I could teleport behind him, but Lucyfar would be right there and I did not want to be close to her. If I took Ray with me, that would be it. I'd pass out.

Ray had another idea. He slapped his palms together to activate his blasting gloves. Chimera responded by spitting, and Ray's gloves shot sparks as he pulled them apart too fast, grabbing me instead and yanking me off my feet. A glob of slime shot past us, burning into the wall.

Projectile acid drool. Lovely. I had enough time to see that Ray had jumped us away from the farm girl when Ray jumped again and my world spun. Another wet sound, more hissing, and now this wall had a smoking hole in it. A hole that for added weirdness looked into another, completely different barn.

We needed a distraction. I had just enough breath back. Maybe I could teleport onto Chimera's shoulder. Even with a hole in it, my tank probably had enough cola for a good slice. Chimera's reflexes weren't good enough to stop me.

Of course, Lucy's were. She lounged on Chimera's hunch back like it was a bed, but now she raised a hand. "Time out for a second. Give up, guys. We'll get the Orb, and we'll lie through our teeth to Spider that we couldn't have done it without you. You're good, but you're losing."

Chimera emphasized her point by taking one lumbering step toward us. At least, he tried. The intimidating effect lost a lot when he winced, reached down, and pulled one of my jacks from the bottom of his hoof. Grunting in irritation, he threw the jack back over his shoulder.

Lucy caught it and looked at it curiously. Maybe she hadn't seen one before? She turned her head, mouth opening to ask me a question.

If she wanted to know what it did, she found out. Jacks imbedded in other spots on Chimera's hide flashed, and they both yelped as electricity arced through their bodies. That gave Ray a chance, not to attack, but to smash his shoulder into the acid-damaged wall and break down a doorway into the other barn.

Not enough of a chance. Lucy clung to Chimera's back in spasmodic pain, but the monster lunged at us. His arm grew, telescoping and adding another joint as it flew at us. We staggered back through the hole, but it didn't matter. The arm missed because Chimera fell crashing to the floor.

The peasant girl pulled her ugly old shovel out from between Chimera's legs, and as if tripping him wasn't enough she jammed the butt end into one of his eyes. Lucy grabbed at the haft of the shovel, and the flat spade end smacked her in the face.

I gaped. I think we all gaped. Chimera recovered fastest, roaring and ignoring the unexpectedly dangerous farm girl, scrambling forward on four legs after us. Behind him, she raised her shovel and yelled something in... French? It sounded like French. That first word sounded like "France," and I caught "angle" as part of the last word, as in English?

No time. I ran for the door, the suspiciously out of place regular wooden door in a severely old-fashioned barn housing one blasé cow and an oil lantern hanging from a hook. I couldn't just run. I had a fight to win, so I grabbed pennies out of my pocket and threw them on the floor behind me. I knew when Chimera stepped on one, because he slipped and hit the ground again. What happened next was painfully obvious. The lamp fell off its hook, the glass shattered, and the hay underneath caught fire.

What happened after that was downright surprising. The cow, no more bothered by fire than strange children or rampaging monsters, stepped on the gathering flames and stomped them into embers.

Tesla's Mystery Safe, that was one smart cow.

And then Chimera, snarling in frustration, spat fire instead of acid and the whole opposite wall went up in flames. What was most important here? That Chimera could breathe fire, that we'd just ignited history, or that my cursed pennies were obviously making him stupid?

Most important was getting out of the barn as fast as possible. Not bothering with subtlety, Ray rammed the door down, and we bolted back into the hallway while I felt for another penny. If I could hit Lucy, we might win this.

We really did end up in the same hallway we'd left. We'd only moved down a door, to the opposite side of Cybermancer and Claire.

They blinked at us. Claire cinched up her oversized rag doll tighter, eyes wide with surprise and worry. Looking away from her had given Cybermancer some focus back, which he used to pull a little vial out of his jacket, twisting the lid to release a spray top button. Giving Claire a direct stare he asked, "You know I know about your power, right?"

She punched him in the solar plexus. He wheezed, bending forward, but under her lumpy bear suit Claire had the muscles of a mad science enhanced athlete. Her knee shot up and hit his chin, then she dropped her doll and grabbed his upper arms. As she did her hands uncurled, flashing purple and blue from her static-cling gloves. When she shoved him back against the wall, he stuck.

"Doesn't help as much as you'd think, does it?" she asked him back, her tone light and playful. Bending down, she picked up her doll and the vial Cybermancer had dropped. Then she spritzed him with his own formula.

The results were all I might have hoped. He turned gray and sagged limply against the wall.

Lucy stepped out of the doorway between us and Claire.

Claire's power had sucked me in. I'd forgotten the fight!

There was no missing the fight anymore. Knives surrounded Lucy, spiraling in a very dangerous-looking shield. I had to backpedal, but the knives didn't bother Chimera. Crouching, he squeezed through the door, then pushed Lucy rudely aside to get at us. He'd shrunk just enough to fit into the hall, but didn't look human. One sharp-toothed furry head snarled and snapped, while giant eyes rolled in the scaly head hanging below it. Bony plates jutted off an oversized arm that he walked on like a third leg, and the other two twitched, flashing claws as long as sickle blades. He had completely lost it.

I still couldn't help looking past him at Claire. Lucy and Chimera ignored her completely as she twiddled with the vial's cap, dainty but determined. When she got it just so, she threw it at Chimera's back. That was too much. It looked like an attack, and one of Lucy's knives flew up to cut the vial in half.

Which, of course, dumped the whole contents on Lucy and Chimera both, coming out in a gray powdery puff. Chimera turned gray and fell over onto his stomach. Lucy turned gray and fell on top of him.

"Is it my turn to win a fight for us?" Claire asked with bright eyes and a coy grin.

We'd done it.

Black fire flickered up off Lucy's body. We hadn't done it.

The fire spread, removing the gray from her body and replacing it with a gleaming, oily black surface that spread into an elegant dress, then oozed up off her back into skeletal wings tipped with knife blades. She started standing up, and I remembered my priorities. I threw the penny I'd collected at her. It smacked into her shoulder and stuck.

Lucyfar pulled herself up completely straight and plucked the penny free of her dress. A black, burning crown roared into existence above her head, and she announced in a strained but just barely calm voice, "I don't know if I've mentioned this, but I am the morning star, the fallen one, the first and most damned child of creation. Magic is the power of creation, children. It cannot harm me."

In case she hadn't made her point, she clenched my penny in her fist. Flames leaked between her fingers, and a painful knot twitched in my belly. I heard a girl's voice shriek in the distance. My voice.

I still was not going to take the self-proclaimed Princess of Lies at her word, and let out a snort. "If you're immune to magic, why are you afraid of the Librarian?"

Lucyfar grinned, and it was the old, playful Lucyfar grin despite the black fire and wings and oozing gown. "Because she can hit me in the head with a fifty-pound book."

"Like this?" Ray asked. He stepped forward, swinging the door he'd broken off to let us back into the hallway.

Lucy's wings lashed out. It didn't help. The hallway wasn't big, and there wasn't enough room around the fast swinging door. Yes, she chopped big furrows in the wood, but the door still slammed into her sideways, knocking her into the wall. Ray pulled the door back and hit her again, and she was too dazed to even try to dodge. Then he pinned the door against Lucy with his foot, clapped his hands together, and pulled out the glowing energy ball he hadn't had time to form before. He shoved it against the door.

Crack! Bits of wood flew everywhere. The door split in half, and the wall crumpled, leaving Lucy slumped under the broken door. All I could see clearly were her limp hands and a section of her stomach where the black dress had disappeared, leaving a regular gray t-shirt.

Ray yelled. Chimera's huge hand had locked around his ankle. The gray, animal bulk shuddered and started to push up.

I teleported two yards up onto his shoulders, stabbed my wand against his back, and turned on the knife. Blood and frothy cola bubbled out, but my swipe didn't even reach his spine before the cola gave way to hissing air. Maybe I wouldn't have to cut his spine. His bulk shook beneath me as he fell back against the floor, making some very ugly coughing gurgles. I must have punctured a lung.

That would kill anyone else. Chimera had already stopped bleeding. To my great relief, Vera floated up the hall to me and I realized I had backup. "Stay down, Chimera, or I'll order Vera to melt you."

Wait. Forget backup, Vera had been here the whole time. I'd had a trump card weapon since the beginning and forgotten to use it!

Or been unwilling to use it. As far as I knew, Vera had no "stun" setting. She only had a "melt" setting.

"I officially vote that we surrender," Cybermancer mumbled, still stuck to the wall.

From underneath the door, Lucy agreed, "Ow, my head. Okay."

Chimera gurgled. The vote was unanimous. We'd won!

Claire giggled. Ray grinned at me. He held out his hand, and I slapped my hand into it and squeezed.

Then I pulled my helmet off, pulled him up close, and kissed him.

A second of Ray's wide eyes staring into mine, and his arms went around my middle, bending me back as he kissed me back harder. After the tension of the fight, suddenly all I could feel was my mouth and his, a warm pressure that made my heart thump in my chest.

I pushed my way out of his grip and caught my breath. Okay, kissing was all it was cracked up to be.

Still staring at me, Ray mumbled, "I should have trusted the card."

Claire's loud groan of frustration interrupted us both. "Finally! Why did it take you two this long?"

I stopped staring at Ray and stared at Claire instead. So did Ray. She gaped at us. "You didn't know. You really never noticed how you're always watching each other. Oh, for pity's sake!" She slapped the heel of her palm against her forehead, and leaned back against the wall opposite Cybermancer with a thump.

Next to my shoulder, Vera's head turned, the thing I'd taught myself to always be alert for. She didn't just move; she dived, down and past me. I spun in place, grabbing at my empty wand, preparing to teleport.

I didn't teleport. Instead, I watched The Apparition rise out of the floor, gray and insubstantial except where her palm met Vera's tiny hand. She'd been reaching out to possess me, but Vera had blocked her.

"How...?" The Apparition whispered, shock enlivening her normally sad face.

I hadn't known, but I wasn't surprised. Conqueror tech seemed entirely compatible with magic. I didn't get to tell her. Vera answered instead with those meaningless bell chimes she had for a voice.

Meaningless to me. The Apparition stared at her, eyes widening further. "That... that can't be true."

Vera rang again.

"For me?" The Apparition asked.

Vera's bell ringing voice went on for several seconds this time, almost a song. As they played, The Apparition's face twisted up. Phantom tears welled up in phantom eyes, and she wrapped both arms around Vera, pulling her floating body close and hugging it tight. Bending her head over Vera, she sobbed, "Yes. Yes, please. I didn't think I'd earned one."

What was I looking at?

I knew the answer as soon as I asked the question. A book about lonely alien beings had inspired Vera's creation. The Apparition was the loneliest alien being I knew. Vera wasn't a tool, or a weapon. She was a gift. This was why I'd made her.

I felt a little like crying myself. Ray slid his arm around my shoulder. As The Apparition's hug loosened, Vera turned her head and chimed bells at me.

I didn't understand the words. I didn't need to. "Yes. You have my blessing. I'll miss you."

I'd miss her for more than just her incredibly useful powers. I'd find some other way to stop bullets. Just a little bit of grief gnawed in the middle of my happiness as I watched The Apparition fly down the corridor holding Vera's tiny hand, ducking past the petrified Librarian, until they turned into the main hall and out of sight.

I'd see them again, right? I hoped so.

I walked around the pile and peered at the wheezing Chimera. "Are you going to live?" I asked. I was pretty sure, but... well, I'd just cut his lung open!

He nodded weakly. That was a relief.

"I'm sorry, but if I'd done anything less you'd be back up in sixty seconds, right?" I asked again.

"Yep," he whispered.

"We're cool, kids. Or at least, we will be as soon as I swallow a hundred aspirin," Lucyfar groaned, pushing the door out of the way of her face. "Thanks for not spraying me with that stuff that eats hair, Bad Penny. Reviled, I think you broke a few bones."

Ray raised an eyebrow. You could just barely tell behind the mask. "Was that a compliment?"

"You bet it was," she chuckled.

The hallway vibrated as crashing thundered out of the main hallway.

Claire jerked upright. "Maybe we missed someone."

"Maybe someone got back up," Ray suggested, pulling his blasting gloves tight.

We inched around The Librarian's statue, taking extreme care not to touch it or her books until we were clear and could run out into the hallway. We got there to find the metal gateway broken down. Rubble lay everywhere. The frozen gods were gone, but a black-furred hand sticking out from under a huge black metal plate suggested Entropy was still out for the count.

Something shrieked, over and over, down the hall past the ruined wall. It came from the jungle spilling out of the pit. We had a clear run to it.

Run we did. As we ran we heard two loud, quick thumps, then a third off-tempo, then a crash. We ran through the trees out onto the landing for the stairs that wound their way down the bowl to the bottom of this miniature jungle. That bottom had been wrecked. Rage and Ruin lay unconscious under broken tree trunks. Claudia was slumped over the pedestal that should have been supporting the Orb of the Heavens. The T-Rex lay on the other side of the bowl, but as we watched it pulled itself up, stretched out its neck, and screeched like a parrot. The rainbow colored feather crest on its head bobbed up and down furiously.

It staggered toward Claudia, mouth gaping. Ray slapped his hands together, pulling out an energy ball, but he hadn't had much time to recharge. I had to do something, so I jumped, teleported, and landed next to Claudia to wrap my arms around her.

That had been a terrible idea. The world spun and went dark, my muscles turned into knots, and I fought for breath. I couldn't get her out of here. Through the black spots I saw the T-Rex loom over us, and a pink and purple ball of energy smash into the side of its head, knocking it on its side.

It didn't get up. Instead, it faded into a skeleton. An obviously fake, plastic skeleton. The library's transformation was reversing.

I got enough breath to wheeze, "Cl—Generic Girl! Are you okay?"

Her eyelids fluttered. I'd woken her up. She groaned. "I stopped Rage and Ruin. I was fighting the T-Rex, when something cold touched me. I blacked out."

"Where did the Orb go?" I asked.

Claudia looked up. So did I. There was a hole in the roof, just about the right size, letting in fresh sunlight now that the fake sky had gone.

Claudia pushed my arms away. I couldn't have resisted her even if I hadn't been achy and exhausted. Without another word, she flew up into the air and sped out through the hole in the roof, the hole Vera must have burned while The Apparition possessed Generic Girl.

The logs on top of Rage and Ruin faded into nothing. So did the grass underneath, leaving them lying awkwardly the floor. The library was reverting rapidly now.

Ray hopped over the remaining debris to me, holding out a hand and carefully pulling me up. He sounded solemn for once. "I think we've left enough witnesses, but if we're here when the police and heroes come, but the Orb isn't…"

I nodded as he trailed off. "Yeah."

He swung me up in both arms, cradling me against his chest. It felt better than ever. "There's a side door on the other side of the Children's section," he suggested.

I gave myself a double check to make sure I looked perfectly normal and civilian as I pulled my bike up in front of my house. On the off chance I'd actually gotten away with this, I crept down the length of the house and crawled back in through my bedroom window.

After all that excitement, this was where goose bumps rattled me, as I opened the door to my bedroom and stepped out into the hallway.

Mom leaned out of Dad's office immediately. "Penny? I thought you were asleep! You'll want to see this."

She beckoned me into the office and waved me to one of Dad's monitors and the TV news showing on it. Dad sat in a chair by his computer, chin on his fist as he watched. Just as I walked in the same reporter who'd tried to interview me downtown came onscreen. "Reports from hostages on the scene confirm the story we've put together. Today, the LA Main Branch Public Library was ground zero of the biggest supervillain gang fight in history. The winners were, incredibly, The Inscrutable Machine, a group of middle-school supervillains who've been crushing every adult in their way. A representative of the superhero community confirms that the prize for this fight was a unique piece of technology kept secretly in the library, although we don't know yet what it was."

I blinked. "No way."

Dad waved a hand at the screen. "The real story is a bit more complicated. The Inscrutable Machine went out of their way to protect innocents caught in the fight, then defeated all the other villains in the building to steal the Orb of the Heavens themselves."

Mom leaned forward in her chair, folding her arms over her lap as she stared at the screen. It failed to offer anything more interesting than distance shots of the library. "I believe they were sending a message. Not to us. The superheroes have accepted them. Now the supervillains have to as well."

Dad looked over at her and frowned. "Do you think they gave the Orb to Spider?"

She nodded. "I think so. I'll contact the Expert and have him contact Spider. It would be unlike either of them to lie about this."

Dad stared at Mom for a few more seconds, then the screen, and then sighed and pushed himself up out of his chair. "I have to get going. Echo is sure the bomb isn't a bomb, but, whatever it is, it's powerful and he doesn't want to move it. He thinks it may be Conqueror technology."

Her face completely expressionless, Mom mused, "Three associations with Conqueror tech in a week. That's a bad pattern."

Dad came down hard on that idea. "One thing Spider wouldn't do is sell us out to the Conquerors. Judging by their performance today, neither would The Inscrutable Machine."

Slowly, Mom nodded, a thoughtful frown replacing her scarier Audit face. "No. They've made that very clear. They're not crazy or rogue. They're thirteen-year-old professional supervillains. We have to accept it."

I'd had enough. I walked out of Dad's office, out the kitchen door, and leaned against the house to stare at the road. The Inscrutable Machine were still supervillains. More supervillains than ever. What had I accomplished today?

The front door clattered as Dad stepped out. He glanced over at the mailbox as he passed, and with a curious frown picked up a pink envelope and tossed it to me. "Mail, Pumpkin."

No return address or postmark. "Penelope Akk," in elegant formal script. It looked like an envelope for a party invitation.

It was another letter from Spider.

While my Dad climbed into the car, then pulled out onto the street, I opened up the envelope and read the letter inside.

Bad Penny,

You most likely expect me to be angry. On the contrary. I owe you a rare and sincere apology. I treated The Inscrutable Machine as children, and you punished me for my hubris, reminding me why respect and courtesy are the best ways to conduct a professional relationship. It is true that I got what I wanted today, but I am very aware that I got it only by luck. In every way that's important, you bested me.

I hope that you will be willing to forgive me, and will work for me by your own willing choice in the future. You have a great future ahead of you as supervillains, and I would like to be part of it.

Sincerely,

Spider

I laid my head back against the bricks. What had I accomplished today? I'd saved a lot of people from being hurt, set yet another record for wildest thing I'd ever seen in my life, had my first kiss, made the person blackmailing me beg for forgiveness instead, had a fantastic amount of fun, and made myself a legend.

I hadn't intended to be a legend as a supervillain, but now The Inscrutable Machine had a reputation to maintain, and a lot of fun to have in the process.

I felt good. I felt so good, I had to laugh.

"HA! AH HA HA HA HA HA HA!"

ABOUT THE AUTHOR

Richard Roberts has fit into only one category in his entire life: 'writer.' But as a writer he'd throw himself out of his own books for being a cliche. He's had the classic wandering employment history—degree in entomology, worked in health care, been an administrator and labored for years in the front lines of fast food. He's had the appropriate really weird jobs, like breeding tarantulas and translating English to English for Japanese television. He wears all black, all the time, is manic-depressive, and has a creepy laugh.

As for what he writes, Richard loves children and the gothic aesthetic. Most everything he writes will involve one or the other, and occasionally both. His fantasy is heavily influenced by folk tales, fairy tales, and mythology, and he likes to make the old new again. In particular, he loves to pull his readers into strange characters with strange lives, and his heroes are rarely heroic.

Thank You
for Reading

Please visit http://curiosityquills.com/reader-survey to
share your reading experience with the author of this book!

A TASTE OF...

ENTRY 1

RECUPERATING!

M y mother had given me these papers when I was eight to fill with a diary or some other drivel, but I feel this collection of pages would best be used to chronicle the adventure in which myself and my new friend, Sherlock Holmes, found ourselves involved. I doubt anyone would be interested in our exploits, but I figure that if anything else I will scribble here for posterity and be done with it. In my golden years, if Holmes allows me to live that long, I will have something to look back on fondly. That is, of course, if I am in one piece long enough to remain friends with Holmes.

I am John H. Watson, aged twelve, and I do feel a bit silly introducing myself in my own journal, but I supposed if other eyes were to find these words then they must know who took the time to cramp their hand and write them out.

I find myself at the end of our adventure, nursing a family of bruises. Though I am glad we survived, I do wish we had been more cautious, but then again my friend Holmes does not strike me as the cautious type. I, on the other hand, am as cautious as a... well, an example escapes me at the moment, but take my word for it when I say that I am most assuredly cautious.

My mother says that I was "born old," whatever that means. Maybe that will stand as an illustration of my cautiousness. I supposed she meant that I was rather mature for my age and I would agree with her, but she failed to give me a suitable explanation. But despite my apparent caution and regard for self-preservation, I find that I share that dastardly trait of the cat. That being curiosity, of course. This sour habit was the thing that brought Holmes and I together, and as much as I regret the mannerism, I must say that I am happy for it. Holmes has become a very dear friend, and in such a short time, too!

I am currently under the covers, huddled in bed, writing as feverishly, but as quietly as humanly possible. The hall monitors are about and after the adventure of which I am planning to relate, their interest in Holmes and I will no doubt be heightened. They will be checking in on us from time to time, and there is much to write. They want me to rest and that is certainly easier said than done. As if I could manage to close my eyes after all the excitement.

I could just blurt it all out in a few pages, but the thrill of the hunt will not be present and the meat of the story's bones would have been sadly worried off and that would be doing a disservice to whoever reads this. If it is you, old Watson, gone now fifty or more years, then how do you? You were a handsome lad, hope you haven't let it all go, my dear sir.

But I digress; there is much to write as I have said, and I suppose I have the time. They won't let us back to class for a few days so we can nurse our scrapes. I would much rather sit in class than stare at the walls, but Holmes is more than happy to mope. He has buried his nose in a book on poisons and is seemingly drinking the knowledge up like a straw. His brain capacity must be infinite, which makes his intellect vast, and thusly makes him a bore at times.

He can be quite the social lemon, but when it comes to his deductive reasoning, I stand by him. He is a genius, though I don't think I would ever say so out loud to him. I imagine he would reply, "But of course, Watson. Don't waste your breath on the obvious things in life."

But you haven't met him yet. Let me begin at the beginning, and we shall meet Mr. Sherlock Holmes together, whoever you are. I think I shall call this first—of what I gather to be many exploits—the *Astounding Adventure of the Ancient Dragon.*

ENTRY 2

FAREWELL CHILDHOOD!

The sky had thickened on my last day at Watson Manor, my home. It had been threatening rain since the day before, but today it seemed as if the forces of nature were amassing to drown the world. The clouds clotted and the sun was gone behind dark, sinister clouds by midday. It pitched the house into a grimmer ambiance than it already had, and soured our moods further.

For the past six or seven months, my mother, Misses Victoria Marie Watson, aged thirty-three years, had grown ill. My father, Doctor Henry Watson, knew more than he was letting on, but decided to keep it quiet around me. Of course, I was all too aware of the change in my mother and soon I began to realise that her thining away was not a good sign.

About four months ago, she needed my father's hand to help her up and down the stairs. This was, of course, when she had tried to put on a brave face for me. A month later, she stopped coming down the stairs at all and remained in her room. I became her nursemaid, and I was certainly glad to do it. I had never been close to my father, who I considered a very serious and stoic man, but my mother had always been a source of warmth, and my love for her was unbounded. I had hoped that the condition she found herself in was a temporary one, and as fate would have it, that would be the case, but not exactly as I had hoped.

It started with the coughing fits and the blood on her sheets. She would sweat to beat the devil, leaving her thirsty, but to make matters worse, she would vomit anything she drank or ate. Her skin became pale and ghostly, so that her blue veins showed underneath like dried snakes. Her eyes grew rheumy, and she began to wheeze with every breath.

But still I held out hope, and I prayed and I begged God to do what he could for my poor, sick mum. I held onto this hope until about a month ago when I heard my father talking to a friend of his, another doctor, who had come to help minister to my mother.

The man in the grey overcoat turned to my father after shutting the door to my mother's room and shook his head, his face set grim. My father, though as stoic as I have mentioned, began to cry. The man in the grey overcoat grabbed onto my dad and supported him as he let out emotions that he had no doubt been keeping in check. I had never seen my father cry before then, and that night I joined him in solitary grief. I ran from my hiding spot at the top of the stairs and locked myself in my room. There I spent the night in tears, and I don't think I slept a bit, or at least I don't remember doing so.

It had finally dawned on me that my mother was dying and there may not be anything anyone could do to make her better again. The fact that Father was a doctor and was helpless in the face of this wasting disease made me angry with him. I withdrew from him even further. He closed his clinic and he spent his days with Mother, wiping her brow, soothing her bedsores. I saw them exactly three times a day. My mother did not allow any of the servants into her room, so I brought her breakfast, lunch, and supper. She would ask me about my day, but my father would always usher me out, saying my mother needed to conserve her strength.

I would leave, but I would wait by the door and listen to her strain to drink up the clear, beef broth, which had become her diet. If she could keep half of it in her stomach, then it was a good day. Even in the face of such terrible sadness, it was important to find things to count as good. At night, I would try to sleep, but my pillow grew wet from tears and I could never quite manage any rest. Soon, both my father and I looked like ghosts and had joined my poor mother in her wasting away to the bone. We neglected to eat, but the maids made sure I had something before going off to bed. We forgot to change our clothes, but the maids made sure we'd keep up appearances. I had neglected my school duties, but no one seemed to care then. Not even my father, who was once so high on my education.

Friends and family stopped visiting and the house grew dark and quiet as if death had settled in with us comfortably and was infecting the whole of the foundation. There was a chill that never left, despite the roaring fireplaces. It would eat into our bones and cripple our fingers, unnatural as it was. We lost a few servants a week before the night in question. The only reason they gave was that they felt they couldn't stand the eeriness of the house, that it felt like a tomb. And yes, I would have to agree that our once warm, glorious manor had indeed become a tomb for the living and the dying.

You'll understand now why the gathering storm clouds on that last night seemed so ominous and portentous. All day, a cold, hollow knot in my stomach kept churning about. There was also a pain in my chest that made me wonder if my heart, so connected to my mother's, was feeling the pangs of separation.

The day was spent as usual, except my father was out of the house for most of the day on an errand he failed to explain. I was told not to bother my mother, but I could bring her food and help her to eat it if she was of a mind to try it. She skipped breakfast, had a bit of lunch, and supper hadn't been attended to by the time my father arrived, looking ruffled.

He disappeared into my mother's room and told me to wait by the door. I took a seat on the bench in the hallway and waited, listening to the muffled voices. I wasn't as shabbily dressed today as usual, thanks to one of the remaining maids, Minnie, who had decided to prop me up in finery for some unknown reason.

I remember this moment as if it was yesterday, and for the rest of my life I believe it will live in my memory as if it had only occurred the day before.

I wiped tears from my eyes and my reddened face as the bedroom door opened and my father stepped out into the hallway. He looked down at me, but I was still busy trying to hide the tears to return the gaze. He bent down and dropped to his haunches, studying my face.

"Your mother would like to see you, John," he said, his voice grave and rough, choked with an emotion I had never previously heard buried within it.

I sniffled.

"Be brave, son," he said, giving me a curt pat on the shoulder.

I stood and disappeared into my mother's room. The once stately bedroom had grown dim and smelled of rotten fruit. The flames in the fireplace seemed feeble against the wild, ominous darkness creeping about the room. My goal was the small, pale figure tangled in the rumpled sheets on the bed.

Victoria Marie Watson, my mother, was once a stunning woman. She used to joke about how my father had to fight off a hundred men to win her affection, but that she somehow always knew father would be her husband in the end. Now, her once lush black hair had grown dull and untamed by a comb. Her warm emerald eyes had lost their fire and were sad, dark-green blots. Her skin, which was once as precious as ivory, was still as pale and thin as I mentioned. Her lips, previously round and crooked in a perpetual smile, had grown small and limp. The face had lost its roundness and taken on the appearance of a skeleton with a wet rag on it. Still, despite the ghastly state my mother found herself in that night, I had grown slowly accustomed to it and I was surprised to find that somehow she managed to retain a sense of regal elegance that knocked the wind from me.

"Come to me, John," she said, waving a small, weak hand.

I moved as if in sand and eventually found my way to the chair by the bed. My eyes drifted away, afraid to stare into the glazed gaze of my mother, and spotted her empty water glass.

"Oh, your glass. Would you like some more water?" I asked, standing up. "I could get you some more if-"

"No, John, it's alright," she said, placing her hand on my shoulder and sitting me back down with the last of her strength. "We need to talk, son."

I remember looking down at the floor; afraid to glance at my mother for fear that my heart would break. The cold, hollow knot began to rise and force tears to flood my eyes. I knew where this talk would lead; I knew it with every beat of my pained heart, and I did not want to be there in the room with my heart bursting. In fact, I started to pray to God to make all of this go away, when she spoke again.

"It looks as if I'm going to be sick for a while, son. Your father is at a loss, and if he can't figure it out, then he assures me that he has friends who can."

"So you will be fine," I said, hearing hope in the words.

"I don't think I will be, my love."

My eyes rose to meet hers, the truth finally revealed. I was so stunned I couldn't breathe.

"I've tried to raise you as an honest and upstanding man, and I've never lied to you, so I don't think I should lie to you now," she said, and the regality of her assured presence took full control. "I'm afraid I'm dying, John."

"But Father said—"

"Your father cannot help me anymore, son. It's just my time to go."

I sprang from the bed like a child of two and hugged my mother, clutching much too tightly. She in turn wrapped her arms around me gently as I cried like a baby, afraid to let go of the one perfect thing in my life.

"You can't go!" I demanded, gripping tighter, making sure death couldn't drag her away.

"If it were up to me, my love, I would live long enough to meet your children's children. But, as it seems, it isn't up to me," she said, her voice as smooth as silk.

"And Father can do nothing?"

"Oh, he'll bring his friends here and they'll try their best, but I'm afraid I hold no hope in their efforts," she finished, and shook with renewed grief. "I don't mean to be blunt, John. But to get through this life, we must face our obstacles head-on, and so you must learn to do so as early in life as possible. I'm sorry it has to be this way, though."

"But what will I do without you?"

This was, of course, the question of the hour. I couldn't fathom an answer for myself and I suppose my mother couldn't either because she began to cry. The tears dropped onto my shoulder, and somehow I welcomed them and they comforted me. She took a moment before she answered.

"You will grow up, son. You will grow into a brave, intelligent young man. You will be proud and honest and a fair friend. You will follow in your father's footsteps and help people of all kinds. You will always be my son, and I will always be with you, John."

We held each other for a moment, maybe hours, I couldn't be sure, and then she gathered herself enough to separate us. She held me at arm's length and looked into my face for what turned out to be the last time.

"I love you so much, and I am so very proud of my son, the future Dr. John Watson."

"I love you too, Mum."

She hugged me again, tighter than she possible could have in her condition, and I still feel her arms around me today.

I was ushered away and found myself in my room. The maids were there, busy packing my one suitcase. We had used it for our trip to France and Belgium, but for the bulk of its cracked-leather life, it has lived deep in my closet.

I looked at my father, who had led me to my room, and he rubbed a smooth hand across his bearded face. He looked down at me and tried a smile. Patches of grey had started to appear around the jaw line, and I hadn't noticed it until then.

"I realise you've been neglecting your schooling, John, and even though your mother's illness has kept us busy, we can't have that," he started, the deep, stoic voice returning. "I'm sending you away to a school, son. It's not very far, and they can take care of you, so I can concentrate fully on your mother."

He already concentrated fully on my mother, so his reasoning was illogical. However, I supposed my mother had made him send me away to keep me from the cold grip of the deathly still house. I can't say I relished going back to school, but as my mother had put it, "it isn't up to me," is it?

The maids closed the suitcase and one of them came over to hand it to me. I took it and wavered under the weight of it.

"Those are a few of your things. In a week's time, I will send along the rest," he said, and I nodded sadly. "I know you understand why this is best, son."

"When Mother—" I started, but mercifully Father stopped me.

"If… your mother… passes away, I will come for you. But she'll be fine. Better in no time, you'll see." I sniffled, and he bent down to stare into my eyes again. "I'm sorry, son. I wish there was another way. I don't mean to send you away to be cruel."

I nodded.

I understood.

"Keep a stiff upper lip, son. We Watson men are made of hearty stuff."

"Yes, sir."

He led me out of my room, and I managed to throw a look back inside my once-pleasant dwelling one last time as the door shut on my wonderfully sheltered childhood.

ENTRY 3

FIRST IMPRESSIONS!

The horse-drawn carriage sped across the countryside, aided by the ghostly blue light from the full moon above. The wooden wheels rutted the dirt road that ran through a particularly eerie patch of forest deep within the countryside. Perhaps the eeriness was due to the fact that I rode alone in the carriage, flying through the dark blue void as the howls of wolves followed us.

Keep in mind, of course, that the sound of the horses' hooves and squeaking wheels was deafening, but still the piercing, awful cry of the hungry fiends could be heard.

I would poke my heard out the window from time to time to try and spot the no-doubt bloodthirsty beasts, but all I saw were the dark, ominous trees speeding past and the glowering moon high above. It was a night for witches, not one for attending to school.

The driver, a gruff dockworker, who smelled of fish, flopped his massive, monkey face around and grunted. I poked my head out again and he pointed at the distance with his knobby fingers.

"We're almost there, boy," he said, shouting over the cacophony of the carriage. "You'll be able to catch your first glimpse of Candlewood as we come up ahead."

The carriage bounded up over a rise in the road and then dipped down deeper than I had expected. As we moved downward in an impossibly vertical state, I did indeed catch my first glimpse of the prestigious Candlewood Boarding School for boys and girls.

My eyes nearly rolled back into my skull as I took in the size of the place. Pitched into total darkness, the actual dimensions could only be guessed at, but by the looks of the monstrous black shape, the building was six times the size of our manor house, with fantastic spires and towers climbing towards the sky. I had read during the carriage ride that the school had been built as a hospital, but after a fire, they had closed it down and then reopened it as a school almost a decade later. They had added a few wings and turrets, but the building had remained in its original state since its construction in the early 1800s.

As we approached the main gates, I spotted the plaque on the wall reading the name of the school and setting the establishing date at 1810. The plaque was bronze, and even in the dim light, you could tell that green oxidization had taken over.

Clearing the main gates, the carriage thundered across the expansive, well-manicured lawn and headed for the magnificent, tall double doors at the front entrance. I got a better look at the building then and saw that the stone work was certainly old-fashioned and gothic, which appealed to my romantic sensibilities, but I took in all these details without further care, since my thoughts were firmly with my mother and her health.

In fact, it was because my mind was on my mother that I first took notice of the figure in white on the front porch with some trepidation. Was this the ghost of my mother come to say her final goodbyes? As the carriage rolled to a stop, I saw the figure float down the stairs and approach. My heart flew up into my throat as fear choked me.

The figure reached up and opened the door. The blue moonlight revealed her face and it was not my mother's, but belonged to a stern, middle-aged matron. Her hair was in a tight bun, stretching her wrinkled skin.

"Young Mister Watson I presume?" she asked, her voice heavy for a woman.

"Yes, Ma'am."

"Mister Watson, I am not one of your teachers, so you will address me as Head Mistress. Are we agreed?"

"Yes, Head Mistress."

"Very well, then. The hour is late. We can discuss your curriculum in the morning. I will show you to your dormitory now. Be so kind as to grab your bags and follow."

The head mistress led the way down the long, ornate hallway lined with oil paintings and tapestries of ancient origin. She held a blazing candelabra and I followed the halo of dripping candlelight through the darkened heart of the school.

Inside the massive structure, I had a moment to appreciate its existence, even if I dreaded being kept prisoner within. The walls were stone slabs and the floors were as well. They were cold to the touch, but the interior as a whole was rather warm. The windows were arched with leaded glass and the ceilings rose to dizzying heights. It was a church more than it appeared to be a school. Or a museum! Yes, that's closer to my first impression of Candlewood.

As for the head mistress herself, she gave off a sense of tenseness and unfriendliness that chilled the blood. She walked in tight formation as if marching, and her manner of speaking was always matter-of-fact. My first impression of the head of the school was not a favorable one because she seemed about as likable as the cold stones around me.

"The Candlewood boarding school is not only the best school in England, but has a tradition of turning out the best minds the world has ever seen. I do hope you will be among those counted," she said, turning slightly back towards me so that her harsh voice would carry down the hallway.

"Yes, Head Mistress."

"There are many rules, which we can go over tomorrow, but the most important ones right now is that bedtime is nine p.m. and breakfast is at seven a.m. This means you must be up by six to make your ablutions and be ready in the mess hall by seven. Correct?"

"Yes, Head Mistress."

"Splendid. I think we'll be getting along famously."

I seriously doubted that, and continued to follow her. We turned innumerable corners and crossed dozens of hallways. I was already lost by the time we made our way up a flight of stairs and she said, "We're almost there. The school may seem labyrinthine at first, but rest assured. You will find your way around quickly. Especially when you have to get to classes."

I moved as if a ghost myself. Still coping with what seemed the eventual loss of my mother and the awful grief that brought with it, plus trying to adjust to a new school environment at the same time, made my head spin. I didn't know whether to cry or scream or laugh or jump up and down and sing a song. I was dizzy with emotions and that certainly didn't help me learn my way around, especially in the groping darkness.

"Here is your point of origin, the boy's dormitory," she said, suddenly stopping at a large, wide, teak wooden door. "Everyone should be asleep, so move about as little as possible, find yourself a bed, and get some rest."

"Yes, Head Mistress."

"I am well aware of your situation and even though I sympathize, I do hope you won't make me regret allowing you late admittance to the school year. Welcome to Candlewood."

"Thank you, Head Mistress," I said as she opened the door and ushered me in.

It slammed shut behind me and I peered into the bluish gloom as I tried to make out the details of the dormitory. In front of me, spread out a long room, lined with cots. Most of the cots were dotted with boys under thin, white blankets, tossing and turning in their sleep.

To my right was a roaring fire in the fireplace, giving out some much needed warmth and light into the expansive sleeping area.

I was drawn to the fire, planning on sitting down by it and thinking, when a creak squeaked. A hand appeared at the armrest of one of the chairs by the fire. I looked up and saw a boy peering back at me from around the chair. A thick book was clutched in his other hand. His face was small and pinched, but carried a sense of confidence with it.

I stopped in my tracks as the boy examined me from head to toe. He looked into my eyes and waved curtly. I nodded in reply and turned to the cots, deciding against the warm fireplace now that I wouldn't be alone.

I made my way down the aisle, between the cots, and plunged into the darkness, away from the firelight. I soon found an empty bed under a large window and threw my suitcase on top of it. I approached the window and looked out onto the darkened grounds of the school.

I was finally still with my swirling thoughts and as the situation replayed itself over and over in my head, I began to cry. I was alone, with no father or mother, in a strange place with no friends. My heart grew heavy and I heaved a sigh as the tears streamed down my cheeks, despite my valiant efforts to hold them at bay.

Suddenly, there came a *thud* on the bed behind me and I spun around, wiping my face with my coat sleeve. There on the suitcase laid an extra blanket, folded neatly. I looked up and saw the boy from the fireplace standing at the foot of the bed, his face unreadable.

"You'll need that, I'm afraid. I'm sure you've noticed, but the cots by the windows are the empty ones. The window cots are unpleasant because the cold seeps in right through the glass. The glass is thin here. No doubt the cheapest possible. So, like I said, you'll need that extra blanket."

I sniffled and wiped my face, unsure of what to say or do. My thoughts were far from niceties and manners at the moment. The boy examined me and cracked a small smile.

"Cheer up, old boy. It's only school after all, a prison as it is," he said, and sauntered back towards the fire.

I sat myself down on the cot and grabbed the new blanket to wipe my eyes with. I was feeling the weariness of the day and the emotions and the travel, so I placed my suitcase on the floor and lay on my cot. I threw the new blanket over the original one and comforted myself with the warmth.

Turning to the fire, I watched as the boy sat in his chair, his nose buried in a book, no signs of sleep evident in his alert, brown eyes. The book seemed heavier than he was, but he managed it with ease as he sailed past the pages. There was a virtuoso quality to his studying of the book as if the volume were finally living up its full potential. He was an intriguing fellow, and little did I know he would become my best friend.

This was how I came to meet Sherlock Holmes.

THE STORY CONTINUES IN...

ELEMENTARY
MY DEAR WATSON

The Astounding Adventure of the Ancient Dragon

JOSE PRENDES

AVAILABLE WHEREVER BOOKS ARE SOLD

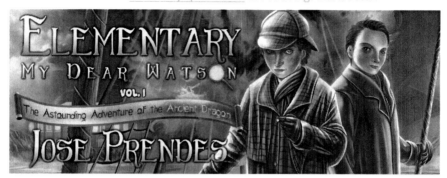

Elementary: My Dear Watson, Book One: The Astounding Adventure of the Ancient Dragon, by Jose Prendes

When 12-year-old John Watson is sent to Candlewood boarding school, he makes quick friends with a boy named Sherlock Holmes, a universally disliked know-it-all and amateur sleuth. Before long, Sherlock embroils his new friend in a covert investigation of the mysterious disappearances blamed on a vengeful ghost. Dodging the meaty fists of the bully Moriarty, and aided by bumbling patrolman Lestrade, they uncover a deadly secret hidden deep underneath Candlewood. But does the duo have the brains—and the brawn—to crack this dangerous case?

Broken Branch Falls, by Tara Tyler

Doing homework for bully ogres and getting laughed at as the butt of pixie pranks, Gabe is tired of his goblin life. When he and his friends step out of their nerdy stereotype and pull a prank of their own on the dragons at the first football game, it literally backfires, bringing a High Council vote to dismantle not only Gingko High, but the whole town, too!

The Book of Ages—hidden handbook of the High Council, filled with knowledge and power—may be Gabe's only hope. With the help of friends old and new, can Gabe complete his quest to find the Book in time to save Broken Branch Falls? Or will he remain an outcast forever?

CPSIA information can be obtained at www.ICGtesting.com
Printed in the USA
BVOW05s1112250115

384766BV00003B/20/P

9 781620 074633